WHEN WE
MEET AGAIN

· CHILDREN OF THE PROMISE ·

VOL. 4

WHEN WE MEET AGAIN

· DEAN HUGHES ·

DESERET
BOOK
SALT LAKE CITY, UTAH

For Brad and Amy Russell,
Michael and David

First printing in hardbound 1999
First printing in paperbound 2006

Visit us at deseretbook.com

This book is a work of fiction. The characters, places, and incidents in it are the product of the author's imagination or are represented fictitiously.

Library of Congress Catalog Card Number 99-74788

ISBN 1-57345-584-9 (hardbound)
ISBN-10 1-59038-588-8 (paperbound)
ISBN-13 978-1-59038-588-3 (paperbound)

Printed in the United States of America
Banta, Menasha, WI

10   9   8   7   6   5   4   3   2   1

Snow had fallen again. It lay glistening over the field of battle.
To Alex Thomas it seemed that nature had chosen to purify
this patch of Belgium, to hide the bomb craters and desiccated
villages. But the elegance of the snow-covered fields, the fences
and barns, couldn't change the truth: frozen bodies—both
American and German—lay under all that beauty. Of course,
every soldier, at times, felt a certain envy: at least the dead had
been delivered from the torturous cold.

The clouds had cleared now, and the night temperatures
were fierce. Alex had told the men in his squad to dig in deep,
but they had marched in heavy snow all day, taken a pounding
from mortars and artillery, and the effort to hack away at the
frozen earth had been more than they could summon. They
had penetrated the ground only far enough to get out of the
wind, and now they lay huddled against one another in pairs.
They were wrapped in blankets, but they were mostly defenseless against the brittle air, and the sweat they had worked up
while digging had turned to ice in their clothes.

Alex and his partner—Private Myron Davis—had not dug
much deeper than the others. Out of exhaustion they had
fallen asleep—but not for long. Alex had awakened, trembling
and suddenly frightened by what he felt from Davis, next to

him. Davis was a strongly built young man, not yet twenty, but there was no fat on him, and the cold seemed to reach him more than the other men. He was shaking so badly that Alex thought he was convulsing.

Alex reached around Davis and pulled the blanket tighter against his wool coat. "Are you all right?" he asked.

"No, I'm not. How could I be all right?"

Alex, of course, wasn't surprised by the bitterness in Davis's voice. The troops of the 101st Airborne Division had spent a month out in this cold, almost constantly. They had been transported to Bastogne without winter clothes or adequate supplies, and they had been greatly outnumbered by German *Wehrmacht* and SS troops. Surrounded and cut off from supplies, they had held their ground, held Bastogne, and now, with other Allied forces, had stopped the "bulge" that the Germans had created in the defense line. The Americans had been battered by heavy artillery, and more than half their men had been killed or seriously wounded, but they had refused to retreat, and now they were pushing back.

It was all the stuff of legend, and it made great headlines in American newspapers, but the men knew little about and felt nothing of the glory they had gained for themselves. They had suffered enough and they wanted out, and yet the word kept coming down that there was no one to replace them; the Allies had to cut off the escape routes before too many Germans retreated behind the Siegfried Line. So E Company of the 506th Regiment was on the march. The company, with the rest of the Second Battalion, had cleared the little village of Foy and was now preparing to attack Noville, which was still held by German troops and tanks.

"This is the coldest night yet," Davis whispered.

"If we get through this one, we can handle anything," Alex told him. He thought of Howie Douglas, the young soldier he had befriended and tried to help during their time in Holland and, later, here in Belgium. Alex had told the boy the same thing a few times, and Howie had made it through. But then, in the attack on Foy, Howie had taken a bullet in the chest and died. Davis was a little older, smarter, and more self-willed than Howie. He wasn't someone Alex could be big brother to in quite the same way. Davis's resentment also ran deeper. He had come into the war idealistic, if not as naive as some, but a month on the front had shaken him, diminished his enthusiasm for abstractions. Life had become a battle with self—with the cold and dirt and hunger as much as with Nazis. And to some degree, the enemy seemed the army itself: those distant generals who kept telling the men to continue when it seemed they couldn't.

Davis had grown up on a farm in Illinois. From what he had told Alex, his life had been rather simple. For fun, he had driven into town to see a picture show, or maybe gone to a dance at the roller-skating rink on a Saturday night. He might have had a beer or two on those nights, or even a snort of whiskey, but most of his days had been sober and full of work. On Sunday mornings he had usually put on a white shirt and tie and gone to hear a sermon at his Methodist church. But if the weather was right, in harvest time, Sabbath or not, he had run a thresher from sunup until sundown. He was stone-hard from the work, and he could, ultimately, survive the deprivation of war; what made no sense to him was the arbitrary way his life was controlled by others. Foot soldiers were never consulted. They rarely knew exactly where they were or what their larger objectives were. They carried out orders, and then they waited. "I feel like a piece of equipment," he had told Alex. "Just not as valuable as a jeep or an artillery piece."

Alex felt all the same things, but he was beyond that first stage of disillusionment. He assumed, every day, that more hardships, more traumas, more losses would come. On the previous morning his friend Jim Gourley had been caught with machine-gun fire as he had tried to jump across a little stream. He had been carrying a heavy load of ammunition and had slipped in the snow. Because of that, he had climbed up the stream bank slower than the others, and two bullets had struck him, one in the groin and the other in the hip.

Tony Pozernac had put his own life on the line, had dragged Gourley through the snow and into the woods. And he had done what he could to stop the bleeding. A medic had helped, had sprinkled sulfa powder in the wound and bandaged him. "He'll make it," the medic had promised, but since then Alex had heard nothing more, and he had wondered how damaged Gourley was, whether he would be able to walk all right when he healed.

Alex had more than that on his mind. In Foy, he and his men had had a chance to get inside for a few nights, and there his mail had caught up with them. Alex had learned from Anna, his wife, that he was going to be a father. It was January, 1945, and the baby was due in June. Sitting by a fire, with friends around him, he had felt the power of this news, and he had cried. But now, back out in the cold, back in the battle, a numbness had returned, filling his head and chest, seeming to rob him of the things he wanted to feel. He told himself every day that he had to be careful, had to stay alive for his child, for Anna, but he knew that there was no real way to protect himself. His end could come at any time, and it would be as unsurprising as any of the other deaths he saw every day.

Alex knew he wouldn't sleep the rest of the night, but sleep was a luxury, not something he ever counted on. He longed for the escape it would provide, but mostly he just wanted to get this night over, to get up and go so his heart would pump some heat into his body. The night before, Lieutenant Owen, Second Platoon leader, had talked to the squad leaders. He had told Alex and the others that the company would attack Noville at first light. "It's supposed to be about 800 meters into town. We'll probably catch hell all the way in there. The Germans have some tanks, and they know we're coming. We need to get down that open road just as fast as we can. Once we get to the houses, we'll have some cover, but up until then, it could be bad."

All the same, Alex wanted the attack to come. It would mean the end of this night, and if he and his men made it into town, maybe they could sleep inside for a night or two. If he—or some of the others—were going to go down, at least they would find out. Waiting and freezing was worse than anything.

Alex kept his arm around Davis and neither spoke again. But the hours ticked away one slow second at a time. Alex felt a kind of disassociation at times, as though he were floating outside himself, but he never entered the blankness of sleep. When Lieutenant Owen finally began to move about and tell the men it was time to get up, Alex felt only relief.

Some of the men tried to eat a little, but most of the canned K-ration food they carried was frozen solid. No one was allowed to smoke, and that only added to the crankiness. Alex wasn't hungry. He knew that if he made it across this open land and into Noville without getting shot or hit with shrapnel, he would feel more like eating. And maybe, in the town, he would find a stove he could use.

"Thomas, where are you?" It was Owen, coming out of the dark, his big body a gray hulk.

"Right over here."

Owen stepped closer. "I went up to Noville to look around last night," he said. "I saw some of our own tanks and thought maybe we had taken the place, but they were knocked-out tanks from when this whole thing started a month ago. Some of our boys were lying around in the snow, all frozen solid, and the Jerries hadn't even drug 'em off somewhere."

"Do you think the Germans have withdrawn?"

"No. They're still in there. I just wanted you to know about those tanks. You'll see 'em as you come into town, right on the main road."

"We need to push off just as soon as we can," Alex said. "I'd like to make it to those buildings on the edge of town before they open up on us."

"Yeah. But we gotta be able to see each other."

"That won't be much longer now."

"I know. Did your boys get through the night all right?"

"They're beaten down, Lieutenant. I don't know how much more we can ask of them."

"Maybe so. But don't let 'em bellyache and cry on your shoulder. It don't do no good for them to feel sorry for themselves."

When Owen left, Corporal Duncan walked over to Alex. "I don't like this one," he said. "Eight hundred meters is a long ol' haul." He cursed softly.

"It's all about speed," Alex said. "We've got to hit fast. That's only half a mile. We can cover it in a few minutes if we keep moving."

"Maybe you can. I ain't no track star."

"You might be today."

Duncan laughed. "Yeah. I just might." But then he put his hand on Alex's shoulder and said, "Good luck, Deacon."

"You, too," Alex said. Something like a prayer passed through Alex's mind, but he didn't try to formulate the words. He had become too fatalistic. God's will was coming, one way or the other, it seemed to him. He and Duncan had been through so many of these attacks together. It was hard not to believe that their luck would run out one of these times.

Dawn was nothing more than a gray hint off to the right of the soldiers when the command came down, whispered along the line. "Move out." Second Platoon—Alex's unit—was heading straight down the road, with Third Platoon on the right, east of the road. Alex watched as the first squad led out, and then he waved for his own men to follow him in a file. He doubted the Germans could see them yet, but he was anxious, and he wished the first squad would move faster. Every second was important to make a good, long thrust forward before the firing started.

Everything went well for a time. The men kept moving ahead, and the half-mile was quickly being cut in half. Alex told himself that this might not turn out to be so bad after all. But then a flare burst overhead, a bright white flash that spread out gray overhead. Almost instantly the first explosion sounded. It seemed to be mortar fire, muffled by the snow, and targeted at Third Platoon, off to the right.

"Go hard. Don't stop. Get to the houses," Alex shouted to his squad.

The men picked up the pace, running now, tromping down the snow-packed road, their gear clattering. A few more seconds passed and all the fire was still to the right, but then a searing light flashed in Alex's eyes and he went down. The concussion slammed against his steel helmet as he fell. He felt the breath suck from him, his ears crackle. He didn't know whether he had been hit or not. He expected pain—something specific—and yet he was already struggling to his feet. "Keep going, men. Keep going!" he screamed, but he couldn't see anything straight in front of him, his eyes still blinded from the flash.

In his peripheral vision he could see where the road was, so he pushed forward, but another explosion sounded to his left. It bowled him over, and this time a sharp pain, biting hot, was in his shoulder, seeming to burrow on through. He grabbed at the pain and rolled onto his side. But he knew instinctively that he wasn't hurt badly, and once again he worked to get his feet under him. This time, though, he heard coughing, choking, next to him on the ground.

Alex grabbed for the man next to him, tried to see him. His vision was beginning to clear, and when another explosion lit the sky, he saw that it was Duncan and that he had blood on the side of his face and on his throat. "Dunc," he yelled, "hang on." And then he screamed, "Medic! Get up here. *Now!*"

Duncan was still choking and sputtering, and Alex didn't know what to do. "You're all right, Dunc. You'll be okay." He jumped up. "*Medic!* Come help this man." Someone was running toward him in the dark. "Help this man. He's hit in the throat."

Alex had to go. He couldn't stop to deal with this, not even for Duncan. "Let's go. Let's go," he shouted, and he no longer knew who was where. He took off, running hard. The explosions were striking beyond him now, but the pounding of a machine gun, the whiz of bullets, was in the air around him. He dove to the ground, rolled over, and then crawled forward. But that was no good. He had to get into the cover of the buildings that were still a couple of hundred meters ahead, looming in the dull light.

Alex had abandoned the road when he hit the ground. Now he angled away from it—since that's where the German fire was concentrated. He charged toward a house on the edge of town. It was a hard run in the deep snow, and every second he expected to be hit, but nothing came his way, and he made it to a little shed outside the house. He dove behind it, lay in the snow, and for a time simply gasped for all the air he could get. Then he got up and looked around the shed, trying to see what was happening. He fired his M-1 at a window in a nearby house where muzzle fire was erupting from a machine gun. He had no idea whether he struck home, but others were firing too, and the machine gun stopped. When it did, Alex burst around the shed and ran to the house. He flattened himself against the outside wall, waited a few seconds, and then looked around the corner.

Up ahead, he could see the Sherman tanks—the damaged ones Owen had told him about. They were just inside the town, on the main road. He ran for them and then dropped down next to one. Just then he heard the rumble and screech of a tank track as it crawled over cobblestones. It had to be a German tank, and it was coming toward him. He rolled under the big Sherman and lay on his back.

Just then another man dove down and also jammed himself under the tank. As he did, he knocked his rifle against Alex's shoulder. Alex felt the pain shoot down his arm and remembered his wound, but he had no time to do anything about it now.

"There's a Kraut tank coming," the other soldier said, and Alex recognized the voice. It was Irv Johnston.

"I know. I—"

But suddenly the Sherman took a resounding hit. The noise slammed through Alex's head as though he had been hit with a flatiron. He couldn't think what had happened for a moment, but then he realized that the German tank had fired into the Sherman, probably to make sure it was disabled.

"Get out," Alex screamed, and he pushed against Johnston. He was afraid the tank might explode.

But when the men slid out from under the tank, they found themselves trapped against a wall. There was no escape route. "Stay here for a minute," Alex told Johnston, but he couldn't believe how badly he had handled all of this. After Duncan had gone down, he hadn't thought right. He had lost his men, and now he had gotten himself pinned down where he couldn't do anybody any good.

Another terrific noise sounded as the German tank took a hit. Someone—from some position Alex couldn't see—had fired a bazooka and struck the big Tiger. It was still operating, but the driver was backing away fast. By then, Alex could see more men streaming into the main street.

"Let's go," Alex called. "We've got to clear these houses."

Alex ran down the street, but when he tried to hold his rifle in front of him, the pain in his left shoulder was much worse than it had been before. He kept running all the same, saw that a number of men were taking the first house on the left, and crossed to the one on the right. Johnston, who was at his side, already had a grenade ready. "Look out, Sarge," he yelled, and then he pulled the pin and rolled the grenade against the front door. Alex and Johnston threw their backs against the wall of the house on either side of the door. The crash sounded and debris flew. Alex waited a couple of seconds and then spun toward the door. Johnston burst inside ahead of him. Alex followed, but all was silent and dark inside. Then, from up the stairs, someone shouted, "Please, no. No shoot."

The accent was French, not German, and it was a woman. Johnston ran to the foot of the stairs and pointed his rifle up the staircase. "Come down. Hands up."

A light came on upstairs, and then, in a moment, two bare feet appeared on the steps. A woman in a nightdress came out of the dark. "No shoot," she said again, and she walked carefully down the stairs.

She was a woman in her fifties perhaps, a thin woman with graying hair tied up in a bun. "Are there Germans here?" Johnston shouted at her.

"No," she said. "They go."

"When did they leave?" Alex asked her. She looked puzzled, and so he asked the question in German. Most people who lived this close to the border spoke both languages.

"This morning," she said. "Two officers slept here for a few nights. But now they are gone."

"We must look through your house," Alex said, again in German.

"*Ja.* That is fine. But someone must take care of your shoulder. I can do it if you like."

Outside, Alex could hear firefights—machine guns and rifle fire, the blast of grenades. He knew what had to be done. "It's not so bad," he said, but he glanced at his shoulder, saw the rip in his field jacket and blood soaking through.

"It's bleeding a lot," Johnston said. "You'd better let her take care of it."

"I can't do that," Alex said. He was thinking that a lot of men were dead. Duncan was down on the road with his throat torn open. Alex couldn't sit down in this warm house and be fussed over, not until everything was over. He stepped toward the door, but just then he heard a click, and his eyes darted to the stairway. He could see the toe of a black boot sticking out from around the wall at the head of the stairs.

"We'll be going," he said. He turned his back, took a grenade from his belt, pulled the pin, counted one, two, then suddenly spun and threw it up the stairs. The grenade blew, sending plaster and wood flying, and a body thudded to the floor. In an instant, Alex was up the stairs, his rifle ready. The man who had been hiding was on the floor, in a heap. He was a big man in a field-gray officer's uniform. Another officer was on his knees, holding his hands to his face. Alex saw the SS symbols on his collar. "Stand up!" Alex shouted. The man did stand, but when he took his hands from his eyes, Alex saw the blood streaming down his face from a gash across his forehead. "Take your pistol out. Drop it on the floor."

The man did so and then clamped his hand to his head again. Alex moved closer and picked the pistol up.

"Can you get help for me?" the German asked.

"Yes. But not immediately. Maybe the woman downstairs can do something." The pain in his own shoulder was getting worse all the time, but he still couldn't take the time to deal with it.

"You speak excellent German," the officer said.

Alex stared at him for a few seconds, hardly taking in the meaning of his words. Then he felt a kind of fury inside himself. "Be quiet," he screamed at the man. "Don't say one more word to me."

Noville fell easily once the half-mile charge had been completed, but a lot of men had been hit coming down the road. As soon as Alex could find someone to hold his prisoner, he looked for his men, got them established in a house, and then walked up the road to a temporary aid station, back where he and Davis had dug in the night before. He was weak now, from the pain and the loss of blood, and he needed to get his shoulder bandaged, but he also needed to know about Duncan. And he feared the worst.

He found Duncan in a tent, bandaged and drugged with morphine. His eyes were closed, but he opened them when Alex spoke to him.

"Dunc, how are you doing?"

Duncan's head moved just a little—a sort of nod.

There were three other men on cots in the tent. One of them said, "He can't talk. Shrapnel tore up his throat."

Duncan took a long, raspy breath and then seemed to choke.

"Don't try to talk, Dunc. Just take it easy."

Duncan pointed at Alex's shoulder. "I know. But it's not bad. They won't ship me out for this." Alex took hold of Duncan's hand. "You'll be fine. They can fix you up. They'll probably fly you over to England. You'll be drinking beer in some London pub in a few days."

But Alex didn't know what to think. Duncan didn't look good. He was white—almost blue—and who knew what might be ripped up in his neck?

"You'll be home before long, and out of all this. I envy you, Dunc. I really do."

But Duncan looked scared, his eyes full of confusion.

Alex didn't know what else to say. He could hardly face the idea of going on through the war without Duncan next to him. He wanted to tell him that, wanted to tell him a lot of things, but he didn't think he could get the words out, not without making a fool of himself. "When we get home, we'll visit each other. We'll talk about all this stuff. Okay?"

Duncan nodded.

"We'll stay in touch. You're the best guy I know, Dunc."

Duncan tightened his grip on Alex's hand, and then Alex saw tears running from the corners of his eyes. Alex said nothing more, but he knelt next to Duncan's cot, and he put his arms around him, gave him as much of a hug as he could. "I'm going to miss you," he said. He stood, and he felt himself—almost an act of his muscles—try to pull himself together. He left the tent, and then he went looking for someone to fix his shoulder. But he felt overwhelmingly alone. He and Duncan had always made it through together. What was he supposed to do now?

E Company spent only one day in Noville—one warm night—and then the battalion made a last push toward the little village of Rachamps. The town fell without too many casualties, and on January 17 the division was finally replaced. The 17th Airborne moved in, and the entire 101st boarded trucks. The word was that they were going to be transported to France. The men all hoped they were going to Mourmelon again for some R and R, but rumor had it they were heading to another front in the Alsace region, along the German border. The Germans had started another offensive, and once again the 101st would have to plug a hole. Whether that was true or not, things didn't look good. Germany was pushed to the wall, and spring was not far away. The final drive across the Siegfried Line would start soon, and the 101st was being kept close. That meant more action.

When the men of E Company climbed into the trucks, only six men were left in Alex's squad. Gourley and Duncan had gone down in this last push, and now Alex and Curtis were the only two left from the original squad. But Pozernac had been with them since D-day, and Johnston and Davis and Ernst were not kids anymore. They had seen a good deal of action themselves.

Alex sat next to Curtis, the two leaning against the cab of the deuce-and-a-half truck. Alex's shoulder was giving him a lot of pain, and the swaying and bumping against the other men didn't help.

"You could have gotten yourself out of all this if you had complained just a little more about that shoulder," Curtis told Alex.

"Maybe. But I would have sat in some aid station for a

couple of weeks, and then they would have shipped me back. I'd rather just stay with you guys."

"I don't want to head into Germany without Duncan," Curtis said.

That's what Alex had been thinking. He felt vulnerable, in greater danger. Duncan was big and strong, but he was also battle-smart. Alex had always conferred with him about important decisions.

The truck passed through Bastogne later that day. The place was battered and damaged, with rubble and bombed-out buildings lining the long main street. But the town had never been occupied by Germans.

"This is something we can tell our grandkids," Pozernac said. He didn't explain, but everyone knew what he meant. All of the men had enough perspective now to know that what they had done in Bastogne would be in history books, would be remembered by Americans forever. Alex knew that, and he wanted to feel some pride as he recalled that night the 101st had entered this town and taken over for the beaten troops on the run. All the same, he didn't think he wanted to tell anyone about it, especially not his grandchildren. In his mind, this would always be the place where Howie had died—and so many others. He didn't want to think about that, let alone talk about it.

"Someone said our company is down to about sixty guys," Curtis said. Alex knew that Curtis was thinking the same thing he was.

"Less than half, and we've had a lot of replacements," Johnston said.

"It's worse than that. Most of the guys still with us have been wounded a time or two," Pozernac said.

"We've *all* been wounded," Curtis said.

2

Wally Thomas had drifted for a time, had actually been close to sleep. The pain had not exactly abated, but if he stayed completely still he could avoid the excruciating stabs that any movement caused. But now something had brushed against his face and brought him back to consciousness. He didn't want to turn his head, couldn't really. Beyond the pain was the weakness that left him feeling paralyzed.

He tried to think what had touched him, what was next to his face. He remembered the bread that the guard had set next to him on the floor by his mat—the bread he hadn't been able to eat. And then he knew, recognized the little scratching noises. A rat was eating the bread, just inches from his cheek. He thought of reaching, of knocking it away, but he couldn't move that forcefully; the pain would be more than he could stand. And he couldn't bring himself to care that much. The rat could have the bread. Wally would defend himself only if it tried to chew on his face.

When the rat scurried over him, across his chest, and then a few moments later returned across his face—the little feet stabbing at his cheeks, touching his lips—the thought of it was disgusting, even frightening, but such emotions didn't register clearly now. To respond he would have to come back to life, return to the surface, and he was deep within himself, buried under the weight of pain and weariness. This rat had little meaning by comparison.

Wally had lost track of time, but he thought he had been in the barracks for three days. He was in the building set aside for sick POWs—that is, the seriously ill. When a man simply could not make it to the mine—and the guards could see it— he was sent to this place, often to die. An Australian doctor tried to do what he could for the patients, but he had no medicine, not even anything to relieve pain.

Wally had a fever of some kind—maybe rheumatic fever, the doctor said—but there wasn't much to do but hold on and hope for the best. He had been working in a Japanese coal mine for the better part of a year, but before he had fallen ill, he had worked for about three weeks in a section of the mine that was ankle deep in cold water. He had managed to stay on the job for a few days after first noticing the fever and had assumed it was just one more illness like so many he had experienced during his nearly three years of imprisonment. But then one night the pain had become intolerable. Wally's friends had pleaded with the guards and had finally received permission to carry him to the sick barracks.

Chuck Adair, the closest of Wally's friends, was already in the same barracks. He, too, had become sick after working in the polluted water. He had vomited until he was dehydrated and had been brought here a week before Wally, almost dead. The last Wally had known, Chuck had started to recover, but Wally didn't know what was happening to him now. His thoughts were a tangle of realities, leaping from dreamlike impressions, in color, to gray-brown visions of free-floating pain.

The rat didn't matter. So many horrible things had happened to Wally, and this was only one more example of loathsomeness—not some new depth. How could he become fastidious now? He had eaten too much rice full of rat droppings, seen too many open sores, gone too many months without a chance to bathe in clean water.

Wally drifted again, never exactly asleep or awake but aware that time was passing. When he resurfaced to a state closer to wakefulness, the room was lighter. The night was gone. He heard nothing next to him, felt no presence. Something else had roused him: he felt something moving down his forehead onto his temples, like the gentle touch of a finger. And the room seemed cooler, bearable.

Doctor Woodburn was there. Wally opened his eyes and looked at the man—gaunt, like all the prisoners, but the doctor had tried to groom his mustache, to comb his hair somehow, to keep as clean as he could. "Wally, your fever is beginning to break," he said. "You're starting to sweat. You should get some relief now."

All that day the water poured from Wally, and Dr. Woodburn made certain that he drank enough water to keep up with the loss. With the sweat, the pain seemed to ooze away too, although very slowly. At least, before the day was over, he could raise his head enough to drink the water. He could also move his knees a little, and his elbows.

And that night Wally slept, actually moved into that inviting emptiness he had been longing for since the fever first struck him. When he awoke, well into the following day, he was beginning to feel some sense of himself again, some returned reality that made him care about his needs. He ate a little rice and his ration of bread. Then, finally, he got up and walked to the latrine, supporting himself always with his hand against a wall or a bed.

Another day later Wally found Chuck, and the two sat on the floor, on Chuck's mat, while they talked. "I thought I was dying," Wally said, finally articulating what had been only a general sense during his ordeal. "What about you?"

"No. The doc told me, after, that I had been in really bad shape. But I always thought I would get better."

"Did you pray?"

"Sure. Did you?"

"No." Wally thought about it. "I think I wanted to die. But I didn't ask for that."

"You didn't stop trying, Wally. That's a kind of prayer."

But Wally didn't remember it that way. He looked at Chuck, whose skin was like old paper, brittle and yellow and shaped to the bones of his face. Certainly Wally had to look at least as bad himself. They were like specters, the two of them, but brothers more than ever. Wally patted Chuck on the shoulder. "We made it, one more time," he said.

Chuck nodded. "Maybe. If they send us back to work too soon, we could have some hard times ahead."

Wally nodded. He knew from experience that their recovery time would be very limited.

A week passed, but that was too long for the Japanese guards. Men could take their time dying if they needed to, but taking time to get well was unacceptable. So Wally and Chuck were put on "limited duty," which meant they could be included in work details around the camp.

Their first assignment, with some other men who were also recovering from illness, was to shovel dirt over a newly built concrete air-raid shelter. The prisoners on the detail were given picks and short-handled shovels and placed under the supervision of an American sergeant. Wally and Chuck worked together. Chuck would grub a little with his pick and loosen some dirt, and then Wally would scoop it up and drop it into the hole. The men were so weak that the work was draining, but the sergeant told the crew, "Look, you guys, just do what you can. I'll keep my eye out for Japs. I'll give you the high sign if I see someone coming."

By afternoon the men were hardly moving, all of them so depleted they could barely manage to stay on their feet. Chuck and Wally knew better than to sit down, but they were both leaning on their digging tools and looking toward the ground when they suddenly heard a loud voice: *"Ki wo tsuke!"*

Chuck and Wally brought themselves straight, stood at attention. Wally wondered what had happened. Why hadn't the sergeant warned them? He and Chuck were in *big* trouble.

But it was worse than Wally had imagined. The man who stood before them, still at a distance, was the Japanese camp commander. Hisitake was his name. He was a short man who strutted about in his fancy officer's uniform with a two-fisted sword strapped to his side. The sword was so long it actually dragged on the ground as he walked, but he seemed unaware of the humor that the prisoners saw in that. He was a serious, brutal man who had shown many times that he could take the life of a prisoner without a second thought.

"Nan no?" he demanded.

Wally knew the meaning of this: "What are you doing?" And so he tried to explain. With motions, and mostly with English words, he tried to say that he and Chuck had been sick, and that they were near collapse now.

It was not hard to see that the little commander wasn't satisfied. He stared at Wally, his eyes intense and hateful, then at Chuck. Finally, he ordered both of them to come to him.

Wally took his shovel, not sure what Hisitake would ask of them. He and Chuck walked forward and stood at attention before the man. The commander reached out and grabbed the shovel away from Wally, and then, without warning, swung it directly at Wally's head. Wally ducked away automatically. He escaped the edge of the blade that would have slashed his face, but the flat side of the shovel struck him across his head and sent a flash of pain through his skull.

Wally went down, but he tried to get back up. As he did, he caught the back of the shovel over the top of his head. He dropped onto his face, and now Commander Hisitake used this chance to slam him again and again, hitting him on the shoulders and back. Wally rolled up as best he could and took the

beating. Over and over, the shovel struck him, the blows sending jolts of pain through his body. But Wally fought to stay
conscious even though his brain wanted the escape.

Eventually the rain of blows slowed. The commander was
breathing hard by then, grunting, and maybe it was that, his
own weariness, that finally stopped him.

Wally felt pain everywhere, but worst in the small of his
back. He wondered whether his spine might be broken.

But the commander was telling him to get up, so Wally
struggled to his feet. He stood as straight as he could, trembling, panting. He glanced at Chuck, who nodded, surely to
say, "Hang on, Wally."

"Come with me," Hisitake said in English, and he walked
toward the guard house. Wally knew the commander's talent
for creative torture, and he knew that something horrible was
coming. Sometimes the man had used electrical shock. Maybe
that's what was coming now.

The commander called two guards outside. He told a
rather involved story, in Japanese. Wally understood his claim
that he and Chuck had refused to work. That was outrageous,
of course, but Wally knew better than to say anything.

The three Japanese men talked and Wally couldn't follow
what they were saying, but one of the guards finally walked
away, and when he returned he was carrying two rough bamboo poles. Wally tried to think what those might be for.

The guards placed the poles on the ground, parallel to each
other, about a foot apart. "Get down!" one of the guards commanded, and now Wally got the picture. He and Chuck were
forced to kneel on one of the poles, with the other one under
their shins. Then the guards stood on Chuck and Wally's feet
to press their bones down hard onto the poles. Sweat broke out
on Wally's face immediately. The pain was intense in his knees
and shins, and it was already shooting up his legs. It was hard
not to resist, but he knew that would be an invitation for further beatings, and maybe his death.

After a minute or two the guards stepped away, but there was no escaping the full weight of their own bodies, pressing their legs against the rough, hard bamboo. As each minute passed, the pain only increased, and Wally knew that the guards would push this torture to some limit of pain—and then beyond. And with that realization came the crucial question: How long could he hold out?

At the moment, the answer seemed to be that he could last another thirty seconds, maybe another minute. But when a minute passed and the pain only deepened, acute at the point of pressure and more general throughout his legs and hips, and especially in his injured back, he told himself that he could go one more minute. Then, if he couldn't stand it, he would simply lie down, and they could kill him. But he wasn't ready to give up quite yet.

Five minutes passed that way, and then ten. Or maybe it wasn't nearly that long; Wally had already lost his sense of time. All he knew was that he couldn't last much longer.

Hisitake finally spoke again, from behind Chuck and Wally, who were next to each other, shoulder to shoulder. Wally understood enough to know that the commander was leaving, and he was turning the punishment over to the guards. Wally also knew, just as he had sensed from the beginning, that this torture was not going to be a matter of a few minutes.

The commander began to walk away and then suddenly turned back. He came around in front of the men. Wally expected another blow from the shovel, still in Hisitake's hands, almost welcomed it as a chance to fall to the ground again and end the pain in his legs. But the commander handed the shovel to Wally, made him hold the handle with both hands. Then he motioned for Wally to raise it above his head. Wally did as he was told, and then Hisitake nodded. "You hold it. No put down."

Wally was already tired from everything else, but he held the shovel high. He tried to lock his elbows, to make this as easy as he could. He was well aware of the new agony that was coming. It was a favorite punishment the guards used—forcing men to hold something in the air for long periods of time until their muscles gave out.

When the commander left, Wally watched the guards to get some sense about what their intentions were, but they were settling in. One of them stood before Chuck and Wally, his legs spread, the butt of his rifle on the ground. He showed no sign of anger, no emotion—certainly no pity. What Wally saw was something like interest or curiosity, as though this were a mild little entertainment, something to change the monotony of his daily guard duty.

Wally was on the edge of breaking down. He knew that. He could see in the guard's face that the man had no intention of stopping the torment any time soon. So why not give up now? Maybe he should throw down the shovel and take what the man had to give him.

But just then Chuck whispered, "I can't do this much longer."

"Yes, you can," Wally told him. And, of course, he was telling himself the same thing. "We'll get numb. It won't hurt so much."

Wally knew that about pain. It was one of the principles he had learned to live by. Every terrible test looked impossible at first, but the body had a way of adjusting, of protecting itself. He was overpowered now, but the spreading pain would finally push him to a state where his mind would refuse to accept so much agony. And then his head, along with his knees, would give way to a deadening numbness.

If he could get past the next few minutes, maybe that numbing would come, and then he could survive for perhaps an hour. It was hard to believe that the guards would push this abuse much longer than that.

Chuck bent forward and adjusted his weight a little, but when he did, the bamboo poles moved, ever so slightly. The effect was like an electric shock. And suddenly, Wally was starting over. The tiny movement had driven the rough ridges of the bamboo deeper into his skin, seemed to freshen the pain, to bring it back to full consciousness.

Minutes kept going by, but every now and again Chuck adjusted his weight, and each time the pain for Wally was like razor blades cutting at his knees and shins. Finally, he said, "Chuck, if you can help it, don't move like that."

Wally didn't have the strength to explain, nor did he dare say much in front of the guard. Chuck only said, "I'm sorry," but he didn't move again, and Wally knew that had to be hard for him. In some ways Chuck had been more weakened by his illness than Wally. The vomiting and dehydration had taken him to the edge of death and kept him there for a longer time. Wally knew it was taking all of Chuck's strength just to hold his position, let alone to accept the pain in his legs.

"Hands up!" the guard shouted.

Wally realized that his arms had begun to sink a little. He pushed upward, locked his elbows again. It was better that way, easier, but it took a certain amount of concentration, and his mind was working its way back to the place where it had been during his illness. His arms were hurting as much as they were going to, he suspected, and so he told himself he could deal with that. The pain in his legs was everywhere now, maybe general enough to deal with for a time. Now it was a matter of removing himself from his body, of not letting the pain reach him.

But an hour went by, or some time that seemed like an hour, and the guard showed no sign of change. He didn't check the time, didn't seem to have any plan to stop what was happening.

Wally realized the truth: there was no end to this, and he shouldn't think about it that way. It was like the imprisonment itself. A prisoner had to take it a day at a time and not think about the future. The pain was something to keep on the surface, accept as the current condition, without considering when it might stop. It was that understanding that got him through the afternoon.

Time kept passing—hours, not minutes—and Wally was barely sentient. Reality had turned into a dreamy sort of blur, outside himself. But when a new crew of guards came on duty, he let this change register in his mind. When the commander had first brought him and Chuck to the guard station, the time had been about 2:15. The shift change was at 6:00. He and Chuck had been kneeling on the bamboo for nearly four hours.

If the first set of guards left, there was no one to tell the next crew when to stop the torture. They might keep this going until Chuck or Wally, or both, collapsed. But what then? It was tempting to let himself go and crash on the ground. Would the guards conclude that they had broken him and let the punishment end? Or would they beat him to death? Shoot him? Make him start again? There was no telling. The one thing he knew was that he was alive, and he could last a little longer. He might give up at some point and then see what would come of it, but right now he would rather deal with the pain than find out what else the guards might do to him if he forced a change.

Wally's vision came back into focus as one of the new guards walked to him. This guard, the one who seemed to be in charge now, had a different look in his eye. He reached out and took the shovel from Wally's hands. Wally lowered his arms and felt the blood pump back into them, which, for the moment, made the pain much worse.

"You take," the guard said to Chuck.

This seemed to be the guard's notion of fairness, that one not have to hold the shovel the whole time, but Chuck gasped, and then he whispered, "Wally, I'm sorry, but I can't do it. If I have to hold that shovel, I'm not going to make it."

So Wally spoke up. "Me," he said. "I'll hold it." He lifted his hands to take it, even though the motion cost him more than he expected—his arms feeling cramped now and unwilling to respond to his new demand.

The guard gave Wally a long look, and then he glanced around to see who was watching. Finally, he stepped over to the guard station and leaned the shovel against the wall. Then he nodded. That act of kindness almost ended it for Wally. He almost broke down. He needed to get back to his desensitized state, not to think or feel. And so he tried to let his mind drift again, to separate himself from the pain in his lower body and to feel some comfort from the end of the torture on his arms.

Hours kept passing, and gradually it was exhaustion that Wally was dealing with at least as much as pain. At one point during the evening, the guard went into the guard station, and when he came out, he had a stick of chewing gum—gum from Red Cross boxes that were supposed to be passed along to the prisoners. Wally watched as the man removed the Spearmint wrapper and the tin foil, then put the gum into his mouth. He wondered whether this was another little nuance of the torture.

But the guard chewed only a few seconds, and then he took the gum from his mouth and stepped close to Wally. Wally watched out of the corner of his eye as the guard, being careful not to be seen, reached the gum toward him. Wally opened his mouth just a little, and the guard pushed the gum in, then stepped away.

It was only a tiny bit of sugar, only the slightest of help to bring some saliva to Wally's mouth, but he knew the guard meant well, that he was pulling for the men, hoping they would survive. After a few minutes, he unwrapped another stick of gum, chewed it for a few seconds, and this time carefully approached Chuck, just as warily placing the gum in Chuck's mouth.

That was a little boost, some indication that this guard might relent at some point. But a thought was beginning to press itself on Wally. Maybe this was a death penalty. Maybe dying would be the only escape from this suffering. He could feel his body breaking down, his strength giving out. He and Chuck had been too worn down going into this. There was no way they could hold any position for much longer, with or without the pain. Without food and water, it was just a matter of time before their body systems simply shut down.

Time kept passing. Wally didn't think about bravery, about the value of life, and not even about his family, the thought of whom had sustained him for so long. And he didn't pray. In this state, hope was a kind of enemy. It was better to accept that whatever was best would finally happen and not to ask for specific relief or even strength. What was different for him now, compared to those horrible days when he had first been taken prisoner in the Philippines, was that he lived with the assurance that God knew his hardships. At times he would start to pass out, and his body would jerk; then his muscles, seemingly on their own, would choose to hold on again. What he knew was something he had learned over all these years of abuse: God was with him even when he felt abandoned. He didn't have to plead for help; he only needed to trust.

"I'm not going to make it," Chuck finally said, after neither of them had whispered a word for hours. "It must be midnight. They're going to keep this up all night."

"Don't think about that. Just deal with now."

"I'm finished, Wally. What's he going to do if I just quit? I don't think he'll kill us."

"He might not, but Hisitake might in the morning. Don't give up yet." And then he did pray for Chuck. "Keep him up, Lord. Hold him," he whispered.

Wally heard a little whimper, and he knew that Chuck had made a decision. He was holding his position. Sooner or later, however, it wasn't going to be a decision. One of them would just go down. Their lives were in God's hands. Only if He wanted them to live would they have a chance.

And then Wally heard an odd whistling sound. His body jerked, reacting to a flash of light and what he thought was a clap of thunder. But the flashes continued in a steady rhythm, as did the rumbling sounds, and by then Wally knew: bombs were falling. One crashed very close, hitting a building in the compound, and others were falling in the city and off toward the mine.

"Americans," Chuck said.

Yes. It had to be. Bombers were striking Omuta. Wally had heard rumors that Japan was being bombed now, but he had never heard or seen any direct evidence of it. But this was it. Maybe there was an invasion going on. Maybe the war was nearing its end.

Wally's reactions were confused. He could be struck by an American bomb at any moment, but he felt no fear. What he believed was that God had sent these bombers now—for him and Chuck—that the two of them were being freed.

"Don't move yet," Wally told Chuck. "Wait."

Wally wanted the guards to release him. He wondered how angry they might be, with bombs dropping. He didn't want to give them any excuses to take out their anger on him and Chuck.

For a time there was confusion. The man who had been guarding Wally and Chuck left for a couple of minutes—or at least moved out of their line of sight. But then he returned, and he shouted, "Stand up."

Wally felt the release, the relief, but he couldn't get up. He put a hand down and lowered himself onto his side. He tried to straighten his legs just a little, but pain shot through his body. He lay still, panting. Chuck was next to him, grunting, crying out at times. Suddenly someone grabbed Wally under the arms, dragged him on his side up some steps and into the guard house. Then the man dropped Wally onto a concrete floor in a dark little room. In another minute or so Chuck arrived the same way. Without saying a word, the guard stepped out, then shut the door and locked it. Wally was still curled up, still in agony, but he also knew the worst was over, at least for now. He looked up at the barred window in the room, and he saw lights flashing, the distant report of continued explosions, and then he shut his eyes and said, "Thank you, Heavenly Father. Thank you."

Chuck was muttering the same words.

3

Bobbi Thomas looked out at the ocean. She loved to watch the emerald waves rise, swell, then break and turn white as they crashed toward the beach. She was sitting next to Richard Hammond just as she had the year before when he had been getting ready to go to sea. He was back now and they were officially engaged, but they were about to be separated again. In another week—the first week of February, 1945—he would be transferred to the mainland. He would be going to San Francisco first, where a specialist, a doctor who did hand surgery, would operate to remove scar tissue and try to salvage more of the movement in his left hand. After that he would report to the Bushnell military hospital in Brigham City, Utah, only about a hundred miles from his home in Springville. He would receive skin grafts there, probably a series of them. What he had learned was that his hand would not be amputated, since he had feeling in it, and it would be more useful than any sort of prosthesis, but he still might lose parts of some of his fingers.

"I wish I were going with you," Bobbi said—words she had spoken a dozen times before but that she was feeling more powerfully every day. Richard was going home, and now she was the one going to sea. She had received an assignment as the head of a burn ward on a hospital ship, the *Charity*. The next time it put in at Pearl Harbor—and that was likely to happen within the next two or three weeks—she would make the transfer. She had volunteered for the assignment when she had desperately needed a change, when Richard had appeared to be lost at sea. Now the transfer only meant a wider separation. The navy had dropped its regulation that had previously prohibited nurses from marrying, but with Bobbi shipping out, there was no way for her to be with Richard, and her commitment to the military wouldn't end until the war was over—and probably not for some months after that.

"Richard," Bobbi said, "I want to talk to you about something."

"Okay."

She looked at the waves, not at him, but she let her arm rest across his knee. The two were in their swimming suits, sitting on beach towels close enough to the water that the remnants of the larger waves sometimes glided up the sand almost to their feet. It was Bobbi's day off, and she had stolen Richard away from the hospital. They were breaking all sorts of rules, but when Bobbi asked her commanding officer for permission, Lieutenant Karras had said, "Just don't tell me anything about it; I don't want to know." Bobbi had borrowed a car from some members of her Mormon ward. She didn't have a driver's license, but she didn't care about that. The police could throw her in jail if they wanted—but only if they caught her on the way *back* from Sunset Beach.

"There's a temple just a few miles from here, you know," Bobbi said, and she laughed.

The two of them had stopped in Laie not two hours before and walked around the temple grounds, so that information could hardly come as a surprise to Richard. "Yes," he said, the word sounding more like a question than a reply.

"We could drive back to Honolulu, track down my bishop and stake president, and get back out to the temple. We could get married before the day is over."

"Elope to the temple? Is that allowed?"

"Richard, I'm serious. Why don't we get married now? Not today—but before you leave next week."

"I'll tell you what I love most about you, Bobbi. You're so subtle."

"You should be flattered." She put her hand on his cheek, turned his face, and kissed him. "It means I *want* you."

"You brazen woman."

"I know. I am." She put her hand on his chest and shoved him, drove him onto his back, and then she leaned over him and kissed him seriously. Or at least tried to. Both were laughing by then.

Richard rolled onto his side, slipped his bandaged hands around Bobbi, and took her in his arms. "So do you think I've never thought about doing just that?"

"I don't know. Have you?"

"Sure. Bobbi, when I kiss you, if you think I'm not getting *other ideas*, you're nuts."

"I'm glad to know it. You never tell me that."

He laughed. "I don't want to shock your delicate sensitivities."

"I'm delicate, all right." She pulled away and socked him in the stomach with her fist.

He grunted, but he pulled her close again, and she loved the feel of his skin. "People make it sound like girls aren't supposed to *have* those kinds of feelings, but I think about it all the time lately—us being together."

"Bobbi, I love you," Richard said. "Maybe if we're married fifty years—or a few thousand—you can teach me to say what I'm thinking, the way you do. It's a good trait."

"I'm not always like that, Richard. Afton's the one who says what she thinks—whether she should or not. I'm only that way with you."

"Why with me?"

"Because I want you to know *everything* about me—and still like me. And I want to know you the same way."

He laughed again, and she liked hearing the deep rumble inside his chest, but he let go of her and rolled onto his back. She rested her head on his shoulder, but she thought she felt some tightness there now, and she heard the hesitancy in Richard's voice when he said, "Bobbi, it's just not like me to reveal myself all that much. It's a good way to be, I guess, but I'll probably never be as open as you are."

"You don't know that, Richard. You've never been married. Don't you think peeling off layers—getting closer and closer—sounds exciting? It's how I've always liked to think about marriage. I want to see you naked, and I want you to see me that way—physically and every other way. It's such a sensual idea to me, and spiritual at the same time."

Richard laughed longer, harder this time. "I suppose," he finally said. "But I always thought girls were shy about things like that."

"I *am* shy about it. I can feel myself blushing, clear down to my toes, even just to talk about it. It's the *idea* that I like."

"And I thought all along that it was *me* you liked."

"Don't laugh at me, Richard. I'm being serious."

"I know you are. But I'm not sure that's how marriage usually goes. Most of the married people I know don't strike me as all that open with each other."

"I know that. But can't it be that way?"

"I really don't know." He wasn't laughing now, and that worried Bobbi. "You're awfully idealistic, Bobbi. I'm not sure I can give you what you need. It almost sounds like you want someone more like that English professor boyfriend you had back in Salt Lake."

Bobbi was suddenly annoyed. She rolled onto her back and looked at the sky. "Richard, I'm not talking about being poetic, or even talkative. I just want us not to hide anything from each other, not be afraid to say *anything*."

Richard didn't respond, and Bobbi wondered what he was thinking. She knew she had to be careful. She had also made up her mind that in a good marriage partners didn't try to change one another. And she *was* too idealistic; she knew that. She reached and found his arm, took hold of his wrist above his bandage. "I'm sorry," she said, without explaining. She shut her eyes and concentrated on the breeze brushing over her body. She reminded herself to be thankful just to have Richard here close to her again.

"Bobbi, I'll try," Richard said softly.

She liked that immensely. She rolled onto her side again, put her arm across his chest, and took hold of his shoulder, liking its firmness now. "I will too, Richard. And don't let me scare you off. I know I get carried away. My dad always said I had way too many fancy theories about everything."

"That's okay. The first thing I liked about you—other than the way you looked—was that you were so interesting to talk to."

"Seriously?"

"Yes."

"Then why wouldn't you talk? I thought you were a statue there for a while."

"Bobbi, that's what I'm trying to tell you. I don't open up all that easily. I don't know why."

"You will. I'll *open* you. But you're changing the subject. You still haven't answered my question."

"What question?"

"Why *shouldn't* we get married this week?"

Richard lay still for a long time before he said, "I don't know how to do that, Bobbi—get married and then leave a few days later."

"But we'd have things to remember, Richard, and things to look forward to. It would bring us together."

Richard didn't respond. One thing Bobbi knew for sure was that she wasn't going to force this on him. Richard was not domineering, but he was also not someone who could be easily cajoled into a new way of thinking. He considered everything, came to decisions after a process, not an impulse. And the truth was, she wasn't sure it was wise to get married now either. As much as anything, she wanted to be reassured that he did want her, as much as she wanted him.

"Bobbi, I have things I have to do. Maybe it sounds strange to you, but I don't want to marry you until I have hands—until these bandages are off and I can feel somewhat normal again."

"Richard, those bandages aren't important to me."

He didn't say anything, but she felt a reaction—the slightest hesitation in his breathing.

Bobbi raised herself on one elbow and looked down at him. "Are you worried about the way your hands are going to look?"

"Sure. To some degree. But that's not the main problem. I still don't know what I'll be able to do and not do. I need to find out what my limitations are."

"Do you think that would matter to me?"

"I don't know. I hope not."

"Then what are you worried about?"

"I didn't say I was worried."

But now a tightness was in his voice, and Bobbi really didn't understand. "Tell me what you're thinking. Are you afraid you can't make a living, or . . . what?"

"I'm not afraid. That's not the point. I'll be fine. I just need some time to get back to normal—to feel like myself again."

"I don't know what that means, Richard. To me, it doesn't seem that your injuries are all that serious. I see boys in the hospital who are going home without eyes, with their arms and legs missing. Or their faces burned beyond recognition. You have no reason to feel *abnormal*."

Richard sat up. And now Bobbi could see that she had said the wrong thing. His jaw muscle had tightened into a little lump. "I don't feel sorry for myself, if that's what you mean," he said. "I'll manage just fine."

"Richard, what are you talking about? I wasn't accusing you of anything. I just don't understand why you don't feel like yourself. I know you can't come back from all you've been through and just suddenly adjust to everything. You've been in battle. Your ship was sunk. You were hurt, and—"

"Bobbi, I need to tell you something right now. You keep telling me you want to be open about everything, but I'm not going to talk about the war. I don't want to think about it anymore, and I certainly don't want to spend the rest of my life discussing it."

Bobbi thought she understood some of that. In the hospital some men talked incessantly about their war experiences, but others refused to say a word. It was a common reaction, and one she thought she could comprehend, but it seemed a change for Richard. "When you were here before, you told me about things you'd seen. You told me about those Japanese soldiers floating in the water—and a lot of other things."

"I was going back to sea then. I was trying to figure some things out. But now it's over. I want to think about the future and put all that stuff behind me."

"But if certain things are bothering you, why not get them out in the open? Won't that help you? I know you don't want to talk to just anyone about it, but why not with me? That was the whole point I was trying to make before."

"And I told you, maybe I can't be the way you want me to be."

There was a hint of anger in his voice, or maybe just frustration. Whatever it was, it scared Bobbi. It was one of those moments when the wrong words could push one of them to say things that might change their relationship forever, maybe even end it. But it was Richard who softened and said, "Bobbi, listen to me. I've seen some things—felt some things—that I don't want to feel anymore. I don't want to talk about them, *ever*. I want to forget them. I'm not all messed up. I'm not some battle-fatigued 'war victim,' or something like that. I just remember the kind of guy I was before the war, back home, and I want to get back to that. I want to go home, get my life going again, and *then* get married. That's all I'm saying."

"All right. I can understand that. Maybe everyone does have to hold certain things inside. We have the right to some part of us that we don't share with anyone."

"But that's not what I'm saying. I'm telling you I don't *want* certain things to be part of me, and talking about them will only make them worse, not better."

"Or will they fester inside you?"

"No. I'm not going to let that happen."

"Okay," Bobbi said, but she wasn't convinced. There was still too much emotion in Richard's voice, too much he was holding back. And for the first time in a long time, she wondered about the two of them. What if he was too private for her? What if she did have trouble, all her life, dealing with his reticence? What if she questioned him too much and he gradually withdrew from her? She had seen marriages that seemed all wrong, as though two people lived in the same house and shared meals and even beds, but apparently little else.

"I think maybe I ought to head back to the hospital," Richard said.

"No, Richard. I won't plague you about this anymore. Let's just relax. We need to laugh."

He nodded, and he even smiled, although that too seemed a little forced. "That's true," he said. He hesitated for a moment and then added, "I think you're getting the wrong impression, Bobbi. I'm fine. I really am. There's nothing bothering me that I can't deal with."

"Okay." But it was the lie she heard so often at the hospital. Many of the men seemed to feel it was a sign of weakness to admit they were dealing with emotional difficulties. She watched men who were so full of pain they looked ready to explode but who would never admit to the slightest problem.

Could she really stand it if Richard would hold her outside himself that way?

But she had to back off, and she knew it. So she and Richard got up, and they waded in the water, walked the beach, talked and joked. The only problem was, none of it seemed quite real, and the pretense kept hurting more and more. Finally, earlier than Bobbi had planned, they began their drive back to Pearl Harbor. Along the way, they talked about nothing important, and it was somehow like talking through a screen door, seeing each other all right, but with a hazy distortion between them.

Bobbi's fear kept building. She didn't mind Richard's vulnerability; in fact, it touched her. But she needed to understand, wanted to help. What exactly was he thinking about—trying to forget? She hated the thought that she would be separated from him, that he would have to fight through this thing alone. And even more, that he wanted it that way.

They took the long way, drove toward Koko Head, and they talked about the beauty of the ocean, of Hawaii. Bobbi could feel that Richard was trying hard to seem self-assured, relaxed.

When they reached the Halona blowhole, Bobbi stopped the car so they could get out and stretch. That's when Richard said, "Boy, I'd like to dive into the ocean and cool off. I can't swim with these bandages on, but—"

"Sure you can. A little salt water won't hurt your hands. When we get back to the hospital, I'll change the wraps."

"All right." He smiled, slowly. And then fully.

That smile always had the same effect on her. She just wanted to forget everything else and be swallowed by his beauty—those pale blue eyes and the tender, quiet way he smiled. "I have a better idea. Forget about the water. Let's kiss some more." She put her arms around his neck and let her body press just a little against his.

But there were people about, and it wasn't his style to make a show in public. He gave her a little peck, but then he pulled away and put his arm around her shoulder. They walked back to the car and drove to a spot up the road where they got out their towels again and then headed for the water.

Bobbi was a good swimmer and not afraid of the surf. She dropped her towel, ran ahead of Richard, and dove in first. He had a powerful stroke, however, and soon caught up to her. The two treaded water for a moment and then set out again, into the waves. When they caught a strong current, Richard said, "Let's go for a ride."

They both turned and swam with the flow of the big wave and then let the surf carry them all the way in to the beach. Bobbi crashed at the end, didn't get her feet under her, and she came up spitting water. Richard laughed at that but managed to get his bandaged hands around her to help her stand in the waist-deep water. She used the chance to put her arms around him again.

"Do your hands hurt?" she asked.

"No."

"Are you tired?"

"No."

"Then let's go again." She turned, dove into the water, and swam once more into the force of the waves. Then, as before, she rode the surf back. And back at the beach, she hugged Richard again, felt the gooseflesh on him as he shivered in the breeze.

They swam that way for maybe an hour, and finally they retreated to their towels, where they dried off. After, they waited as the sun sank toward the ocean, and they watched as it set. Some long, lean clouds, hanging almost on the water, were turning orange and gold, and the waves were picking up the tint.

"The world *is* beautiful, Richard," Bobbi finally said. "We need to remember that."

"People are okay, too. They're just a lot more complicated

than I used to think they were." He hesitated. "Bobbi, I'm going to be all right. I promise you I will. I feel happier right now than I have in a long time."

"That's good. Do you feel like yourself?"

"No. Not really. But maybe that's just some idea I have about who I used to be. Maybe I would have changed during these years no matter what I had been doing. We all change."

"I'll never again be the Bobbi who left Utah three years ago. But that's okay."

"Sure. That just makes sense."

"Let's not think quite so much, okay? Let's just stay happy. What I need to remember is that a couple of months ago I thought you were dead, and I didn't know how I was going to make it through the rest of my life. How can I feel bad just because we've got some challenges ahead? At least I know I *have* you—even if we're going to be away from each other for a while again."

"I thought I was going to die, Bobbi. I could have, very easily. And I kept telling myself, 'I've got to make it. I can't let Bobbi down.'"

"Really? You never told me that before." He nodded and touched her neck with his wrist, and a little chill ran through her.

"We got back to each other, Richard," she said, "and now we'll make the best of it. We're going to be all right."

Richard nodded. Then he took her in his arms and held her, and he didn't seem to worry whether anyone was looking.

Finally, rather late that night, they drove back to the navy base, and Bobbi redressed Richard's hands. It was actually the first time he had let her look at them. "They're not bad at all," she told him. "I've seen so much worse."

He held his hands out and looked at them. "When the explosion went off, I covered my face with my hands. It was just a reaction. But that's why the back of my hands got burned.

The doctor said that's a lot better than getting them burned on the palms."

"You protected your face, too. And your eyes."

"Not completely. I had some bad burns across my forehead, but they healed pretty well."

"I know. I can still see the scars right along here." She touched his forehead, and then she lifted each hand and kissed it. As she did, she felt his response. He didn't say so, but she knew he was relieved that she had accepted that much of him.

Bobbi was glad their time together was not quite at an end. She wanted to build on the feelings they had expressed later in the day, and not see him leave with all the tension they had felt at Sunset Beach. When she got in bed that night, she lay on her side and hugged her pillow, as though Richard were with her there, and she reminded herself again that she had prayed for him to come back, that his return had been the greatest gift of her life. But behind the thought lay a certain uneasiness. Could she have prayed so hard, been so thankful, and all along been wrong? What if the two of them really were too different? She tried to dismiss the thoughts, to tell herself that she was just being her usual overly analytic self, but she didn't rest well, couldn't seem to relax all night.

· C H A P T E R ·

4

LaRue Thomas was on a date with Reed Porter. Everyone at East High now considered her Reed's girlfriend even though the two had only been going out for a few weeks. Reed was the golden boy of the high school, the star of every sport, and a heartthrob, too, with his wavy blond hair and childishly shy smile. He was like a cowboy movie star—soft spoken, with a tendency to look away when complimented, his heavy eyelids drooping as though to cover his embarrassment. He and LaRue were with two of his basketball teammates and their dates, and they had all just come from the Centre Theater, where they had seen *National Velvet* with Mickey Rooney and Elizabeth Taylor. LaRue had found the show a little too dripping with sweetness, but everyone else had liked it.

Now they had driven to Fred and Kelly's, a malt and hamburger place on Eleventh South and State in Salt Lake. When the jukebox began to play Jo Stafford's "Whatcha Know, Joe," LaRue suddenly jumped up. "Come on, Reed, let's dance to this," she said.

"Wait a sec. I don't want my burger to get cold."

"Oh, come on. It'll be all right." She jerked on his arm, almost dragged him out of the booth they had been sitting in. She knew the truth, that he wasn't confident about his dancing. Nor should he be. The guy had no sense of rhythm at all. But LaRue didn't care. She *was* good, and she liked to dance where others could watch her. She was wearing a great outfit tonight: a straight skirt, short and gray, with a white blouse; a bright red, sleeveless sweater; and a matching red ribbon in her hair. She knew she looked cute, and she was well aware that Reed—as well as the other boys in the group—had been watching her all night. She loved every minute of that.

"Just step when I do," she said. "I'll show you the beat."

He grinned. "Are you trying to tell me I can't dance?" he said.

"I wouldn't say anything like that." She winked at him. "I just like to lead. You need to get used to that."

"I think I found that out already."

LaRue began to jitterbug, stepping emphatically at first, showing him the rhythm. After a few repetitions, she spun under his arm, then out, and then, as she had sometimes done with her friend Ned at the USO, she spun under Reed's arm again, but this time she wrapped all the way around his back, made a full turn, switched hands, and spun back out on the other side of him.

Reed was baffled by all that, but he laughed and held on, and then LaRue moved him back into the rhythm. By then almost everyone in the place was watching them—or at least her. She wished Reed knew how to lift her, or slip her through his legs. Those were tricks she just couldn't do without his help. All the same, she clung to his hand and tried all the variations on the turns she knew, and when the song was over, she told him, "See, you're *good*, Reed. I'll make you a great dancer if you stick with me."

"Hey, I'm happy to stick *to* you," he said, and he slid his arm around her waist. LaRue knew that this was his idea of a clever line, but there was almost no wit in the boy. He did well in school—taking tests and writing term papers—but he was certainly not a deep thinker. LaRue, of course, had never been a scholar of any great merit herself, but she did think about the world, and she did raise questions.

"Careful there, boy. Don't get sticky with me." She jabbed him in the ribs with her finger.

He was still clinging to her, so she twisted away and faced him.

"Let's dance this slow one," he said.

"What about your hamburger? I thought it was getting cold."

"It is cold now. What the heck?" He reached around her again and tried to pull her close. The new style for dancing at East High was to hold the girl very close and bend way over her. It made for awkward dancing, at best, and in Reed's case it also made for smashed toes.

"Oops. I think my malt is melting." LaRue pulled away and headed back to the table.

Reed followed, seemingly unfazed, and the two sat down to their food. The other two couples had to shift to make room in the booth once again. LaRue and Reed sat facing one another.

Reed's buddies, Rex Davis and Clint Chambers, were sitting next to their dates. Rex and Clint were seniors, but their dates were both juniors, the same as Reed. Rex was with Evelyn Creer, a cute girl with dark hair and deep dimples. She was one of the school yell leaders. Clint had been dating Connie Fawson for more than a year, and they didn't hesitate to tell people that they planned to marry once they were out of school. Connie wasn't all that cute, in LaRue's mind. Her front teeth stuck out a little too much, and she didn't know how to dress. But she was nice—not so stuck on herself as Evelyn was.

LaRue was the youngest person there, the only sophomore, but that didn't bother her. What did concern her was that the other two couples had apparently begun to talk about the war while she and Reed had been dancing. The last thing she wanted was one of those boring discussions about who was winning where, and when the war might end. That's all anyone ever talked about, it seemed, and yet no one knew the answers.

"The Germans are going to be finished off before long," Rex was saying. "We'll never get in on the war in Europe. But I'd rather kill Japs anyway. Me and Clint are going into the Marines right after graduation. We'll be hitting the beach in Japan and shooting all the little yellowbellies we can, and poor Reed will be stuck back here, still in school."

"Reed's got time to get in on it, too," Clint said. "It's going to take a long time to mop up the Japs."

LaRue hated this kind of stuff: the way boys tried to take on such manly, know-it-all tones when they talked about the war. She had a notion she might be a better Jap killer than any of them if she only had her chance.

"I just might go with you," Reed said. LaRue saw the solemn, almost tragic look appear in his face.

"Really, Reed?" Connie said. "Aren't you going to stay around for your senior year?"

"I don't see how I can," Reed said. He leaned forward, placed his elbows on the table, and cast his eyes down. "It just doesn't seem right to be having a good time while so many boys are out there fighting and dying for our country. I'm afraid the war will end, and I'll never get a chance to do my part."

"But East High needs you," Evelyn said. "We won't win at *anything* if you're not here."

Reed looked up again—at LaRue, not at Evelyn. "I've thought about that," he said. "I've tried to consider all the people I'll let down, no matter what I do. But I just feel like it's my country that needs me the most."

"I guess the war will end a *lot* sooner if you're there," LaRue said.

LaRue had used a sincere tone, and it took Reed a few seconds to realize that she was making fun of him. But he took it well. He smiled and cocked his head a little to the side as he looked at her. "Let's just say that with me and Clint and Rex there, we ought to be able to end things a year or two ahead of schedule."

Clint didn't laugh the way the others did. He waited for a few seconds, and then he said, "Rex and I had to decide what to do last year. But we wanted to finish high school. If I were you, I'd do the same thing, Reed. Your senior year of sports is something you'll never forget."

LaRue burst out laughing before she realized that no one else saw any humor in Clint's comment. She looked around, still smiling, and then finally said, "I'm sorry. I just thought you were going to say something about *graduating*. But I guess to you guys, sports *are* what high school is all about." She laughed again and then added, "You'll always have that game last night to remember."

This was the worst thing LaRue could have said. The Leopards were in second place, and their chance for the championship had gone down the drain the night before when they had lost to Granite High. The boys had vowed, early in the evening, not to be glum about it, certainly not to talk about it.

So there was a long silence, but Connie, who was an officer in the pep club, looked hurt. LaRue saw her put her hand on Clint's hand and pat it a couple of times.

Clint only gave LaRue a long, curious look. At six-foot-five he was the tallest boy on the team, the center. But LaRue thought he looked awkward on the court. She had grown up watching her brothers play, especially Gene, and she knew the grace of a really fine athlete.

It was Reed who jumped in and tried to save LaRue. "Hey, we all put school first. All three of us want to get a college education when we come home. But to me—like our coach says— sports are just part of getting a four-square education. We have our academics, then our physical side, and—" He glanced at Rex. "What are the other two sides of that square he draws?"

LaRue was the only one laughing again.

"Social and spiritual," Rex was saying, his voice reverent.

"So is that what we're doing tonight?" LaRue asked. "Filling in one side of the square? Maybe we should read the Book of Mormon for a little while now. Then you guys would be all squared up."

Evelyn was staring at LaRue as if to say, "What in the world are you talking about?" Or maybe even, "Fine talk for a stake president's daughter."

Reed tried again. "I just feel like, to be a well-rounded person, you have to—"

"I thought you were going for a square."

"What?"

"How can you be well rounded and make this square you were telling me about?" LaRue took a sweeping look around the table, and she realized she was making a mess of things. It was time to back off. So she took hold of Reed's arm and then said, trying to sound sincere, "Reed, I'm only teasing you. I think it's great that you're willing to give up sports for the sake of our country."

"Well, I haven't made up my mind for sure. My parents still think I should wait another year."

It was all LaRue could do to keep a straight face this time. She knew that Reed would be out there on the football field next fall, not landing on any beaches.

But then Reed said, "I guess you all know that LaRue's brother Gene, one of the greatest East High athletes ever, lost his life as a Marine."

Of course they all knew. And of course they all nodded, with grave faces, but they didn't have the slightest idea what they were doing. Gene's death wasn't inspiring; it was devastating. And she found it offensive that Reed would use it as part of the little act he and his friends were performing.

But she let it go. These kids wouldn't understand what she was talking about, even if she tried to explain. It wasn't worth the effort. She danced some more, and after, when Reed dropped the others off before taking her home, she knew that she could expect the final scene of the play. Now that he had shown her what a fine young man he was, sincere and ready to sacrifice his life for Old Glory, he could surely expect her to kiss him goodnight.

But she was still annoyed. She slipped quickly from his car so that he had to hurry just to catch up to her. And at the porch, as he moved in close, she joked with him, tried to keep him off balance.

Still, he put his arms around her and said, "LaRue, you're very special to me. If I do decide to go into the service this next year, I'll miss you most of all."

She wanted to say, "Reed, I see through all this. I spent too many nights at the USO. I know all the lines." But the truth was, she suddenly felt sorry for Reed. He was trying so hard. On an impulse, she decided to let him have his little victory. She looked up, turned her head so he had the correct angle, and let him kiss her. His lips were a little too tight, too hard; he wasn't very good at kissing yet. Still, he seemed pleased with himself when he stepped back, looked her quickly in the eyes, and couldn't stop himself from smiling.

But after, when LaRue went inside, she was mad at herself. Why had she allowed a kiss when she didn't really care that much for Reed? She had only done it to string him along, and she knew it. What did that make her? But she didn't like the question, didn't want to think about it, so she walked upstairs and went to bed.

On Monday, LaRue saw Reed at school. By then, she wasn't posing hard questions to herself. She teased him, touched his shoulder, leaned close, and whispered in his ear. And all those little techniques worked enormously well. His face got red, and he could hardly think what he was saying. If she had said, "Now, dear Reed, tie yourself in a knot for me," he would certainly have gone to work on the project.

But he had to get to basketball practice, and she was on her way out the front doors onto Thirteenth East. It was warm outside, for February, and she was glad to get out into the air. She was even glad for the walk home alone. She often walked with some girls from her neighborhood, but in her dawdling with Reed, she had missed that group today.

She was walking rather leisurely when someone overtook her. "Hi, LaRue," a deep voice said. She glanced up to see Cecil Broadbent step alongside her. He was a boy from her ward, a year older than she was, like Reed. She had known him all her life, and she sort of liked him, even though he was her opposite in most ways. He was something of an egghead—and a loner. He didn't go to the high school games or dances, didn't even join the science clubs. In Sunday School he would say nothing at all most of the time, but then, without warning, ask a question that would not only baffle but sometimes anger the teacher. "How can God listen to millions of prayers at the same time?" he had asked when he was maybe nine or ten, and the question had bothered LaRue ever since. She rarely prayed without wondering who else was on the line.

"Hi, Cecil," LaRue said. He was a tall boy, and his long legs were about to carry him on by, but LaRue, for reasons she didn't really understand, said, "What's your hurry?"

"I'm not hurrying," he said. "I'm just walking." But he did slow down.

"I guess you have to get right home so you can dive into a book."

Cecil smiled. He wasn't a bad-looking boy, actually. He had mild problems with acne, and his eyebrows were a little too weighty and black, but he had straight, white teeth, and a wide smile that appeared suddenly, whenever it did appear. "It's not fair to judge a fellow by his reputation," he said. "For all you know, I have a great intrigue planned. I just might be on my way to Smokey Joe's, where I play saxophone with a blues band."

"You're right. I could have you all wrong. You might be

another Baby-Face Nelson. You could have a bank heist scheduled."

Cecil laughed. "I'll tell you the sad part—and now I'm going to let you in on something I usually don't reveal."

She waited and smiled.

"I have two books I'm reading right now. And I was just asking myself which one I wanted to dig into tonight, after I do my homework. So I guess my bad reputation is based on a certain degree of fact."

"What kinds of things do you read?"

"Everything. Russian novels are my favorite. But I like history, too, and in my heart of hearts, I'm a scientist."

"Is that what you want to be?"

"Yeah, I do. I'll probably end up in chemistry or physics—something like that—when I go to college."

"What about the war?"

"What about it?"

"Won't it keep you from going to college for a while?"

Cecil let out a puff of air, and the steam blew away in the breeze. "I keep hoping the army will reject me—for some reason. I wish I weren't so disgustingly healthy."

"Don't you want to be in the service?"

"Let's see. This is a hard one. Do I want someone to shoot at me, throw hand grenades at me, drop bombs on me, or all of the above? I think I can live without those things, thank you very much."

"Hey, most of the guys your age can't wait to get out there. That's what they tell me, anyway."

Cecil laughed. "I can tell you believe every word of it, too."

"Cecil, how dumb do boys think girls are? They all want us to tell them what big, strong heroes they are. I'm sick of hearing it."

Cecil nodded, but now he was smiling, not laughing. "LaRue, I'll never figure you out," he said. "You've always known what's really going on. But you go along with everything anyway. I remember in elementary school, that club that Beth Ellison and VerLynn Burney started. You made fun of the whole thing—and then you joined."

"And got myself elected president, too."

He laughed hard, and for a time he looked away, as though he were trying to think back to that time. "But why do you do that?" he asked.

"If I play a game, I play to win."

"So is that what everything is to you? A game?"

"What is it to you?"

"I see the games. I just don't play."

"You're way too serious, Cecil. The games are what make life fun."

"No. I don't buy that. I don't think you do, either." They had come to a corner, and a car was waiting at the stop sign. Cecil stopped and waved the driver on by. The man nodded his thanks and pulled on through, and then Cecil and LaRue crossed the street. "Sometimes you go too far, LaRue. It can't possibly be worth the price of admission for this latest game you've gotten yourself into."

"What's that?"

"Going with Reed Porter."

"What's the price?"

"Having to spend time with him."

"Reed's a nice boy."

"Reed is a *very* nice boy. But he's never had an original thought in his life. He wouldn't know one if it was chewing on his leg. He thinks *football* is life."

"Not now. It's basketball season."

"True. I lose track of these things."

"That's your own game, Cecil."

"What?"

"You don't play games you can't win. You aren't good at sports, and you don't know how to be Mr. Popular, so you pretend you don't care. But if you didn't pay any attention to that stuff, you wouldn't even know I was going with Reed."

Cecil shrugged and looked away.

LaRue saw his confusion, and she knew she had him, but she was sorry that she had stabbed so deep. She hadn't meant to hurt him. "Look, Cecil, I just don't take things as seriously as you do. Reed is cute, and all the girls want to go out with him. So I want to be the one who wins. But I wouldn't ever marry a guy like that. I couldn't stand to be around him all my life."

Cecil didn't reply. LaRue worried that she had driven him back inside himself. He had never, as long as she had known him, said so much to her.

LaRue glanced up toward Mount Olympus, where clouds, sheer as wedding veils, were clinging to the peak. The sky was blue otherwise, at least in the east. When she looked toward the valley, between the houses along the street, she could see a thick haze of rust-colored smoke hanging over the city. Dirty snow was piled up in melting mounds along the sidewalks. Something about the day was suddenly depressing even though she had felt rather cheerful when she had first come out of school.

"You might be right. Maybe I am jealous of guys like Reed. But . . . things are about to change. When I get out of high school, brains will no longer be a disadvantage. I'm about to come into my own." He smiled with satisfaction, and once again LaRue was struck with the idea that he wasn't so bad looking when his face came to life.

"Sorry to tell you this, but the University of Utah isn't so different," LaRue said. "They just play the games on a little higher scale over there. If you're not in a fraternity or sorority, you're nobody."

"Are you going to join one?"

"I don't know. Probably. I guess you never would?"

"Naw. I couldn't do that. I wouldn't even know how."

"Hey, if you need lessons, you've come to the right place."

"Tell me—seriously—how do you know what to do?"

"Hey, it's just instinct. You have it or you don't."

He shook his head with obvious disgust, but she could see that he was actually rather intrigued.

"Take clothes, for instance," LaRue said. "It's crucial to wear the latest things, but your timing has to be right. If you wait too long and then start wearing a certain outfit—even if it's stylish—everyone knows you're just copying the really 'with it' kids. I'm at the point now where I can buy something new and *start* a new trend—at least with the sophomore girls. Now that's power. It's almost liking changing the course of history."

"Wow. Important stuff." He rolled his eyes.

But LaRue paid no attention. She waved her hand in front of herself. "Under this coat is a dress every girl at East—and not just sophomores—would die to have bought first. I have on the new 'Heartbeat Casual,' in melon green. It cost me eleven dollars, but don't tell my dad."

"Didn't he pay for it?"

"Not exactly. I worked for him, and he paid me, but it was my money by then, not his."

"So what's so fancy about this dress?"

"It isn't fancy. It's *casual*." She unbuttoned her coat and opened it so he could see. What LaRue liked about the dress was the way it buttoned all the way down the front, like a long shirt. "I saw it at ZCMI and knew it would be the new thing this spring. So I wore it today, to get ahead of everyone. By March, imitations will be blossoming like daffodils."

"I never understand styles. If my clothes are still holding together, I just keep wearing the same ones."

"You don't have to tell *me* that. I know. I see you all the time. And by the way, if you want to be popular, don't admit to things like that."

Cecil shook his head. He sounded serious again when he said, "I still say the price is too high. From my point of view, you're selling yourself way too cheap."

"I don't even know what that means."

They had arrived at the corner where LaRue had to turn. Cecil usually continued on for another block. The two hesitated at the corner for a moment, and then Cecil turned and walked with LaRue down the hill toward her house, obviously because he wanted to continue the conversation—although he didn't say so. "I don't understand you, LaRue. You're smart, but you've always gone out of your way to avoid letting anyone know it. It's like you've decided that being so beautiful, you'd rather use your big brown eyes than your head to get what you want."

"Beautiful? Cecil, do you think I'm beautiful?" She was smiling, flirting.

"Don't do that, LaRue. You know how pretty you are. You'd be better off if you *didn't* know."

LaRue knew she was being complimented and, at the same time, cut to the bone. Who was Cecil, of all people, to be telling her how to operate in this world? But he seemed to know her secret—the one so obvious she was always surprised more people didn't pick up on it. She was almost never sincere, almost always calculating. But then, Cecil didn't have to be brilliant to see it; everyone else just had to be stupid.

"It sounds like you don't like me, Cecil."

"Don't do that either."

"Don't do what?"

"Don't try to get me to say what you want to hear."

LaRue took a long breath and then didn't deny his accusation. She even liked the fact that he couldn't be manipulated that way.

"I've already told you that you're beautiful and that you're smart. That ought to be enough."

"You've also told me that I'm shallow and that I'm selling myself too cheap."

"Well, yeah. Something like that. But I guess that means I think you're worth more than you're getting." He ducked his head, and then he added, "LaRue, I've liked you for as long as I can remember. Since clear back in grade school. Just like all the other boys. I don't like to admit that, but it's the truth."

LaRue was surprisingly flattered. She would never go out with Cecil, of course, or even think of him that way, but she was surprised by how much she liked talking to him.

The two had arrived at LaRue's house. As she reached her front walk, she stopped. Then she turned and looked at him. She was about to say good-bye when he said, "So. What do you think? Do you want to go steady?"

"I don't think so."

"I thought not." They both smiled. "But I would like to talk some more one of these days. I never have anyone to talk to."

"We will, Cecil. We'll talk some more."

He nodded, but the smile didn't return. In fact, LaRue saw a wistfulness in his eyes—some longing that she knew she could do nothing to repair.

"We'll go somewhere and have a really long discussion one of these days," LaRue said.

"Okay."

But she didn't mean it. She had enjoyed the little chat, but she didn't want him to think she would go out with him. She would feel funny if people saw them together, and besides, she was wary of his little penetrations into her head.

Anna Thomas was at the London office of the British Secret Intelligence Service when her supervisor asked her, "Would you like to take on some additional work?"

"Yes, I would," she told him. "I could use the money."

"Well, it's a bit different, this. The American boys, over at OSS, need a good translator, and they asked us for a recommendation. I told them about you, and they want to have a chat with you, just to see how it might go."

So Anna walked to the American OSS office, just up Grosvenor Street, and she sat down with a man who told her it was better that she not know his name for the present. He was an impressive man, however. He seemed educated, well spoken. He interviewed Anna carefully, learning everything he could about her background in Germany and about her American husband, and yet Anna had the feeling that he already knew everything she told him.

Eventually the man said, "Mrs. Thomas, I'm willing to hire you, based on what we've talked about, but you must understand that you'll be required to come here, never to take your work home as you have done for the M-6 fellows at SIS, and you won't be able to speak a word about what you learn—not to your mother, not to *anyone*. This is top-secret material, and we don't like to put it in the hands of civilians, but it's information coming out of Germany, and our own people simply don't have the background they need. You know the country, the nuances of language, landmarks, culture—all in a way that our people never will."

"I understand."

He folded his arms across his chest. He was wearing a white shirt, with the sleeves rolled up to his elbows, and a dreary tie, dark blue, that was loose at the neck. Anna thought that before the war he might have been a professor, certainly not a military man. There was something contemplative and distant about him, even as engaged as they were in conversation. "But let me explain a little about these transmissions," he added, "and you'll understand why no word of this material can ever leave the building."

Anna nodded.

"Mrs. Thomas, the British have never done much to penetrate Germany. We have far too little reconnaissance information about the effects of our bombing, about troop movements, fortifications and buildups, civilian morale—all kinds of things. For the past few months we've been getting some people into the country. Most of them are native German speakers, and some don't speak much English, so many of the transmissions are in German. The operatives use a radio system we call Joan/Eleanor. Joan is the ground radio, and Eleanor is the receiver that picks up messages. The radio directs a signal, straight up. It's a narrow signal at the ground level, but it fans out. We fly over the area, at high altitude, in a small, fast little airplane called a Mosquito. The pilot circles over the radio signal and records the information. This method is far less dangerous to the ground operative because German detection equipment can't pick up a signal that is directed straight up, and the airplanes are high enough that they're rarely noticed."

"Will I translate the radio messages?"

"Yes. The messages are recorded on a spool of wire. You

can play them back on a machine I'll show you how to operate. Sometimes the signals break up a little, but most of the recordings are pretty clear. Let me have you listen to one. Come with me."

The agent got up from his desk and motioned toward the door, but in the hallway he walked on ahead. Anna had had time to get nervous by then. She wondered whether her English would be adequate to give him what he wanted. And she wondered what "nuances" were. She would have to look the word up when she got home.

The man led her to a little room only large enough for a desk and chair. He held the door for her and then closed it behind him. On the desk was a little recording machine. The man showed her how to load the spool of wire, and how to play and rewind it.

"This is a new recording," he told her. "Listen, and see whether you can understand it all right."

The two listened for maybe half a minute before Anna said, "Yes, I understand it very well."

"Good. Some recordings are not quite so clear, but you'll do fine with them, I'm certain."

"Sir, I'm worried about one thing."

"What's that?" He turned toward her, lowered his head a little, seeming patient.

"I think my father is in Germany. No one has ever said that to us, and he couldn't tell us, but I'm almost sure that he's one of your operatives. If that's true, and there's a problem with my knowing that, say so now."

The man took his time but finally said, "What you know is that your father is working for our office and that he's away. We have informed your mother, from time to time, that he is all right. I want to say nothing else."

"But perhaps I could hear him on one of these—"

"I want to say nothing else."

"It's good. But I thought you should know."

"Yes. I'm not surprised that you would draw the conclusion that your father is in Germany. But you must understand that it isn't my position to confirm it."

That did seem, actually, a sort of confirmation, but Anna didn't say so. She only said, "I understand."

"If you don't mind starting right now, we need this recording translated today. If you can't stay, we can—"

"No. It's fine. I'll do it now."

The agent opened a drawer and got paper and pencils out for her, and then he left, but she didn't write anything at first. She decided to listen to the recording once, all the way through, before she began to translate.

What she felt as she listened was something she hadn't experienced lately. She heard the hurried descriptions of bombing raids, of reconstruction efforts, of troop movements, even of resistance work. But beyond the words, she heard the speaker's anxiety, the same trepidation she had lived with for such a long time when the war was lurking nearby. In Berlin, she had known the horror of the blanket-bombing raids, and in London, the threat of rockets. But for Londoners, now, the threat of attack was mostly over, and it was easy to lose touch with that terror of present danger.

She thought of her father moving about in Germany perhaps, relaying transmissions, putting his life in constant danger. She thought of her brother, Peter, perhaps in jail, perhaps on the run. And Alex, for whom troop movements were life, not symbols on a map.

All those feelings were on her mind when she wrote to Alex that night. She couldn't tell him what she was doing for the OSS, but she could try to make herself real to him and hope that it helped in some way. Before she wrote her letter, however, she read, one more time, the last one she had received from him:

Dear Anna,

I can tell you now that I'm no longer in Belgium. I'm in France, not away from the battle front exactly, but in a place that's pretty safe, by comparison. I took a shower when we first got here, and you can't imagine how great that was. I would need to take a hundred more and sleep in a bed for a few months before I could ever feel like my old self, but a good shower at least brought me back to life a little. I sleep inside now, too. The building I'm in is something short of the Ritz, but it has most of its walls, and a stove, so it's a big step up from what I've had for the last couple months. I even saw a movie, "Rhapsody in Blue." They brought it out to us, and we moved back from the line to watch it. It was almost shocking to hear music and see people acting like people. I suppose it wasn't very real, in one sense, but it looked like the life I remember.

I think every day, almost every minute, about our baby. I guess I'm like every dad. I figure my kids are going to be the greatest ever—smart and good and as beautiful as their mom. But I'll have to say that I worry less about greatness than I probably would have back home. I'll settle for some happiness, some togetherness. I will admit, I dream of playing catch (that's baseball) with my son, or throwing a few passes to him (that's football—American football), but I could sure enjoy a little girl putting her arms around my neck, or letting me do her braids for her.

All of that is so difficult to imagine, even to believe in, here, and that's why I concentrate on it so hard. We'll make it happen, Anna. I only pray that I can be with you when the time comes. Can you send me a picture? I want to see you all round and motherly. I want to hold you in my arms and feel our little child between us. Before long, I want to be fussing about scraped knees and chickenpox, not about everything I see over here.

I love your letters, Anna, and I should start receiving them much faster now. So keep them coming and I'll do the same. Talk to our baby, tell him (or her) all about me. By the way, have you been sick? You didn't say anything about that. I remember how sick my mother always was, when she was expecting.

I love you. In the middle of this endless night, your letters come to me like flickers of light across the channel, and it lets me know, always, where home is. It's not in Utah, not in any place. It's with you.

Love, Alex

The letter had come only the day before, but Anna had almost memorized it, she had read it so many times. Still, it made her cry again. She wrote back to him:

Dear Alex,

I am happy to know that you are in a safer place and that you are out of the snow and mud. You sounded more like you in your last letter, and that made me very happy.

I have not been sick. I am lucky, I must say. But my great joy is that the baby moves within me all the time now. For a long time, I waited for a change in me. Now I'm getting fat and ugly as an old Hausfrau, with apple cheeks, and I don't like that so much, but I like to feel the baby kicking and turning like a school child not liking to be in his desk at school all day. I believe it's a boy, so active he is, and I believe he is handsome, with your dark hair. That's how I see him when I try to think what kind of boy he might be. Maybe it's a girl though, strong and quick, like a German girl. You always say you like my eyes, so if she is a girl, I hope she has such eyes for you to love just as much.

Alex, I am busy, and I am doing good things—things that will help with the war, perhaps. I can't say more than that in a letter. But I feel very close to you. If you could hold me in bed tonight, and curve your strong body around the bend in me, I would hold on and never let go, I think. Once I have you again, I never want you out of my sight forever. I don't want to be a flicker of light to you. I want to be your sun. I want you to be my world, with only our little baby to fill it up. I know that life has problems, but if I have you with me, nothing will ever be so bad again. At least that's what I feel and hope. Be safe, my beloved one. Think of me tonight.

Love, Anna

* * *

Once again Richard Hammond had boarded a ship, and Bobbi had watched him sail out of her life. He had only waved once—probably because of his bandages—so Bobbi hadn't waved much either. She had merely stood on the dock and stared at him, tried to memorize him. Bobbi was about to give up everything familiar and once again be alone. She had learned now that the *Charity* was to dock at Pearl Harbor in just a few days. When it returned to sea, she would be on it. That meant losing Afton and Ishi, her beloved Nuanunu family and all her friends in the Waikiki ward.

She had now worked her last day in the naval hospital and had a few days off until her ship arrived. One afternoon she was in her room sorting through her uniforms and few possessions, trying to decide what was worth keeping and what she would need in the close quarters of a ship. She was holding up a rather seasoned white nurse's dress and wondering whether it could last her a while yet when she heard a knock. She opened the door and saw the young receptionist who normally sat at the desk downstairs. "There's someone here who wants to see you," she said, and she smiled. "A Marine."

"Who is it?"

"He told me not to tell you his name. He said, 'Tell her to come down and see for herself. She won't believe it if you tell her.' All I can say is, he's kind of cute."

Bobbi was intrigued. She tried to think of the Marines she knew. Before she walked downstairs, she took a minute to run a comb through her hair, but she didn't put on any lipstick. She was wearing a civilian dress—a little linen sun dress that needed to be thrown out with the rest of her worn-out things, but one she had thought would be comfortable on a work day like this.

When she reached the main floor she saw the Marine, but he was looking out the window, his back to her. She couldn't think who it was. He was a slim man, not one of those big-shouldered types she often saw in Marine uniforms.

Then he turned around—and the air went out of her. It was David Stinson. "Hi," he said, and he grinned in that childlike way of his. "I'll bet you didn't expect to see me."

"You're a *Marine*?"

He nodded, still smiling, and then he walked to her. "I know you're engaged, but I'm still going to kiss you." He only gave her a little peck on the cheek, but Bobbi was amazingly self-conscious about it. She thought of that night she had talked with him in his apartment, back in Salt Lake, and he had kissed her and set off such confusion in her life.

"I'm off to the war," David said. "I managed to stay out of it for a long time, but my patriotic zeal was finally too much for me. Besides, they were about to draft me." He leaned his head back and laughed. He was the same old David, but he looked so strange with his hair cut short.

"But why the Marines?"

"Oh, you know me. I always go for the best." He was still holding her hands. In some ways he was more appealing than ever, a little more filled out, and in spite of what he was saying, more subdued. He didn't seem quite so arrogant, either.

"Let's walk outside," Bobbi said. There were things she wanted to ask him, but not with the receptionist listening. "I hope you won't be ashamed to be seen with me. I look a fright."

"Bobbi, you're beautiful. I was just thinking how good you look. Is it all right if I tell you that?"

"You can tell me anything you want. But you always did make things up." She took David out to the lawn, where they sat on the grass, facing each other. David crossed his legs and leaned forward with his elbows on his knees. Bobbi, a little embarrassed by her bare legs—and her freckles—tucked her legs under herself. "How did you know where to find me?" she asked him. She found herself pushing her hair behind her ears, trying to smooth it.

"We got in last night. As soon as they let me off the ship this afternoon, I walked up to the hospital. They told me you were shipping out in a few days, but they also told me where the nurses' quarters were. By the way, what's the name of that red-haired nurse I saw at the hospital? You know—just in case I need a checkup before I leave town."

"David!"

"Hey, she could just check my pulse and my blood pressure. That's all I had in mind."

"It sounds like your heart is beating just fine." She looked him over, wondered who he was now. "David, what's going on? What's this all about?"

"What? Going off to war?"

"Yes."

"I don't know. When I realized I was going to be drafted, it just struck me as a great joke to become a Marine. I'm a kind of parody, I suppose, but I rather like the idea of having a go at heroism. I want to be Jason. Or Hercules. I want to *live* a little life, not just read about it."

"To be a hero, you have to believe in what you're doing, David. That's part of the deal."

"Oh, I'm a *true* believer. I hate all our enemies, and I'm *fierce* with anger. Can't you see it in my eyes? I love liberty, freedom, and above all . . . General Motors."

She did look at his green eyes—remembered all the moods she had seen in them, but what she saw now was nothing but irony. "When did you become such a cynic?"

"I'm not, really. It just seems too maudlin to admit that I actually do feel some commitment to what I'm doing. The truth is, I haven't been very happy these past few years, but this seems right—what I ought to do."

"Why haven't you been happy?"

"Ahhhh. Well . . . that's something we can talk about later."

He pulled a blade of grass slowly from its roots, then stuck it into his mouth. Bobbi watched him, remembered how his hands worked, his shoulders, always with more motion than was needed, as though his body were bursting to do, to act, no matter how much he preferred to think. He wasn't as good-looking as Richard, but there was something electric about him. His thoughts were always fascinating to chase, and his moods were like little eruptions, changing almost a sentence at a time. "Tell me about this fellow you're going to marry. What's his name again?"

"Richard Hammond."

"Is he a thinking man, Bobbi? Will he keep you interested for a whole lifetime?"

"A whole eternity, I hope."

He laughed. "That's right. Mormons sign a long-term contract. Do you really want to be around him that long?"

"Richard's not like you, David. He hasn't read *everything*. But
he's curious, and right now, sort of perplexed by life. He's asking lots of questions. But he likes answers. You always liked the
questions better than the answers."

David smiled. "You do know me, Bobbi," he said. "But
lately, I must admit, I've longed for a few answers. I guess I'm
getting old."

They looked at each other, and Bobbi was surprised. She
saw the sadness in his eyes, and with it, his affection for her.
She looked away.

"Well . . . I hope this one's not like that last guy you got
engaged to," he said.

"No. He's not like Phil. He's gentle, and smart, a little more
correct than I am, but very kind hearted. Before the war, he
didn't care that much about ideas and books. He was one of
those engineering students at the U that you used to make fun
of. But now he tells me he'd like to hole up in a library and read
for a few years."

"Don't try to make me like him. I refuse to do that."

Bobbi hadn't expected David to say something like that—
not even as a joke. She didn't want this to be awkward. "You
would like him," she said. "But you two are nothing alike. He
holds back; I have to dig inside him to find out what he feels."
She smiled. "That was never your problem."

"True. But I'm not like that with most people. I talk a lot,
but I don't *admit* very much about myself. You were the one
who brought that out of me." He hesitated, and then he added,
"Bobbi, what intrigued me about you was your goodness. Lots
of religious people toe the line, but you really are good, and
that always disarmed me. I'm sure I told you about me just so I
could hear more about you."

"You overrate me," Bobbi said, and she meant it.

"No. I don't think so. I spent my years in Utah laughing at

Mormons. There's just something so self-conscious about the way your people live their religion. But to me, your impulses always seemed right—even though they were so deeply tied to beliefs I couldn't take very seriously."

"I don't know how you can say that. You're the one who had the right 'impulse.' I was ready to make a mistake, and you sent me packing."

"Funny you should say that. It's crossed my mind a few thousand times in the past couple of years that breaking it off with you was the biggest mistake I ever made."

"No, David. It was right. I'm just thankful to you for recognizing it."

"Well, let's see. You've just thanked me for *not* marrying you. That could almost be taken as an insult."

"But it isn't meant that way, and you know it. It was a noble thing you did, David, and very wise."

"So much for wisdom. I won't try it again." He tried to laugh, but then he looked down at the grass. Bobbi had to resist the desire to bend forward and touch his hand. "Will Richard give you room to think for yourself, Bobbi? He's not one of those guys who'll 'exercise his priesthood' on you, is he?"

Bobbi smiled. "He never tries to boss me—if that's what you mean," she said. "But he's independent. I'm not going to get away with telling *him* what to do either."

"How well do you know him?"

"Not as well as I need to, David. I love him; I really do. But I haven't had a lot of time with him yet."

"Well, then, let me ask you one more question." He grinned. "Since I'm so wise and all—like a dear old uncle—I'm still looking out for your welfare."

"That's kind of you. What's your question?"

"Are you *sure* this is the right guy for you to marry?"

"Yes. I'm sure this time," Bobbi said, and she tried to keep her voice as light as David's.

But then he said, "Bobbi, I'm serious."

Bobbi tried to say the words with conviction, had them ready, but they didn't come out. Instead, she found herself saying, "I think everything will work out all right, David. But I have been a little worried lately. I don't know how to read Richard sometimes. He's going through a hard time, and he won't let me help him. Sometimes I wonder whether he'll ever be as open with me as I want him to be."

"Don't compromise on that one, Bobbi. There are too many married couples in this world who live in the same house, go about their business, and hardly seem to notice each other."

"I know. But I don't think it would be like that."

"What do you mean, you don't *think* it would be. Don't you know?"

"David, when I'm with him I don't worry as much. It's harder when we're separated like this."

"You don't worry *as much?*"

"Come on, David, you know me. I worry about everything."

"Maybe so. But I don't want you to be unhappy. I didn't give you up for that."

Bobbi couldn't do this any longer. She didn't like the muddle of emotions she was feeling. What would Richard think if he could hear this conversation? "You needn't worry about that," she said. "I'm sure everything will be fine." And then she changed the subject. They talked about Chicago and what David had been doing, about the Thomases, and about all the changes that had come because of the war. Two hours passed quickly, and then David was saying that he had to get back to his ship.

"Bobbi, I don't know how long we're going to be here," he told her. "I don't even know whether I can get off the ship again. But could I see you again? I would at least like to see Honolulu, maybe eat dinner."

That sounded like an evening together—a date—and Bobbi wasn't sure. But she did want to see him again. "Sure. We could take the bus into town. I'm not working now, until I go. But I could be leaving some time next week."

"Yeah, the same here. If I can't get off my ship, I'll get word to you. But if I can get shore leave again, I'll call. All right?"

"All right."

Bobbi was surprised by her own emotions—by the excitement she felt—but she didn't want to give him the wrong idea. "David, it's just . . . you know. I mean . . ."

"Sure, sure. We're just old friends. Don't worry. I won't bother you any more about Richard. I just like seeing you. I've missed you. Every single day."

Bobbi took a long breath. "David, don't—"

"I'm sorry. I won't." He got up, suddenly, quickly, brushed his fingers through his hair, as though he thought he still had that lock of hair that had always fallen into his eyes before. He was smiling. "If you want, you can bring that redheaded nurse along—you know, just for a chaperone."

Bobbi liked that better. "I doubt you're ready for her. She only dates captains and admirals."

"I should have known."

"Well . . . do call me if you can. I have plenty of time." But that sounded much too inviting. As Bobbi walked back to her quarters, she was almost certain she had done the wrong thing.

6

Alex was living in a stone farmhouse that had been damaged by artillery fire, but he was out of the worst of the cold. The men in his platoon had scrounged a little wood stove from somewhere, and that took the chill off the place. His battalion was now stationed in Haguenau, in the French Alsace, a part of France that had been German territory at times in the past, and where most people spoke both French and German. Haguenau, sliced in half by the Moder River, was a town of about 20,000 people. On the opposite side of the river from where Alex and his platoon were quartered, the city was still occupied by German forces. All a man had to do was walk outside to draw sniper fire. If two or three walked out together, they might attract a round from an 88-millimeter gun. Well back from the line, the Germans also had an enormous 205-millimeter railway gun. When it fired, the incoming shell made a sound like a flying truck. Anyone upstairs had plenty of time to run all the way to the basement before it struck, but if one those big shells had ever hit the house dead on, nothing would have been left of anyone, whether in the basement or not.

The house the Americans occupied was serving as a forward observation post. Lieutenant Owen could call in artillery on targets across the river, or he could inform headquarters

about any troop movements on the other side. In truth, however, everyone was quite certain that no counterattacks were
coming. The Germans had made a push just before the 101st
had been pulled out of Belgium, but the brass now believed
that had been only a feint to draw some Allied troops south,
away from the retreating German forces in the Bulge. Right
now, in Haguenau, everything was on hold on both sides.
When spring broke, the Allies would unquestionably begin a
major offensive, and paratroopers would assist in the operation.
But for now, all the signs pointed to both sides sitting tight.
Alex had received a couple of replacement soldiers, which
meant that the position was being bolstered, not abandoned.

The replacements were not as young as the last group, but
they were still wide-eyed and fresh out of jump school. One
was a fellow named Darwin Pugmire, who was something of a
kindred spirit to Alex. He was a blond-haired fellow, tall and
strongly built, with a tendency to smile, subtly, even when
there seemed no reason to do so. He had graduated from the
University of California in engineering and had held down a
job in a defense plant for a time. He was married, too, and had
a little boy. The arms factory where he had worked had begun
to cut back the previous year, and when he lost his job, he was
suddenly vulnerable to the draft. The army was taking more
fathers now, but he and Alex were the only two married men
in the squad. That linked them in some ways, but beyond that,
they shared an interest in history and in the politics of the war.

The other new man, Eliot Kaplan, was from New York
City. He was a tough-talking little guy, and something of a
philosopher, with an opinion about almost everything. He
liked to double up his fist when he talked and hammer home
his convictions. Alex liked having a couple of men around who
could talk about things that were going on back in the States,
and men who had some interesting ideas to discuss.

Neither of the new men was impressed by the quarters. But
they were the only ones. The soldiers who had survived the

Bulge thought they were living in a palace. The windows in the old house were blown out, the plumbing didn't work, part of the roof was blown away, and the floors were covered with trash—ration cans and cigarette packages thrown among the plaster and bricks and broken glass—but the men could cover the windows and heat the place a little, and they were out of the snow and wind. For a time, right after they arrived, the weather had warmed, but lately, in early February, snow was falling again. Still, the men were happy not to be digging fox-holes and sleeping in mud.

Alex and his men, shortly after arriving, had had the chance to take showers. They had stood in temporary canvas structures and let the water—not hot, but at least not freezing—run over their dirt-crusted bodies. Pulling off their long underwear, after almost two months without changing, had been tedious and painful. The hair of their legs and chests had grown through the cotton fabric, and it was impossible to undress without ripping a lot of that hair out. But once they had stripped down and soaked themselves, soaped up and scrubbed, they felt human again. And now, with a place to hunker down, out of the elements, they were living in comparative luxury.

After Alex had shaved, he had stood and looked at himself in the mirror. He was surprised to realize that his face hadn't changed any more than it had. He expected to look older, more haggard. His dark eyes and long eyelashes, the sculptured bones of his face, seemed almost effeminate to him now—after looking into hard, rough faces for so long. The way he felt inside, it seemed a sort of deception to look so much like his old self.

One afternoon Summers, on assignment from the company commander, came to see Alex. He was still the executive officer of the company, but his promotion had come through. He was *Major* Summers now. He and Alex shared a lot of history, all the way back to basic training in Georgia, and Alex respected the man more than any other officer in the company, but he didn't like the look on Summers's face today. Summers talked to Alex's platoon leader first and then came to Alex. The two stepped outside, away from the view of the Germans across the river, and they talked for a long time. When Alex walked back into the house, he could tell that he must have taken on the major's expression. Pozernac immediately said, "What do we have to do now?"

"I've got to get some people together, and then I'll tell you," Alex said. He went looking for the men he wanted. When he had gathered his "volunteers"—twelve soldiers—into the living room, he stood in front of them. They were sitting on the floor or leaning against walls. All the furniture in the room had been burnt in the wood stove, long ago.

"I've been asked to put together a patrol," Alex said. Most of the men moaned, and Alex didn't blame them. "My squad is going, and I chose you other five men because I know you've been around for a while. Your squad leader gave me permission to ask you."

Alex watched Pugmire and Kaplan. He wondered what they were thinking. But they kept looking him in the eye, probably trying to communicate that they weren't afraid.

"We're going to take a couple of rubber boats across the river. We know where there's an outpost in the basement of a building, just on the other side. We're going to go in fast, grab a couple of Germans, and bring them back. The S-2 isn't excited about sitting here with no idea what the Germans are doing over there. He wants to get hold of some soldiers he can interrogate. Sooner or later, we have to cross that river, and he wants to know what we're going to be up against."

Alex heard one of the men from another squad, a man named Ed Lyon, mumble something to the soldier next to him.

"What's the trouble?" Alex asked.

Lyon looked at Alex for a time, and then he apparently decided to say what he really thought. "These intelligence guys . . ." He cursed them. "They get tired of sitting around, so they put *our* lives on the line for a little information. I don't think we're going to learn much from a couple of German soldiers, and we're just about sure to get some of our men killed."

"I can't answer to the value of the mission, Corporal," Alex said. "What I know is that I've got an order, and I picked some guys who can carry it out. We've got a good plan. We'll hit quick and get back, and we've got all kinds of firepower backing us up. But if you don't want to go, just say the word. I'll get someone else. That goes for all of you. Just raise your hand if you want out."

Lyon swore again, but he didn't raise his hand. No one did.

"We're going to train with the boats in the morning, and probably the next day—but not where the Germans can see us. Be ready at 0800 tomorrow, and we'll get trucked to a place where we can make some practice runs. The mission itself starts at 2200, day after tomorrow. I'll fill you in on the whole thing in the morning."

Alex let the men go then, but what he felt was that Lyon was probably right. He wasn't at all sure that Intelligence could learn anything, and there was no question that the mission was dangerous. He also had to wonder why he was the one chosen to lead the mission. Summers said it was because he spoke German, but virtually every soldier knew how to say *"Hände hoch"* or *"Komm mit, schnell!"*

For two days the men trained with the boats, and then, as 2200 approached on a cold night, the men crouched by the river and prepared themselves to make their quick assault. It was cloudy, with no moon or stars. Most nights the Americans shined searchlights at the clouds and lit up the front along the river, but tonight there were no lights. The Germans put up some flares from time to time, and as usual, at random times, fired off a volley of artillery shells, but for the most part, it was a quiet night. From the American side, however, every German stronghold had been targeted, and a rifle team, machine gun, mortar tube, artillery gun, or some combination of all of those was ready to go into action should the patrol need the backing.

The crossing was to take place right in front of the stone farmhouse. The river had been high, even out of its banks a couple of weeks earlier. It was back to a normal width now, only about thirty meters across, but it was running swiftly. Alex was to take the first boat, with six men, row hard, and carry one end of an attached rope across. They would hook that up to a tree on the opposite side, and the second boat would use the rope to get across. Then, on the return trip, both crews would have the rope available for a quick escape.

When Alex and his men pushed off, they soon found that the water was even more swift than they had expected, but they worked hard, got across—even though they were carried well downstream—and Alex jumped out first. Just hanging onto the boat was a tussle, but the others soon leaped out and helped, and then they quickly carried the boat up the river to a place more directly across from the OP. They found a sturdy tree, tied off the rope, and signaled for the second crew to come across.

While Alex waited for the second boat, he surveyed the area, watched, and listened for any sign of movement. But all was dark. As soon as all his men were with him, he whispered, "All right. Let's go."

He moved quickly, without running, and all the men stayed in a tight group because of the dark until they reached a house where they knew a number of Germans were holed up. Just as the patrol had practiced, everyone fanned out, and then the designated men pulled their hand grenades loose and got ready. Pozernac fired a rifle grenade through a basement window, and then the others tossed their hand grenades in. Alex and a young private named Les Hartley were waiting, down a short flight of stairs, at the basement door. When the grenades went off, they both threw themselves against the door and smashed it open.

One of the grenades may have been a second behind the others, or maybe Alex hit the door an instant too soon. What he felt as the door gave way was the impact of flying debris against his uniform, his helmet. He had ducked his head, and he wasn't hurt, but he heard Hartley scream and drop to his knees. He had obviously been hit by shrapnel from a grenade.

"Come out with your hands high," Alex shouted in German. And then to the men behind him, "Hartley's down. Someone help him."

Two of his men ran down the steps, picked up Hartley, and carried him back. Alex stepped back outside the door, and he shouted, again in German, "Come out now, hands high, or we'll kill you all."

In a moment a German soldier appeared at the door. Just as Alex had hoped, he had been far enough away to survive the grenades, but he seemed to wobble, probably still stunned from the explosions. Another man was behind him. As the two stepped through the door, they hoisted their hands in the air.

"Come forward," Alex demanded. "Are there more?"

"*Alle sind tot,*" the first man said.

But that wasn't true; not everyone was dead. Another man appeared, the front of his uniform dark with blood. He was gasping for breath. Alex could hear by the wheezing that a grenade fragment must have penetrated his lung.

"Come. Come," Alex yelled at him. But this man was a problem. He needed medical attention right away.

Most of Alex's men had already disappeared in the dark. They had taken the two prisoners with them, and they were hurrying to the river. Everyone knew there would be a reaction just as soon as German gun crews knew where to target their shells. If the men in the patrol wanted to stay alive, they had to get back across the river fast.

Irv Johnston grabbed the wounded soldier. "He's not in

good shape," Alex told him. But Johnston was already pulling him down the little incline toward the river. "Who's got Hartley?" Alex yelled.

"I do," Curtis called back. "He's got a chunk of shrapnel sticking out of his forehead." It was a horrifying image, but worse was Hartley's anguished wailing. Alex ran to Curtis and they picked Hartley up, one on each side of him with their shoulders under his arms, and they hurried down toward the boat. They could see very little until they were almost on top of their own men.

The first boat crew was loaded, the men had one of the Germans with them. They had just begun to pull their way across the river, using the rope, when a flare lit up the sky. A second later, machine-gun fire began to snap, and tracer bullets darted like strings of light toward the river. Alex clung to Hartley, who was crazy with pain. His arm was around Alex's neck, and he was squeezing with tremendous power. "We'll get you help in a minute," Alex told him.

Somewhere behind Alex, he heard Johnston say, "This Kraut is in bad shape. He's collapsed. I don't think he can make it."

"Leave him," Alex said. "His own medics can help him."

By then, the first boat was out of the way, and Alex's crew was pushing their boat into place. Two men had hold of the second German prisoner, and they took him onto the boat. Everyone else helped to carry Hartley on, and then they started pulling across the water.

Another flare flashed over the river, and a few seconds later a mortar shell crashed into the water, close by. The boat rocked to the left, and just as it was coming down, an explosion struck on the opposite side. Most of the men had lost their hold on the rope, but Alex clung on, knowing it was their lifeline. The others grabbed at it as soon as the water settled a little, and they began to tug toward the bank again. Machine-gun tracers were still whipping through the air. The men pulled hard and were across the river in a minute or less, but getting out of the boat was not easy, with Hartley still screaming and flailing. "Kill me," he had begun to scream. "I can't stand it."

Just as Alex stepped out onto the bank, he heard a thud next to him, and instantly, a grunt. One of his men had dropped into the mud by the river. "Help me," Alex yelled. "We've got another man down, right here."

Alex heard men coming but could hardly see anything. He helped get Hartley up the steep bank, and then, with three others, carried him around the farmhouse. The man continued to scream, and Alex wondered how long it would be before he would lose consciousness. The shrapnel had to be through his skull, into his brain.

Once all the men were behind cover, several men held Hartley, and one of them got out a syrette of morphine, broke off the glass top, and then plunged the needle into Hartley's arm. He calmed rather quickly after that, but Alex held out no hope that he would live.

The bombardment was going crazy now, from both sides. American guns were firing into German positions, and all around the OP, mortars were dropping in, the building itself taking a couple of hits. The men stayed close to the wall and waited for things to quiet.

"Do we have those Germans secure?" Alex yelled between explosions.

"They're not safe with me here," Lyon shouted back at Alex. "I'm going to kill them both." He cursed, and Alex knew what he was feeling. Hartley was Lyon's best friend.

"Who else went down out there?" Alex yelled.

Pozernac was next to Alex. He said, "It was Pugmire. He got hit in the back. He's dead."

Alex suddenly felt sick. The guy hadn't been up front a week yet. He had a wife back home, a little baby. Alex took a long breath, and then he stood up. "Get inside," he demanded.

"We need to get into the cellar until all this fire stops. We could get some big stuff in here any minute now."

The men moved inside and then hurried down the steps into the cellar. There was no electricity in the house, but the men from the other squads were downstairs already, and they had lit a lantern that cast a pale brown light around the room. Alex told the German soldiers to sit in a corner, on the floor. He watched them, noticed how hard they seemed, how fearless. He saw the SS insignias on their collars. One of the men was an *Unterscharführer*—a buck sergeant in the military SS— and the other an *Oberscharführer*, or staff sergeant. They sat calmly, quietly, and they showed no sign of emotion.

A couple of the men had stayed upstairs with Hartley. The barrage of fire was continuing, and Alex worried about them. After a few minutes he walked upstairs to see what was happening. Lyon was kneeling by Hartley, whose breathing had become so shallow it was difficult to discern. "How's he doing?" Alex asked.

"We used the line to HQ to call for medics, but he'll be dead before they get here," the other man said, a corporal named Donaldson.

"For *what*?" Lyon asked. He turned and looked at Alex.

Alex didn't answer. "You men need to get to the cellar," he said, "so we don't lose you, too."

"He's our buddy; we'll stay with him," Lyon said.

A shell hit nearby, thumped into the field to the north of the house. And then, in the silence that followed, Alex heard Hartley take a long draw of air and let go. "That's it," Donaldson said.

Lyon got up. He turned and walked to the door and then trudged down the cellar steps. "Come on, Corporal," Alex said. "Let's get downstairs."

But just then Alex heard a commotion in the cellar, heard Lyon shout, "You did this! You did this!"

Alex hurried down the steps. By then, Pozernac had hold

of Lyon, but Lyon was still kicking at the two Germans, who were cowering in the corner. One of them was holding his face, and Alex knew that he had taken a punch—or a kick—in the head. Lyon was still fighting, swearing, trying to get in another blow.

Davis had moved in now. He helped Pozernac drag Lyon to the other side of the room. But Lyon's eyes were crazy with anger. "I want to kill someone," he was yelling. "Someone deserves to die for this."

Alex knew what Lyon was thinking, that maybe it was an American who deserved the death penalty—maybe the intelligence officer who had thought this mission up, or maybe Alex, who had chosen the participants. Alex walked to Lyon and put his hand on his shoulder. "Stop it," he said.

Lyon did stop his shouting, but he looked at Alex defiantly, the anger still raging in his eyes.

"Sit down and be quiet," Alex said. "Don't go near those Germans again."

"Then get them out of here."

"A couple of Battalion S-2 officers are coming over to take them. They'll be here as soon as things calm down outside."

"This wasn't right, Sergeant. I told you that before we ever started."

Alex had no reply. But he was relieved that Lyon was beginning to collect himself. Alex walked across the room, and he looked down at the two Germans. "We lost two lives capturing you," he said in German. "You *must* answer all our questions if you want to live. I *promise* you, these men will come after you if they learn that their friends died for no reason."

This was all said quietly but with a certain controlled anger. One of the Germans, the buck sergeant, was a young man with a stubble of dark beard. He appeared much younger than the other. Alex thought he saw some fear in the boy's eyes.

In the next half hour or so, the shelling from across the river slowed and then stopped. The S-2 officers, two lieu-

tenants, showed up looking entirely too young and inexperi-
enced, and they took the German sergeants away. Once they
were gone, Lyon and Donaldson and most of the other men in
the cellar decided to go upstairs and get some sleep, but Alex
kept his men downstairs. They were still riled up, not ready to
sleep yet, and Alex wasn't sure the shelling was finished for the
night.

The men sat around the edges of the cellar on the dirt
floor, all leaning against the whitewashed rock walls. Alex knew
they were feeling the same thing he was: the sickening sense
of loss now that they had time to consider what had happened.
And surely, too, the fear that always set in after surviving such
mortal danger.

"Pugmire shouldn't have been here at all," Pozernac said
after a time, as though he knew what everyone was thinking.
"He has a little kid at home who's never going to know him."

"I trained with Pugmire, right from the first day," Kaplan
said. "The guy was like a big overgrown Boy Scout. He was
always saying, 'After the war—this; after the war—that.' That's
all he thought about—getting back to his wife and his little
boy."

There was a long pause, and all the heads stayed down.
Finally Pozernac, clearly preferring anger to this excruciating
sadness, said, "I'd still like to shoot both of those SS sergeants
right between the eyes."

Alex tried to think how he felt about that. What he knew
was that flashes of the same emotion had fired through him
tonight.

"I could kill them and not bat an eye," Pozernac said.

He waited and got no reaction until Irv Johnston finally
asked, "What about when you get back home? Would you
remember something like that? Would it start to bother you?"

That was not the sort of thing the men usually talked
about. Johnston was probably the only soldier in the squad
who would pose such a question. Alex was pretty sure it wasn't

something good to talk about, but he hesitated. He was curious to hear Pozernac's response.

"It wouldn't bother me a bit," Pozernac said.

"It's the kind of stuff we accuse the Germans of doing—killing prisoners, shooting men who try to surrender."

"It *is* what they do."

"So we should do it too?"

"Shut up, Johnston. Just shut up. I get tired of all your . . ." But he couldn't seem to think of the word he wanted.

Johnston glanced at Alex. He had those strange pea-green eyes, and the lantern cast a yellow glow on his face. "I shot a guy the other day," he said. "A German over on the other side of the river. He was way off, and I didn't think I could hit him. I was mostly just bored from sitting around. So I allowed for the distance and squeezed off a round. And the guy went down. He didn't move either. I think I killed him."

"That's what we're here for, Johnston," Pozernac said. "Maybe you don't understand that."

"I understand. But that guy was just leaning against a building, having a smoke. And I took a pot shot at him for the fun of it. I gotta say, since I did that, I've been wondering what's wrong with me. I've got a feeling that ten years from now—*fifty* years from now—I'm still going to be thinking about that guy."

"That's stupid, Johnston. Really stupid. He'd kill you without giving the idea a second thought. This is war, not Sunday School."

"That's right. But when you get home are you going to go to church—sit there with all those decent people and act like you're just the same as they are?"

"What's that supposed to mean?" Pozernac started to jump up, but as he did, Ernst grabbed him, held him.

"That's enough," Alex shouted. "Both you guys—just be quiet."

"Hey, I'm just curious," Johnston said. "I'm not—"

"I said be quiet!"

"Okay. Fine."

"Let's go upstairs and get some sleep."

Alex got up, and the men tramped silently up the steps to the room where all of them slept in close quarters, their bedrolls spread out on the floor. Pozernac was still mumbling, telling Ernst what he thought of Johnston, but Johnston didn't seem to care.

Alex lay down, with only a blanket around him. That was not a problem. He had slept plenty of nights that way. What he feared was that his mind wouldn't stop. He could push Johnston's questions aside—he had been doing that for a long time—but he wasn't sure he could stop thinking about everything else that had happened that night.

It took a few minutes for the men to settle down, but soon after they did, Alex heard a sound outside that he couldn't identify. The broken windows were covered with torn-down curtains or burlap sacks. The coverings cut out the wind and some of the cold, but not the noise. Alex could hear a buzzing sound rise to a whistle, hesitate, then repeat itself. The pattern continued for some time before it was interrupted by a sound that Alex did know, instantly. It was a gurgling, loose cough.

"It must be that German—trying to breathe," Curtis said. He was lying next to Alex, and he had obviously been wondering about the noise too. "The one with the fragment in his chest."

Pozernac cursed. "I'm not going to listen to that all night," he said. But now he sounded as though he were trying to cling to his anger, the passion of it gone.

Every soldier feared, more than anything, a slow and agonizing death, with no help, no painkiller. And alone. The man was out there on the riverbank, and the Germans hadn't found him the way Alex had thought they would.

The wheezing continued for a couple of minutes before Ernst said, "I'm going out, Sarge. I'll throw a grenade across the river and finish the guy off."

"No. You'll draw fire."

"Yeah, but . . . I think we owe him that much."

Alex, of course, was already thinking the same thing.

"He was SS, the same as those other guys," Pozernac said. "Let him suffer."

But the wheezing didn't stop, and every draw of breath sounded like a cry for help. Then the coughing would come again, and sometimes a moan. Each time the breath held, hesitated, Alex hoped that was the last, that the poor guy could die. But on and on the sound continued, and Alex could not will himself to ignore it, to sleep. He kept thinking of Pugmire, of Hartley.

Maybe half an hour passed, and the room was silent, but Alex heard very little of the snoring and deep breathing he had usually known in this room. He was confident he wasn't waking the men when he finally said, "Okay, Ernst, go throw a grenade. Put the poor guy out of his misery."

Ernst got up without saying a word, and he thumped down the stairs. It was a couple of minutes before the grenade exploded. After, no one in the room moved. But the desperate breathing continued. Ernst had obviously waited and listened, even though he was in a dangerous spot. Moments later, another explosion sounded, and this time Alex waited, his own breath holding. And he heard nothing.

"That did it," Curtis whispered.

Ernst returned before long, and he lay down. "I'd want someone to do that for me," he said, and Alex was struck by the kindness in the boy's voice.

But Alex still lay awake. Every time he shut his eyes, he saw the same image: Hartley, his face full of agony, that thick sliver of steel sticking out of his forehead, blood pumping from around it. And he kept hearing the thud, the sound when Pugmire had taken that bullet in the back. There were other pictures too: his friend Duncan, with that jagged cut across his throat; Howie, face down in the snow.

Alex didn't sleep much all night. And he didn't feel like eating in the morning. It was almost 0900 when Captain Summers drove up to the OP in a jeep. He came inside and said, "Thomas, I need to talk to you. Step outside with me."

And then, once outside, Summers said, "Great job on that patrol last night. That younger German talked a blue streak. We know what they've got over there now—troops, guns, tanks, everything—and we learned a lot about the fortifications in the Siegfried Line along this sector. When we cross the Moder and attack that line, we're going to be a lot better off."

"We lost two men," Alex said.

"I know that. But we saved a whole lot more. We can't go on the attack without that kind of information."

Alex nodded. He hoped that was true. "Can I tell the men that? Some of them are pretty upset."

"Of course you can tell them. But Thomas, we're pulling you out of here."

"Where are we going?"

"Not your squad. Just you."

"What do you mean?"

"The army is looking for German speakers. All kinds of intelligence information is being gathered from inside Germany now, and it all has to be interpreted. I don't know what you'll be doing exactly, but you'll get some training, and then an assignment."

"I'd rather stay, Captain. I don't want to leave my men."

Summers laughed. "I remember back in the states, about a hundred years ago, you told me that you didn't want to be a squad leader. You wanted to get into Intelligence so you wouldn't have to kill anyone."

Alex knew that, but he also knew how he felt now. "I want to stay with these men. The young guys need someone experienced to get them through."

"Bentley knows the ropes. So does Pozernac."

"Neither one is quite right to lead the squad, Captain. I want to stay. I'm serious."

"I know that. But it's not your choice. You're being promoted to second lieutenant—effective immediately. That's a battlefield commission, one of the greatest honors that can come to a soldier."

"Please don't do this."

"Get your gear."

Alex stood his ground, silent for a time. But there was nothing he could do. He walked inside, and he found Curtis. "They're pulling me out," he said. "Sending me to some kind of Intelligence school."

Curtis stared at Alex as though he hadn't understood.

"I'm sorry. They won't give me a choice."

Curtis was one guy who never seemed to change, never seemed to look any older. But when tears began to drop onto his cheeks, he looked like a little boy.

7

David Stinson called Bobbi on a Saturday afternoon. An hour later they were sitting next to one another on a bus, on their way to Honolulu, and Bobbi was feeling guilty every time his elbow touched hers. She didn't think Richard would mind her spending this bit of time with David. What troubled her was the turmoil she was feeling, the excitement she kept trying not to show. She didn't want to give David the wrong idea.

She walked with him in town and took him to the Iolani Palace. Then they caught another bus to the beach at Waikiki. David took off his shoes, rolled up his uniform trousers, and waded into the water. Bobbi thought that surely must be "against regulations" or "out of uniform," but David didn't care. And when he strolled too deep and got caught in a wave, he didn't seem to mind that he got wet all the way to the waist. "Come on in!" he kept shouting back to Bobbi, and finally she took off her sandals and let the water run over her feet a little, but she was wearing a pretty white skirt and didn't want to get it wet. Still, she laughed at David as he splashed about, daring the waves, and then running from them.

"This is great," he said, when he finally walked out of the water. "I haven't played in the ocean since I was a little kid."

He was pulling his stockings from his pockets, so Bobbi

handed him his shoes. "We should have planned better," she said. "We could have brought our swim suits." But she had thought of that earlier and decided not to suggest it. The last time she had gone swimming, she had been with Richard.

"Naw. That was enough. I'll be back in the water again before long. Only next time I'll be charging onto some beach—with bullets flying past my ear. Now *that's* what I call excitement."

"Is that really what you're headed for?" Bobbi asked.

"Sure. That's what we heroes do. And it doesn't scare us, either. We whistle 'The Marine's Hymn' the whole time."

"Keep your head down while you're whistling. Okay?" Without exactly meaning to, she had touched his arm, and she saw him react, take her in with his eyes the way he had always done back when she was his student. She had always loved that, the longing for her she felt from him. Richard had told her that he wanted her, but never with the passion she felt from David.

She turned away. "Should we go get something to eat?" she asked.

But he was looking down the beach, toward Diamond Head. He suddenly threw his arms out, as if to reach wide enough to grasp it all. "At least I got to see this. The Marine Corps gave me that much. It's almost worth the price." Bobbi thought his voice was a little loud. People on the beach were turning to look at him, smiling. "I want to eat some poi and roast pig and—hey, where can we find a luau?"

"I know a restaurant that serves real Hawaiian food, but you can't go there with your pants all wet. It's a fancy place."

"Okay. Then I'll dry off. Let's sit down somewhere."

Bobbi knew a bench near the beach. It was a place where she had often sat with Richard, but she took David there now, and the two sat where they could look out over the ocean, see the swimmers and watch the sailboats on the water.

David was still taking it all in. "Look at the color of the

ocean out there," he said. "The Atlantic is never blue-green like that, at least not where I used to see it."

"I've been here so long that I forget how beautiful it is," Bobbi said. "You make me see it all over again."

He turned to her, rested his hand on her shoulder. "When I found out I was coming here, I decided it was fate—that the cosmos wanted me to see you again."

"Another few days and I would have been gone."

"I know. It *is* fate."

She could see in his face, in those fervent green eyes, that he was serious, at least to some degree, and she worried about the conversation that would follow.

"Bobbi, I made a big mistake. I can't find anyone else like you, and I want someone to share my life with. I'm not happy. I haven't been happy since that day you got on the train in Chicago."

"It was the right thing, David."

"I'm not so sure about that anymore. And I'm not entirely convinced that you are either."

"David, don't do this. I need to make up my own mind."

"Are you saying that your mind *isn't* made up?"

"No. It is. I'm just not quite sure about the future, the way things are right now. Richard is so hard to read sometimes."

"Okay. I'm just going to say this, and then I'll slip out of your life again." He took hold of her hand. "If you go home and he turns out to be something less than you think he is—and if you're still single when I come home—will you think about our giving it one more try?"

"David, our problem hasn't gone away. You told me that my church was the center of who I am—that you would rob me of that if we got married. That's still true, however much it hurt me at the time to hear it."

"Maybe I'll become a believer after all. You know what they say about atheists in foxholes." He tried to laugh.

"I wish you could believe, David."

"Do you mean that?"

"I only mean that it's what you need. It would make you so much happier."

"Okay, here's the truth. I have been praying. I don't believe in it, but I want to believe in something—just because I've felt so empty lately. I'm a skeptic at heart, and I can hardly keep a straight face when I pray, but something sent me here before you left. Believing in fate is something like believing in God, isn't it?"

"I don't know. You used to tell me you believed in God in your own way."

"Sure. But that's like saying I believe sap rises in the trees each spring. Call it Mother Nature, or whatever you will, I only believe some force is at work in the world. I also know what will happen if a Japanese gentleman, of the Shinto faith, shoots his rifle at me, a man of Christian upbringing. If his aim is good—no matter who is praying for what—I'm going to die."

"I've had some experiences in the last year that make me more sure than ever that prayer works, David."

"Well . . . maybe I could live on your faith—as long as I got the rest of you to go with it."

Tears were suddenly on his cheeks, and Bobbi hadn't expected that. She gripped his hand tighter. "I'll pray for you," she said.

"Please do," he told her. "I can almost believe that might make a difference."

"You shouldn't be a soldier, David. You're the last person I know who should shoot at anyone."

"No. I can do it. You don't know all the sides of me." He looked back out toward the ocean. "I'm not asking anything of you, Bobbi. That wouldn't be fair. But I'm pretty scared. Maybe I'm just trying to cling to something. I want to go into battle with a fantasy in my head. You know, that I'll come marching home, and you'll still be there—and we can work something out."

"David, I am planning to marry Richard. You have to know that."

"I do know it." He turned back toward her and gave her a little slap on the back—like a buddy. "But it's my fantasy—so I can dream up anything I want. Hey, let's get a hamburger. I don't want to wait to dry."

So that's what they did. And after, they walked again before they took the bus back to the base. Then he left. He didn't try to take her in his arms. He merely bent toward her and kissed her on the cheek, and then he walked away. Bobbi, by then, was wishing that he had never come. She didn't need this confusion, and she feared she had only opened an old wound for David.

On Sunday Bobbi spoke in sacrament meeting. She thanked the members of her ward for her experience in Hawaii. "I have learned so much from you," she told them. "You may not see a great change in me outwardly, but I feel different. I would like to find joy in life and not worry about the things I can't control—as Sister Nuanunu has tried to teach me. I'm not good at that, but at least I know it's the better way."

After the meeting, virtually everyone took turns hugging her—men and women and all the kids. She not only accepted the embraces, but she also enjoyed them, hugged the people back, and she wept with all these dear friends who told her how much they loved her.

When Bobbi finally left, she took the bus to Ishi's house, along with Ishi and her children and Afton and Sam. It was not an easy time for any of them. They ate dinner together and tried to laugh, but after, when Bobbi was getting ready to go, Ishi clung to her and said, "You've gotten me through this terrible time. I don't know how I'll get by without you now."

"Oh, Ishi, the war in Europe can't last much longer. Daniel will come home before long, and then you'll have your life back."

"We've said that for such a long time. It's hard for me to believe it really will happen."

"I know. But let's not worry so much. I mean it when I say I'm going to try to be better about that."

Ishi laughed, with tears still in her eyes. And Bobbi cried all the more when she hugged and kissed Lily and David. And they cried too. Little Lily clung to Bobbi and kept saying, "You're my best friend, my very best friend."

Bobbi knelt and told her, "We'll still be friends. We always will be." But it was a weak truth, if true at all, and certainly Lily knew it.

Sam and Afton drove Bobbi back to the base and dropped her off. Bobbi did her final packing, but it all went much faster than she expected, and suddenly, when she had nothing else to do, her loneliness struck her full force. She had been so home-sick when she had first come here, and now she was hardly sure where home was. She wished she could finish out the war in this little cubicle of a room with Afton and the things she knew.

Bobbi walked outside into the soft, moist warmth of the Hawaiian evening. She knew the time she had spent here, even with the war and the worry, was a lovely addition to her life. She felt, a little to her own surprise, that almost everything she knew, she had learned here.

She walked around the base, collecting images she wanted to store in her mind and take with her, even stopped by the hospital to say good-bye to the nurses on duty and a few patients she had grown close to. When she returned to her room, Afton was there. The two sat on their beds, across from one another. "They're going to put another girl in here, Bobbi," Afton said. "Golly, I just can't stand to think of it."

"You'll get to know her. You'll like her."

"It won't be the same. She'll never understand me the way you do."

"At least she won't try to *mother* you."

"I could use a mom right now."

Bobbi knew what she meant. Afton had finally written to her parents that she was serious about her relationship with Sam. She had gotten back a frantic letter from her father. It was full of warnings about interracial marriage. "Come home first," he had pleaded. "You've lost touch with how things are here. Don't do anything until you've had some time back here with us."

"What are you going to do, Afton?"

"We're going to get married."

"When?"

"I don't know. I want to write my parents again and tell them what this means to me. I'd like to have their blessing, but if they won't give it, I'm going to marry him anyway."

"I think Sam might make a better roommate than I've been."

Afton smiled. "I doubt it. You keep everything in its proper place. He's pretty messy."

"He still might be better to wake up to in the morning."

"Right now, I'm thinking more about going to bed with him at night." She giggled.

"Where are you going to live, once you get out of the navy?"

"In Honolulu, I guess."

"Will you miss the mainland?"

"Sure. But I don't know what else to do. No one gets everything, Bobbi—not exactly the way we want. But I'd rather give up Arizona, and even my home, than give up Sam. He means too much to me now. And it's not just that he's handsome. He's exactly what my parents want, if they only knew."

"Well, you won't miss me, once you have that big lug around your house."

"When the war is over, you and Richard can come here on vacations—and we'll have some great times together."

Bobbi nodded. Afton knew that David had been to see her,

but Bobbi had reassured her that she was still committed to Richard. It was Richard's commitment to *her* that she had been wondering about. And maybe David's notion about fate—although she didn't tell Afton that.

"'When the war is over.' Isn't that what we always say?"

"What will we have to dream about when it really is over?"

"I don't want to think about that, Bobbi. I don't want to be realistic. I just want to believe that everything will be better."

"I can't imagine that other times will be as hard as this has been. But I think this time will always be a good memory for me in most ways—and that's, as much anything, because of you, Afton."

"I'm closer to you than anyone else in the world, Bobbi. Even Sam doesn't know me as well—not yet, anyway. We can't lose each other. Okay?"

"Okay."

But that was another half truth, at best, and Bobbi knew it. Life was changing again. And there would be no going back.

A week later the *Charity* docked in Guam, with Bobbi on board. Then it joined a large task force and shipped out again. No one on the medical staff knew where the task force was headed. Bobbi spent her time getting ready—training staff, organizing medical supplies, thinking of things to worry about. On the third day out she had almost finished her lunch in the officer's ward room when Dr. Kate Calder, her new friend, approached the table. "May I join you?" she asked.

"Sure. But I've got to head back to the ward before long."

"No you don't. Take a few minutes. You're pushing yourself too hard."

Bobbi laughed. "I've never been in charge of anything before. I'm worried all the time that things won't be organized right when the action starts."

So far, Bobbi had no patients aboard, so life might have been easy, but she had a big staff of corpsmen, many of whom were young and new, and she had very few nurses to help her train them. She knew that when the wounded began arriving, all these young men would be tested to the limit. The task force was certainly headed into battle, and since the troop ships were stacked deep with Marines, it was obvious that a beach landing was going to take place. That meant casualties, and lots of them—or at least that's what all the experienced personnel told Bobbi.

Bobbi wished she had Kate's confidence. Dr. Calder had graduated from Radcliffe and Johns Hopkins Medical School. She was a tall woman with a presence about her. When she walked into a room, people turned toward her. Some of that came from the self-assurance in her voice, but it also had to do with the way she moved. She took direct paths, stood straight, stepped forward like a commander. She had told Bobbi right after they first met, "Don't let these male officers scare you. They'll run right over you if they think you're a shrinking violet."

Kate was a pretty woman, too, though she did little to enhance her appearance. Her light hair had a lovely texture and pretty tones, but she cut it short and didn't curl it. She had wonderful eyes, very brown for her light complexion, but she wore little wire-rim glasses that weren't very flattering.

Bobbi looked across the ward room. Four male doctors were sitting at a table. They were laughing rather boisterously, as they often did. This was a strange world Bobbi had entered. She hated the confinement, the gray paint everywhere, the closed society. She could never get away from the military atmosphere the way she had in Honolulu—didn't have her civilian friends in the Church. There were three corpsmen on board from Utah and Idaho who were LDS. One of them seemed to be running from the Church, but Bobbi and the other two had held a little service, of sorts, on Sunday. Still, there was no chance to meet people she could relax with. The officers were mostly older and more experienced. Their talk, their lifestyles, their drinking, their attitudes—everything about them—made her uncomfortable. The rest of the ship was filled with young men she couldn't "fraternize" with. She liked a couple of the nurses, and Kate, but she felt alone most of the time.

Kate was bent forward with her elbows on the table. She was eating, with seeming satisfaction, a meatloaf that Bobbi had found barely tolerable. "Have you ever thought about medical school, Bobbi?"

Bobbi had finished all she wanted to eat; she pushed her tray back. "No. Not at all," she said. "My father pushed me into nursing school. I was an English major my first two years of college. Dad thought I needed a degree in something 'useful.'"

Kate laughed. "That's interesting. Literature is my other great love. I had to make the same choice. But at least I made it myself. What about when you get married? Are you going to let this Richard fellow you're engaged to decide what you do with your life?"

It was the same question David had asked. "I don't think he's that way, Kate. But the thing is, I'm not sure I know what I want to do anyway. I'm not much of a cook, and I can't sew a stitch, but I suspect I'll end up being a mom, and doing it pretty much the way my own mother did."

"That seems sad to me."

"Why?"

"I don't know. If it's what you want, it's fine, I guess, but women are going to have a lot more choices from now on. It seems like someone with your talent ought to make a mark in the world."

"Raising kids is making a mark."

"Sure. One kind. But there's no reason we can't do everything men do. Women will come out of this war with some confidence and experience, and with some new doors open. More med schools are opening up to women every year. Even Harvard has started admitting women now. When I came up, it was tough enough to get in, but then, when I said I wanted to be a surgeon, I heard nothing but 'you can't do that.' And that just made me all the more sure that I not only could but would."

"I will say this," Bobbi admitted, "I've always felt that I had a pretty good brain, and maybe some ability to do something special with my life. I've just never been very sure what it should be, or whether I was arrogant to think so. I—"

"See, that's exactly what we have to get past. What man ever thinks it's arrogant to go after his dreams? 'You stay home and feed the kids, and support *me*,' they tell us, and then they go out to slay the dragons while we wipe runny noses and feed the chickens. The truth is, there's too much testosterone and stupidity in this world. Women need to step forward and have their say."

Bobbi laughed. She liked Kate's ideas, even if they seemed a little dangerous to her. Still, she didn't think she could be, or even wanted to be, quite like Kate.

In the middle of February Bobbi's ship anchored a considerable distance off the shore of a small island. For the first time in her life she heard the pounding of artillery shells, could even see the distant flash of muzzle fire from the big navy battleships. She saw, too, flights of bombers, just tiny spots in the air, the flicker of explosions, and then, after a delay, the subtle rumble that rolled across the sea.

There was something strangely pretty about the little fireworks show, but the idea of it was horrifying. Bobbi watched the bombs detonate, saw the smoke drift off in the tradewinds, and she wondered how many people would die. Who were they? What made this little spot in the open sea worth fighting over?

Later that day, one of the ship's officers told her that the island was called Iwo Jima. It was one of the Volcano Islands, and a Japanese possession. "It's halfway between Guam and Japan," the officer told her. "My guess is, we need it for a B-29 base, so we don't have to fly so far to bomb Japan."

That made sense—the kind of sense a newspaper report might make—and Bobbi had always followed the war closely in the newspapers. But what she could see was a dark spot, like a gray stain on the water, and all around it the vast green Pacific. It was so hard to imagine why humans would need to kill each other for such a tiny dot on the planet. She could see the endless armada of American ships between her and the island, and she knew that any time now young men would be clambering onto that little chunk of land, and the killing and maiming would accelerate. Then she would have to see these boys. They wouldn't be names in a newspaper this time, but real men with real wounds. One of them could even be David.

Again the next day the shelling and bombing continued until a long plume of dust and smoke was steadily floating from the island out to sea. And then, on the next morning, February 19, word spread throughout the ship that the landing had begun. Bobbi walked out and watched the distant wave of little specks—landing craft, moving toward the beach. And she saw that in spite of the tremendous barrage of fire that had been directed at the island, the Japanese gunners had survived, and their own barrage was lighting the horizon now.

The next couple of hours were frantic and yet slow. Bobbi kept trying to think of last things: preparing instruments, gathering bandages and medicines, placing everything where it could be reached quickly. She knew that the burn ward would be crucial for some of the patients. Burns had a way of taking their victims slowly. A badly burned man would sometimes suffer for two or three days, seem to be doing better, and then suddenly die of the shock and loss of skin. Often it was the action in the first few minutes or hours that saved lives during the following days.

Eventually, she felt the ship's big engines start, and then the *Charity* steamed closer to the island and anchored again. Shortly after, someone shouted, "We've got a landing craft on its way, and it's loaded down."

Bobbi prayed, and then she waited. It was some time before the first patient was processed through triage and sent down, but he was a battered young sailor. He had come off a ship, not the beach, and he had been far too close to some sort of explosion. The problem was, he was pierced with shrapnel, and his whole upper body and face were covered with bandages and blood. A corpsman carrying one end of the litter shouted, "The doc said the burns are worse than the wounds. But we have to hold the bleeding while we start the debriding."

The corpsmen set the young sailor on a table, and two doctors went to work immediately removing the bandages, looking to see what they were dealing with. Bobbi stayed close. She had seen a lot of boys brought in off hospital ships after days or weeks of care, but never anyone still this bloody and black with burns. The tag on his foot said that he'd had a shot of morphine, but the boy was moaning, low and anguished.

His face and hands were burned worse than his chest. When the doctors pulled the bandages loose, the boy's fingers were bent and bloody, like claws. There seemed no flesh left on the bones. But another patient was coming, and she needed to help him. And then everything started to mushroom. For the rest of the day patients came in bunches, the flow never exactly letting up. Bobbi worked with the corpsmen, debriding skin, applying bandages that were embedded with Vasoline and salves, guiding the doctors to the men who were in the worst shape.

Soon blood was everywhere. Sometimes the triage doctors and nurses had to make fast choices, and they sent down men who needed surgery more than care for their burns, but in many cases, Bobbi knew, the patient was not going to live, no matter what. When Bobbi could see that there was no hope, she would tell the corpsmen to give the patient plenty of morphine and to provide what comfort they could. Then she would have to walk away.

A priest kept returning to the ward. He gave last rites to

men who looked at him, wide eyed, perhaps realizing for the first time that they were not going to live. Or he prayed over men who were, in truth, already dead. But he also spoke to the living, and Bobbi saw how desperately some of them clung to him for solace.

Early in the afternoon a Marine was carried into the ward. He was wrapped in bandages from his chest to his thighs, and his face was black with burns and glistening with a salve that the corpsmen at the front had applied. He seemed older than most, but certainly not more than twenty-three or four. His eyes were darting about as though he were frantic under the haze of all the morphine he must have in him.

Bobbi looked at his tag and noticed he was an officer. At the same moment, she heard Dr. Spencer, the youngest of the burn ward doctors, curse in language that surprised her. She looked up to see that the doctor had cut away and folded back the bandages over the man's middle. She caught a disgusting smell—feces, perhaps, and something else, sour and putrid. The man's abdomen was wide open, and his insides were exposed. One hip was torn up so badly that the bone was showing. "What's this man doing down here?" Doctor Spencer shouted.

By then Bobbi was spinning away. She was going to run, but it was too late. She lurched forward and vomited on the floor. She stayed bent for a moment, and she took a long breath, but she knew she couldn't do this. She just couldn't. She was the head nurse in this ward. But already she was retching again, and another splat hit the floor. She wiped her mouth with her hand, spat, and then she looked up, expecting everyone to be staring at her. But most were too busy, and no one seemed to pay much attention. A corpsman was mopping, had never really stopped all day, and he came quickly. The vomit was only one more fluid on the floor, and he wiped it away quickly.

Bobbi ran to the women's head, washed her face and hands,

rinsed out her mouth, and then hurried back. She went to the officer and took hold of his hand. Doctor Spencer had moved on, but he glanced over his shoulder from the next table and said, "There's nothing to do for him. I don't know how he ever got this far."

Bobbi saw in the man's eyes that he had heard, that he understood. His body had been blown up some way. Something had torn away at him, opened him up, and still his heart was trying to live. She looked into the man's eyes, nodded to him. "Are you in pain?" she asked.

He stared at her for some time, and then he whispered, "Please."

That was all he said, and she didn't ever find out what he had meant. Please make the pain stop? Please save me somehow? Please let me die?

In any case, he did die—later. For now, Bobbi gave him another shot of morphine, and then she had to move on.

For two days the pressure rarely let up. That first night Bobbi took two little naps, maybe half an hour each time, and the second night she finally slept for about three hours. But the casualties kept coming, and eventually the doctors in the burn ward were doing surgeries, removing limbs, extracting shrapnel, sewing up wounds. They left the belly and chest wounds to the surgeons, but they handled almost everything else. On the third morning the ship's captain got approval to move out. The vessel was loaded to the brim, and the doctors couldn't handle any more patients. They would carry these men to the hospital in Saipan and then perhaps return for more, depending on how long this battle lasted.

There was no real letup, and with so many burn victims needing continued attention, Bobbi had hardly eaten for two days. She wasn't hungry, but she was weak, and Doctor Mickelson, the senior medical officer in the burn ward, told her to eat something and then rest for a little while.

Bobbi trudged to the mess hall, rejected the sausage and

scrambled eggs she couldn't bear to look at, and took instead only some slices of toast and a glass of milk. She found a table away from the few other officers who had found time for breakfast, and she sat before the toast, taking a bite once in a while, but hardly finding the energy or interest to do more than that.

Kate was across the room with some of the other doctors. When she got up from the table to leave, she spotted Bobbi and came over. "How are you doing?" she asked. "You look beat."

"I'm tired. Who isn't?"

Kate sat down. "The first time is the worst," she said. "From now on, at least you know what to expect."

Bobbi nodded, but all she could think was that experience wouldn't really help in this case. If anything, she dreaded the next go-round more than she had the first.

"We could save more of these boys if we had the time."

"It's so crazy, Kate. We watched those poor kids head for that island, and then we sat here and waited because we knew exactly what would happen to them. What kind of sense does that make?"

Kate reached across the table and touched Bobbi's shoulder. "Back home," she said, "the parents get the body, all cleaned up. They bury it, and they talk about honor and glory. We don't hear military bands over here. We see these kids when they're quivering and begging for help."

"Kate, I vomited—in front of my nurses and all the corpsmen."

"I've never been through one of these evacuations without seeing someone do that. I've seen doctors with lots of experience lose everything, right next to the table where they were operating, and never stop. I've been lucky enough to make it to a head whenever it's happened to me, but a couple of times just barely."

"I'm used to burns, but not . . . all this."

"It adds up, Bobbi. All the smells and the blood and the images just keep accumulating. I can promise you that you won't sleep well for a while, no matter how tired you are."

Bobbi hadn't noticed that Dr. Spencer had walked in. When she glanced up, she saw him standing behind Kate. He had washed and changed, but there were little dots of blood on his glasses that he apparently hadn't noticed. "How are you holding up?" he asked, but he didn't wait for an answer. "Wait just a second. Let me get a cup of coffee, and then I want to tell you something."

Dr. Spencer walked to the big coffee urn. He was a tall man, big in the shoulders and even in the hands. At times he could be rather gruff with a nurse or corpsman who didn't respond the way he wanted, but there was also an obliging, docile side to him. Bobbi had seen him put those big hands on a suffering patient and calm the man.

When Dr. Spencer came back to the table, he sat down next to Kate and took a sip of his coffee. He shuddered and said, "Ugh. Nasty stuff." But then he said, "I talked to a young Marine just a few minutes ago. The boy had some minor burns, and he had taken a bullet in his thigh. I told him he was lucky, that he had gotten off pretty easy. Now he could rest in a hospital for a while. You know what the kid told me?"

He looked at Bobbi and then Kate. They both shook their heads.

"He called me a filthy name. He told me his buddies were dying out there, and he wanted to be with them."

"Really?" Kate said.

"He said some Marines had made it to the top of that volcanic mountain, down at the end of the island, and they had put up an American flag. Then he said, 'You guys out here, you've got no idea what that means. A lot of hard-nosed old Marines broke down and cried when they saw that flag up there.'"

"Wow," Kate said. "I don't know how he can see all this and still feel that way."

Dr. Spencer took another sip of his coffee, set it down, and looked away, across the room. "We see the gore. But these guys put their lives on the line, and they have to believe it's worth it or they couldn't keep up the fight. What we can't forget, in the middle of all this mess, is that it *is* worth it."

A few days later, Bobbi's ship docked near the hospital in Saipan. She looked out across the beach and knew that somewhere on that island—on a beach like this one—Gene had been shot. Maybe he had died on the beach; maybe he had made it to a hospital ship like hers. She didn't know. What she did hope was that someone like her had been there and given him comfort in his last moments of life. And she hoped Doctor Spencer was right—that the loss of her brother had been worth it.

8

"Sign this, both of you, and then you can get out of here."

Wally Thomas took the sheet of paper from the Japanese interpreter—*Mister* Okuda, he liked to be called—and read what it said: "I, the undersigned, under the peril of death, agree never again to attempt to overthrow the Imperial Japanese Government."

Wally looked at Chuck, who had just read the same statement. Chuck shook his head and smiled. "What's this?" Wally said, looking back at Okuda. "We were both sick. We rested for a few seconds. That's the only thing we can be accused of."

"Don't sign it then. You can stay in this little cell for as long as you like. But if you sign it, you can get out."

Wally knew better than to trust this man. Okuda had lived in California at one time and sounded like an American. He pretended to be on the prisoner's side, but he was devious and would betray a man without hesitation. On the other hand, since the night that Wally and Chuck had been tortured, they had been held in this miserable little jail cell in the prison guardhouse. In all the chaos, after the bombing, Hisitake seemed to have forgotten all about them, but the conditions in the cell were unbearable. "How will this be used against us?" Wally asked.

"It won't. You'll return to your barracks and to the mine. But if you ever cause trouble again, you won't be spared. It will be the death penalty for you."

Wally glanced at Chuck and saw the dismay in his face, but he also knew that neither one of them would last much longer if they didn't get out of the guardhouse. They had received very little to eat in this place. "I'm going to sign it," Wally said.

Chuck nodded, and Okuda led the two of them out of the cell to a little desk, where he handed Wally a pen. Wally dipped it in a bottle of ink and then signed. Chuck did the same.

"All right," Okuda said. "You can go back to your barracks. But don't expect to sit around any longer. You'll go back to work in the morning."

Wally was too weak, too preoccupied to let Okuda bother him. He was thinking about the days ahead. He would receive nothing to eat until that evening, and there would be no extra ration, no way to recover from what he and Chuck had just gone through. His body was still beaten up, and he wondered how he could get through the coming days in the mine. But it was like everything else he had survived for such a long time. He would simply have to find the strength one more time.

As Wally and Chuck stepped out into the light, they stopped for a moment and shaded their eyes, but then they trudged on across the compound. Wally's knees were still shredded from the hours he had spent kneeling on the bamboo poles. The wounds were beginning to heal, but the soreness made it difficult for him to walk. His back was worse, however. When Hisitake had beaten him with the shovel, he had injured something in the small of his back. Wally still wondered whether something weren't broken in his spine. He hunched forward and shuffled across the compound.

Chuck was in pain too, and very weak, but at least he hadn't taken a beating. "Can I help you, Wally?" he asked.

"No. I'm making it."

But by the time they reached the barracks, Wally was exhausted. He lay down, thankful that he still had one more day to rest before he had to return to the mine. What he discovered in his room, however, was disturbing. Some of the prison buildings had been destroyed in the bombing, and now the prisoners were forced into tighter quarters. Fifteen prisoners had shared a room in the past, but now thirty mats were crowded together. Wally knew that the men would be sleeping almost on top of each other. The nights were cold, so that was actually not so bad for now, but he could imagine the misery in such confined areas once the heat of summer returned.

Wally and Chuck slept much of the day, and then they limped to the mess hall and received their usual ration—a little rice and a bowl of weak soup. When they returned to their barracks with the other men, now back from the mine, they learned more about the bombing raids. No POWs had been killed, but little was left of the city of Omuta. Incendiary bombs had set off huge fires and wiped out buildings for as far as the men had been able to see as they had marched to and from the mine. Even the buildings at the mine opening had been destroyed.

"A bomb got the mine god," Don Cluff told Wally. "He's dead as a doornail."

"So what did they have you do when you got to the mine the next morning?"

"Nothing. They just sent us on down. I guess they figured that any god who couldn't look out for himself wasn't worth bothering with."

The men laughed, but Art Halvorson asked, "How bad was it, you guys?" and the room fell silent. Everyone knew what the guards had done to Wally and Chuck. Many had seen them out in the compound, kneeling on the poles, and word had spread about all the hours of torture they had been forced to endure.

Wally was lying flat, trying to rest his back, but he was in a lot of pain. He rolled his head to the side and looked at Chuck, who was on the next mat, close to him. "I guess it was the worst thing the Japs have done to me," Wally said. "I thought I wasn't going to make it."

"Yeah," Chuck said. "It was probably the worst thing I've been through."

No one had to be told any more.

"Someday these guards are going to pay for all this," Eddy Nash said. "One of these days troops are going to land, and we're going to get out of this place. But before we leave, I'm going to get some of these guys—especially Hisitake."

"I want Okuda," a man across the room said.

For a time the men talked about the guard or the mine supervisor, or even the American collaborator, all of whom they wanted to get revenge on. Wally didn't enter the conversation, but he thought of the things he would like to do to Hisitake: maybe rip that sword off him and make the haughty little creature kneel across the blade for a while. He told himself he wouldn't really do such a thing, but he liked the idea of threatening him, making him plead for mercy.

As soon as the men quieted, Wally went to sleep, but in the middle of the night he moved just a little; pain shot through his body and woke him up. He had slept a great deal the past few days in the jail, and that had been a blessing, but now his body was angry with pain. He knew that before too long he would have to pull himself off the mat and make it to work. He was cold now, the little blanket and even Chuck, next to him, not enough. His knees were throbbing and so was his back. He tried to find a better position, but nothing took away the pain.

Wally was awake and suffering when he heard thunder. And then he realized that the sound was repeating in a pattern, that it wasn't thunder but bombs dropping. Slowly the noise increased, the crack of the explosions becoming more defined. But just when he thought the bombs might become a threat, the noise stopped. He was sure the city had been bombed again, and he liked the idea. That had to mean he had a right to hope for an end to all this agony before too much longer.

All the same, the next couple of hours passed slowly, and then, when it was time to get up, he had to roll onto his side and struggle to his feet. Chuck and Don helped him, but his first steps hurt so badly he couldn't imagine walking all the way to the mine. Still, he made his way outside with the others, stayed on his feet through roll call, and then, after eating a ration of rice, began putting one foot in front of the other the way he had been doing in one way or another for almost three years. By the time he reached the mine, he felt that he had expended all the energy he had, and yet he had a full day of work ahead of him.

Wally's crew was still assigned to an area of the mine that was flowing with cold water. Most of the men found a high spot and sat down, and then they ate their midday ration of rice from their *bento* box. Wally ate his rice too, but he didn't sit. His back hurt too much to get up and down.

He was standing near the other men, aware mostly of his pain—his deep weariness—when he noticed that the supervisor was sitting by himself. He was bent forward, his arms on his knees and his forehead against his arms. His body was quivering, and Wally thought maybe he was sick. But then he realized that the man was sobbing.

Wally didn't know the supervisor's name, didn't know anything about him. What he noticed was that he had come to the mine without shoes. That was strange, and Wally had to wonder what was happening. He picked up his lamp and walked to the man. "Are you all right?" he asked.

The supervisor looked up. Wally was holding out the lamp. It cast a rust-colored light across the man's face. Tears were on his cheeks.

"Can I help you?" Wally asked.

The supervisor showed no reaction, and Wally wondered

whether he knew any English at all. But then he said. "No. Nothing you can do."

Wally nodded. He didn't know what to say.

"Bombs come. Kill children."

"*Your* children?"

"Yes."

Wally stared at the man. He couldn't think what to say. The supervisor nodded as if to say, "Yes, you heard right," but then he put his head back on his arms.

"Why are you here?"

The supervisor looked up again. He didn't answer, but Wally understood. He hadn't been given a choice.

"I'm sorry," Wally said. He thought back to the night before when he had been happy to hear the bombs drop. He hadn't meant to take joy in something like that—not in the death of children. Certainly not in the loss of *this* man's children.

Wally, in spite of the pain, bent enough to touch the supervisor's shoulder. The touch seemed to move the man; he cried harder.

* * *

Alex Thomas was in Lyons, France, or at least close by. But he wouldn't have known that if someone hadn't told him. He had seen nothing of the city. He had spent his time camped in a tent at an airfield. Every day for two weeks he had been told that "very soon" he would know what was going on, but that he should "sit tight for the present." He had gone through much harder times, but never a period that had made him more nervous. All the hours with nothing to do—and no idea what he would be doing—had been torture for him.

Finally one afternoon early in March he was asked to report to the office of a Lieutenant Colonel DeSantos—someone he had never heard of. When he reached the office, another man was already waiting in the outer office. He was a dark-haired man, shorter than Alex and more slightly built. He was wearing a civilian suit that was clearly European, and Alex assumed the man was French. But when Alex announced his name to the sergeant at the desk, the civilian stood up and said, in German, "I'm Otto Lang—your partner."

At the same time the sergeant said, "You two can go on in. The Colonel is waiting for you."

Alex had no idea what was going on, but he followed Lang into the office, where DeSantos had Alex and Lang sit down across from him, near his big desk. "Did you two get a chance to meet?" the colonel asked.

"Yes. Only just now," Lang said, in English.

"Lieutenant Thomas, I'm sure you're wondering what's going on."

"Yes, sir."

Colonel DeSantos was a slender, dark man with a thin face and a long, narrow nose. He seemed a little rough around the edges, more like a blue-collar worker than a gentleman officer. His teeth were stained dark, and his shirt was too big around his neck. He took a puff on a huge cigar and then set it across a glass ashtray on his desk. The office was almost empty. It was a crudely thrown together shelter with wall studs and ceiling rafters showing. The big cherrywood desk was the one sign of elegance in the room, and it seemed out of place.

The colonel leaned forward and looked directly at Alex. "I understand you speak fluent German."

"Yes."

"You were a missionary. Right?"

"Yes."

"Well, we've got a mission for you. But it sure ain't religious. The report I have is that you don't soldier like a choir boy."

Alex didn't reply.

"I'm an atheist and a communist, myself," Lang said, and he laughed, almost silently, his breath sucking in. "I can look out for the missionary."

DeSantos glanced at Lang and seemed a little less than pleased at the remark. "Well, in any case," he said, "we have a tough assignment for the two of you. Lang here has been through OSS training. He just flew in from London. He's going to be the team leader. Thomas, if you decide to take this assignment, we'll give you what training we can before you make your jump, but for the most part, you *will* have to rely on Lang to get you in and out."

"In and out of where?"

"Well, yeah. I'm getting a little ahead of myself. Let me tell you, quickly, what's going on. You'll get more details before the mission begins. But you need to know, this is absolutely top secret. Don't tell *anyone* what's going on. Don't write home even a hint about it. Do you understand that?"

"Sure," Alex said, but he thought the warning almost funny. He wasn't allowed to leave the field, and he had already been told that even though he was an officer every letter he wrote would be read and censored.

DeSantos picked his cigar up, took a draw on it, leaned his head back, and blew the smoke into the air. Alex hated the smell of it. "The British Second Army and the Canadian First are going to cross the Rhine before too much longer—we don't have an exact date yet, but in a couple of weeks—and to do that, we're going to drop the Seventeenth Airborne, along with the British First and Sixth Airborne divisions, on the other side of the river. They'll knock out some guns and establish a salient where the crossing can take place. We won't tell you where this is going to happen for right now, but here's what we want you to do. You two will drop in by parachute a few days ahead of the main drop. You'll locate the artillery in the area and let the paratroopers know what they're up against. You'll also identify the best drop zones for the troopers and the best landing zones for gliders. We have pictures of that area, but we've learned on past drops there are things you can only spot when you're down there at ground level. That's why we want to send you, Thomas. We need someone with airborne experience who can also speak German."

Alex nodded, but he suddenly felt light-headed, dizzy.

"We have a safehouse set up for you. Resistance in Germany isn't strong, but some of these workers in the Socialist Workers union are willing to help. They're going to run some sabotage operations to slow down trains, blow up power stations—that kind of thing. They'll also put you up and help you with your cover story."

Alex was hardly hearing any of this. He was thinking about Anna, about the baby. What would his chances be of getting back to them?

"Now listen to me. I mean this. I've told you just enough to give you an idea what you're up against. But I don't want to send you in there against your will. You're the best man we could find to pull this off—but some things a man shouldn't be forced to do. If you want out of this, say so right now. No questions asked."

Alex hesitated, tried to think whether he could really say no.

"You're married, right? Got a baby on the way?"

"Yes."

"So do you want to do this?"

"No. Of course not. But if I don't go, who does?"

"I don't know. We'd try to find someone else. But it's hard to find a man with your experience who also speaks German."

"I speak fluent German, but not without an accent. Anyone who hears me will know immediately that I'm not a native German."

"We know that. We're not stupid around here, Thomas. I'm not with OSS, but I'm with the army Counter Intelligence Corps. We've been putting teams into Germany for several months now. We've got a story ready for you. You won't talk any more than you have to. Lang here will deal with anyone who questions you—as much as possible, anyway. If a question comes up, you'll say your mother is an American, and you were raised in Nebraska or Iowa, or wherever it was—the whole thing will be scripted for you. You'll claim that your family moved back to Germany, and you were in the Hitler Youth, and you saw the light—or something of that sort. You get the idea."

Alex nodded. "Will there be details? Where I lived in Germany and—"

"Sure, sure. And we'll have all the fake papers made up. That's exactly why I'm talking to you now. We need to know who's going so we can get everything ready. We're going to send you in there with full military papers, wearing *Waffen* SS uniforms."

"Isn't that against the Geneva treaty—wearing an enemy uniform?"

"Thomas, don't start that. The Germans did it in the Bulge, and they've done it in other places. We need to have you moving around once you get in there, and who can move around better than a military man? You'll claim you fought in the Ardennes. And now you're on leave."

"If we are caught, they will shoot us," Lang said.

"No question. Especially you, Lang. You're a traitor from their point of view."

"I'm a traitor from any point of view." He laughed that airy laugh of his again, and he looked at Alex. "The OSS recruited me from a POW camp."

"So what are you, Lang?" DeSantos asked. "Some kind of anti-Nazi?"

"Certainly," Lang said, but he laughed again, and then he said to Alex, in German, "They promised me I could migrate to America. That's all the anti-Nazi training I needed."

Alex thought he understood. Most Germans knew the war was lost, and they also knew how bad conditions in Germany would be once the war was over. Lang was obviously worried more about himself than he was about politics. His honesty was appealing, in a way, but Alex didn't think he liked his flippant attitude.

"Well, anyway, that's the outline of things," the colonel said. "So what about it, Thomas?"

Alex wondered. Maybe he owed it to Anna to refuse. But who didn't have someone at home? How could he say no and cause some other guy to go? "I'll do it," he said, but the words almost made him sick. He thought about the few minutes he had spent across the Moder when he and his men had taken those German prisoners. He remembered the terror he had felt at being in enemy territory.

"Aren't you going to ask me the obvious question?" DeSantos asked.

"Yes, sir," Alex said. "How do we get out?"

The colonel smiled. He stuck the cigar back into his mouth and leaned back in his chair. "That depends. If all goes well, Allied forces will get across the Rhine quickly and overrun the area where you'll be operating. We have code words you'll use. So you'll approach the lines, give your password, and be allowed to go on through. Then you'll come back to us, and we plan to use you in the CIC."

"Sir, I just left the front lines. If a soldier meets up with a couple of men in SS uniforms, he isn't going to wait long enough to listen for a code word."

"You can approach one of the checkpoints our boys will have set up. By then, lots of Germans should be surrendering. I don't think it will be a problem." He hesitated. "Hey, you know what I mean. I'm not trying to tell you this is a cakewalk. I'm just saying things are worked out. We expect you to get out when it's over. You shouldn't be in there longer than about ten days. We aren't sending you out to sacrifice your lives."

Alex wondered. He knew that operatives were expendable—part of the numbers game of war. If two men could save thousands of lives, their lives were worth gambling. Alex didn't disagree with that idea; he just didn't feel a lot of comfort about being the expendable commodity.

"One more thing. We're moving this whole operation. We're

going to be flying out of Dijon, a little north of here, from now on. So we're sending you two up there by jeep this afternoon. Thomas, you'll be trained by Lang and some other OSS boys. We usually give a man eight weeks of training for a job like this, and you're going to have to learn what you can in two. So work hard. Anything they teach you might save your life. I'm not going to wave the flag at you, but I gotta say, you men are heroes. You could shorten this war by months if you do your job right."

With that, he stood. Alex and Otto stood too, and Alex saluted. Then he and Lang left the room. Once outside, Lang said, in German, "I think we just got a load of manure dumped on our heads."

"What do you mean?"

"Let's just say that the likelihood of living through something like this is not very good."

Alex turned toward Lang and took hold of his arm. "Listen to me, Lang. You go ahead and die if you want to, but I'm coming back. My wife is going to have a baby in three months, and I *must* get back to her."

"That's fine with me," Lang said. "All in all, I would rather live than die." He laughed in his strange way again, drawing in lots of air. "And call me Otto," he added.

But Alex didn't like any of that. This was no game. Alex needed someone at his side who was just as intent on living as he was.

* * *

Peter Stoltz stood at the farmhouse door and waited. He was taking a great chance, but he knew nothing else to do. He had to get something to eat. When the door opened, a woman was standing before him—a little woman, maybe forty, maybe younger. Her hair was covered with a brown scarf, and she was wearing a faded brown house dress, the shape of it gone. She stayed back, held the door, seemed ill at ease.

"I am *Polnisch*," he said—the German word for "Polish." "I work. You give food."

The woman smiled just a little, but she shook her head. *"Nein,"* she told him. And then she spoke in Polish. Peter understood a few words. He had been traveling among Polish refugees for the past few weeks. They had shared their food with him, however meager their own supplies had been, and they had let him sleep by their fires.

This German woman was turning him down. He caught enough words to understand that, and he also understood her problem. There were so many refugees and so little food. A woman like this had to look out for her own children.

He turned to go, but she spoke in Polish again, and he didn't comprehend her meaning. She might have been offering food, but he wasn't sure. At least she had sounded apologetic. *"Danke,"* he said, and he hesitated, waiting to see what she might do.

She repeated some of the same words, but he couldn't put the ideas together. She must have seen his confusion. "You're not Polish," she said, in German.

"Danke," he mumbled again. He decided he'd better move on. If she guessed who he really was, he could be in trouble.

"You're a German boy. You've run from the army."

He stepped off the porch and set out walking, meaning to get as far away as he could before she tipped off some local party official or policeman.

"Wait."

He kept walking.

"I can use the help here. And I'll feed you. I don't blame you for what you've done. Soon everyone will have to run."

He stopped and considered. Maybe she was baiting him, tempting him to stay so she could report him. But he needed to eat. So he walked back.

"I only wish my husband had run. He was killed last fall."

"Where?" Peter asked.

"I don't know. No one ever told me. Somewhere on the eastern front."

"We were all dying there."

He hadn't meant it quite the way it came out, but the idea was right. Peter had died there, he was quite certain, and now he was alive again. Or maybe he was someone else. It was hard to think that he was the Peter Stoltz who had gone to battle.

"Spring is coming. I need to plant. I've never done it by myself. If you will stay here and help me, I'll tell people . . . something. I'll think up a story. Do you have papers?"

"No. Only military papers."

"You could be wounded. You could be my nephew. We'll think of something."

"I've never farmed. I know nothing of planting."

"I know a little. I need help—and some strength."

He smiled. "You're stronger than I am, I think." He didn't say it, but he felt as though he might pass out.

"Your face is like ashes. You haven't eaten, have you?"

"No."

"Come in and sit down. I have bread and *Wurst*. You eat that, and then I'll cook something more."

Peter walked into the little farmhouse. The front room was dark, but in the kitchen the afternoon sun was filtering through sheer white curtains, and the place seemed something like his home, the apartment he had grown up in—or at least the kitchen did.

"Sit down. Tell me your name."

"Peter." He didn't know what last name he would use, but he chose, for now, not to offer one. He slid a chair back and sat down. He knew that he was filthy, and he ought to wash, but he needed to eat a little, to feel some strength before he did anything else.

The woman brought bread to the table on a bread board, cut slices of it, the dark slabs folding over. It was all he could do not to grab for it. But he waited until she brought the *Wurst* and a little block of cheese. She sliced these, too, and still he waited. When she set a board in front of him, a knife and a

fork, he finally took a slice of bread, set it on the board, and
then some cheese and some slices of the *Wurst*. He ate as he
had long ago, in his home, cutting with his knife and fork,
combining the bread and cheese and meat, but eating small
portions. When the woman brought milk, he didn't gulp it but
took long drinks, feeling the smooth coolness of it.

"How old are you, Peter?"

He hadn't thought of this for a long time. He stopped to
consider. "Eighteen," he finally said.

"Where are you from?"

"It's better not to tell you these things. If I have to run
again, it's better that you not know."

"That's true. But if you tell me things, I won't reveal them."

He nodded, kept eating. The bread was soft and fragrant,
the *Wurst* pungent with flavor. "Thank you," he mumbled. "This
is the best meal I've eaten for . . . I don't know. Maybe ever."

She laughed. "Have you been through a lot, Peter?"

Peter was suddenly struck by the affection in her voice, the
way she pronounced his name. It was like hearing his mother.
But it hurt, too, and unexpectedly, he felt tears on his face.
"Yes," he said. "No one should have to do what we did."

"This war was wrong from the beginning, Peter. Hitler was
wrong. My husband said it ten years ago, and he was right."

"My parents said it too. More of us should have said it
louder. We should have stopped him before he led us into this."

"Yes," she said. "That's what we should have done. But no
one dared."

"Hitler has done terrible things. I heard stories in Poland.
He killed people by the thousands. Maybe millions."

"Jews?"

"Yes. Many Jews. But Poles and Russians too—anyone he
feared."

"I hear these things now. But we didn't know this, did we?"

"We knew enough."

"We didn't, Peter. I didn't."

"Where did you think the Jews were going when the Gestapo took them away?"

"To camps. I didn't know the Nazis would kill them."

Peter didn't want to talk about this. In the past few weeks he had seen so much. He had passed through a town called Treblinka, and there he had heard the stories. Jews were being gassed and then burned in ovens—thousands, every day.

He was still eating when a girl came into the house through the kitchen door. She was skinny, a teenager, and she seemed surprised to find a stranger in her kitchen. She looked like the woman—who was obviously her mother—with round, black eyes that bulged. They were pretty eyes, actually, but strange.

"This is Peter," the woman said. And she told the girl the little she knew about him. Then she said, "Peter, I haven't told you my name. I'm Frau Schaller, and my daughter's name is Katrina. I have two sons, both younger. You will meet them soon. We have a room in the attic of our house. There's no bed there, but I can give you plenty of blankets. You will be warm and maybe not so uncomfortable."

"It sounds fine," Peter said. But in fact, it sounded much better than that. He was sitting in a kitchen, eating good food, and he was in a family, almost part of it, it seemed. He had never thought something like this could happen to him again.

Heinrich Stoltz was sitting in a small train station in the little town of Landau, not far from Karlsruhe. It was a dismal morning, with a heavy mist in the air, and the smell of burning coal from the trains was so strong and sour in the air that he felt a little ill. Or maybe it was just that he was nervous.

A few early morning travelers sat on the benches in the waiting area, all of them bundled up in heavy coats because the train stations were not heated these days. Brother Stoltz waited until he saw a man approach—a man with a newspaper in his left hand. "Do you mind if I sit here?" the man asked. "My feet are aching."

"Not at all," Brother Stoltz said. "Give your feet some rest."

The man was bigger than Brother Stoltz had imagined he might be, almost brutish. He was wearing worker's clothes—a mechanic's coveralls and a worn-out cap—and his massive jowls hadn't been shaved for a few days. But he had carried the paper in his left hand, had given the proper code words—the statement about his aching feet. Perhaps his appearance was something of a disguise.

"They tell me that you want to help? What are you, a professor?" The man kept his voice down, but it was deep—as though spoken from a cave.

"I was a teacher at one time in my life."

"This may not be the right work for you, *Mein Herr.* We're not professors, our people."

"It doesn't matter. I want to do my part. What should I call you?"

"My code name is Wolf." He turned and looked directly at Brother Stoltz. "Can you crawl about, by night, and blow up train tracks? That sort of thing?"

"I have no expertise in such things, but yes, I will work with others if they can show me what to do."

"I guess we'll take what help we can get, but you're not what I would go looking for."

"I want to bring Hitler down, to end this war as soon as possible. Isn't that qualification enough?"

The man looked about. A train was approaching on one of the tracks outside, the sound building as the rhythm of the engine slowed. "Keep your voice down," he said. And then he asked, "Are you a socialist?"

"No."

"Most of us are, you know. Very few people will fight this man. They're all too frightened. But those of us who want a better world, we are willing to fight for it."

"You want to team up with this butcher, Stalin, and make a better world that way?"

"Listen, if you can't work with us, tell me now."

"It doesn't matter. I want to do *something,* so I'll know all my life that I didn't just sit by and let Hitler have his way."

"You've waited a long time. We needed more resisters long before now."

"Yes. Yes, I know."

Brother Stoltz glanced around the train station. The few people—mostly men in military uniforms—looked half asleep, worn down by everything they had been through. He wondered what such men thought of Hitler now. He heard less enthusiasm these days, less reverent talk of "the Führer," but he also never heard anything he could call criticism. There was so much stoicism now, even fatalism, recognition of the dark time ahead, but people didn't speak openly of that either. They simply kept surviving, staying alive each day. If they cursed anyone, it was the pilots who bombed their cities, but even that kind of talk had diminished. Everyone in the western cities knew that those same Allied forces who bombed their homes would soon be crossing the Rhine, occupying the area. And the fear of Russia was much greater than fear of the Allies.

"The crossing will begin soon," Wolf said. "The Allies will make a major move before long. Everyone knows that, of course, but we know the points where the crossings will take place. We are in contact with Allied operatives working here in the country. We are to bomb railroad tracks and power stations, knock out guns, make things easier for the invading troops."

Wolf surely knew Brother Stoltz's connection to the OSS. Georg had put the two in touch with each other, and he certainly would have told him that much. It didn't seem wise, however, to say anything more than necessary. The fact was, Brother Stoltz knew nothing of the invasion, and Wolf did. "If I engage myself in such sabotage, will I have to kill innocent civilians?" Brother Stoltz asked.

"Possibly. I can't guarantee that will never happen. But we take precautions. We don't blow up tracks when trains are approaching. For the most part, all we do is delay the train. The railroad people have learned to repair tracks quickly. They are used to it. But a delay of a few hours, in certain circumstances, can make a significant difference. If we can keep troops or ammunition from arriving fast, the invasion could go much better."

"I want you to understand—I know that lives must be taken in a war. And I have taken my stand. I stood up to the Gestapo. My son and I fought an agent, injured him badly. I am no coward. But what I want is to save lives, not kill."

Wolf nodded, and he seemed impressed. "You surprise me," he said. "You fought a Gestapo agent? That is more than I have done." He laughed. "You have some shoulders on you, and good arms, but you look too gentle."

"One of my shoulders was broken by a Gestapo agent. And my knee. I'm no fighter, and I never was. But I will do what I have to do. I know you need younger men, ones who can carry heavy loads and run fast. I can't do those things, so if you don't want me, just say so. But I want to help if you will let me."

"It's good. I can use you. How shall I call you?"

Brother Stoltz laughed. "If you are a wolf, perhaps it's best to call me *Hase*."

Wolf laughed. "A hare? You said you couldn't run."

"That may depend on how scared I am."

He nodded. "There's good reason to be frightened, my friend. There is a certain amount of danger to others, as I said, but most of the danger is to us. I hope you understand that. The tracks are guarded these days, and the *Abwehr* is always trying to track us down. Once you join us, you are on the road to death. Perhaps, now, the Allies are close enough that we can hope to survive, but for years I have expected every day to be picked up and shot. Many of my friends have met that fate."

"I understand. I thought about all of that before I made my contact."

"All right, then. We know how to reach you. We have someone in Karlsruhe. He will contact you on the street, probably as you leave the bakery where you work. I will tell our man to mention a hare in some way, and that will be your way of knowing him. It won't be long now."

"Good. I'll be waiting for your contact."

Wolf got up and walked away. Brother Stoltz would catch the next train back to Karlsruhe. He was glad that he had finally made this contact, but he was ill at ease. For such a long time he had wanted to do something more, strike a blow of some kind. At the same time, he knew how dangerous this was.

Perhaps he owed his wife and family better than that. But then, that was what most Germans were thinking, and that's why so few had taken a stand.

So Brother Stoltz waited, and he returned to Karlsruhe, and each day, as he left the bakery, he wondered whether someone would approach him. He was always a little relieved when it didn't happen, since he was apprehensive about taking a step into deeper danger, but he also knew that the sooner the action came, the sooner the Allies would cross the Rhine and penetrate the Reich. And then, Hitler would fall.

* * *

LaRue had study hall in the library every day right after lunch. As often as not, she spent the time talking to her friend Verla Sumsion. LaRue actually wasn't doing badly in school—at least for someone who rarely studied. She had raised her grades since fall, when her father had gotten upset with her about all the time she spent at the USO. LaRue had been more careful since then about handing in all the little busywork assignments she hated. What she didn't bother to do was read her textbooks. She got through by listening to what was said in class and by bluffing on tests. Algebra couldn't be bluffed, but it was easy for her, so she managed to get by with little effort there, too.

Today she was sitting across the table from Verla, and the two had been gabbing about this and that—mostly the basketball team, or more specifically, the boys on the basketball team. But then Verla surprised LaRue by asking, "Did I see you walking down my street with Cecil Broadbent the other night?"

"You might have," LaRue said. "I did go for a walk with him." What she didn't admit was that she had gone for a walk with him not just once but three times.

"Why?"

"I don't know. I've known him all my life."

"You don't *like* him, do you?"

"Not really. Not like you mean. But he's kind of fun to talk to. He's really smart."

"He's not very cute."

"He's not so bad."

"I don't think he's cute at all." Verla was looking across the little library room. One table was filled with boys, most of them seniors. They were playing a game, like hockey, with pencils and a wad of paper. Mrs. Shurtliff, the librarian, had been to their table twice already, warning them that they could lose their study hall privileges. But they were at it again. They kept laughing and watching out for Mrs. Shurtliff.

"Those boys are so ridiculous," Verla said. "They never take anything serious."

"Most of the seniors who amounted to anything dropped out to go into the service last year."

"That Nealey boy—Duane—he's kind of cute."

"He's dumb as a fence post, Verla. I'd never go out with him."

"Since when did you care about that? Is that what you like about Reed—that he's an A student?"

"How did you guess?" LaRue said, and she laughed. But she decided that maybe she should get a little reading done for her English class. That was the hardest class for her to fake her way through. She opened her copy of *Silas Marner.* "I'll tell you the truth about Reed," she said. "He does his homework, so he gets pretty good grades. But he's not a whole lot smarter than that basketball he bounces around."

Verla giggled. She was a tiny girl with hair that looked reddish in the sun, but here in the library it seemed less than blonde, too light to call brown. She had pale, almost colorless skin, except for a smattering of freckles. But she did have a cute round face, with big eyes, and a lively sort of smile. She was not beautiful, but she was very popular. She never missed a school dance even though she didn't have a steady boyfriend.

"If I looked like you, LaRue, I'd pick out the best-looking

boys in the whole school—and wrap them around my little finger."

"Hey, I've got Reed wrapped up, nice and tight. And there are some other guys waiting in line." She laughed, and then she breathed on her fingernails and rubbed them in a polishing motion on her sweater. In some ways she liked this image of herself. On an impulse, she stood up. "Watch this," she said. "I'm going to test my powers on those boys."

"Oh, brother. Look out," Verla said, and she giggled.

LaRue walked across the room toward the table where the seniors were sitting. As she approached, all six heads came up. "Young men," she said, and she gave them a sly smile, "you are distracting those of us who want to take our studies seriously. How can we girls think when all you big strong boys are over here drawing our attention away from our books?"

"Come here," a boy named Tom Denkers said. "Sit down by me, LaRue, and I'll study you—or I mean study *with* you."

That got a big laugh from the boys. But LaRue waved her finger at him and said, "Naughty. Naughty. Now that's just what I'm talking about. We need a lot less laughing around here and a lot more attention to the things that matter."

"I can see what matters," a boy named Brig Evans said. "I'm giving it *all* my attention."

She stepped closer and began to pet his hair. "You're such a cute little kitty," she said. "Let me hear you purr."

He leaned his head against her side and made a buzzing noise. All the other boys howled with laughter, and suddenly Mrs. Shurtliff was on her way. LaRue decided she'd better make her getaway. She added a little extra swing to her stride as she walked back to Verla—and she knew that she had twelve eyes locked onto her. When she sat down, Verla asked, "What did you say to those guys? They're all about falling out of their seats."

"It's not what you *say*, Verla. It's how you say it."

"LaRue, you're really something. I could never do anything like that."

LaRue laughed, and she did enjoy the sense of her own power. But when study hall ended and she walked down the hall to her next class, Brig caught up with her and tried to pursue the little conversation. The problem was, his attempts at wit were obvious and stupid, and now she knew that she would be getting phone calls from him—and invitations that would force her to lie. Sometimes she thought she would be better off to announce that she was going steady with Reed. But that would get back to her father and cause a fuss, and it would also lead to more and more tedious evenings with the boy. The only problem was, she really didn't think she knew anyone else at East High she wanted to go with.

That afternoon, when LaRue got home, she did resolve that she was going to dig into *Silas Marner* and at least get enough read to give herself a fighting chance on the test the next day. But she had been reading for only a few minutes when someone knocked at the front door. Beverly yelled up the stairs, "LaRue, it's for you."

LaRue had an idea she knew who it was, and she was surprised at how pleased she felt. She walked downstairs. "Hi, Cecil," she said when she saw him through the screen door. Beverly had left him standing on the porch.

"I wondered, would you like to go for a walk?" Cecil asked. "It's pretty warm outside."

All the snow was off the ground now, and even though the trees weren't budding out, hyacinths and tulips had begun to stick up from the ground. LaRue liked the way the earth was beginning to smell, like winter's back was finally broken.

"I'd better not," she said. "I need to get a book read for English. I have a test tomorrow."

Cecil laughed. "When LaRue Thomas turns you down for a book, you know you've gotten the brushoff," he said. "Okay. I'll see you later."

LaRue was disappointed he had given up so easily. "Let's sit on the porch for a minute," she said. "But not long. I've got this whole book I should read tonight. I was supposed to start it about two weeks ago."

"Which one is it?"

"*Silas Marner.*"

"Hey, it's short. It won't take you two hours to read."

"Apparently I don't read as fast as you do, Cecil."

"Do you want to know the plot?"

"Sure." Suddenly LaRue realized she had a good thing going.

"Okay. Go for a walk with me, and I'll tell you the whole story—complete with the symbolism Mrs. Drake will find in it, and the likely essay questions, with answers."

"Cecil, my boy, just let me grab my coat."

LaRue ran upstairs, got her spring coat from her closet, and ran back down. She told herself she didn't care who saw her. Cecil would only add a little complexity to her image. "Okay, tell me the whole story," she said, as she stepped out the door.

"All right." He grinned. "Silas is an old weaver with bad eyes. He's been hoarding up gold all his life. Meanwhile, back at the ranch, these two brothers, who are rich and spoiled, get into a lot of gambling debt and . . ."

He told the story in dazzling—but rather confusing—detail. LaRue could hardly follow it all.

"So this poor woman is wandering around or something, and she dies, and her baby daughter toddles off to Silas's house. He thinks she's his bag of gold, but—"

"What?"

"Remember, he's got bad eyes, and she has golden hair."

"Are you making this up?"

"No, no. He raises this little girl, and then the rich brother wants her back. But the little girl—Eppy—she sticks with Silas, and she marries her childhood friend. Oh, and they empty the pond for some reason, and Silas gets his gold back."

"You must be kidding."

"No. It's not so bad. Mrs. Drake will ask you to describe the 'theme' of the book, and all you have to say is that Silas is a simple, pure man—be sure to use that word—and he receives his just reward, which is far better than gold. He finds out gold doesn't mean a thing compared to his love for his lovely Eppy."

"Oh, brother. It's lucky you came along," LaRue said. "I could have actually read that book."

"I shouldn't make fun of it, really. It's not one of my favorites—as you can tell—but it's not as bad as I make it sound."

"I'd rather go to the movies."

Cecil laughed. LaRue could see he was looking up toward Parley's Canyon, probably thinking how beautiful the snow was. She didn't care. She just wanted spring to come, and golden summer, when she would be out of school.

They walked east, and then south on Thirteenth East, past town, and out toward the farms and orchards that lay beyond. LaRue loved the clear air, the feel of the sun on her face and hair, but she wondered what the walk was doing to her new saddle shoes. She wished she had changed them before she had left the house.

Cecil talked mostly about essay questions that Mrs. Drake might come up with. LaRue pretended to be excited about all the information, but in truth, she felt guilty. She knew exactly what her MIA teacher, Sister Galbraith, would say about her cheating this way.

Cecil was wearing a gabardine jacket that made him look like an old man. He took if off after a time and swung it over his shoulder. And then, obviously trying to sound casual, he asked, "So what's happened to that boyfriend of yours, LaRue? The one at the USO?"

The question took LaRue by surprise. "How do you know about him?"

"I don't know. Someone told me you had a boyfriend from the East somewhere."

"He was just someone I danced with. I didn't care that much about him—until he left."

"Do you write to him then?"

"Yes."

"Sounds kind of serious."

"I don't know." LaRue was starting to get warm too. She unbuttoned her coat to let a little more air in. "He was really nuts about me, Cecil. I think he actually does love me. Reed might have a crush on me, but it's all kind of kids' stuff. Ned wanted to marry me."

"At your age?"

"It was stupid, in a way. But it was pretty nice to have someone feel that way about me."

"So what's going to happen? Is he going to come home after the war and take you away?"

"I doubt it. For a while, I thought maybe I'd be interested in him. But his letters are full of spelling mistakes."

"Oh, no!" Cecil leaned his head back and laughed. His voice was strong, usually, but when he laughed hard he made high-pitched little squeaks that delighted LaRue.

"No, wait," LaRue said. "You didn't let me finish."

"Oh, all right. But for a girl who doesn't like to read, and who likes movies better than literature, you're suddenly sounding a lot like Mrs. Drake."

"I don't care about the *spelling* exactly. I probably misspell words in my letters too. But it just reminds me that he's probably never going to go to college, never make anything of himself. If I ever get married, I want a husband who'll let me . . ." She wasn't sure whether she should finish her sentence. She thought it over and then said, "Okay, I'm going to tell you the truth."

"All right."

"I want to be rich. And I want to get that way myself. I

want to own a company and run it—like my dad, only something bigger than his little plant. I want to be the boss. And I want to live in a fancy house and have *tons* of nice clothes. And I want to go on trips to Europe and have a cook and a housekeeper and . . . I don't know. All the things rich people have."

"Maybe you'd better read *Silas Marner* after all."

"It's too late. I want all the gold I can get. My dad wants to bring my brothers into his business. But he never thinks about Beverly and me. So I want to start my own company and make his look like small potatoes. The problem with Ned is that he's just going to get a job somewhere and work all his life. I want more than that." She looked at Cecil and smiled. "I know what you're thinking," she said.

"What?"

"That I'm shallow."

"Well, yeah. But I already knew that."

She turned and punched him in the shoulder—hard.

Cecil pretended to suffer from the blow, but he was at his worst when he tried to play around. He just didn't know how to do it, and he ended up looking goofy. To make things worse, he put his jacket over his shoulders without slipping his arms into the sleeves, as if trying to look like a movie star. But he was looking serious by then, and he said, rather carefully, "But now I'll tell you the truth about me. I'm just as shallow."

"Oh, good."

"But not quite in the same way."

"Not so good."

"I want to be famous. I want to be a scientist and make some incredible discovery that will put my name in history books forever. And it's all about revenge. I want to come back here to Sugar House someday, walk down the street, and have my old school friends say, 'Look. It's *Cecil Broadbent*, the famous scientist. I actually went to school with him.'"

"Their kids will all want your autograph."

"Hey, that's a great touch. I'm going to add that to my fantasy."

"Reed Porter's fourteen empty-headed sons, all stars of various sports teams, will say, 'Dad, you actually *knew* him?'"

"No. They won't be smart enough to understand what I've done."

LaRue laughed at that, but she felt guilty again. She knew that Reed was no genius, but he was sweet—and he read more books than she did. She knew she had no right to make fun of him.

"Do you want to know my whole plan?"

"Sure."

"First, I don't want to go to the U. I want to get away from here. That's one of the reasons I study so hard. I need a scholarship. I want to go to Harvard or MIT or maybe Columbia. I want to live in Cambridge or New York, and I want to be around people who won't mind if I'm smart. I never want to live here again after next year."

"But you'll make a trip here once in a while, just to be admired."

"Yeah. I guess. But the main thing is, I want out. And I want to do something really big with my life. I know I'll probably get stuck in the war for a while, but I think someone will decide to put me behind a typewriter, not in a tank, and I'll get through that."

"All that sounds good to me, Cecil. Maybe that's what *I* should do."

"Go to war?"

"No. Study. Get a scholarship. Go away to college."

"How are your grades so far?"

"My grades aren't all that bad," she said. "I just don't know anything. Maybe I'll start reading my assignments."

"*Silas Marner?*"

"No. I don't want to be that pure and good."

Cecil chuckled. He pointed down at a muddy spot in the pathway. They were beyond sidewalks now. LaRue walked around the mud, and then she looked off toward the west where a cherry orchard, the limbs of the trees still bare, made crooked scrawls against the fading blue horizon. She wanted time to pass, wanted the leaves to bud out, and then she wanted a year—no, two—to pass away quickly. She wanted the war to be over, and she wanted to qualify for real life. What she didn't know was how she would live, exactly, when all the choices were up to her.

That suggested another question. "What about the Church?" she asked Cecil.

"What about it?"

"Is it going to be part of your life?"

"I don't know. To me, right now, it's just part of this place I hate so much—what I want to get away from. I'm not religious, to tell the truth. But maybe I'll feel different about that someday." He hesitated and then added, "Your dad would be shocked if he heard me say that."

"It doesn't take much to shock *him*," LaRue said. But she was thinking about Cecil's dreams. She didn't struggle with her dad as much as she used to, but the idea of being on her own, of making decisions without answering to her parents—it all sounded appealing. Maybe she would try to go away to college too.

"What about you? How do you feel about the Church, LaRue?"

LaRue knew that she believed in guilt, in God, and in prayer, more or less in that order, and that she had even felt moved a few times in her life by the presence of something refined and right—especially at Gene's funeral. She knew she believed in a life after death, and that Gene still existed. But the Church, for LaRue, was meetings and rules and Dad. Right now she thought she could settle for a little less of all three.

An image came to LaRue's mind: she saw herself with those senior boys in the library earlier that day. She had loved that moment when she had basked in their attention, manipulated their reaction to her. But she didn't like that side of herself, however much she played upon it. She liked herself immensely better when she was with Cecil. And yet he, finally, was not the answer either. She longed to feel that she was not faking, not exploiting, not trying to satisfy someone else. She had no idea what it would take to feel that, entirely, but she had an idea that getting away from home might be the right first step. And it wasn't only rebellion. Maybe she would finally get to know God if he weren't sitting on the stand at Church every week, wearing a white shirt and tie.

"My problem isn't with the Church," she said. "Not exactly. It's mostly with me."

They walked for some time in silence after that. And then Cecil said, "LaRue, I'll say this much. You're *not* shallow."

She smiled, and she nodded, and then she took hold of his arm.

Alex and Otto rested, even slept a little, and watched as the sun came up. They had parachuted into a field during the night, early Monday morning, on March 19, and then they had retreated to the woods and buried their parachutes. For a time they had worked their way through the forest, moving steadily toward their objective: a village called Brünen, near the town of Wesel. But they had come to an open area, with a village in the middle, and they knew better than to be caught moving about in the night. So they waited for morning. Once the sun was up, and they saw people stirring at a farm not far off, Alex and Otto hurried out to the road and then walked on through the village.

Some of the people there—a grocer, a woman sweeping her front walk, a farmer in a cart—greeted Alex and Otto. Alex was reminded of his days in Germany as a missionary. There was no sign of war here, with common folks going about their business as usual. A little boy walked from his house, shut the door behind him, and stepped through a trellis that arched over his front gate. The limbs of a climbing rose, still bare of leaves and blooms, covered the trellis. As the boy walked away, Alex noticed a lightness in his step, as though he might start to skip at any moment. He was wearing a satchel on his back to carry his schoolbooks. It was astounding to think that at least here, life could continue so placidly.

Alex and Otto made it through the village without incident and hiked on down the road toward Brünen. The morning was cool and misty, with fog hanging in the valleys, but the skies promised a lovely day. Alex didn't like to think why he was here; he wanted to enjoy the pretty countryside and listen to the birds. The reality was, however, that this area would become a war zone before long, and the village Alex had just seen would almost surely be caught in the combat. That lovely little boy with the satchel on his back wouldn't see the Allied paratroopers as saviors but as invaders, killers. Alex hoped the boy wouldn't be hurt.

In the next few days Alex and Otto had to gather information from contacts, locate artillery positions, choose drop zones and landing zones for gliders, advise resistance groups on sabotage targets, and communicate all this information to army intelligence units through radio contacts. And then, one pretty morning like this one, hell would explode around these people.

As a missionary, Alex had promised never to be an enemy to the German people. In Holland, in Belgium, he had forgotten most of those feelings, but now, here in Germany, he knew that he didn't hate Germans. He had only hated those moving targets, the figures out there in the snowy fields who wanted to kill him before he killed them.

"Where I lived, it was like this on a spring morning," Otto said.

"But it's colder there, isn't it?"

"Yes. Spring comes a little later."

Otto was from a village not far from the North Sea, outside Bremerhaven. He and Alex had talked about his family. Otto's father had owned a small hardware store at one time but had been called away into the army in 1943. He had returned a year later with one arm blown off, his hearing mostly gone, and deeply changed by his experience. By then, however, Otto was already in the army himself. He had fought in the east, had been wounded with mortar shrapnel near Minsk, and had spent a summer and fall in a hospital in Munich. He had been released in time to be sent to the west, to the Battle of the Bulge. It was there that he had been trapped between the closing Allied forces and taken captive, and there that he had agreed to work for the American Office of Strategic Services. He had told Alex that he had become a communist during his time in a Munich hospital, that a fellow patient had convinced him that only a revolution would give working-class people a chance to live as they should. But even as he talked of such matters, Alex never felt any intensity or commitment. Otto's father had been fairly well off, and Otto knew little, in truth, of the struggle of the classes that he spoke of.

"Is your village all right so far?" Alex asked.

"Yes, the village has been spared. No bombs have been dropped there. But the men are mostly gone—many of them dead."

"What about Bremerhaven?"

"It's like all the cities. Or worse. It's been bombed over and over—especially the shipyards."

"Don't the people hate us, after all that?"

Otto laughed in that breathy manner of his. "Oh, certainly. They hate *you*. The last I knew, they thought I was a fine fellow."

But Alex didn't want to talk about that. He was still a little nervous that Otto might cut and run the first time he got a chance. That had happened before with some of the POWs who had been sent in to spy on their own country.

The two men were dressed in field-gray SS army uniforms. Alex wore corporal stripes, and Otto the V-shaped stripes of a sergeant. Both were carrying packs on their backs. Otto had hooked his thumbs through the straps, and he was walking along confidently. But then he glanced over his shoulder and stiffened. "Look out," he whispered. "Trouble! Don't look back."

For a moment, Alex didn't know what Otto meant, but he heard a vehicle coming up behind them.

"Let me do the talking," Otto said.

"Who is it?"

"Military police."

In a few more seconds, a German armored car—a roofless vehicle—pulled alongside them and stopped. Alex and Otto stopped too, and Otto greeted the soldiers.

Two policemen climbed from the car, one from each side. As the driver came around the front, he asked, "Where are you two going?" He didn't sound all that concerned, but Alex knew the danger, and he felt almost rigid with fear.

"We're soldiers," Otto said. "We're on leave for a few days. We're heading home."

"What's your military unit?"

"Two Hundred Twelfth *Volksgrenadier* Division, Eighty-Fifth Corps, Brandenberger's Seventh Army."

"Who is your company commander?"

Otto answered without hesitation. He and Alex had memorized many names of leaders, but the fact was, a policeman of this sort would not know whether they were right. The trick was to answer confidently.

"Where is this unit?"

"We fought in the Ardennes offensive. Most of our men didn't make it out. We're being re-formed soon. We are to report not far from here, near Aachen."

"Where did you fight in the Ardennes?"

"South of Bastogne."

"Then you didn't fight very well."

Everyone knew the story. This was the area where Patton's Third Army had broken through. But Otto didn't hang his head. He raised his chest a little and spoke directly into the policeman's face. "Our men fought with valor. No one can say we didn't. Not you, not anyone."

The officer nodded. Otto's pride seemed to please the man,

but he didn't back away. For the next few minutes, Otto answered lots of questions, and he and Alex presented their papers. Otto's cover name was Erhardt Becker, and Alex's was Kurt Steinmetz.

Alex said as little as possible, but he knew better than to remain completely silent. Finally, the older man, the driver, faced Alex. "Why did you receive a leave at such a time? This is not common."

"Our commander gave us a few days to go home, that's all. Not many of us survived. As my friend told you, our unit is being re-formed. Many new soldiers will join us soon."

"And where is this home of yours?"

"In Brünen—not far from here."

"But you are not a native German."

"My mother is an American. I lived in America as a child. I know both languages."

"Perhaps you lie in both languages, too."

"Only when my mother asks me what I did last time I had a leave." Alex laughed.

The officer smiled just a little. "A mother's boy, are you?"

"Oh, yes. That's where I'm going—for some home cooking."

"American cooking?"

"Yes. Sauerkraut and potatoes."

The man laughed, but he said, "Get in the car. We'll give you a lift to Brünen. I want to meet this American mother of yours."

"Good. You'll like her. With any luck, she'll feed you, too— if she has anything to serve."

"What weapons are you carrying?"

"We have our pistols in our knapsacks," Otto said.

"Throw the knapsacks in the back of the car," the driver said. "Then get in."

As Alex got into the car, he looked about himself for a way to attack the officers and make an escape. He sat down in the back seat. Otto tried to follow, but the driver told the other officer to take the back seat, and he directed Otto to the front. He obviously didn't trust them completely—not yet.

The driver was a thin man, and a little older than one might expect. His partner was stronger looking, more typical of most policemen in the German army. Otto and Alex had answered all the questions correctly, had known the right details about their unit and travel, and their papers were in good order. But Alex felt the suspicion, and that was probably based mostly on his accent.

Otto glanced back and gave Alex a barely perceptible shake of the head, enough to say, "Don't try anything." Alex wondered what he had in mind. Maybe Otto thought they could still bluff their way through this situation. He certainly was making an attempt to sound relaxed. He questioned the officers about the news, about the progress of the war, the weather. It wasn't long until the policemen were talking in friendlier voices. Otto asked them where they were from, and when he learned they were both from southern Germany, he began to tell them about people he knew in Brünen, things he had done growing up there. It was an amazing performance, but Alex kept wondering where it would all end. Sooner or later, the bluff would be over unless Otto had some idea how to escape.

Just as the car was entering the village, Otto suggested they all stop for a beer at a *Gasthaus* he spotted, but the officers weren't ready for that. The driver said, "We don't have time for that. I'll drive you to your homes." Clearly, he was going to play this all the way out, but his tone suggested that he was pretty well satisfied that Otto and Alex were telling the truth.

"Yes, yes, you're right," Otto said. "I could use a good beer right now, but I should go home. I live just a little outside the village, on a farm. I'll tell you where to turn."

"I think we should take your friend home first. I want to meet his mother."

"That's fine," Alex said. "Either way."

"Actually," Otto said, "we live fairly near each other. I'll give you directions."

And so the driver followed the instructions that Otto gave, and Alex was amazed at Otto's confidence, as though he knew the village well. He guided the driver beyond the village, and then along a country road. "So, are you two farmers?" the younger man asked. He was actually just a big kid, Alex had decided. He couldn't have been more than nineteen.

"Yes," Otto said. "Our fathers both farmed at one time. But my father was killed in Africa—at Kassarine Pass. It seems long ago now. My mother rents out the land, but she keeps the house. This is the place—the one you see coming up here."

"Your house?"

"No, no. Kurt's. Mine is just beyond here a little way."

The driver turned into the lane at the front of the farm. Alex looked for people, wondered what would happen next. But Otto was still talking. He chatted about the little hollow beyond the fields. "That's were Kurt and I spent many a summer day—swimming down there in the little stream in that valley." He got out of the car. "I'll walk in with you. I want to say hello to Frau Steinmetz. Don't go through the front door. No one does. Come around this way."

Alex could hear his heartbeat, like a bass drum, pulsating in his ears. He knew now that the string was out, and Otto was about to make a move. Alex had been trained for the past two weeks on methods of killing by hand, but it was all training. He had never really expected to take anyone on, but once Otto made his move, Alex would have to help.

Otto waited for everyone to get out, and then he tried to hang back a little and let Alex and the officers walk ahead. But the older officer hadn't dropped his vigilance entirely. He motioned for Otto to walk ahead of him.

Alex led the way, as seemed natural, and he didn't look back. But that was terrifying. How would he know what was happening behind him? What would they do if someone came out of the house? Otto had obviously thought this out, and Alex was willing to let him make the move, but he wished there were some way for the two to communicate. He walked along the side of the house, but as he reached the corner he turned enough to glance back. "I'm not sure my mother is here," he said. He saw Otto raise his hand, move his finger, seem to point forward. Alex looked ahead again.

"*Ach*, what's this I've stepped in?" Otto said, from behind. Alex kept going. Perhaps one full second passed before he heard motion, then a grunt and a muffled but agonizing wail.

Alex spun around, saw the look of terror in the older policeman's eyes, saw him sinking. Otto had stabbed the man in the ribs, it appeared, then stepped behind him. Now a knife was flashing through the air. There was a moment of realization, of stasis, when the knife hung before the officer's face, about to slash at his throat, and in the same moment, Alex's own reactions took over. The younger officer had turned back toward the commotion, his back now to Alex. Alex grabbed him, spun him around, then drove the heel of his hand directly into his nose. Blood spattered, and Alex felt the bone break. As the officer fell backward, Alex was about to follow through, to drive the bone of his nose into his brain, but Otto was on him. He grabbed the officer around the head and jerked his knife hard and deep across his neck. Blood sprayed in all directions—all over Alex.

The young man dropped, and Otto released him. "We've got to get out of here," he told Alex. "Someone might be in the house."

And so the two ran hard, back around the house. Just as they jumped into the car, Alex saw a man come around a shed at the back of the farm. He was looking toward Alex and Otto, but he showed no sign yet that he had spotted the policemen. Otto was trying to find the right key on the ring. He tried one that didn't work, and Alex felt the panic. He grabbed the door

handle and was about to take off running when the next key
slipped in and turned. Otto seemed to know these vehicles. He
hit the starter button, the engine barked once, then roared
alive. Otto backed away quickly. Then he spun the wheel and
turned back toward the village. Gravel sprayed, rattled under
the car as the wheels dug into the dirt road and then caught
and shot them ahead.

"We can't be seen in town," Alex yelled to Otto over the
sound of the engine and the rushing air. "We've got blood all
over us."

"I know. I'm turning off on a side road I spotted down here.
We'll dump the car somewhere and get cleaned up. We still
have to get into Brünen. Our contacts are the best people to
hide us."

Alex was astounded at Otto's self-assurance, at the way he
had already thought everything through. They drove toward
the village until Otto spotted the dirt road he had spoken of.
He turned into it and then drove too fast, the car bouncing and
lurching through the rocks and deep ruts. They headed down
into a little valley, at the bottom of which was a stream that was
lined with trees. There was no bridge, just a crossing, but when
Otto reached it, he turned upstream and drove into the shallow water. He gunned the engine and kept the car jostling and
splashing through the water until he rounded a bend in the
creek where the car would be out of view. Then he stopped,
suddenly, and turned the engine off. For a few moments both
of them listened, but they heard nothing.

"I couldn't see anyone following us," Alex said. He was out
of breath, and his heart was still pounding against his rib cage.

"All right. We need to wash this blood out of our clothes.
Then we might as well stay here until dark."

"We shouldn't be moving about town in the dark. Someone
will stop us for sure."

"We're going to have people looking for us anyway, Alex.
If we walk into the village in daylight, we're dead men. Let's get

away from the car and get down this stream and into those woods we saw just outside Brünen. Then later, we'll have to sneak in and not get ourselves caught."

"Maybe we ought to head away from here."

"If we do, our mission is destroyed. That farmer didn't get much of a look at us. He just knows there were two of us in an armored car. Our papers are still good. Only those two dead men saw them."

Alex didn't know. The only thing he knew for sure was that he and Otto would be strangers in a small village, and he had an American accent. The farmer might have seen, too, that they were wearing army uniforms. He wasn't sure that he and Otto had much chance of surviving in an area where they had just killed two military policemen.

But of course, he also knew what he had been sent to do. If Otto had said he was ready to give up the mission and run, he might have been tempted himself. But Otto was staying with the plan; Alex knew he had to do the same.

The two washed their hands in the stream, grabbed their packs, and then hurried downriver, walking in the water for a mile or more. Eventually they stopped and took off their uniform tunics, which they washed in the water. After that, they got out carefully, on a grassy bank, where they wouldn't leave tracks. Then they moved into the trees. In the forest they both hung their tunics and pants and socks up to dry. The air felt cool to Alex now, stripped down as he was to his shirt and army underwear. But he and Otto found a clearing and lay in the sun, and from time to time they checked their clothes. The wool, however, dried slowly in the damp air.

None of this was easy. Alex tried to shut his eyes and relax, but the fear made that impossible. He kept thinking that someone might be able to track them, and he felt vulnerable out there in the woods without his clothes on.

All afternoon Alex and Otto heard vehicles moving up and down the main road, and at one point they thought they heard a truck on the dirt road they had used to get into the little valley. "They're probably looking for us," Alex said.

"Maybe. But you have to remember, everyone knows that the big Allied push is coming soon. People who live in this part of Germany have a lot more to worry about than two dead men."

"Maybe. But we'll also be a lot more noticeable than we would be in Berlin or Frankfurt."

"Sure. And military police around this area will be upset. But everyone else has more to worry about."

Alex told himself that was true. He had to believe he was going to find a way to get out of this mess and get home.

As night came on, he and Otto put their damp trousers and tunics back on. They waited, sitting next to each other. "Where did you get the knife?" Alex finally thought to ask.

"It was in my boot. Don't you carry one?"

"No. One of the trainers told me that if we were searched, a concealed weapon might give us away."

"Yes. True. But not having one scares me more. I'm glad I had it."

"So what's this, for you, the beginning of your communist revolution?"

"No. It's the beginning of a fine adventure. What more could we have hoped for?" He laughed. "The most exciting thing in life is to skirt the edge of death—and live."

Alex watched Otto, tried to perceive whether he really felt that way. But there was always something mysterious about Otto, as though he had no real emotions. Maybe everything he said was as invented as those stories he had told the policemen. The man frightened Alex.

Night was falling fast, but a moon was rising. "We'd better go now," Otto said. "Before the moon is up too high."

And so they moved into the edge of the village. They not only knew the address of their contact, but both had memorized the streets of the village. They knew exactly where they had to go to find the house. They followed shadows, waited for long periods until streets cleared. And eventually, they found their way to the house. When they finally slipped into the *Hof* out back and knocked on the door, a man appeared. He was large, seeming to fill the whole door, and his face, in shadow, seemed angry more than welcoming.

"We have the cabbages you ordered," Otto said.

"Yes, yes. Come in."

The man pulled Otto by the arm, and both hurried inside. When he shut the door, he said, "Two military policemen were killed today. Do you know anything about that?"

"Yes. Of course," Otto said. "We were honored to make their acquaintance."

"This is very bad. I don't know whether I can protect you."

"Should we move on?" Alex asked.

"No. But we'll have to change our plans."

"We'll do what you tell us. Do you have the radio equipment?"

"Yes. That's not a problem. But you'll be noticed now. There are people looking for you."

"We understand," Alex said, but he had hoped for some protection and reassurance here, and there was nothing of that in the man's voice.

The three men were standing in a dark entrance. There was a kitchen down the hallway with a bright light shining. Alex wished he could turn the light off. He wanted to find a cellar or an attic—somewhere to hide.

11

"Have you eaten anything?" the man asked.

"No. We're starving," Otto said.

"Sit down, then. My wife is in bed, but I'll find something. My name is Werner Rietz. Don't tell me your real names—only the ones you are using. And tell me your cover."

"We have German military papers," Otto said. "We have passes, too, to show we're on leave. We told those military policemen that we were from Brünen, but they are the only ones who heard that story—and they won't tell it now."

"This much I already knew. But what else should I know about you?"

Werner placed a round loaf of black bread on the table, on a cutting board. He was a powerful-looking man, with a huge, round chest and a neck like a tree trunk. His face was square and set, seemingly emotionless. He stepped back to a cupboard and then brought out a large cut of cheese.

"I'm an American," Alex said. "You can hear that, I'm certain. My story is that my mother is American, and I was raised there until I was fifteen."

Werner swore, but then he only said, "Go ahead. Eat."

"With uniforms on, we won't be bothered," Otto said. "There's no need to be concerned. We can answer any questions put to us." He told Werner a bit of his cover story, which was based on his real experiences: his fighting on the eastern front and then in the Ardennes. He named his units, his officers.

"Why are you here, according to this story?"

"To pay a visit. You are my cousin."

"No. This will not do. The Gestapo have been watching me. They questioned me last week."

"Why?" Otto asked.

"We have done some resistance work here. Some sabotage. They know I'm a member of the Socialist Workers Union, and they realize that most of the resistance comes from labor leaders and communists."

"I'm a communist myself," Otto said. "You should know, Alex doesn't think well of people like us. He's a capitalist."

Otto laughed, but Werner didn't. "I don't want to hear any of this," he said. "I warned you, tell me only your cover names and nothing else about yourselves."

"I'm Sergeant Erhardt Becker," Otto said.

"And I'm Corporal Kurt Steinmetz."

"It will be a miracle if you got here without being seen. We may be raided tonight, or in the morning. If we are, I doubt that any story will save us. If no one comes, I want you to stay in my attic all day tomorrow. I will go about and learn what I can. This killing you did, it has everyone on edge around here."

"We had no choice," Otto said. "It was that or die ourselves."

"I only wish you had. I was opposed to your coming. We could do better without you, and we would be in much less danger. The *Wehrmacht* has been building up for days now, bringing big guns in on trains and trucks. They know the Allies are gathering across the river. They know that parachutists are coming—and this flat lowland is the most likely spot. Axis Annie has been telling the Seventeenth Airborne, along with the British units, where they're going to land—probably before they know it from their own army. I don't know what you can learn that we don't know already."

Alex thought he understood Werner's feelings, but it was hardly what he wanted to hear. Alex told him, apologetically, "I'm a parachute trooper myself. I understand about drop zones. Thousands of men will be landing. The American army didn't want to trust the decision about drop zones and landing zones for gliders to someone who doesn't know these things."

"We are not stupid. We could be told what to look for. I told them this. But all they would talk about is sending someone to me. My life was in danger before. It is probably finished now. I have a wife. Two sons. What will they do when I am put to death by the Gestapo?"

"If the Gestapo suspect you, why don't they just shoot you now?" Otto asked. "That's how those people work."

"I work at a steel plant. I'm a master at what I do. The plant manager has saved my life so far. He tells them he needs to produce steel if the war is to continue, and he needs me to keep the plant running."

"Perhaps you're safe then."

"I might have been—until you killed those military policemen. If I can be connected to that, in any way, the steel won't matter."

Alex could see the pallor in Werner's skin, as though his worries had drained him of blood. "I'm sorry for this trouble," Alex told him. "But the invasion is coming very soon. Then you should be all right."

Werner was standing by the cabinet, his arms folded over his chest. "Maybe. Maybe not. If someone thinks I'm involved, they may take revenge on me."

"We can make certain you're protected."

Werner smiled. He obviously didn't believe that. "Eat something," he said. "Then go to bed."

The men ate the dark bread, the good cheese, but Alex, even after the long day without food, had little appetite. He wondered now whether he and Otto had been as careful as they thought they had been. Maybe they had been spotted entering this house. Maybe Gestapo agents were gathering now, or military police. Or maybe a watch would be kept all night, and then the raid would come in the morning.

When Alex and Otto finished their meal, Werner led them to the attic. He brought them blankets, and then he said, "Don't come downstairs in the morning. I'll bring you food, or my wife will. By tomorrow evening, if we haven't been arrested, I'll have a better idea what we can do."

Alex sat down and pulled off his boots, but he slept in his clothes. The house was not heated at night, and the attic was especially cold. Still, Werner had given them plenty of blankets, and Alex managed to make himself fairly comfortable. But then he didn't sleep well. He heard every sound in the house, and time and again, as he drifted off to sleep, he would jerk back awake as the rafters creaked.

When morning came, a soft-spoken woman opened the attic door. She had more bread, more cheese. "You don't have any coffee, do you?" Otto asked.

"No. We can't get that now. Nor chocolate. I can give you hot milk." She was a big woman, plain, with rough, red cheeks. Alex could feel her animosity.

"Yes, yes. That would be just fine," Otto said.

"I'm sorry for your trouble," Alex told her.

She looked at him for a second or two, and the doubt in her eyes was obvious. *You have no idea the trouble you are causing me,* she seemed to be thinking. But she said nothing aloud, and she left. After a time she returned with the milk.

The day was long. The attic was not lighted, and so there was nothing to do but sit and wait. Or sleep. Alex finally did fall into a better sleep than he had all night, but he awoke with a start and with a strange dream lingering in his head. Crowds of angry people had gathered about him. They wanted to kill him but kept holding off. Alex would try to run, but in every direction were the masses of people, who pushed at him, held him from getting away. He fought through them as best he could, but there were always more.

All day Otto was less talkative than usual, less arrogant. "I don't blame Werner for the way he feels," he told Alex. "We're a big problem for him."

But that evening Werner seemed a little more hopeful. He invited the men down, and Margarita cooked for them this time. Their two sons, Willi and Erich, who were twelve and nine, sat at the kitchen table with the others. While they were there, Werner said nothing about his day, but after, when the boys had gone outside to kick a soccer ball about, he said, "I heard less talk of the killings than I expected. Some men are saying it's spies, advance people coming ahead of the troops, before the big push across the Rhine begins. But I saw no sign that anyone is suspecting me. No one followed me this morning, or again tonight."

"Can we go out?" Alex asked. "Will we be stopped?"

"I suppose you can. We can try that—saying that one of you is my relative. But if you wander about too much, I don't know how you will explain what you are doing."

"The landing zones we're considering are a few kilometers from here, near Wesel. We thought, if we had bicycles, we could pedal to them."

"And what if you are stopped? How will you justify this riding about?"

"We've talked about that," Otto said. "We'll claim we're hoping to make trades with farmers. We could trade for eggs or a chicken. Or maybe last year's potatoes, from farmers' cellars."

"That kind of bartering is illegal."

"I know that. But it's done all the time, and few policemen try to stop it. As soldiers, if we get stopped for doing something like that, it won't be a problem."

"But what could you trade?"

"Tobacco? Military cigarettes?"

"I have no source for this. Nor do you."

"We have money," Alex said. "Wouldn't soldiers on leave have some money in their pockets?"

"Yes. This is possible. But it isn't the usual thing—staying with a cousin, going out looking for food. Soldiers have other things in mind."

"Perhaps so," Otto said. "But we have good papers, and I can always think of a story. I can talk about all the bad food in the army, how nice it is to eat an egg—that sort of thing. I can make it work."

"Just one slip and you will be dead men."

"We can manage. Do you have bicycles we can use?"

"I have one. I can get another."

"Then we'll go in the morning."

"If you are stopped, leaving this house, how will you say you got here?"

Otto was the one to answer again. "We came last night—but we had to walk the last few kilometers. The trains were stopped by air attacks."

"Where?"

"You tell me."

Werner thought for a moment, and then he said, "Near Dorsten. It's far enough away that someone here wouldn't know whether it was true or not. But it's too far to walk. Say that you caught a ride with someone—a passing troop truck."

"All right then. We have no worries." Otto slapped Werner on the shoulder.

"Don't laugh at this," Margarita said. "I have sons to raise." Her heavy face, the rough skin, was flushed with anger.

"I'm sorry," Otto said. "I didn't mean it that way. I'm only saying that we can do it."

"If you can't, what happens to us? And if you can, what do I have to show for it?"

"The war can end."

"It will end in any case. And then we will be occupied. Do you think my husband will be honored for what he has done? Not by Germans, and not by the Allies either. He will be a filthy socialist to them. This is all for nothing, if you ask me."

"Never mind," Werner said, softly. "Maybe it will be all right."

But Alex was haunted by her words that night. He wondered whether this mission was worth the trouble it might create. In the morning, when he and Otto left the house and pedaled down the street, he had the ominous feeling that someone would stop them at any moment. But the two of them made it out of the village, and they rode their bikes toward the projected drop area near Hamminkeln, just north of Wesel.

Along the way they did manage to buy some eggs, which they carefully placed in Otto's knapsack and lay in the basket on the front of Alex's bike. They eventually hid the bikes in a wooded area and then moved about through the trees to a point where they could observe some of the projected drop zones and landing zones. Alex spotted some problems that hadn't been evident from aerial photographs. There were fences and electrical lines that needed to be avoided, and some marshy areas that would be dangerous, especially for gliders. He didn't dare carry maps with him, but he made mental notes for adjustments he would recommend.

By afternoon Alex felt good about the observations he and Otto had made. But they hadn't done the dangerous work. The Allies needed to know as much as possible about anti-aircraft guns in the region. Guns could be easily camouflaged and therefore be invisible in photographs. Even on the ground they were hard to see without getting close. That meant Alex and Otto would have to nose about in wooded areas well away from roads—and away from farmhouses—so their cover story would not hold up, should they be spotted. Any gun knocked out, just before the drop, could save hundreds of lives, but any mistake, now, could not only get Otto and Alex killed but could also compromise the entire operation. Spies in the area would be a sure signal that something was coming right away. Additional guns could then be rushed to the area.

Alex and Otto stayed in the woods and looked around as best they could, but they found nothing. Finally, they decided they had better not push their luck any longer for one day. They returned to their bikes, watched carefully, and then hurried back to the road. They rode back into the village and then on to Werner's house. Along the way, Alex saw no sign that anyone was paying special attention to them.

Werner seemed a little more relaxed that evening. "This matter with the military policemen is dying down faster than I expected," he told them. "I'm not exactly sure why. It may be that the local Gestapo agents see the end in sight. They're probably starting to worry about their own lives."

Everyone ate fresh eggs that night—a wonderful cheese omelet that Willi and Erich in particular liked. Alex slept much better than on the previous night, and the next morning he and Otto biked into the countryside again. They stopped at a farm and bought a roasting chicken, which a young man killed for them. They placed it in their basket and then followed the same road as they had the day before. This time, however, they had to range farther around the drop zones, and twice they crossed open fields to penetrate little wooded areas that could hide a big gun. They found AA guns all right, but only a few, and Werner's people had observed lots of them coming off trains recently. Alex and Otto knew that plenty more had to be out there somewhere. They weren't finished yet. But as they returned to the village that afternoon, a local policeman waved them down. "I don't believe I know you two," he said.

"No, we're not from here," Otto said.

Alex took a deep breath and hoped for the best. He wouldn't speak unless he had no choice.

"So what brings you to our village?"

"We had a few days' leave and no time to head home, so we

came to visit relatives of mine. Look at this nice chicken we bought today. I haven't eaten a fresh chicken for a long time. You people who live in the country, you eat much better than the rest of us—especially better than us soldiers. I envy you."

"And where did you buy this chicken?"

"From a farmer, off down that road. I don't know his name. We hoped to buy some vegetables, too, but no one had anything left over from last year's harvest. Do you have any idea where we could purchase some nice potatoes, or maybe leeks, for a good soup?"

"No. I cannot say. These farmers are not supposed to sell food this way. It is needed at the front."

"Yes, I know. But they keep something for their families, and there's no harm in their accepting a little cash, as I see it. You wouldn't begrudge them that, would you?"

"I'm not the one who makes the laws."

"I know. I know. You've caught us. We're lawbreakers, all right. But I'll wager you've fought in this war yourself. You probably know what it means to eat something fresh for a change."

The policeman finally smiled. "We ate well in the beginning. I was in the early campaigns. When we took Paris, we did as we pleased—ate like kings. But then they sent me to the Balkans, and we ate our share of army bread—hard as cobblestones. I took a bullet in the knee over there besides. I still don't walk very well."

"We know what you mean. We fought in the Ardennes. Lots of our boys paid a price there, too. Many a brave man."

The policeman was nodding now, seeming friendly. But still, he asked, "Where are you staying here?"

"With my cousin."

"And who would that be?"

"Werner Rietz."

The policeman nodded, but some of his ease seemed to disappear. "Could I see your papers, please?" he asked.

Otto and Alex got out their military paybooks and their leave papers. The policeman looked them over carefully, and then he looked back at Alex. "Are you foreign?"

"No, no. I'm German. I grew up speaking English and German both."

"And where was that?"

"In America. My mother is an American."

The policeman clearly didn't like that. He took a long look at Alex.

"He's lucky," Otto said. "His father moved his family back to Germany when he was fifteen. And then he was in the Hitler Youth. He learned what this country is all about."

"Yes," Alex said. "And I know all about America. The people themselves are not bad, but this Roosevelt, he's a monster. It means nothing to him to bomb our cities, wipe out civilians by the millions."

"How long will you be here?"

"Three days, at most," Otto said. "Then we return to our battalion. We'll fight again before much longer. And we'll stop those *Amis* at the Rhine, I can tell you that. They'll never march into your home. That's my promise to you."

The man was studying them now. There was no telling what he was thinking. "Go ahead," he finally said, and nothing more.

Alex was uneasy about all this, but Otto was pleased. "It couldn't have been better. Now we are known. We've told our story. I don't think we'll be bothered again."

When Werner heard the story, he was not nearly so sanguine. But he said little and let Otto's version of it stand. Alex had the feeling that he didn't want to worry Margarita. He did ask, "When are you scheduled to transmit?"

"Tonight," Otto told him.

"Good. Tell them what you know, but don't return to the country tomorrow. In fact, I would leave Brünen."

"We need to do more surveillance," Alex said. "There must

be more anti-aircraft positions. I'm thinking that they're closer to the river, near Schneppenberg, and we haven't searched that area yet."

"Be satisfied with what you've been able to do. You must remember, just before the invasion, we in the resistance will blow up the two railroad lines that run through that area. That will delay reinforcements. And we've targeted a power station—to cut off lights and create confusion. We can do our own search for guns, too. I can relay the information myself, if we find anything."

Alex didn't assent to that, but he also didn't argue. He decided to give the matter some thought overnight, and he did agree that it was time to transmit what they knew. So that night Alex and Otto slipped out onto the roof of the house. They turned on their transmitter and waited for a response. It was almost an hour before a Mosquito spy plane picked up the signal and made contact, but once it did, Alex quickly whispered his reconnaissance information. A few seconds later, a voice announced that the message had been recorded. Otto and Alex put the radio back into its case and slipped through the dormer window, back inside. Then they hid the radio in a compartment that Werner had created between the attic floor and the downstairs ceiling.

Alex was relieved to know that that much had been accomplished. What he didn't feel was that he had done enough. If he and Otto left, he wasn't sure how diligently the resistance people would search for guns, and he didn't want to learn later that the Airborne units had been decimated during their landing. He knew what kind of information he would hope for if he were making the jump himself. So in the morning he convinced Werner that he and Otto had to make one more trip to the country.

As it turned out, this day *was* more productive. Alex and Otto were hampered in the morning by some troop movements in the area—large trucks rolling down the country road—but the two of them hid out for a time and then rode their bikes along a little back road that ran between Hamminkeln and Schneppenberg. Close to some railroad tracks, they spotted a double set of camouflaged field guns, so they worked their way along the tracks, staying in the woods, and found another emplacement, this one with three guns, probably 88 millimeter. They were quite certain that other guns must be placed farther down the tracks, but an open pasture lay between them and the next woods, and they didn't dare walk across it. Railroad tracks, especially with anti-aircraft gun emplacements nearby, would certainly be guarded at various points along the way.

By then, because of the early delays, the trip had extended way too long into the afternoon to be easily explained. Alex told Otto they had better head back. Otto wanted to search another area, but he didn't push the matter, and the two returned to Brünen. This time Alex was relieved not to see the policeman or anyone else who might want to check their papers. But as they were setting their bikes in the *Hof* behind the house, the back door flew open. It was Margarita. "Leave!" she whispered. "As fast as you can. Werner has been arrested. Men were waiting for him when he came home from work."

"Gestapo?" Otto asked.

"I don't know. You must leave *now*."

"Did they mention us?"

"No. But they were rough with him this time. If they torture him, and he breaks, they will be back for you."

"I'm sorry," Alex said. "I'm very sorry."

"I've lost him. They'll kill him this time." Tears rolled down her cheeks, but it was rage in her voice, not sorrow.

"I'm so very sorry," Alex said again, unable to think of anything else. He thought of her boys.

Otto was already leaving, pushing his bike, and now Alex followed. At the street, Otto stepped onto his bike and pedaled away, calmly, slowly. Alex understood. He did the same.

The two had almost reached the street corner when Alex saw an armored car speeding down the road toward them, the tires whining on the cobblestones. Military police.

Otto suddenly began to pump hard. He accelerated around the corner and down a hill toward the east. Alex was right behind him. Halfway down the hill they dodged into an alley. Otto yelled, "Follow me!" He darted behind a building and cast his bicycle aside. Then he vaulted over a fence and ran through another courtyard. He was heading up the hill to the west, back to the street the armored car had been coming down. He was obviously trying to double back and cross up the police. Alex understood the ploy, but he also knew they were returning into the village, and they needed to get outside and into a forest somewhere. That was their only hope to get away.

Otto suddenly stopped, grabbed the door to a shed, and jerked it open. "In here," he said.

"No." Alex grabbed Otto, pulled him forward. "Once we stop, they'll throw a ring around us and hunt us down—with dogs. We have to get out of here *now*."

This time it was Alex who led out. He rushed around the house and out to the street. "Walk," he said. "That car went down the hill after us. They're heading the wrong direction."

"They'll backtrack before long."

"I know. But let's head back down the hill on a parallel street. We need to get out of town."

The difficult thing was to control themselves, to walk—and not attract attention. When they reached the corner, they turned downhill, to the east again. Alex knew the edge of the village was only about half a mile away, and then there were fields for another half mile—less than that probably—and finally a little valley, filled with trees. That was the only place he could think of to hide.

The two kept walking—and watching. What would the men in the armored car do? Would they think of the alleys and head back? Would they find the bicycles? If they did, what would they assume? Would they keep driving about, or would they try to get help? Would there be a delay as help was gathered?

"Let's cut down this alley," Otto said.

"No. Keep going. We'll make a break down an alley or into a house if we have to. We're better off to keep moving for now."

Otto was in charge of this operation, but Alex trusted his own instincts this time, and Otto seemed to accept the rightness of them. When the two men passed people on the street, Alex nodded and greeted them. And he kept from glancing back too often. Otto was doing enough glancing for both of them. They reached the edge of the village in ten minutes, maybe less, and they hadn't seen the armored car. But ahead of them was a dirt road that cut through open fields. Everything was flat—with no place to hide.

"Let's walk inside the fence line," Otto said. And Alex understood. They could keep moving east, but if the car appeared, in the distance, they could dive down next to the rock fence. Of course, if they were spotted first, hiding out there would do no good at all. They had to make it to the trees—and right now the woods seemed ten miles off.

Another few minutes passed—and every second Alex expected to hear Otto say, "There they are." But Alex was sure they had done the right thing. Most people, in the same situation, would have found a hiding place, and that was what the pursuers were probably thinking. They must be searching in the village.

"Drop!"

Alex hit the ground, but they were only about fifty yards from the woods. He wanted to make a dash into the trees.

"I don't think they saw us. Crawl!" Alex took off, not in a military crawl, but up on all fours, going as hard as he could while keeping his backside lower than the rock fence. He had cut the distance to the woods in half when he heard Otto shout, "Never mind. It wasn't the armored car."

Alex didn't care. He stayed down, kept crawling. And then, finally, he was descending a grassy hill toward a creek and a little valley full of brush and willow trees. Beyond that was a larger wooded area that extended north along the creek. He jumped up, finally ran, and tromped on into the creek, then turned and followed it to a place thick with growth. He climbed out of the water and burrowed into some brush and ferns under a little stand of trees. "All right. Now let's wait," he told Otto.

Otto was laughing, but he pushed into the bracken and sat down next to Alex. "You were right," he said. "This was the smart thing to do."

"Yes. But now what? Where do we go? What do we do?"

Otto, of course, didn't have the answer. Until now, Alex had thought only a few minutes ahead; now he had no idea what his next step should be. He lay back on the grass and took a couple of deep breaths.

But as soon as he felt a bit of relief, he thought of Werner, of Margarita and her little sons. What had he and Otto done to them?

I 2

Anna Thomas was placing a new spool on her recording machine. Sometimes the static on the radio dispatches made the messages difficult to understand and she would have to listen several times, jot down the words in German, and then, when she had it all, translate the whole thing into English. She spent her time closed off in her little booth at the OSS office, where others couldn't hear. As this new recording began to play, she was ready to listen for German when she realized that the recording didn't have to be translated. It was in English. In those cases, she was still supposed to write out the text. Then she used her maps to locate any geographical landmarks the speaker had mentioned.

The sender, in this case, was recommending a series of adjustments to the drop zone for "Operation Varsity." The recording was difficult to understand at times, the voice only a whisper. Anna was writing quickly in her own version of shorthand when she suddenly stopped. She heard something familiar in this strained, muffled voice. She listened for a time without writing.

"We know there must be more AA emplacements in the area, but surveillance is very difficult. We plan to make another reconnaissance pass tomorrow. If we learn anything, we'll report again. We do have a problem. My partner and I were forced to take protective action against a couple of military policemen. Our contact feels that his security has been compromised. We may have to leave this safehouse. If we are unable to transmit, employ these new coordinates for the drop zones and go forward as planned."

By the time the message had ended, Anna was almost certain she knew the voice. She recognized the intonation even in this faint and unclear transmission. She kept saying to herself that Alex wasn't in Germany, that the voice couldn't be his, but she couldn't convince herself.

Anna needed to know—absolutely. She left her booth and walked down the hall. She stopped at the door to her supervisor's office and said, "Mr. Coleman, I need your help for a moment. Could you listen to a recording for me?"

Roger Coleman was leaning over his desk. He was studying a map. "Just a moment," he said. And then, after maybe half a minute, he stood up. "What's the trouble?" he asked, and he followed Anna down the hallway.

"I need to have you listen to a message and help me understand. It's in English."

She stepped into her booth, rewound the wire, and then started it again. She watched Mr. Coleman. He had his head down, prepared to listen carefully. The messenger's first statement was, "This is Driftwood."

Suddenly Mr. Coleman's head came up. He looked at Anna carefully for a moment, and then he said, "I can't answer any questions, so don't ask."

"I know who it is."

He looked down at the floor. "Of course you do. I've known this day was coming since I hired you. But I didn't know what else to do. We needed someone with your background."

"Can you tell me where he is, or what—"

"I can't tell you anything."

"He's in great danger, isn't he?"

"All our men are in danger, Anna. You know that."

"May I leave now? I'll work an extra hour tomorrow."

"Yes, of course. If that's what's best. But Anna, don't worry too much about this. These men are well trained. We aren't sacrificing them. They have ways of returning."

"Why wasn't I told?"

"You know why."

But she didn't know. She knew the answer Mr. Coleman would give, but she didn't accept it. Alex was wrong to have done this without talking to her about it first—no matter what the army would say about that. She listened to these messages almost every day, and she always had the feeling that she was hearing boys at play. The agents here in the office, the ones in the field—all of them seemed to love their little games. Why would Alex do this to her? He had promised to be careful, to get back to her. She knew that a high percentage of these operatives were being lost.

"You could have stopped this. You didn't have to let them send *my* husband."

"Not really." He seemed to consider, and then he dropped his pretense. "I didn't know who he was until they were ready to place him. But why would I want to stop him? Someone has to do this."

"I hope that's true, Mr. Coleman. I really hope that's true. My father is over there somewhere, too, and that's too much. It's unfair to send them both."

"Anna, the people who penetrate Germany all agree to go. Most of them are German expatriates—Nazi haters who want to help us. Sometimes we borrow military men because we need special knowledge of one kind or another. But they aren't forced into anything. They have to know German, and Germany, and not many people have that background. It just happens that you have two in your family who could do this—and were willing."

"It's still not right." She left the booth, got her raincoat and umbrella, and walked out into the cold. The rain had stopped for the first time in two days, but the air was heavy and damp. She walked to the Underground station at Victoria Station and rode to the Baker Street Station.

When she entered her flat, she wanted to break down and cry, to tell her mother everything, but she couldn't do that. She went to the kitchen to say she was home. After, she planned to disappear into her room. But she found her mother at the kitchen table with Mildred Stewart, their new boarder. The Dillinghams, the couple that had lived with Anna and her mother for many months, had decided to move in with their daughter-in-law now that their son had returned to the Royal Air Force. Mildred was eighteen and alone. Her parents had been killed during the blitz in 1940, and her older brother was in the army. He was with General Montgomery, in Holland.

Anna saw immediately that Mildred was upset. Instead of passing on through the kitchen, Anna stopped and asked, "Is something wrong?"

"Not really. I'm right enough," Mildred said, unconvincingly.

Mildred was a small young woman who looked even younger than she was. She had red hair, which she rolled under at her shoulders, and bronze-colored eyes. In truth, she wasn't all that interesting to talk to, but she was pleasant enough, and certainly an easy person to have about the house. She worked an early shift at a military ordnance warehouse, where she dealt with the complicated paperwork involved in shipping supplies and munitions. She was tired when she came home each day, so she usually went to bed early.

"Mildred reads the war news in the paper," Sister Stoltz said, in English. "I tell her, 'Don't do that.'"

Mildred looked up at Anna. "Bernard is going smack in the middle of things, I fear. Everyone says the boys are gathering now, getting ready to attack the Siegfried Line. I was reading in the *Times* just now that thousands of Monty's troops will be lost—there's no escaping it." This was all said with a certain objectivity, as though Mildred wanted to sound perfectly in control. It didn't take much perception, of course, to know that she was feeling much more than she was admitting.

Anna glanced at the newspaper spread across the kitchen table. The headlines announced that General Patton had crossed the Rhine. Montgomery's troops were prepared to do the same, farther north. Russian troops had reached the Oder River and were closing in on Berlin. Germany was surely about to fall, and if Anna hadn't learned what she had today, these same headlines would have reassured her that the worst was almost over. She might even have hoped that Alex would be back in England before the baby came.

"It is a worry, Mildred," Anna said. "But for every boy who's lost, there must be ten who make it back just fine. Or twenty. I don't know. There's no use thinking the worst. The war, at least in Europe, really is nearing an end." But Anna was saying this for Mildred. Her words couldn't relieve her own mind.

"I don't want to think the worst," Mildred said. "It's just that he's the only one left in my family." She looked off toward the kitchen window, which was filled with dull gray light.

"I know. I understand," Anna told her.

Sister Stoltz reached across the table and patted Mildred's hand. "We both understand," she said.

Anna thought what an understatement that was. She and her mother actually had more reasons to worry. But she didn't want to talk about any of that. She wanted to get away now. If she couldn't tell them what she knew, she didn't want to tell them anything.

"I know you've already gone through more than I ever will," Mildred said. She, of course, knew some of the stories about the Stoltzes's past.

"No. That isn't so," Anna said. And she suddenly felt ashamed. "You have already lost much more than we have. We still have hope for our family to return."

"But for me, it was over in an instant. And then I knew what I had to face. You've faced such a long ordeal."

"It has been long," Anna said, and then she walked to her room. She sat on her bed and thought of it all. July, 1941. This coming summer it would be four years since she had fought off Agent Kellerman, four years since her family had been forced to go on the run. Since then, never a day had felt normal.

Fear and worry were so much a part of Anna's life that it was difficult to remember what she had been like as a young woman. She knew that she had been smug, even disrespectful, and sometimes she felt a certain gratefulness for the changes that had come to her. But she couldn't think that way today. What she wondered was how much more she could take. She knew that if Alex made it back, she would ask for little more out of life, but now the odds seemed so greatly diminished. She wrapped her arms over her bulging middle, tried to feel the little soul inside her. But it only made her angry to think that she and her child could be left alone, and that Alex had had a choice not to go on this mission. She thought of his last letter, and now, for the first time, she understood some of what he had meant.

She got up and walked to her desk, where she took the letter from a little bundle she kept in a drawer. She read it one more time.

Dearest Anna,

I'm sorry I didn't write for a few days. A lot has been happening. I've been moved again, but I'm not allowed to tell you more than that. I hope you understand.

I want you to know that I may not be able to write for a time. Don't let that worry you. In certain situations it is difficult to mail letters. I tell you this so you won't think something is wrong, and so you won't be alarmed when my letters don't come. Anna, it could even be weeks before you hear from me again.

I have some things on my mind tonight—things I don't say much about, usually, but some things I want to tell you. I've thought a lot about the war lately. I've had a little more time to do that than I usually do. Sometimes, on the battlefront, the politics seem to mean nothing, but tonight, as I consider the whole thing, I do believe that what we're doing is right and necessary. I hesitate to say that the war is a struggle of good against evil, there's too much evil in all of us to make that kind of claim. But if Hitler or Tojo, or both, were to hold the power in our world, all possibility of justice would end. Evil would be placed in a position of control. America has its faults, just as dear old England does, and Stalin is a dangerous man himself, but Hitler would take away our humanity, given the chance. He does have to be stopped. No compromise is possible with him, no truce. We have to fight this out to the end.

I say all this only to tell you that what I'm doing is worth it and must be done. I've doubted that all winter, and at times even concluded that I didn't believe it. But for the last few days I've stepped back and tried to look at the meaning of the war—not just the immediate experience—and I've felt better about what we did in Bastogne, for instance. American troops are mostly a bunch of civilians who got pulled into this thing, not trained warriors, but what we believe turns out to run pretty deep in us. Right now, what I remember about Bastogne is mostly the snow and cold and misery, but we held our own when things looked really bad, and once I have time to reflect, I think I'll be proud of that the rest of my life.

What I'm thinking about tonight, as I'm sure you can tell, is the cost of everything we have gone through. I know I'm not the same man I was, and I don't like some of the changes. I sometimes wonder what you will think of me, whether you will want me back. But what I ask myself so often is whether or not this is all worth it, especially if I don't survive. I want you and our baby to know, if that should happen, that I'm feeling at this point that it is. That would be something for my son or daughter to know, to cling to, if something did happen to me.

But don't misunderstand. I plan to get back to you. And I hope it won't be long before that happens. During the time you don't hear from me, remember that. I have a picture in my mind that never leaves me entirely, and keeps me going. I see you from a distance, and I run to you. I grab you up in my arms—and know that it really is all over. And then I just hold onto you and feel absolutely nothing but your body in my arms. From that point, I *just put all this behind me, and I never think about it again. I hope that will be soon, and I hope when it happens, you'll still be round and schön so I can be there when our baby is born. Let's think mostly of that. Please don't worry about the other things I've said.*

I love you,
Alex.

Anna understood the letter now, but she wished that she didn't. The tone of this letter was different from most that he wrote, and a little strange, and when she had first read it, she thought she noticed some confidence between the lines. Now, knowing where he was, she saw the letter the way he must have seen it. He had told himself, "If I don't make it through this mission, what kind of letter will I want Anna and my child to have as my last statement to them?" He had wanted to sound noble, wanted to convince her that his sacrifice had been worth it. But she found that infuriating. She took out a sheet of her stationery and wrote:

Dear Alex,

I am angry tonight. Angry at you. I shouldn't say that, I know, but it is what I feel. Today I was doing my work and I heard your voice. Do you understand what I say to you? I had no idea you were doing something of this kind, and then, there you were. Now I'm angry about the things you said in your last letter. I want no good-bye letters from you. I want you to come home.

Maybe you think I should be angry with the army, but I know more than you think I do. I know where you are. You had a choice, and you decided to go. Don't tell me why the war must be won. I knew this long before you did. What I know is that you have given three years of your life. It's enough, Alex. It's time to think of us. Me and your baby.

You may think me selfish, but I don't care. I'm tired. Here in London I see the soldiers who work in offices, who go each night to drink in the pubs or spend the night with their English girlfriends. I have heard them joke about the war, say what a good time it is. Those are the ones who should be doing what you are doing. They should have their turns.

I know everything you would say to me. I know the way you think.

You put your duty first. But that means you put us—me and your baby—last. Alex, I don't want to be alone. I don't want to raise our child by myself. Think what you owe to us, and don't tell me about evil. When this war is over, evil will still be with us. It will be forever, no matter how many wars we fight. I want to find a place where we can make a family and we can try not to be evil ourselves. That's the only war we have a chance to win.

But now she was crying. And so she put her pen down, cupped her hands over her eyes, and blocked the tears from running down her face. She didn't want to cry; she wanted to stay angry. But she couldn't cling to that. She sobbed for a time, and when she picked the pen back up, she wrote:

Alex, I go too far. I'm sorry. I do think you have done your share, and more, but I also know the truth. I'm angry because your heart is pure. You are like the young warriors in the Book of Mormon who fought with pure hearts. You tell me this is not so. But I know you accepted this mission because of who you are. Don't tell me about Hitler or politics. You had to go because you knew that if you didn't, someone else would. That's your goodness, and I wouldn't love you so much if you weren't this kind of person. But, Alex, I do want an end to all this. We've given enough to this war, and I don't want to give any more.

Anna sat back. She couldn't send this letter. It was all a muddle, and if Alex ever read it, she would regret some of the things she had said. But she couldn't put it aside without ending it the way she knew she should:

Alex, please find a way to get back to us. All my anger is only because I can't stand to think of living without you. I love you.

> *Anna*

Suddenly she was angry with herself, not at Alex, not even at the war. She didn't have to be so weak; it wasn't what Alex needed now. She tore the letter into shreds and threw it away. Then she stood up and tried to think what to do—how she could get through these coming days. There would be no letters now, perhaps for quite some time. And she would know nothing, have so much to worry about. She had to think of a way to deal with this.

Suddenly, on impulse, she walked to the kitchen and said, "Mildred, would you like to go for a walk with me?"

"No. I don't think so," Mildred told her. "I'm tired tonight."

"Please. We need to get out. We need to do something. I would take you to a pub and buy you a beer—except that I don't go to pubs and I don't drink beer."

Mildred laughed. "I'd settle for a nice bit of chocolate—if we could buy one."

"No. I doubt we can do that. But we could walk in the park."

"Yes, and look at the roses, all gone wild."

"I know what we can do. Let's go to the cinema. All three of us. Let's take the Underground to the West End—and see something silly."

"Abbot and Costello," Mildred said, and she brightened.

"You two go," Sister Stoltz said. "I don't understand those two. It all makes no sense to me."

"Then we'll find something else—one of those tap-dancing movies. Fred Astaire."

Sister Stoltz smiled. "I do like those," she said. "I don't understand what they say so well, but I like to see the dance."

"Then let's go. We'll stop somewhere for fish and chips so we won't have to cook tonight."

"Oh, yes. Now I like this," Sister Stoltz said, and she laughed.

"And Mildred," Anna said, "if you see a nice-looking soldier, and want to flirt with him, you don't need an old lady and a pregnant woman with you. We can walk away."

Mildred denied any thought of that, but she was laughing now, too.

And so everyone got ready. They took turns in the bathroom, each quickly fixing her hair, applying a touch of lipstick. As they headed out the door, Sister Stoltz said, "Anna, this is a wonderful idea. I'm glad you came home in such a happy mood today. It was just what we needed."

· CHAPTER ·

13

Alex and Otto slept in the woods the first night after their escape from Brünen. They didn't know how avidly they might be sought, but they felt that if they could avoid detection for a few days, they had a good chance of surviving. What they knew was that the invasion was coming soon. The OSS had been unwilling to give them an exact date. If they were caught, it was better that they not have that information. Still, everything they had heard convinced them that the drop wasn't more than a few days off. A bombardment from airplanes and big guns across the river was likely to come a day or two before the invasion. Then the airborne troops would drop behind the German front lines, attack toward the river, and provide support for the Allied troops who would make the crossing. If all went well, Allied soldiers would occupy this area around Wesel and Brünen in less than a week, and then Alex and Otto could approach an outpost and make themselves known.

The problem for the moment, of course, was that they had nothing to eat. For the first night and day the fear of being caught outweighed their hunger, and they stayed in the dense, overgrown spot they had chosen for a hiding place. By the second night their hunger was becoming the more pressing matter. Otto wanted to find a village and break into a grocery store or a *Bäkerei.* "That's a sure way to get ourselves caught," Alex told him. "Let's find a farm. A chicken coop. A few raw eggs will hold us over."

"I've got a better idea. I have matches. Let's snatch a chicken. We can make a fire and cook it."

"I think we'd better stick with the eggs—or maybe some vegetables from a root cellar, if we can find one. We don't want to light a fire that could give away our position."

"Raw eggs and raw potatoes?" Otto laughed. "I think maybe I'll try a *Gasthaus.* I'd rather eat *Wienerschnitzel.*"

By the time the two approached a little farm north of the spot where they had been hiding, however, Otto wasn't laughing. As they drew close, they got down and crawled on their stomachs. The moon was fairly bright, and Alex could see the yard behind the house. "I don't see a chicken coop," he whispered.

"What? No raw eggs?"

"What's that in back of the house? A rabbit hutch?"

"It could be."

"Maybe we *could* take a chance on a little fire—and cook a rabbit."

"That's the kind of talk I like."

"But we've got to go right up to their house, and there's a light on upstairs. What if they have a dog?"

"Chances are, they do. Let's move in a little more. If it barks, we can slip away."

And so the two nudged themselves forward a little at a time. They crossed a rock fence and then worked their way across a garden that was plowed but not yet planted. There was no sound of a dog, and now, if one did set up a fuss, the two were too close to make a quick getaway.

"If something happens, don't go back the way we came," Otto said. "The back fence is closer, and there are some trees to hide in, just beyond it."

"All right. I just hope these rabbit pens aren't empty."

They crawled a little closer, and then, very carefully, Alex stood up. The moon illuminated things quite well, but inside the hutch, he could see nothing. When he turned the wooden latch, however, and opened the wire door, he heard something move. He waved his hand inside, felt fur, and grabbed on. But he got a leg, and the rabbit, in its panic, put up a wild fight. It kicked and squealed and thrashed against the wood and wire.

In only a moment, Alex had the rabbit tight by the throat, and after a fierce squeeze, the flailing stopped. The animal twitched a few more times and then went limp and silent.

Alex stood his ground and listened. No dog. But then he heard something—just a subtle creaking sound that might have been a screen door opening. He waited, didn't move. A little breeze was blowing, and he wondered whether the sound had been something outside.

He waited a full minute, perhaps, before Otto whispered, "Let's go. Move slowly. Head to the back."

Alex stepped toward the end of the hutch and was about to walk around it. Just then a firm, low voice said, "Halt. Halt or I shoot."

Alex froze. He felt Otto bump into him and then hold, tense and still.

"Step out a little," the voice said. "I want to see you."

As Alex stepped forward, he could see a man's silhouette against the white stucco of the house, but not his face. It crossed Alex's mind that some Gestapo agent or military policeman had traced them here. But the voice said, "What are you doing behind my house? What is it you want?"

Alex was trying to think what to say when Otto said, "Food. We stole one of your rabbits—because we're starving."

"You don't look underfed to me," the man said.

Alex and Otto were under the moonlight, not shaded by the house the way the farmer was. He could see them better than they could see him. Alex wondered whether the man would really shoot. Maybe they should rush him now, before he called the police.

"I've killed a rabbit," Alex said. "I'm sorry. But we're hungry."

"Who are you?"

"Soldiers," Otto said. Alex decided he would let Otto make up the story. He had a better knack for it.

"What are you? Deserters?"

"Yes, we are. But many are running. You can't believe what it's like at the front now. It won't be long until we're all over-run. You will have *Amis* tramping across your land before another week goes by."

"Maybe they will have their own food—and won't be steal-ing my rabbits."

"My friend, we've spent years at the front. We were in Russia and East Prussia. Both of us were wounded there. The army let us heal a little and then sent us to the Ardennes. You have no idea what we've been through. We've had enough. Call us cowards if you want. Maybe we deserve the name. But a man can only take so much. I'm sorry about the rabbit, but we're desperate. We haven't eaten for days."

The man was quiet for a time. Alex couldn't see his face at all, so there was no way of knowing what he was thinking. It seemed to Alex that Otto had gone a little overboard, and the man might not believe a word of the story. But finally he said, "Come inside. I'll give you food. Walk to the side of the house and then stop at the door."

Alex and Otto did as they were told, but when they reached the door, the farmer stepped in front of them, making himself vulnerable had either one wanted to knock him down. He opened the door and yelled, "Berta, I'm bringing two sol-diers inside. They're hungry." And then he said to Alex, "Drop that rabbit there by the step. Don't mention it to my wife."

He led the way in, and all three were in the lighted kitchen before Alex realized that the man had no gun. "Sit down here at the table," he said. "My wife will see what she has to feed you."

She appeared at the door in just a moment. She had pulled on a worn flannel robe over her nightgown. Her gray hair was wrapped up in a bun at the back of her head. She was barefoot. "Our dog woke us up, but we didn't know what was going on out there," she said. "Were you knocking at the door?"

"They were about to," the man said.

"I didn't hear a dog," Otto said.

"Oh, he doesn't bark," the woman said. "He runs about, growls, acts nervous, but he's scared of his own shadow. He wouldn't run off a thief if we ever got one here."

"We're sorry to get you out of bed."

"I wasn't asleep. I read until late most nights. I'm not good at sleeping." She laughed.

She appeared to be around fifty. Alex looked again at the farmer, who seemed a little older. There was something simple about him. He was big, and he seemed strong, but he was relaxed now, without any apparent suspicion. He was wearing a short wool coat and a baggy, worn pair of trousers, with his pajama bottoms hanging out below the cuffs.

"What do we have, Berta?"

"Bread and some cold things. Maybe they would like some rose-hip tea."

"Yes, I would," Otto said, "if you don't mind."

"Don't trouble yourself," Alex told her. "We're sorry to intrude."

"It's fine," she said. "You must eat." She busied herself, pulling out the food from her cupboard. She stoked the stove, added a stick of wood, and then set a kettle on to heat. "Our name is Richartz. Tell me your names."

"Erhardt Becker," Otto said. "And my friend is Kurt Steinmetz. We're both from northern Germany, not far from Bremerhaven."

"Were you separated from your company?" the woman asked.

Now Otto had to return to his story. "We're not proud of ourselves," Otto began. "Things have turned crazy at the front. The Allies are bombarding our positions, and our company has been devastated. What is left of it is scattered everywhere. We finally decided to save our lives. We took off."

Otto's story was plausible enough. Lots of fighting was now going on just west of the Rhine, and German troops were being driven back. Of course, Otto had been careful not to name a particular sector where he and Alex were supposed to have been fighting.

What Alex saw was that the woman did believe the story—and he couldn't help but feel some guilt about their lying to her. "Things are falling apart," she said. "I hate to think what lies ahead for all of us."

Alex nodded. "Within a few days, you can expect Allied troops here," he said. "You may want to move back, somewhere east."

"I'll wait right here and take my chances," Herr Richartz said. "I don't think the English or the Americans will harm us if we offer no threat to them."

Alex wondered, but he didn't say so.

Frau Richartz was placing bread and cheese and cold meat on the table. Alex was hungry enough to be eager, but he tried to be polite. He took a slice of bread and then used a knife and fork to take some meat and cheese.

"I was in the last war," Herr Richartz said.

"That was a bad one too," Otto said.

He nodded, and his wife said, "He was wounded. A bullet tore a piece of his leg away. And an explosion broke his eardrums. He has a terrible time with his ears, especially in the winter."

Herr Richartz was sitting at the table with Otto and Alex, but he was looking away. "I was at Verdun. I saw thousands of

German bodies out there in the mud, sometimes stacked on top of each other in piles. All just boys. And not one of us knew what we were fighting for. I wanted to be a patriot, to show I could be a man, but sometimes, at night, I whimpered like a boy. I was only eighteen in the beginning. I guess I *was* a boy."

"I don't know what we're fighting for this time," Otto said.

The room became silent. Alex saw Herr Richartz glance quickly at his wife, and then he said, "There are things better not to discuss."

"Maybe so. But Hitler lied to us. That much you have to admit."

Herr Richartz was sitting with his arms folded across his chest. He glanced away, then back, as though he were taking time to make up his mind, but then he only said, "I love my country. I always will. I have nothing more to say."

"Countries are not worth loving," Otto said. "It's all just a piece of ground. I care about the people—the common people like us. The workers and the farmers."

Alex had no idea why Otto wanted to talk this way. He half expected the Richartzes to order them from the house. They glanced at each other, and Alex detected a certain stiffness in them. Finally, Herr Richartz said, "Certainly, people are most important. Since I came home from the Great War I have been a farmer and have only wanted that peace. But I try to do what I can to help my neighbor. We believe in the Bible, the two of us, and we try to live by it."

"That's as it should be," Alex said, and he stared hard at Otto, who seemed to get the message. He laughed and shook his head, and then he went back to his food.

Frau Richartz came to the table and sat down. "What do I hear in your voice? What is your dialect?"

"I was raised speaking mostly English," Alex said. He wondered whether he should invent a new story, but he stayed with the one he had been using. "My mother is an American. I lived in the United States when I was growing up."

"My, my. That must be strange for you."

Alex found himself looking at the floor, at Frau Richartz's bent toes, the hard edges of her feet, the calluses. They were the feet of someone who had worked hard, who had not been pampered, and what occurred to him was that he owed her his respect. He didn't want to lie to her. He said, simply, "War is like that. Sometimes we do what we have to do."

"Yes. A young man in your situation, you're not asked to choose a side. The choice is forced upon you."

"I do love Germany," Alex said, and of course, he meant it. "I love both countries, the people in both lands. I never wanted to choose between them."

"Do many of our boys have these feelings, this confusion about the war?" Herr Richartz asked.

"No. I think not," Alex said. "Our men fight valiantly. They are patriots, just as you were. You can be proud of them."

"Was it bad in the Ardennes?"

"Terrible. But your soldiers fought like lions. They died by the thousands. I respected those men. They knew that their beloved fatherland could soon be occupied by foreign troops, so they sacrificed themselves. They never stopped until they were overwhelmed. Every meter was paid for by bitter fighting. In the end, the Americans and British had too many troops, more weapons, and they had air support. But Germany can always be proud of those young men. I will always honor them."

Alex had gone too far and he knew it. But he wanted to say these things.

There was a long silence in the room, and then Herr Richartz asked, "Who are you men, really?"

"We'll eat, and then we'll go," Alex said.

"Yes. It's better that way. I'll ask nothing else."

"Herr Richartz, there are people all over the world who believe in the Bible. Once this is over, maybe we can all try to do as you say—try to live by it."

"Yes. This is our hope."

Alex ate again, and he looked across the room. He saw a picture of the Richartzes when they were younger, and seated with them three children—two boys and a girl. "You have three children, I see," he said.

"We have a son in a hospital in Vienna. He's lost both his legs. Twenty-six years old, and now a very hard life ahead of him."

"Our daughter is married," Frau Richartz said. "But her husband hasn't written for many months. We hear nothing from the military, so we have no idea whether he's lost in action, dead, or perhaps imprisoned. Our daughter is almost crazy with worry."

"Was her husband on the eastern front?" Otto asked.

"Yes."

"Things are insane there. No one knows where anyone is, or who is dead or alive."

"This we know," Herr Richartz said. "At least we have the hope that he *is* a prisoner, and maybe the Russians will release him when the war is over. One never knows with those people."

"What about your other son?" Alex asked.

"He's a soldier too," Frau Richartz said. "But he couldn't possibly be a good one. He left us when he was sixteen, and he cried like a baby all the way to the train. So far he's been lucky. He's with the troops in Denmark, and he's never faced a day of battle. We pray every day that he will never have to fight."

It hurt Alex to think of it all: this boy without legs, a frantic daughter, a frightened young boy. It had been so long since Alex had seen the face of his "enemy." During the battles he had been through he had tried not to think of who the German soldiers were, but now he was glad to be reminded. When the war was over, he wanted to feel like a brother to them again.

Otto and Alex ate quickly. When Alex had eaten only half

of what he wanted, but enough, he stood. Otto took a last drink of his tea, and then he stood too.

"There's something else I need to tell you," Alex said. "When the Allies come, there will be bombing first. You will hear it. You won't have much time after that. If the troops march down this road, past your farm, it's possible they will force you out and take over your home."

"We've talked of this," Herr Richartz said. "We won't resist. We'll let them sleep in our beds—and hope they pass quickly on through."

"It may not be that easy. Let me warn you not to leave anything of value in your house. Take out your best furniture. If you have money or jewelry—anything of value that can be carried away—take it outside and bury it. Most of the men would never harm you, but war does strange things to people. You can't assume that you are safe. If soldiers want your house, turn it over and leave. Don't argue with them."

"Thank you for this advice," Herr Richartz said.

"I wish we could stay, so we could be certain that you're protected."

"You would be welcome to stay."

"Actually, that could put you in danger of another kind."

The Richartzes clearly understood. They both nodded. "Will you do one thing for us?" Herr Richartz asked.

"Yes. Of course."

"If you are picked up, will you say that you forced your way in here and took our food?"

"It's not exactly a lie," Alex said. "I'm sorry. But I do want to give you some money for the food—and for everything."

"No, no. We want nothing."

Alex hesitated, his hand already in his pocket, but then he said, *"Danke schön."* He shook both their hands. "Where will you sleep?" Frau Richartz asked.

"Out in the open. We'll find a place." Alex knew better than to be specific. It was better that the Richartzes know nothing they would have to deny, if it came to that.

"You can sleep in our barn."

"No. That would put you in danger. We'll clear out and let you have your peace for now."

"I have some old blankets. Take them. I don't need them."

"They could be traced back to you."

"I don't know how. And it doesn't matter anyway. I can give a blanket if I want. If that's a crime, then I'm a criminal."

She disappeared and went upstairs, and when she came back, she had two tattered quilts. She also set about putting the remains of the loaf of bread and the cheese and meat in a flour sack the two could carry.

"Thank you so much," Alex told her. "We came to take away your coat, and you have offered us your cloak as well."

"You do know the scriptures."

"Before I was a soldier I was a missionary."

"God bless you, young man," she said. She shook his hand again, and then she patted his cheek with her big, rough hand.

Outside, Otto said what Alex already knew. "You said more than you should have. You might have put us in danger."

Alex laughed. "Oh, yes, it would be terrible to be in danger. We've been so safe up until now."

Otto laughed too, but he said, "If someone stops by here, asking questions, trying to trace us, what will they say?"

"Nothing. And someday, if I can come back here after the war, I want to sit down with them and make friends."

"You like Germans, don't you?"

"I like people. And I understand Germans. I was close to lots of people when I was here."

"But not many American soldiers care about Germans. They know nothing about us, and yet they talk of us as though we were dogs or pigs."

The two were retracing their steps. They climbed the fence and angled off across the field toward the woods where they had slept the night before. Alex was holding the blanket over his arm, and the smell of it was the smell of the Richartz's good house. "It's easier to kill if you don't know the enemy—if you think of reasons to hate the people you fight."

"So how do *you* kill?"

"I try to act, not think," Alex said.

"Can you do it—keep from thinking?"

"Sometimes."

"It's a harder war for you than it is for most," Otto said. "You're braver than most men."

"Braver?"

"Sure. You fight your enemy, and you also fight yourself."

"You're the brave one, Otto. You don't fight for anything. I couldn't stand to be here if I didn't think I was fighting for what's right."

"I don't fight for *words*, Alex. I want a full stomach when the war is over. I want a job in America, and a pretty little American girl for a wife."

"That's fair enough. I took the prettiest girl in all of Germany for myself."

"See. That's all I ask of *your* country."

"America doesn't want to import communists. You might have to forget about all that."

"Consider it forgotten. I'll become a capitalist if the girl is pretty enough."

Alex had to laugh. He couldn't think of anyone more different from himself than Otto. But in a way, he liked him.

14

Heinrich Stoltz was shaking with cold and fright. He and his contact—a man who used the code-name Albert—were waiting in the damp woods not more than fifty meters from the train tracks. In the distance, the bombardment continued. For two days bombs and artillery had been pounding the area near the Rhine. By now the German military would be rushing ammunition, tanks, and artillery to the front, west of the town of Wesel. The timing had to be right. If the resistance knocked out the rail lines too soon, there were expert crews in the area who could repair the tracks in just a few hours. The important thing was to cause at least that much delay at the right time, and to get the airborne troops on the ground before German forces could amass more firepower. Way too many additional guns had already been brought in, but to have begun sabotage efforts too early would only have alerted the German military that the forward thrust was about to begin.

So Brother Stoltz and Albert waited for their signal. If a supply train passed the train station in Dorsten, men were waiting to hurry out of town and flash a blinking light. The signal would be sent quickly up the line and would reach Albert in just a matter of seconds—and then the charge, already set, would be ignited. Brother Stoltz had traveled with Albert a considerable distance, from Karlsruhe northward into the Ruhr valley to be part of this operation. But it was worth the effort. There were few resisters in Germany, and no Allied effort needed resistance support so much as the crossing of the Rhine. Word had spread among the Socialist Workers organization that Patton had gotten some troops across the river near Mainz, and American troops were also streaming across a bridge that Germans had failed to destroy at Remagen. But this operation, called "Varsity," was the largest planned crossing and would be the beginning of the end for Hitler. If Allies could take the Ruhr region—and all its factories—the capacity to wage war would be almost ended for Germany. Brother Stoltz had hidden in a delivery truck, driven by Albert, and Albert had had no difficulty getting past roadblocks since he made a trip to Düsseldorf once a week in this same truck. From Düsseldorf, they had been transported in another truck, driven by another resister, also part of the union. In Dorsten, and other towns near Wesel, the men fanned out to do their work, mostly on back roads, riding motorcycles. What Brother Stoltz knew was that if he were stopped, his compromised papers might not hold up—and he was *very* frightened—but he felt this was something he absolutely had to do.

Nothing was happening for the moment, no signal. Albert had warned Heinrich that crews constantly moved up and down the tracks and checked for damage. "I find this waiting very difficult," Brother Stoltz whispered.

"It's always this way," Albert said. "It's like waiting for your personal firing squad to arrive. I never get used to it."

"Why did you start doing such a thing?"

"Revenge, mostly."

"Revenge for what?"

"The Gestapo killed my brother. For no reason. They heard rumors about him, and they didn't care whether the information was true or not. They wanted to make a show of strength in our town."

"Did they beat him to death?"

"No. At least it was quick. They shot him."

"The Gestapo beat me up—broke my bones."

"Did they give a reason?"

"One of them insulted my daughter. I ordered him out of my house."

"Yes. That's all it takes." Albert looked off to the east, as he did every few seconds. He seemed to be a man of about forty, but Brother Stoltz knew very little about him. His hands were rough and stained, probably from grease or oil, but he had the face of a scholar, even the eyeglasses.

"If the Allies get across the river and take the Ruhr, the war will end quickly, don't you think?" Brother Stoltz asked.

"One would think so. If they push on to Berlin, and Russia does the same, maybe Hitler will finally see that he has no choice. But who knows how this man thinks, he and his henchmen? The SS troops are ready to fight to the bloody end, no matter what happens."

"What about this talk that Hitler will create a redoubt in Austria and hold out in the mountains?"

"He might try it. It would be like him to fortify a stronghold of some kind—especially there, at his Eagle's Nest. And some fanatic Nazis would flee to such a place with him. If he commanded it, they would go, and they would die for him."

Brother Stoltz wondered. Maybe the war could drag on for months if Hitler tried a last stand of that kind. Still, it seemed likely that Brother Stoltz would get a chance before long to make contact with Allied troops and escape Germany. The only problem was, he wasn't sure that's what he wanted to do. Maybe Peter would have the sense to move toward the American lines himself. If he could be taken prisoner by the British or Americans, and not by Russia, Brother Stoltz might be able to find him and gain his release.

"Did you hear that?"

Brother Stoltz hadn't heard anything, but he listened now, and he detected a sound, although he couldn't identify it.

Albert remained silent for a time, and then he said, "It's an inspection crew on one of those pump cars."

"What should we do?"

"Let's wait. It's still too soon to blow up the tracks."

"But what if this crew finds the explosives?"

"I can't let them do that."

Brother Stoltz knew what that meant. He and Albert were sitting by the plunger box. If the explosives or the wires were discovered, the two of them could be dead men. The sound of the pump car was getting louder, but the car was moving slowly. "Some are probably walking and checking the tracks," Albert whispered. He said nothing more, but he placed his hand on the plunger.

In a few more minutes voices were in the air, still at a distance. The slow pace of it all was almost more than Brother Stoltz could stand. "Maybe we should get away now," he said.

"No. We hid the wires well. I've seen men walk right by these charges and never spot them. We have to wait until they give us no choice. If we don't delay the supply trains, we've accomplished nothing."

Brother Stoltz nodded. He shifted his weight a little, got into a better position to get up quickly. The pressure on his bad knee was painful, but he knew he couldn't shift around again.

As the voices, the sound of the car, came closer, finally Brother Stoltz saw movement through the trees, saw the glare of the lanterns the men were carrying. Shadows were working their way along the tracks. A man with a deep voice said, "Anyone else ready to stop for a smoke?" Another man made some sort of joke, and the others laughed, but they didn't stop yet. Brother Stoltz thought he heard at least five men, maybe six, but it was hard to make out that many distinctive shadows.

The crew was coming even with the wire now, and Brother Stoltz felt himself breathing in little gasps. The men seemed to be passing by, however. Brother Stoltz let his breath seep out, ever so slowly. But then he heard a startled voice, heard someone say, "What's this?"

At the same moment, Albert drove the plunger into the box, and everything erupted. Brother Stoltz saw the flash and, for a second, the silhouette of bodies lifting off the ground, turning over. The debris slashed through the trees, and a concussion struck Brother Stoltz in the chest.

"Run!" Albert was shouting. And the two were already up.

Albert couldn't hold himself back. He was in better condition, didn't have knee problems. They hadn't run far before Brother Stoltz was alone in the woods. He tried to hear Albert ahead of him, confused the sound with his own thrashing in the underbrush, but he kept pushing forward, no matter how much pain he felt.

And then he heard Albert. "Come on! You have to run faster. This way."

Brother Stoltz wasn't certain what to fear. Were some of those men alive and well enough to chase them? Or was it the noise that worried Albert—the rush of troops to the area? All Brother Stoltz knew was that Albert was in a panic, and the terror was enough to send him bolting into brush he couldn't see, to accept the scratches on his face and the rips in his clothing.

And then they broke out of the woods. Albert leaped a rock fence, which Brother Stoltz had to climb onto and jump off. Then they ran hard through a pasture and down a hill. At the bottom, in a little cove filled with trees, was the motorcycle they had hidden. Albert was on it and had it started before Brother Stoltz could reach him and climb on behind.

"Hang on tight," Albert commanded, and then he gunned the accelerator. The motorcycle leaped ahead, spraying rocks and dirt. They charged down the road, without a headlight, swerving through ruts and banging into holes. Brother Stoltz could see no road, couldn't imagine how Albert was choosing his path. He ducked his head against Albert's back, partly to streamline the wind flow, and partly not to see. He expected at any moment to be hurtled across the ground.

But Albert never hesitated, kept the motorcycle going all out. And then, as he reached a paved road and turned onto it, he swore bitterly. "We may have failed," he said. "They'll have another crew in there before long. They'll fix those rails. We just have to hope they can't get it done before morning."

That brought the horror to a focus. Brother Stoltz saw the picture in his mind again, the flying bodies. All those men had to be dead or badly hurt, and for what?

"Why did you push the plunger?" Brother Stoltz shouted into Albert's ear.

"What do you mean? To save our lives, of course."

But that was not what Brother Stoltz had intended. He had wanted to save the lives of the paratroopers who would be landing in the morning. And he wanted to save German lives. That's what all this had been about. He was helping to end the war more quickly. That had meant delaying a train, nothing more. Now he and Albert had killed those men, and Albert was saying it could all be for nothing. Brother Stoltz kept his head down, felt the air rush over him, and he needed that; he was getting sick to his stomach.

* * *

The bombardment suddenly intensified in the middle of the night. Big artillery guns were zeroed in on the German defenses on the east side of the Rhine, and the noise the guns made was beyond anything Alex had ever heard before. The roar, even from a safe distance, was constant, as though thunderbolts were striking several times a second, with never a hesitation in the clamor. Closer to morning, flights of bombers, with fighter escorts, came in waves by the hundreds.

Alex and Otto had awakened in the forest to all this chaos. After that, Alex lay awake and watched the explosions light up the western sky. But the bombs began to drop closer. He and

Otto were not far from Wesel, and the town was obviously taking a pounding.

"We'd better move out of here," Otto told Alex. "If one of
those bombers overshoots its target, we're in a bad spot."

"But where can we go?"

"Let's head north, away from Wesel, and then we can loop
back to the west and watch for the drop."

So the two set out in the dark. They worked their way
through the trees until they felt safe, and then they waited for
the sun to come up. The airborne troops would be taking off
now, flying from France and England. It would be midmorning,
Alex supposed, before the drop began. Until then, he was certain this barrage of fire would continue.

For the moment there seemed little chance that anyone
would be looking for Alex and Otto, but it seemed strange to
be moving about in German uniforms at a time like this. Once
the Allied troops landed, Alex wished he had some way to dis-
card the clothes and put something else on. There was no way
to do that, however, so Alex and Otto simply tried to move as
close to the drop zone as they dared so that once the battle was
over they could try to make contact with American or British
forces. They were able to climb to the top of a hill, well out of
the action but close enough that as the sun began to come up,
they could see the dust fly and the trees burst as the bombing
and artillery fire continued. The fire was aimed into the areas
all around the drop zones, but in all the smoke and dust, it was
hard to say whether German AA guns were being knocked out.

"By now, the first wave of ground troops should be across
the Rhine," Otto told Alex. That was true, according to the
plan. Alex just hoped that the men hadn't been shot up and
stopped.

It was breathtaking and dreadful to watch the formed-up
flights of bombers come over, to see the devastation on the
ground. And it was hard to imagine that anyone in the middle
of it could survive. But Alex knew better. If troops were dug in

and didn't take direct hits, they would be waiting when the paratroopers began their drop. He knew how long a parachute drop could seem when a man was watching tracer bullets flashing toward him. He wished now that he could have done more to pinpoint the sites of the German strongholds. This would be the largest airborne drop in history, even larger than D-day, and that meant a lot of men had to make it to the ground. Alex just hoped they weren't falling into a trap.

It was just after ten o'clock when Alex saw the great armada approach. First came fighters, not transports: P-47s diving toward the landing zone, racing across the open areas, and then strafing the surrounding woods. Finally a big, lumbering transport, one of the new C-46s, appeared. At the same moment, Alex saw black bursts begin to fill the air, and now he knew for sure that anti-aircraft guns had survived the Allied fire.

What he saw in the next few minutes, however, was beyond anything he could have imagined. Hundreds of fighters were in the air, and scores of big transports. The paratroopers, with their khaki-colored parachutes, would bloom into the blue sky, in chains, like strings of pearls—slipping from both sides of the C-46s. Before long the entire sky was filled with the little blossoms, all drifting gently toward the ground, but beneath them the very air seemed to be exploding. Bursts of black were smattering the blue with increasing regularity, and a layer of smoke was covering the ground. The parachutes would disappear into all that chaos and dark, and they seemed to be swallowed by it. The sense Alex had was that this was an utter disaster, that every one of those boys was dying.

The explosions in the sky were also sickening to watch. The flak was reaching the transports, which were coming in at only five or six hundred feet. The pilots were holding to their course as their airplanes were tossed about by the concussions. Many were taking hits, and several blew up in the air, suddenly turning into immense balls of fire as their fuel tanks ignited.

Some of the airplanes blew up before they got their jumpers out. But once the jump had been completed, the pilots would try to climb above the flak. The big crafts labored, and a number of them took hits as they climbed, then nose-dived, and finally exploded into the earth.

On another field, parallel to the parachute drop zones, gliders were drifting toward their designated landing zones. Others were still coming, pulled in pairs, two behind each tow plane. As they released and then angled toward the ground, they took a tremendous barrage of flak and machine-gun fire. Alex saw one of the big wood and canvas birds lose a wing and then spin toward the ground. Another landed hard, bounced in a cloud of dust, and then flipped over onto its back. Before long there was too much dust and smoke to see what was happening on the ground, and Alex wondered if any of them were making it all the way down to a safe landing.

Time and again Alex would look away, unable to watch, but then would look again, in spite of himself. He didn't say it to Otto, but what he felt was that he was watching a great tragedy, an enormous failure of the Allied effort. But after a time, he began to see men, looking like insects from this distance, emerging from the smoke. They were gathering into groups. They were moving out. Even out of the dust and smoke of the glider landing zones, an amazing number of troops were appearing. Some men certainly *were* dying, but most were getting down, and they were showing their toughness—not hunkering down somewhere but getting organized to fight.

Alex felt a tremendous surge of pride. These were his airborne brothers, and they had crossed the great natural boundary of the Rhine, which had been impossible in previous wars. These were not men who had planned on military careers. They weren't even flag-wavers. They were merely doing a job that had to be done. Alex had seen so much, had felt so disillusioned all winter, but this was a sight he never wanted to forget. He had never seen courage manifested so tangibly on such a grand scale.

For two hours the landing continued. As the fighters zeroed in on the artillery sites and attacked them, the flak diminished, but the drop still had to be an ordeal for every jumper. By the second hour, however, Alex could see that the troops were moving, attacking the machine-gun emplacements, opening a broader salient. Eventually supplies were dropping, and there was less and less interference. Alex knew that Allied forces were moving not only south and east toward Wesel but also back toward the west and the Rhine. They were hooking up with the men who were crossing the river, and they were driving out the German defenses between them.

Alex and Otto finally ate what was left of the food the Richartzes had given them. And then, as the evening came on, they settled down to sleep one more night in the woods. What they now had to fear, with their German uniforms, was that they might be overrun and shot before they could identify themselves. But it was heartening to see American troops so close. Alex slept fairly well, and in the morning, as he looked down from his hilltop position, he could see an American outpost, a roadblock, with MPs in charge.

"Let's go. I'm starving," Otto told Alex.

"All right. We need something for a white flag." Alex tried to think what he could use.

"I had nothing white when I surrendered last time," Otto said. "We merely set down our rifles and raised our hands in the air. We can do that, and you can shout in English. They'll recognize that you're an American."

"All right. Let's walk off this hill and into the road. Then we can walk straight at the roadblock with our hands high in the air. They'll see us from well off and know we're giving ourselves up. Once we get close enough, we should both start saying, 'Varsity Coach.' Someone at the blockade should know the password."

"Even if they don't, it shouldn't matter. They'll process us through, take us to a camp of some type, and we'll have a chance to explain who we are."

Alex was less confident about that. He had no papers except for his German military ID. He hoped there would be no problem. But he started down the hill, and he told Otto, "Okay, this is it. Once we make this last step, we're home free."

"It was a good operation too. Things are going well for the Allies."

Alex glanced up as he walked through the trees. The sky was a wonderful pale blue, the temperature already warming. It was a lovely day, the kind he remembered from the spring of 1939. He could hear birds in the trees, and the grass was beginning to turn green. Before long, Germany would be at the height of its beauty. It was strange to feel all that warmth and renewal and to know that this spring the war would rage across every part of the country. "Tell me the truth," Alex said. "Doesn't this feel a little strange for you?"

"What?"

"To be on the other side—after fighting for years for Germany?"

"Sometimes, for a moment, I get confused about what side I'm on. I see those American planes—the shape of them and the insignias on their wings—and my instinct is to fear them, to think of them as the enemy."

"They're killing Germans. Doesn't that bother you?"

Otto had come to a thicket of undergrowth. He stopped and looked around to spot the best way down the hill. "We saw more Americans being killed than Germans," he said.

"So where was your heart? Which side are you on, deep down?"

Otto laughed. "You still don't understand me, Alex. I try to tell you, but you don't believe me."

"What? That you don't care?"

"Alex, I'm on *my* side. I don't think much beyond that."

"So what do you believe in? Really?"

Otto broke through the thickest growth and stepped into a little clearing. The sun was shining down through the locust trees, the taller oaks; it was a beautiful, peaceful spot. Otto looked at Alex for a time, and then he said, "Early in the war, the British began to bomb Berlin. A bomb dropped into an apartment house in the Kreuzberg district. Only one person was killed—and that person happened to be my grandmother, the person in this world I loved the most. So I asked myself why. Why did this bomb happen to choose, from all the people in Berlin, this one good person, this one harmless woman? And the answer was obvious to me."

He stood and waited until Alex finally said, "What answer?"

"There was no reason at all. It was random chance. Once I saw that, I told myself, nothing means anything at all. Meaning is something we try to give to life only because we can't face the idea of no meaning. But I have accepted this meaningless-ness. And so I say to myself, 'Make sure you're not the one the bomb drops on. That's the only thing that matters. All the rest is just talk.'"

"Then you shouldn't have come here. There's more chance of getting killed."

"Yes, but that's the other sad truth. Once you see no mean-ing in life, it seems rather tedious. Sporting with fate is the only fun left."

"I don't think you really believe any of that. You want to end this war—and you want to stop all the bombs from falling on all the grandmothers."

Otto looked away, up toward the filtering light in the tops of the trees. "Well . . . I will say this much. Most of the people dying are not the ones who deserve to die. It's these Nazis—who like death so much—who should taste more of it."

He turned then and continued down the hill until he reached the edge of the woods. Beyond the trees was an exten-sive pasture. Alex and Otto stood and looked out across the open acreage. "I guess we just hold up our hands as high as we can and walk toward the road," Alex said. "I don't see anyone yet, but when they do see us, we need to be sure they know that we're surrendering."

"Once we get to the road, they'll see us from the outpost," Otto told him. "They should have field glasses on us. They'll know what we're doing."

"All right, then. Let's go." But both hesitated. This was an act of trust, and it ran against natural instincts to walk into the open. Finally, Alex stepped out and Otto followed. They walked the full distance of the pasture toward the road. They kept their arms stretched high in the air, and they heard nothing, saw no one.

As they neared the road, there was a barbed-wire fence to cross. The two stood with their hands up and looked around them in all directions, and then Otto put his foot on one strand of the fence and pulled up on another one. Alex stepped through, and then he held the wires for Otto. But just as Otto was stepping away from the fence, Alex heard a burst of machine-gun fire. He dropped, instinctively. "Don't shoot," he screamed. "We're Americans."

Another burst of fire followed, and Alex yelled again. "We're Americans. We have no weapons."

There was no reply, but Alex could hear movement, and then he saw a man running up the road. "Don't move. Stay down," the soldier yelled, and Alex felt a sense of relief. The man kept running. He was carrying a carbine, and when he finally stopped, he trained it on Alex. "I'm an American," Alex said. "I was dropped behind enemy lines to choose drop zones for Operation Varsity. Our password is 'Varsity Coach.'"

"That's a German uniform you've got on, buddy. That's all I see."

"We had to use these for cover."

Alex couldn't see the boy's face, could only hear how young he sounded. "As far as I'm concerned, you're a Kraut.

And you're surrendering to me. So get up slow, and don't try anything."

"That's fine," Alex said, and he slowly got to his feet. But Otto wasn't moving. Alex turned toward him and saw that the back of his uniform was covered with blood. "Otto," he said. "Otto." He dropped back onto his knees.

"That's a German name," he heard the boy say, and then he felt a slam in the back of his head.

Alex knew some time had passed when he came back to consciousness. He was lying on his back, looking up toward the sun. There were four faces over him now, and one of the men said, "Get up. You're a prisoner of war."

"I'm an American."

"You can tell that story to someone else. We're going to turn you over."

"What about Otto? He's a German, but he's working for us."

"He's not working for nobody now. He's dead. Now get up."

Alex was still dazed. He didn't try to get up, but the men jerked him to his feet. He felt his head spin and his knees go weak. He almost dropped again, but the men were holding him. "Don't you know the password?" he said. "It's 'Varsity Coach.' We were supposed to use it to get back behind the lines. We put our lives on the line for you guys."

"Look, buddy, I don't know no password," one of the soldiers said. "No one told us to check with all the Krauts for passwords before we shoot at 'em."

"But we had our hands in the air. We have no weapons."

"Shut up, okay? I still might shoot you." Then he spoke to the others. "Go back to our outpost. I'll take this guy in."

The other three disappeared, and Alex kept walking. He wasn't sure whether this sergeant who still had hold of his arm might not take this chance to shoot him and get rid of him.

"All right," the sergeant yelled ahead, "I've got me a Kraut who speaks English like he was born in America." He walked to two MPs who were standing by a jeep, which was parked sideways across the road. "He's talking about passwords and saying he was doing reconnaissance, but he's got a Kraut uniform on and he had German papers on him. He called his friend by a German name, too. So I don't know what's going on."

An MP cursed Alex and then grabbed him and shoved him up against the jeep. "Turn around!" he demanded.

"We searched him already," the sergeant said.

The MP ignored this. He kept patting Alex's pockets, and he checked his legs, his boots, for anything concealed. "I'm in intelligence," Alex said. "I'm a CIC officer. I was trained in Dijon and then dropped in here last week. I was a sergeant in the 101st until they pulled me out for this mission. I'm Airborne, the same as you guys. I was trained at Taccoa. I jumped at Normandy and up in Holland. I fought in the Bulge. I'm from Salt Lake. My name is Alex Thomas. I don't know what else to tell you. Can you get an S-2 down here? Maybe he'll know the password. They told us all you guys would know it."

"Just sit down right there," the MP said, "and stop running your mouth. *We'll* decide whose side you're on. No one would *ever* talk me into putting on one of those stinking uniforms, no matter what the reason."

"What about to save *your* life?"

"Shut up."

But the MP got on the radio, and he called for someone to pick up a prisoner. Then he added, "Someone from Intelligence needs to talk to him. The guy claims he was dropped in here to do reconnaissance, and he speaks good English."

When he got off the radio, he looked back at Alex skeptically. "Just sit right there. Don't move," he said.

"There was no reason for those guys to shoot at us," Alex said.

"I told you. Shut up."

LaRue and Beverly usually worked at the family factory on Saturdays. When there was nothing else to do, they helped in the packaging department, where they boxed airplane parts and readied them for shipping. But more often, lately, Bea Thomas had been teaching them to track orders, check to make sure shipments were correct, and then type shipping labels. Beverly did most of the labels even though she hadn't yet taken a typewriting class at school. She pecked away with two fingers and seemed to lose herself in a task that LaRue found far too tedious.

At noon Beverly got out the picnic basket that she and her mother had packed that morning. The girls sat at a big oak desk with Grace Pearson, her mother's secretary. "Come on, Mom," LaRue called several times, but every time LaRue looked into her mother's back office, Bea had a telephone to her ear or she was studying the sheets of paper on her desk. Finally, however, she did walk to the outer office. The girls had already brought a chair to the desk for her, and they had set out a sandwich and an apple on a sheet of scrap typing paper.

"I'm sorry," Bea said. "I swear, I'm going to cut the line on that phone someday. Everyone needs everything *right now*.

What ever happened to courtesy? Is that another casualty of war?"

"We're like those people in a Charlie Chaplin show—all running around, herky-jerky," Grace said. "But I'll have to admit, I kind of like it. I think the commotion finally got to Millie, but I don't let it bother me."

That was a bit of an awkward subject, and LaRue was surprised that Grace didn't know it. Millie Ellertson had worked for the family for the past year or so, but she had recently left to take another job. Millie had been Gene's girlfriend, and Gene, the third Thomas son, had been killed in the war. Now Millie was dating someone else. The Thomases all felt that she had wanted to separate herself a little from the family now, and that was understandable—but still sort of awkward, and to LaRue, a little sad. At one time, Millie had seemed almost like another sister, and LaRue had found herself hoping that she would never marry, that she would "wait" for Gene. It seemed that maybe Gene deserved that—although he wouldn't have thought so himself.

"Millie talked to me about this boy she's dating," LaRue said.

"Really?" Mom said. "What did she tell you?"

"She said she likes him, but she doesn't love him the way she did Gene. So she doesn't know what to do. He wants to get married, but she hasn't told him she will—not yet, anyway. I think she probably will, sooner or later."

"Well . . . I think it's for the best. I hope she does marry him. She deserves the chance to have her own family."

"Is this boy a Mormon?" Grace asked.

"Well . . . yes," LaRue said. "But I guess he started smoking while he was in the service—and he hasn't been back to church since he got home. Millie's trying to get him going, but she doesn't know for sure whether he'll be able to take her to the temple."

"Oh, dear. She can't be thinking that," Mom said. "I need to talk to her."

Silence followed as everyone seemed to realize at the same time that Mom had said the wrong thing in front of Grace, who was not LDS. But LaRue laughed and said, "That's right, Mom, you take charge. You can tell her what to do."

"I didn't mean it that way."

"Mom thinks she has to solve all our problems," LaRue told Grace.

"She does a good job of it around here."

"Oh, come on, girls," Bea said. "You make me sound like a busybody."

"How did you end up in charge down here, Bea?" Grace asked. "It doesn't even sound like you wanted the job."

LaRue and Beverly both began to laugh. Bea shook her head at them, and then she said, "Grace, you know very well I'm not *in charge.*"

Now it was Grace who laughed. "Who do you think you're kidding?" she said. "Even Mr. Thomas told me the other day, 'You'll have to ask Bea about that. I just don't know.'"

"Hey, it's the same at home," LaRue said. "Dad struts around like the only rooster in the henhouse, but Mom is the one who keeps things going. Dad's hardly ever home."

LaRue saw Mom—and Beverly—duck their heads. Mom always worried about giving Grace a bad impression of the Church.

Grace was a young woman from Denver whose father had been transferred by the Union Pacific railroad to Salt Lake City. He was a manager of some sort, and pretty well off. Grace had moved to town in time to finish school at East High, and she had married a local boy, a Mormon, but she had gotten a divorce after only a couple of years. At times she expressed her disgust with "local attitudes," and from what LaRue knew, some of her conflicting points of view had been at the heart of her marital problems. For one thing, her husband's family had never been very accepting of her.

LaRue also knew that Bea, from the day she had hired Grace, had been hoping to soften her opinion of the Church. LaRue had heard her tell Dad, "If she would join the Church, I really think that marriage could be patched up. It's just a shame for Grace to be on her own with that cute little boy of hers." And then she had mentioned some things she had told Grace—things she hoped would help her understand the true principles of the Church and not the ones she had extrapolated from some rather narrow and unkind behavior she had witnessed.

"LaRue," Sister Thomas said, and she sounded careful, "your dad has important responsibilities, and so he's gone in the evenings quite often. Maybe I do make a lot of decisions about little things around the house, but no one knows better than you that it's your father who sets the spiritual tone in our home."

LaRue saw all kinds of ironies in that statement. Mom made the daily choices, all right, but then Dad would come home and make *pronouncements*. Once he did, the appeal process always set in. It was a matter of working around him—begging or bargaining. In the end, he was never so tough as he liked to let on, but he also never dropped the procedure. He started from a strong position and then let the negotiations begin. Every now and then, when he was upset or cranky, he would suddenly clamp down. Bea wouldn't get the money she needed for some purchase, LaRue would have to listen to a long lecture, or poor Beverly would find out that she read too much and ought to get out and exercise, that she ate too little and ought to be thankful for the good vegetables set before her, or that she needed to speak up for herself and not always let LaRue run over her. This last one always amazed LaRue: "Do as I say; think for yourself," he seemed to be telling poor Bev.

"Say what you want, Bea," Grace said. "You're not only in

charge, but people like it that way. Everyone says you're fair. And you know this business better than anyone." Grace gave the desk a little rap with her knuckles for emphasis.

LaRue liked Grace. She was a stylish young woman who liked to experiment with hairdos. She wasn't overly pretty, but she was dramatic—someone people looked at as she walked by in her bright dresses and high heels with fancy straps, her stunning red lipstick.

"Grace, you exaggerate. I feel like I'm in over my head around here every single day." Sister Thomas was eating her sandwich quickly, obviously feeling some haste at the moment, maybe as much as anything to end this conversation.

"I'll tell you what," Grace said. "When this war is over, it's going to be women like you who have turned over the old apple cart—without even meaning to do it."

"What apple cart?"

"You're showing men what women can do—and you're showing us girls at the same time."

"That's right!" LaRue said. She reached over and gave her mom a pat on the shoulder.

"Dear, dear, don't blame something like that on me," Bea said, and she laughed. But LaRue could see that her mom actually rather liked the idea. "I will say this: In some ways, when the war is over, I sort of dread the idea of just being home all the time."

"Oh, oh," LaRue said. "Look out, *President* Thomas."

Everyone laughed at this, even Mom, but she was quick to say, "Now, LaRue, don't misunderstand. I still say the most important thing a girl can do is raise a family. You know that's how I feel."

"What about Grace?" LaRue asked. "She *has* a little boy to raise. She has to work *and* raise a family."

But Grace took LaRue by surprise. "Not really," she said. "My former husband is good about taking care of us. We have enough to get by. I just like working better than being home with a baby all day. My mom takes care of my little boy, and that gets me out of the house."

This was stunning, even to LaRue. She had never heard a woman say something like that. And Bea, who had obviously been taking some joy in the things Grace had said about her, looked downright worried. She seemed to wait long enough for her words not to seem a direct response, and then she said, "Well, the war has, as you say, upset the apple cart in some ways. And maybe part of that is good. Maybe we've all had to change the way we think a little—especially men. But not everything that's coming out of this is good. When I was a girl, families seemed a lot more stable. The men farmed, or they went to work, and the women were close to their children. Everyone sat down together for dinner, and after, they had some time in the evenings to sit on the porch and talk, or play some games. Nowadays the kids run around so much more than they used to. Families don't spend enough time together. When they do, half the time they just sit and listen to the silly radio."

"Maybe families *were* better, Bea," Grace said. "I don't know about that. But men got away with way too much. The man I married thought women ought to be like children—seen but not heard."

"Well . . . I know," Bea said. "Some men do have attitudes like that."

"Especially *Mormon* men."

LaRue was intrigued. "Are Mormon men different?" she asked. "Aren't all men sort of like that?"

Grace took a deep breath. "Oh, I don't know. I hear all kinds of things. My friend tells me that Catholic men are the worst of all. But she's married to a Catholic, so that's where she puts the blame. All I know is, a lot of women are getting fed up with the way things are, and women here in Utah are behind the times."

"Grace, we believe in inspiration," Bea said. "And we

believe that men have the stewardship to lead their families. Things work so much better that way."

"That *sounds* good, Bea, but my husband was stubborn as a mule. He'd make some stupid decision, and then—when I questioned it—get all upset because I was trying to wear the pants in the family. So I said, 'Good. You wear the pants. And you can keep them on in bed at night, too, if that's what you want, because you won't have any need to take them off when you're sleeping with me.'"

Grace had clearly gone too far. Bea's round face was suddenly bright pink. Grace was smiling, but she was ducking her own head. And Beverly was clearly mortified.

A lot of chewing took place for a time, but finally Bea said, "Grace, I know that some men think they have a right to boss their families around. And the girls could tell you that Al and I have had some . . . *discussions* about that." She glanced at LaRue and smiled. "Al can get a little that way himself."

"A *little?*"

"LaRue, that's enough. You happen to think *I'm* too bossy, too."

LaRue laughed. "Well, that's true."

"Men were raised that way, the same as I was. That's just how things have been. But Al and I have had some very good talks, and he's treating me more like a partner than he used to. I can't ask for anything more than that. He's admitted that he's been wrong at times—and I have too—and now we're trying to work to make things better. To me, that's what marriage is all about."

"But, Bea," Grace said, "my husband wouldn't give an inch. He told me I had no right to question his decisions. And I wouldn't live that way."

LaRue thought she understood that. She knew that her dad had made some changes. He did seem to be trying. But every time he took a couple of steps forward, he would take at least one back. His instincts just hadn't changed very much. LaRue could never be married to someone like her father.

"In case you haven't noticed," Grace said, "I don't spend my time moping around. Most women around here think you have to be married and have a dozen kids to be happy. Well, I've changed just enough diapers to know there are better things in life than that."

LaRue wanted to agree with that, too, but she was surprised by her own discomfort. Grace suddenly sounded selfish and self-centered. LaRue knew, when all was said and done, she did want a family.

"Oh, Grace," Bea said, "I think you're saying more than you mean. I know how much you love your little boy."

"Sure, I do. I'm just saying that I don't feel sorry for myself. I stay home with Jimmy most nights, and I don't mind. But I'll tell you, there's a lot more going on in this town than most of you ladies think. And there's some awfully good-looking soldiers on the loose. There's no use letting the boys have *all* the fun in this life."

Beverly was staring. Bea was swallowing, trying hard not to looked shocked. LaRue was laughing, in spite of herself. What she said was, "Now you're talking," but she was almost as shocked as her mother.

Later that afternoon, LaRue and Beverly took the bus home. Mom told them she was going to have to stay a little longer than she usually did on Saturday, but the girls should go ahead without her. On the way to the bus—in fact, almost as soon as the two were outside—Beverly said, "Do you think Grace does bad things?"

"Bev, don't talk like a little girl. You're thirteen now. You can say what you mean."

"You know what I mean—what she said about those soldiers."

"It's not our business. She can do what she wants. That's

what Mormons always do: judge people and act like they're better than everyone else."

"Things are right or they're wrong, LaRue."

LaRue let her breath out. It was a blustery day, almost April now, but the wind made it feel more like February, and heavy clouds were piled up along the mountains. LaRue could see that it was snowing up there, and she felt some fine sprinkles of rain in the wind, too. Beverly was flushed by the cold, her cheeks pink. She was like Bobbi, fair-skinned with light, wispy hair. No one would have guessed she was LaRue's sister.

The girls had come to their bus stop. LaRue stopped and turned her back to the wind. She was wearing a heavy wool coat, one she had put away at one time but had gotten back out that morning. She turned the collar up around her ears.

"LaRue, *you're* a Mormon."

"What?"

"You talk about the way Mormons do things—like you're not one. You said, 'That's what Mormons always do.'"

"Okay, *we* do too much of that."

"But that's not what you mean. You think that you don't do it—just the rest of us."

LaRue was getting weary of all this. She turned and looked to see whether the bus was coming. The rain was starting to fall a little harder. She had a date with Reed that night. She needed to get home in time to wash her hair and put it up, so she hoped the bus would hurry. "Beverly, when I worked at the USO, I found out how people think about us. Most of the soldiers who came to live in Utah thought we were a bunch of narrow-minded busybodies. They used to say, 'Live however you want, but don't try to tell us what to do.'"

Beverly turned a little. LaRue could see how frustrated she was. "You don't have to agree with everything *they* say. Maybe Grace didn't have a very good husband, but you didn't have to make Dad sound so bad."

"What did I say? He *is* bossy."

"What Mom said was right. She talked to him, and he's doing better."

"I'm sorry, Bev, but I don't think he's changed very much."

"What about you? At Christmastime, you told me you weren't a very good person and you wanted to be different."

"I know I did."

"Well, what happened? Now, you're just the same as you used to be."

"And how is that?"

"You're LaRue—the same old LaRue."

"I never said I wasn't," LaRue said, and she tried to sound unconcerned, but she felt the stab. The bus pulled up soon after that, and the two got on, but they didn't speak again. LaRue was remembering how she had felt that day when Ned had told her off, accused her of caring only about herself, of not being the wholesome person a Mormon girl ought to be. She had seen her own selfishness that day; it had come into focus, suddenly, the way a movie did sometimes when the projectionist suddenly twisted some knob up in the booth and a picture that had seemed clear enough showed itself to have been blurred all along.

But what was she doing now? Reed was so kind and compliant, so nuts over her, that she took advantage of him constantly. She told herself not to do it, but he always let her little manipulations work. She controlled him, tested his commitment, tried things that she knew were only to see how far she could push him before he finally told her to get lost. But he never did.

She waited until the bus had reached its stop and the girls were walking home from Twenty-First South before she said, "Bev, I do need to change. I tried there for a while, but I'm not doing very well lately."

"I'm sorry," Beverly said. "I shouldn't talk so mean myself."

The girl could be so endearing, so simple. "Bev, you're not

the problem," LaRue said. "I am. Like you said—what's wrong with me is that I'm LaRue."

"Everybody loves you, LaRue. You're popular. Every boy wants to go with you." She walked for a time before she added, "I'll never have a boyfriend."

It was such a strange response, and yet the leap of logic was easy enough to follow. "You'll have boyfriends," LaRue said. "And you'll find a good husband and have a nice family. Everything will be just fine for you." She didn't say the last part, not out loud: "I'm the one who's making a mess of things."

When they turned the corner near their house, Beverly said, "Look who's at our house."

LaRue had just noticed the same thing. Grandpa and Grandma Thomas's Hudson was parked in front of their house. Grandma and Grandpa had apparently gone inside. The Thomases never locked their doors. LaRue wanted to be happy about seeing her grandparents, but she had let her feelings dip too low for that.

When they reached the door, however, she heard her grandma, in that husky voice of hers, shout, "So there you are, finally. Where's your mother?"

The girls stepped inside, and Grandma walked to them. She was wearing a flowered dress, all yellows and greens, and looking like spring, not like this miserably cold day. She threw her arms around Beverly and hugged her. And then she turned to LaRue and wrapped her in those long, wild arms that always seemed a little out of control.

"Mom had to stay late. She had some things she had to—"

"Oh, that woman. She'll never learn. She never has known enough about having fun." She stepped back and grabbed LaRue's shoulders. "We need to talk," she said. She spun around. "Grandpa, you talk to Beverly for a minute. LaRue needs me right now." She took hold of LaRue's hand and marched up the stairs, taking two steps at a time, pulling LaRue along.

And then, as she opened LaRue's bedroom door, she said, "So tell me what's wrong."

"Wrong? Nothing, Grandma. It's cold outside, and—"

"Don't give me that load of manure. This is your grandma talking to you."

LaRue smiled. She took her coat off and threw it on the bed, and then she sat down next to it. Grandma grabbed her desk chair and pulled it up close to the bed. "I'm okay," LaRue said. "I'm just a little bit down today."

"Why?"

"I don't know. Listen, I have to wash my hair right now. I've got a date tonight."

"With that basketball player?"

"It's baseball season now."

"He's no genius, is he, LaRue? I tried to talk to him, and I thought his tongue was going to break off. Why do you keep going with him?"

"He's cute, Grandma. You said that yourself."

Grandma let her eyes widen. "He *is* that. But you're not only beautiful, you're brilliant. You can do a lot better."

LaRue folded her arms and looked down at the floor. "He's nice, Grandma. And I'm not. *He* could do a lot better."

"Oh, hogwash. I won't listen to any of that." She got up and came to LaRue, sat down next to her and put her arm around her shoulder. "Why would you say such a thing?"

"I don't know how to explain it to you. But it's true."

"All right. Now you listen to me." Grandma walked back to the chair, pulled it closer to LaRue, and sat down directly in front of her. "LaRue, your father, my dear son, takes life *much* too seriously. He's spent his whole life telling you kids all the things you ought to feel guilty about. You need to take that man with a grain of salt." She leaned her head back and laughed in a loud burst.

LaRue smiled.

"I'll tell you what you are. You're wonderful. You're feisty—

and I like feisty. You're quick. You're clever. And I'll tell you what else you are. You're as sweet as clover honey. You don't know that about yourself. You think you can't be feisty and sweet at the same time, but you can. If I had had your looks, your brains, your goodness, I would have knocked the world on its ear, little girl. I did pretty well, and I was plain as an adobe shack."

"You were gorgeous, Grandma. I've seen the pictures."

"Well . . . I wasn't too bad. But I wasn't half as smart as you, and I never was nearly so nice. Since your father got called to be stake president he's been way too pious. Sometimes I think I ought to poke that boy in the nose just to take him down a notch. He has no right to take the fire out of you. You're going to do great things with your life—and then he'll want to take all the credit for making you so wonderful."

LaRue was amazed by all of this. She never knew what to expect from Grandma. "Dad's not really so bad, Grandma," LaRue said. "He wants to be a good father and a good stake president, and he worries—"

"Way too much. I know all that. But I remember the kid he was. He was a lot more rebellious than you can ever imagine. I watch how hard he tries to do the right things, and he breaks my heart. It's like he knows who he would really be if he ever let go for a few minutes. And maybe that's all right for him. But he can't break your spirit, LaRue. You just be who you are, and you'll be fine."

"I use people, Grandma. I take advantage of them."

Grandma nodded. "I know," she said. "But you know that you do it. Your problem is, people fall at your feet, and it's hard *not* to take advantage of that. But you're only fifteen. Your impulses are right. You'll grow into yourself."

It was a wonderful thought. LaRue slid off the bed and dropped her head into her grandma's lap. "I love you," she whispered.

"See, that shows how sweet you are. And smart, besides."

LaRue laughed, but she still wondered about herself. She knew she didn't like what she was now, but she didn't know who she wanted to be, either. In some ways Grace appealed to her, but so did Mom, and the two were nothing alike. And strangely, she felt that Grandma was being a little too hard on Dad. Maybe he understood her better than anyone did—saw the same faults that she saw and only wanted her to be what she should be, could be.

But at least Grandma thought LaRue was all right, and that seemed important right now. It was nice to think that someone could know her so well, understand her, and also really like her.

It was April 1, 1945. Bobbi had been awakened in the night by the sound of artillery, airplanes, bombs. The Americans were softening up another island for a beach landing. This one was called Okinawa, one of the Ryukyu islands. The war was moving ever closer to Japan, and everyone said this island would be an important air base in the final onslaught. All Bobbi knew was that her ship was likely to fill up with wounded and burned men before the day was over.

She stayed in her bunk, but she lay awake and listened to the tumult. Gradually the room began to lighten until, through her porthole, she could see the orange glow of morning. And then she remembered that it was Easter. The thought took her breath away.

For each individual Marine or soldier arriving on the beach, this day represented a solemn gamble. But for Bobbi, for everyone on her ship, the focus was not on which boys would be hit; what they knew was that *many* would die or be wounded. It was, of course, much worse to be out there, offering one's life on that island, but it didn't change the reality that the war was coming to the *Charity*. Bobbi remembered the exhaustion and the wracking empathy she had felt last time, and she hated to go through all that again, but what she knew now was that it didn't end in a day or two. The pain continued, the nursing, but more than that, the visions of it all—the blood, the smells, the screams of pain—would be stamped inside her forever.

But Easter? She never liked to think of Christ on the cross. For her there was something disturbing about a crucifix. It seemed a kind of sensationalism, throwing the ugliness of Christ's death into her eyes. What she liked to think of was Christ's tender moments with Mary Magdalene. She liked to remember his gentle voice, his telling her, and later the apostles, that he had risen. She wanted, this day, to see past the blood and hold onto the promise that Christ offered.

She got up and looked out her porthole, across the water, but the island was on the opposite side of the ship. At times the light intensified, and she realized that the flash of artillery was meeting the light of the sun, mixing with it. She thought of a poem she had read in college, one by John Donne: "Good Friday, 1613. Riding Westward." The narrator of the poem laments that he is moving away from Christ, not toward him. He wants the Lord to call him back. "O, think me worth Thine anger, punish me," he says. "Burn off my rusts and my deformity." Long ago, before she knew anything at all, it now seemed, she had cried at those words. She had felt her own lack of spirituality and longed to have the Lord touch her, maybe shake her by the shoulder when she needed it. But today, the idea took on a new perspective. She was so far from home and the things she found comfort in, and she was about to do something sacred: offer her healing touch. She wanted to bring her spirit to this act, so that these boys, some taking their final breaths, would know that life wasn't only ugliness and hatred. She wanted them to know that nobility also existed—goodness and kindness. She didn't want to get caught up in all the bandaging and tugging bodies here and there and forget that it was Easter.

But the day didn't turn out exactly the way Bobbi expected. The terrible rush of litters didn't happen. It was almost noon before the first patients arrived, and these men spoke of light resistance at the beaches. Bobbi hoped it meant that the island would fall easily and quickly, but an officer, a young lieutenant, who had broken his ankle and was furious that he had had to leave the battle because of an awkward misstep, told her, "The Japs decided not to take us on at the shore, but they're dug in deep. They've got caves and tunnels up in those hills, and they're going to make us pay for every inch of territory we take on this island. It's going to get worse each day, not better."

And that turned out to be exactly right. By midweek, the steady arrival of LCMs full of broken boys was less rushed and chaotic than at Iwo Jima, but the reality was clear: the shooting was going to continue for a long time. Many of the men were being burned in explosions. The Japanese were using lots of artillery, including several big 150-millimeter guns. They were also launching a steady barrage of 81-millimeter and even gigantic 320-millimeter mortars. One young Marine told Bobbi that the soldiers called these big mortars "flying ash cans," and he told her about the tremendous flash they made when they went off. "I couldn't see a thing," he told her. "The corpsman got to me, and he covered my eyes. I don't know if I'm blind or not."

It was hard to think of Christ by then, even though Bobbi kept trying. She knew the Lord would restore the boy's vision, that in the next life this young face would be made whole, and the boy would be as handsome as he ever had been. But right now his skin was gone, his nose and ears. What mercy he would receive would come later, but for a long time now, he was going to suffer. She told herself that life was a learning experience, and that suffering was actually a kind of sacrament, a holy experience to lift a person to a higher plane, but when she looked at the boy, she could only wonder what he would think when he finally saw himself.

"What's your name?" she had asked him.

"Verl Carpenter."

"Where are you from?"

"Afton, Wyoming. Or close to there."

"That's Star Valley, isn't it?"

"Yeah, sure. Do you know that area?"

"I'm from Salt Lake. We used to make the drive up through Star Valley on our way to Yellowstone. I love that country."

"It's the best in the world," he said. His speech was slurred, and Bobbi knew he was speaking through the haze of the morphine in his body. Still, she heard a sound of longing that touched her.

"Say, are you LDS?" he asked.

"You bet. My dad's the stake president out in Sugar House."

"No kidding? I knew you were real nice, right from the beginning."

"I won't be so nice if you don't do *exactly* what I tell you. And right now, the best thing you can do is give in to that morphine and sleep for a while."

"Aye, aye, sir." He raised his bandaged hand in a clumsy attempt at a salute, and then he laughed a little. Bobbi knew that the morphine was making all that possible, but he had some miserable days ahead.

The *Charity* stayed off Okinawa most of the week, moving in close by day and retreating out to sea at night, but on Thursday the crew finally pulled up anchor and shipped out for Guam. The scuttlebutt was that these patients would be passed along to the hospital there, and that the ship would then return to Okinawa. The soldiers all said this island would take months, not days, to conquer, so Bobbi knew she might make the round trip more than once.

On the first night underway, she finally got something like a full night's sleep, even though she had to be out of bed early. With so many burn patients, the process of redressing the burns, debriding, and keeping the pain under control represented an overwhelming amount of work. Burn patients were usually at their worst a few days after the initial injury, and they had to be watched constantly for shock. Many of the men had their hands burned, or their eyes, and so those who did feel well enough to eat often couldn't feed themselves. The feeding kept the corpsmen busy, and Bobbi might have left that to them, but she tried to take part in every aspect of the work—and work harder than anyone. It was her idea of leadership to let the other nurses and the corpsmen know that she wasn't asking anything of them that she wouldn't do. She remembered Lieutenant Karras, who had remained so distant from the actual functions of nursing, and she didn't want to be that kind of administrator. But more than that, she wanted to keep the part of nursing she liked best: making life a little easier for the suffering men.

Bobbi paid special attention to Private Carpenter. Verl. She felt a kinship with him and maybe some extra responsibility. She took the time to sit by him and feed him. He was working through some pain now, and he wasn't joking, not even talking very much. Nor did he want to eat. Bobbi stayed after him, however, and got some applesauce and some liquids into him.

When she was about to leave, he said, "Can you stay here for a minute?"

"Not long, Verl. We're really busy this morning."

"Am I going to be able to see?"

"I don't know. In Guam, they'll unwrap your eyes and take a good look at you. You'll have a better idea then."

"Okay."

Bobbi tried to think of something to say, some hope to give him, but she didn't know his prognosis, and she didn't want to mislead him. He might have to get used to the idea that he wouldn't see again. She had watched dozens of boys make that adjustment in the past two years. It was always difficult, but she had learned that people have a way of going on, of doing what they have to do.

"Are you as pretty as you sound?"

"I look like your drill sergeant. I'm big and I'm mean."

"No you're not. Your hands are small—and soft as calfskin. Have you got a guy back home—or in the war somewhere?"

She looked down at the bandages that covered Verl's face, the clump of short brown hair showing at the top. She knew he was searching for something good to come out of this. She had seen it so many times, the way the injured boys liked to cling to a certain nurse for comfort and hope. "Verl, I'm engaged, but my fiancé is going through the same thing you are. He got his hands burned. He's had some surgery, and he's going to have some more. At least the war is over for him."

"But it didn't get his face?"

"No. Just a little."

"He's lucky."

"Yeah. But some get hurt a lot worse than you, Verl."

"Oh, sure. I know. I'm not whining."

"Do you have a girl back home?"

"Well, yes. I do. The only trouble is, she married a guy from down in Montpelier, Idaho, and I don't think he would like it if I came home to her." He tried to laugh, but his voice was turning to gravel. Bobbi knew she needed to end the conversation.

"That's rough, Verl. I'm sorry."

"Well . . . that's not too important. She's better off, as it turns out. I don't know anything but farming, so I'm not sure I could support a family now. What am I supposed to do if I can't see?"

"Verl, you're worrying about things you don't know yet. Find out what you really have to deal with before you start jumping to conclusions. You're man enough to do that."

"Touch my arm, Bobbi. Above where I'm bandaged."

"Verl, I—"

"I'm sorry. I didn't mean to embarrass you. I wasn't trying to—"

And so she put her hand on his arm, rubbed her palm along his elbow and up toward his shoulder.

He didn't say a word, but she knew he was crying in his soul, whether his tear ducts still worked or not.

Later that day Bobbi had a few minutes to talk to her friend Kate. They walked out on the main deck, and they breathed a little, looked out across the water. The ocean was quiet.

"I talked to the radio man this morning," Kate said. "He says the word coming out of Europe is that Germany could surrender any day now." She was wearing a surgical cap, but she took it off and shook her head. Her short hair ruffled in the breeze.

"I'll believe that when I see it," Bobbi said. "I don't think the war will end over there until they get Hitler himself."

"Maybe. But the Russians are close to Berlin, they say, and now that we've broken across the Rhine, our troops are moving fast. The radio man said we'll have Germany cut in half any time now. He says there's no way Germany will be able to keep fighting much longer."

"I hope that's right. If I knew Alex had made it through, that would be a big load off my mind."

"Do you know where he is now?"

"No. My mom wrote and said he had been pulled out of France, but he couldn't say where he was. Instead of thinking that the war is ending over there, I always think, 'What if something happens now, so close to the end?'"

"To us, it seems like *everyone* is bleeding."

"Or burned."

"Or both." Kate didn't smoke very often, but she lit a cigarette now. She rolled it around in her fingers and looked at it. "Are you holding up okay?" she asked.

"Sure," Bobbi said. "This go-round hasn't been quite so intense. I do have a bit of a problem, though."

"Problem?"

"There's a boy from my part of the country. A Mormon fellow. He's kind of latched onto me."

"Bobbi, let me tell you something. You know it, but I'll say it anyway." She took a draw on her cigarette.

"Yes, doctor."

Kate smiled. "Bobbi, you can't let this stuff get inside you too much. I know it's hard, but you just can't. When I was in med school, we used to work on cadavers. They weren't people to me. They were just 'things.' Sometimes, now, when I'm up to my elbows in blood, I have to think about these bodies that come across my table exactly the same way. There's a hole in some guy's belly, and that means a repair job I have to do. I sew up the holes, just like darning a sock, and then I see what's wrong with the next body they put on my table. As long as I handle it that way, I do a whole lot better."

"What about when you walk around and see these guys after the surgery? When they're awake and talking—and in pain?"

"I try to do the same thing. I find out where it hurts and decide whether there's anything I can do about it. Half the time I can't. But I've sewn up the hole, and they're alive. If I lie in bed at night and think about their pain, I can't stand it."

"It's not the pain that I struggle with, Kate. It's their stories. They all want to tell me their stories. You don't get as much of that."

"They may not tell me as much, but it's not hard to figure out what their stories are. Just before we left Okinawa, we got a boy in who was all blown apart. If we tried to do everything he needed, he was going to die on us. So we got his insides fixed up, and we let his limbs go. Finally, we had to take off both his legs, one above the knee and the other just below. Then we took one of his arms, above the elbow. When we did it, it was simply what we had to do. If we'd had a lot of time, and some specialists, we might have saved his arm, maybe even one of his legs. But we had no choice in those circumstances." She tossed the cigarette away, half smoked. "But then, this morning, I talked to him. He was realizing what was going on and starting to ask questions. I didn't know . . ." Kate's voice pinched off. Bobbi saw her brown eyes fill with tears, saw her distress magnified by her thick eyeglasses. "What was I supposed to say to him?" she asked, and she choked as she tried not to cry.

Bobbi put her arm around Kate's shoulder, and they both cried. It was a relief. Bobbi wished she could go to her state-room, lie down, and let it all come out. But not a minute had gone by before Kate said, "I can't do this, Bobbi. I have too much to do. We can't let it inside us. We just can't."

"I've been trying to think about Easter," Bobbi said. "That helps me some."

But Kate looked surprised. "All I saw was irony in that. It made me furious that we started the battle that day."

But Bobbi was thinking the opposite. What if they had fought this battle without an Easter, without any promise at all?

* * *

Alex was back in Dijon. At the front, once he had finally talked to the Intelligence people and found someone who knew his password, he had been treated well. A driver had taken him to the Rhine in a Jeep. It had taken awhile to cross, going against the stream of traffic into Germany, but he had begged his way onto a returning rubber boat, one that had been used to bring supplies across, and then he had found a truck heading into Luxembourg. From Luxembourg City, his CIC unit had made arrangements to have him flown to Dijon. His commander, Major Grow, had given him a night to sleep, and then he and Alex had spent a full morning together going over everything that had happened on his mission. Afterward, Alex had spent the afternoon writing everything down, docu-menting what he had seen of Operation Varsity, but also the actions of the resistance, Otto's death, and all the rest.

It was difficult for Alex. He had learned in the past year to deal with things by not looking back. But now, having to write his report, he had to consider what had happened. He thought of Otto, of Werner, the image of all those parachutes amid the smoke of AA guns. He couldn't think what he might have done to protect Otto. Should he have waited longer, taken a different route, sought another roadblock? It had all looked so simple, and actually it had been. But someone had pulled a trigger, and that was Otto's life. As Alex described the scene, on paper, he found that he was shaking. He wasn't breaking down, wasn't going to pieces, but the reality of what he had passed through had gotten inside him now, and the trembling in his hands, his stomach, wouldn't stop.

Alex took his report to Major Grow's office the next morning. The sergeant at the desk saluted, and for a moment Alex was surprised. He still didn't think of himself as an officer. As he returned the salute, the sergeant said, "Colonel DeSantos wants to see you. Report to him at 0900."

Alex was actually happy to hear that. He was at a loss right now, not knowing what was going to happen next in his life. So at 0900 he was waiting at the headquarters building, and soon after he was called into the colonel's office. When he entered, DeSantos stood up. Alex saluted him, and the colonel returned the salute, but then he came around his desk and shook hands with Alex. "I'm telling you," he said, "I'm sure happy to see you. When you send a man out on a mission, you never know whether he'll come back or not." Then he seemed to catch himself. "I felt terrible to hear about Lang," he said. "I guess someone got a little trigger happy."

"Yes, sir."

"It happens, Lieutenant. The hardest thing in the world is to tell a soldier *not* to shoot. I never blame a guy too much who makes that mistake. It's the ones who don't shoot I have a quarrel with."

Alex thought of Howie, who hadn't wanted to shoot. But he merely said, "Yes, sir," once again.

"Sit down." The colonel went back around his desk. Alex sat across from him. "Lieutenant Thomas, you're going to get a medal for this. I understand you received a DSM in Normandy. I'm not sure what to put you in for this time. But you'll get something."

"Won't this mission be classified?"

"Normally, it would be. And we won't tell the whole story. But there's always a balance. We need to let the folks back home know some of what's happening out here. They need heroes back in the states. That's what sells bonds, keeps people feeling like they can live with rationing tires and sugar a little longer."

"Sir, I don't want that. Choose someone else. I'm not a hero."

"Listen, I know what you're saying. We all feel that way. We're just doing our job, and we don't want to blow our own horns, but the decorations aren't up to you. I say you deserve one, and I'm putting you in for it."

"It's not that, sir. Nothing went right over there. Otto is dead, and Werner probably is too. And when the troops dropped, the sky was absolutely full of flak. I don't know that I accomplished a single thing."

"Thomas, when you walk out of here, you're never going to say that again. It's important. People die on dangerous missions. That wasn't your fault. You gave us key data about the landing zones. It made all the difference. The Germans knew we were coming. They saw our troop movements, and they knew where we were lined up. They rushed a lot of artillery in at the last minute, and some of it was so well hidden we couldn't see it from the air. But what we needed was a go-ahead on the drop zones and landing zones. In Normandy we came in over hedgerows twice as high as we expected, and we ran into poles that Rommel had put out there to stop gliders. But we knew what was going on this time. This landing wasn't easy, but what could we expect? We were landing in Germany—across the Rhine. No army has ever accomplished that before." He swore and slapped his hand on his desk. But then he softened his voice. "Thomas, you *are* a hero. A genuine hero. That's something you should never deny, not out of humility or any other reason."

Alex was actually touched by that. He wanted so much to believe that what he had done had had some worth. But he wasn't a hero; he knew he would never think of himself that way. "Sir, could I at least ask this much?"

"What's that?"

"Otto didn't have to go over there, sir. But he was the one who made most of the smart decisions. He kept us alive about four different times. I'd feel a lot better if you gave him the credit somehow. He's really the one who pulled it off."

"He was a German, Thomas. I don't know all the reasons he did what he did, but I wouldn't want to trust some guy who turned against *us*. I'm not going to say much about him when I write up my report. You're the American. You're our guy."

"It sounds like advertising, Colonel—like we've got something we think we have to sell."

"Look, Thomas, you've been around this mess for a long time. Don't talk to me like some Boy Scout. War is profane. But if you want to win, you don't say that to the people who pay the bills back home. You wave the flag. You put a few tears in their eyes. It's always been that way."

Alex had no idea how to respond to that. "Is there any chance, sir, that I could return to my unit? I'm not really—"

"Of course not. We don't do that. Germany is going to be finished in a few more weeks. You're in the CIC now. We're going to need every German-speaking soldier we can find. When we take over Germany, there's going to be more to do than you can believe. For us, in Intelligence, one of the biggest things is to catch as many of the high-ranking Nazis as we can. We need to make them pay for what they've done before they find some way to hide out."

"Why? Once the war is over, what difference will it make?"

The colonel stared at Alex for several seconds. "Lieutenant, I think you're worn out. I think you're still in shock from what you've been through. But you know as well as anyone that Germans have to pay for what they've done. These men have caused the death of *millions* of people. Have you seen the pictures coming out of Ordruff?"

Alex had seen them. A camp had been discovered, and in it were vast piles of corpses—along with living, walking skeletons. The Nazis had been working and starving people to death, killing them systematically. Word was coming from Poland that the Germans had been gassing Jews and then burning them—perhaps millions of them—in special ovens. However terrible Alex had known Hitler and the Gestapo to be, this was beyond his imagination. He had known of camps, had heard about killings, but he had never suspected anything on this scale. But revenge was the last thing he needed personally. He just wanted the atrocities to end. And above all, he didn't want to be involved in continuing the killing when the cease-fire finally came.

"Listen, Thomas, here's what I'm going to do. I'm going to make arrangements for you to receive a thirty-day leave. I'm not sure how soon I can push this through, but you get some rest in the meantime. The truth is, I don't know quite what to do with you right now—until Hitler tosses in the towel. Your wife is in London, isn't she?"

"Yes, sir."

"Well, good. I want to give you some time with her."

"She's going to have a baby in June."

"I can only get you thirty days, Thomas. And the way things are going, I'll need you back by then. But it would be nice to get over there for a while, wouldn't it?"

"Yes, sir. Of course."

"Well, you deserve it. It might be a week or so before I can get you out of here, but I'm pretty sure I can work it out."

Alex couldn't believe it. It was what he wanted, of course, but the idea was also frightening. He wasn't sure he was ready to see Anna. He wanted to be more whole, more under control, not quivering inside, when he finally took her in his arms.

Bea Thomas was sitting at her desk when her husband walked in. "Come here a second," he said. "I have something to show you."

"Just a minute. I—"

"No. Come right now. This is exciting." So she walked into his office, which was the largest office in the back—even though President Thomas now spent much less time at the plant than Bea did.

When President Thomas reached his office, he picked up a thick document and handed it to his wife. But he didn't let her look through it to see what it was. "It's a contract," he said. "A big one."

"For what?"

"Washing-machine parts. Bendix. We're not going to miss a beat, Bea. Just as fast as we can do it, they want us to start switching over. In five years we could be twice the size we are now. Everyone in America is just waiting to start buying appliances. The old ones are worn out, and people haven't been able to replace them. The other thing everyone wants is a new car. I'm going to be ready for that, too."

Bea smiled. She was happy for him, pleased for the family. She wasn't sure why she wasn't as excited as her husband was.

President Thomas sat down at his desk. Bea knew he wanted her to sit down too, to revel in this. The fact was, she had a letter from Boeing, in Seattle, telling her that her last order had never arrived, and she knew that wasn't true. She had the paperwork to prove it, but she wasn't going to be able to sleep that night if she couldn't find it. Still, she stayed.

"Bea, think about the opportunity we have." He leaned forward with his elbows on his desk. He had started to put on a little more weight lately, and his white shirt was straining a bit in the shoulders and over his chest. "Alex and Wally are essentially set for life." He held up his hand immediately. "Don't even say it. I know. I can't make up their minds for them. They're going to have to decide if they want to be involved."

"No. That isn't what I was thinking. I just have a hard time imagining a future like that until I actually see them here, safe and well."

"I know that. An hour never passes that I don't think about that very thing. But I'm just saying that a door is being opened, and the war is winding down. I want to believe they'll soon be back here and looking for a path to take. Maybe both of them will tell me they don't want a thing to do with all this. But Bea, we've built something, and I can't imagine that they won't want to be part of it." He nodded emphatically, and Bea had to think of the Al Thomas she had met so many years ago at the University. He had seen nothing but bright skies in the future, and she had fallen as much for his visions as for himself. It was nice to see some of that spark back, but Bea couldn't feel the same joy—not yet.

"Al, I know what you're saying. But who is Wally now? I see pictures of these skeletons they released in the Philippines, and I wonder what the starvation has done to them. I keep telling myself he's alive, but we have no proof of it. And what kind of attitude does he have by now? Won't he be bitter about everything? When he left here, the last thing in the world he wanted was to be in business with you."

"Bea, look at me. I've thought every one of those thoughts. But it's not what I believe. I know I rant about our heritage and the kids laugh at me for it, but Wally is a Snow and a Thomas. I believe that boy has gotten stronger, not weaker. If I'm wrong, I'm wrong, but I believe it's what the Spirit is telling me."

The words were touching to Sister Thomas, and she thought she felt her spirit verifying them. But she also knew that it was what she wanted to believe.

"Here's another thought," President Thomas said, and Bea could tell he had been running all this through his head long before the contract had come. "LaRue has a way of stopping me short. She always says, 'What about me? Don't Bobbi and Beverly and I get in on all this?'"

"That's a fair question, too."

"Well, sure. Those girls just might marry young men who want to make it on their own—not get stuck in the in-laws' business."

"Or someone who doesn't want to be in business at all, whether he makes a lot of money or not. I think that's how Richard is."

"Richard is smart, Bea. He may have his own plans, and I don't want to interfere. But on the other hand, what if some of the kids are really well off and others aren't? Richard isn't going to be able to work with his hands, but he could manage one of our businesses. The way I see it, there's no limit to where we can expand. We have a reliable reputation now, and production in this country is going to go wild. We could make parts for refrigerators, cars, trucks, bicycles—who knows what."

But all this made Bea nervous. She was wearing a suit she often wore to work: blue-green, with a double-breasted jacket. She looked down at the skirt, smoothed it a little. "Al, I know you mean well about all this. And maybe you're right. But Richard is one egg we'd better not count before he's tucked away in our basket."

"What do you mean?"

"He's got it in his head that he has to be successful—to meet some standard he thinks *we* have."

"I'll talk to him about all that. I'll sit down with him and talk man to man. I'm going to need good managers. Why shouldn't they come from my family? I'm sure we can work things out." President Thomas leaned back, the way he often did when he thought he had pronounced the final word on a subject.

"Just go a little slow with him, Al. Bobbi could be gone for a long time yet, and for now, I think Richard needs to go to school and get some things behind him."

"Oh, sure. There's no rush on any of this. LaRue and Bev are the same way. I'm just talking about the future, as this thing starts to mushroom for us. But here's the thing about LaRue. She's not going to be happy if she marries some fellow who doesn't make a good living. She needs a husband with some push to him. And all I'm saying is that if a boy like that comes along, and he wants an opportunity, we'll have one for him."

"What if it's LaRue who wants to be part of the business, not her husband?"

President Thomas laughed. "You and your daughter. I can always see the next question coming."

"Since when? You're still talking about her husband and not LaRue."

President Thomas began to twist his swivel chair back and forth, fidgeting. Sister Thomas knew she had to be careful. All this meant so much to him, and she really didn't want to throw cold water on his enthusiasm.

But he was still smiling. "Bea, LaRue is going to grow up. She won't feel the same way once she's old enough to get married. All this business about being a big shot—she'll forget about that. She'll always be a little spunky, but she'll start to understand what it means to have a family and to be a mother. I worry about her sometimes, but I really do think she'll come around."

Sister Thomas nodded. Some part of her said that was right. When women had children, they did have a responsibility to them. She hoped that LaRue would tone down some of her "attitude" about things. But something in Bea wouldn't let all this drop quite that easily. "Al, do you think being a father is different from being a mother?"

"Of course I do. Different roles."

"But both of them owe their first responsibility to the family, don't they?"

"Bea, look, let's not do this today. I know what you're telling me. I haven't been home as much as I would like. I haven't always—"

"No. That's not what I'm saying. I just wonder. I know some women who teach school, for instance, and raise their children too. I don't know how I feel about that. I didn't do anything like that, but I never really considered it. LaRue is going to think about it, and I'm not sure what to tell her. Maybe she could start her own company—or do some of those things she thinks about. Maybe there's nothing wrong with that."

"It's not God's plan, Bea."

"God's or men's?"

"Bea, please. You know better than that."

She saw his eyes narrow, his breath draw in. Sister Thomas made a decision. She wasn't going to start anything. She wasn't even sure what she had been about to get into anyway. The fact was, she really had been asking a question, and she didn't know the answer. "Well," she said, "we'll have to see what happens. It's nice to know that the plant won't fold when the war ends."

"That's right. And honey, it's going to be good for you and me, too. I'll step back from it a little at a time. And you can get out of the rat race."

She tried to hold to her decision not to say anything else, actually almost got out of her chair, but she couldn't seem to help herself. "So, do you have everything planned out for *me*, too?" she asked.

Now some air blew out of him, and she knew exactly what he was thinking: "Here she goes again." But he was careful to say, "Bea, I'm going to need you around here for quite a while yet. We don't have anyone who could even start to step in and take over. Including me. But won't you be glad to get away from this place when you can?"

"In some ways. I get tired of keeping up with it all. But our home is going to be empty in another few years, and I'm not sure I want to knock around that big old house all by myself. I've spent a long time as the 'bishop's wife' and the 'stake president's wife,' but around here I'm Mrs. Thomas, or I'm Bea, and I have a lot of people out on that floor who think I know what I'm doing. I like that."

President Thomas nodded. "I can understand that. I've always gotten a lot of that kind of attention in my life—so much so that I hardly think about it. And maybe it would be hard to set it all aside. I just didn't think that sort of thing mattered to you."

"I'm not sure it does. Or that it ought to. I just try to picture the day when I get up in the morning with no kids in the house and know that I'm going to be there alone all day. I find myself thinking that one of the kids might take this operation over and make a mess of it. Alex did all right with it before he left for the service, but a lot of things were way too messy when I came to work here. This is a much smoother operation now, if I do say so myself."

Al laughed. "No question about that. I'm proud of you, too."

"Well, I need to get back to work—or it won't be such a smooth operation much longer. I have a hundred things to do." She stood up. But something was still bothering her, and she wondered whether she should say it.

"Let's go out tonight," Al said.

"Out? What do you mean?"

"Let's go get some supper somewhere. Or go dancing."

Sister Thomas stared at her husband. She couldn't believe what she was hearing. "Al, we haven't gone dancing in *ages*."

"Of course we have. We go to the church dances."

"That's not 'going dancing.' That's 'making an appearance as the stake president.' You spend the whole time talking to people."

"I know, it usually turns into that. That's why I'm saying we ought to go somewhere else. Somewhere I won't get called 'President' a single time the whole night."

"We might have to drive out of state to find a place like that."

"No, no. Can't we just go to one of these dance halls around town?"

Bea was standing at the desk. She leaned over, put her hands on the surface, and said, "Al, the last time we went to the Rainbow Rendezvous, you didn't last half an hour. You said there was too much smoking and drinking."

"Well, that place *has* turned into a mess. The wrong element has taken it over. A lot of it is these military people who are stationed around here."

"There was always a lot of drinking at that place, long before the war. You just didn't let it bother you when you were younger."

"Well . . . that's probably true. But I don't want to go down there. Let's go to the Empire Room. We can order a good meal, and they usually have a nice band—not one of these jivey, loud things I hear on the radio all the time now."

"Everyone there *will* know you."

"Not everyone. Or even if they do, we'll still dance."

Bea laughed. "Well . . . okay," she said, and suddenly the idea did appeal to her.

"If you wanted, you could take off early and stop in town— buy yourself a new dress."

"What *is* this?" Bea came around the desk and put her hand on her husband's shoulder. "You haven't been nipping a little whiskey yourself, have you?"

President Thomas laughed. "Not that I remember," he said. "Look, I don't know. I'm just tired of having to be so serious all the time. We worry too much. We work too much. We hardly ever do anything fun."

"Al, that's my speech."

"I know. But today I'm feeling that you're right. We just got a contract that could be worth—who knows?—maybe a million dollars, in time. We can spend fifty bucks on a dress and a pair of shoes."

"For fifty bucks I can get a handbag, a hat, and a pair of gloves to go with them."

"No. If you want all that, spend a hundred. I mean it, Bea. I feel guilty about all you've done down here and how little you have to show for it. It's time we start thinking about building us a new house." Suddenly, he did the last thing she expected. He wrapped his arm around her waist and pulled her onto his lap.

"Al, someone could come in."

"So what? I believe we're married, aren't we?"

She didn't pull away. In fact, she put her arm around his shoulders, and she kissed him on the forehead. "Al, thanks," she said, "but I love our house. I don't need another one. And I don't know how to spend a hundred dollars in one store. I couldn't do it if I tried."

"Practice, my dear. Practice. Maybe I can send LaRue with you. She could figure it out."

Bea loved all this, and she hated it. She was glad to see her husband happy and feeling generous, but she didn't know how to change that much, even felt uncomfortable with the idea of it. If they were going to have more money, she didn't want to show it off. She didn't want her neighbors to think that she considered herself too good for them. And she never wanted to leave her neighborhood. She even worried just a little that Al was losing his head, thinking a little too extravagantly before the money was actually in their pockets.

"I'll tell you what," Bea said. "I don't have time to go shopping today. But I do need a nice church dress, and one of these days I'll buy one. And yes, I will go dancing with you tonight as long as you don't keep me out too late—because I do need to come down here in the morning." She stood up and pulled away from him.

"It's Friday, Bea. You can sleep in a little on Saturday morning."

"I'll sleep in as long as you do."

"Bea, I can't sleep in. If I could, I would, but you know I can't."

"And what would you do if you got up and had to make your own breakfast?"

"I'd do just fine. I can fry an egg."

"Not without burning it up."

"I can eat a burnt offering one Saturday morning."

Bea was touched. And what affected her more than anything was that he was trying so hard. He seemed to be saying, "I know I need to loosen up about certain things. I want to be a nicer person to be around."

There was still one thing wrong with all this, and try as she might, she couldn't get it out of her head. She stepped to the door, but then she decided she wasn't going to leave the office without saying something. The two of them needed this out of the way if they were going to go dancing. "Al," she said, "why didn't you talk to me about that Bendix contract?"

"I did, didn't I?"

"You mentioned that you were making contacts and that Bendix had shown some interest. But this was a complete surprise to me today. How could you negotiate a contract, *sign* it, and never even let me know?"

"I wanted it to be a surprise."

"Al, you surprise someone with a gift—a birthday present. But this is different. You must have been working on this deal for a long time. You must have hired a lawyer to work on the contract, and you must have spent a lot of time working out all those details." She pointed at the contract on his desk. "And yet, you haven't *ever* talked to me about it."

"I just didn't know whether it was going to come together, so I decided I wouldn't get you excited and then have it all fall through."

"It's you who would worry about that—not me."

"But Bea, you don't even seem to get the point. We've done well during the war, but I've always wondered when the bubble might pop. Now, we're in the driver's seat. And you know how my mind works. I'm thinking about politics, making a difference in this state. I can be an important influence. Certain things take money, Bea, and now we know for sure that we have it."

Bea leaned against the door frame and shook her head. She had never wanted to be an "important influence" in anything. She didn't even know what that meant. And she was a little uneasy about her husband's motives. Was he talking about having power, being a big shot? He had always talked about having a righteous posterity, but this seemed to be about becoming a wealthy, prominent family. "Al, for the last year I've become the expert around here on our government contracts, our deals with big companies. I've tracked our production, trained new hires, paid the bills, met the payroll, listened to the girls cry on my shoulder about their boyfriend problems, negotiated with suppliers—everything from top to bottom."

"I know that. I've told you a lot of times, 'Do what you think is best. I'll trust your judgment on this one.'"

"But I've always consulted with you about *everything*. Now, you come in and tell me you've put this whole deal together without getting my opinion about anything. At the very least you could have let me review the contract."

"Bea, it's a lot of legal lingo. I don't understand much of it myself. The lawyers took care of all that."

"But why not use your best resource? I could have helped you see some dangers. I could have given you some history on things that haven't gone well with the companies we work with. I know I could have told you *something* that would have helped." She was standing straight now, and she felt her own stiffness.

"Maybe so. I'm sorry. I guess I didn't want to jinx the deal by telling anybody about it."

"I'm not *anybody*. I'm your wife. Did you discuss it with your dad?"

"A little. Not much."

Bea shook her head. And she tried not to cry. But then she said, resolutely, "Al, I don't want to go dancing with you tonight."

She left the office and went back to her desk. She stared at the papers in front of her, but she couldn't focus on anything. After a few minutes Grace walked to the office door and said, "Bea, I found the paperwork on that order. We definitely sent it on time. What I can't find is any confirmation that it arrived."

Bea looked up, but she didn't hear the words. What she was thinking was that she was the one who had dealt with all the problems at the plant for a long time now.

"I'm going home," she told Grace. "Check with Al about that. He'll know what to do."

"He hasn't been involved with—"

But Bea got up and walked to the coat rack. She got her spring coat and draped it over her arm as she walked out. She needed a new coat. She had told Al that, and he had told her to get one. But she hadn't had time to shop. She hadn't baked enough for a long time either, and the girls complained about that—although they didn't bake anything themselves. She was secretary of the ward Primary, too, and needed to start thinking about the yearly penny drive. She didn't mind doing it, but it was "one more thing" in her life. She wondered what the bishop would say if she told him she had been in the Primary a long, long time, and she wouldn't mind a change. But the bishop never knew what to do with her. After all, she was the stake president's wife, and he didn't want to give her a calling that might put too much stress on her family.

The stake president's wife. Sister Thomas. That's who she was. Everything about her was defined in that title. She never played that role, never tried to figure out what she should do to fit it. But she didn't have to. Everyone knew who she was whether they knew *her* or not.

Bea wished she had the keys to the Hudson—her *husband's* car, really—and she could just take off and go somewhere by herself for a few days. But of course, she couldn't do that. A *stake president's wife* would never do such a thing.

She took the bus and headed home, and that was surely something she would end up regretting—because the work would keep piling up. She liked the rebellion in her act, but she knew her mood wouldn't last long. It wasn't in her to do something really dramatic. She would go home and have a couple of hours to herself, and then she would go about life the way she always had. What she hated most was that her husband would come home and apologize but never really understand what he had done. And she would accept the apology, only so there would be peace, and then life could go on.

What she felt more than anything was deeply, deeply tired. She got up every morning thinking of her children who were so far away. There had been no letters from Alex lately, and she had no idea what that meant. Wally had become like a great blank spot in her consciousness. There was so much to worry about and so little to know about him. The ache was so old that it seemed it ought to soften, but it never did. And now there was Bobbi, off on the other side of the world, close to the battle. There was no guarantee that a hospital ship would always be safe. Every time someone knocked on the door, she walked toward it with a subtle trepidation in her chest, fearful that another telegram might have come. But Bea had never liked being around self-centered, self-pitying people. She wasn't going to melt into any sort of self-indulgence herself now. She had already been a little too petulant, walking out on Grace the way she had. And the irony was already becoming obvious: she didn't know what she would do when she got home. She certainly wasn't going to bake anything, and she wasn't the type to sit around in a bubble bath. What she would do, once she calmed down a little more, was try to think where the rest of that paperwork could be filed—and give Grace a call.

The problem was, life was like a giant river—too forceful, too channeled to affect very much. She could throw her little tantrum, or whatever it was she had done, but all she could make was a ripple on the surface. Nothing would change. Al was Al, and life was life, and that was that.

She looked out the window. She was riding up Twenty-First South by then, and every store, every stop sign, every crack in the sidewalk, it seemed, was as familiar as her own worn face that reflected in the window. But when she tried to tell herself how unhappy she was, she knew that she was trying a little too hard. There was a certain comfort in the sameness, and she knew it.

She got off the bus at Eleventh East, right in the heart of Sugar House, and as she did, she heard a little voice: "Hi, Sister Thomas."

She looked around to see a girl from her ward, the Nichols' daughter, Kathleen, who had to be about ten now. Bea had known her since the day she was born. "Hi, Kathy," Bea said. "How are you, honey?"

"Fine. How are you?"

"I'm fine." Bea touched Kathy's hair, and then, suddenly, she was fighting not to cry. She walked away, but the affection, the warmth, in little Kathy's voice was lingering in her head. "Sister Thomas" *was* a nice title. At least it *could* be.

What Bea found at home was what she half expected, and feared. The Hudson had arrived ahead of her. And Al was on the porch, waiting for her. She would be all right soon, had even started to feel that way. But she didn't want to hear this.

"I'm sorry," he said. Of course.

"Al, I know. But I don't want to talk about it yet. Don't worry. I'll be back at the plant in the morning. In fact, I'll go in and call Grace right now."

"Bea, what I told you wasn't true."

"What?"

"I thought I was telling the truth when I said it, but I wasn't being honest with myself." For the first time she realized that he hadn't taken that strong stance of his, his feet set a little too far apart. He looked small, diminished. His head was down.

"What are you talking about?"

"I'm not used to thinking that way—that I ought to consult you about things. I just went ahead without giving much thought to whether you needed to know or not."

"I know."

"And then . . . well, this is hard to say."

Bea waited. He had his hands in his pockets, the wings of his double-breasted coat open and flopping to the sides.

"Bea, it's not easy for me, the way you've handled the plant. I walk in there and people treat me like I'm a visitor. I've had the foremen say to me, 'You might be right about that. I'll ask Bea what she thinks.' Things like that. I'm not so sure I didn't negotiate this Bendix deal just to show you up a little—let you see I'm still the provider around here, the guy who gets things done."

Bea nodded. She saw how honestly chagrined he was, and deflated. *President* Thomas had just taken a mighty step down— off a high pedestal. She couldn't imagine how much it had cost him to say these words, and even more, to discover them in himself.

"So what do we do about that?" she asked.

"We don't do anything. I just have to think about things a little differently."

"Al, what if I want to stay involved—after the war is over?"

"That's fine. It's up to you. Except, we both need to step away some and find more time for each other."

"Time for each other? Are you serious?"

"I love you, Bea. I miss you. We've let too many things get between us."

Bea reached inside his coat, took hold of his suspenders, and pulled him closer. Then she wrapped her arms around his thick body, inside his coat. It had been a long time since she had felt this close to him, had *liked* him this much. "Do you still want to go dancing tonight?" she asked.

"Sure I do," he said. He held her for a time, and then he began to hum, "I'll get by as long as I have you."

President Thomas kept *Sister* Thomas close, but he took hold of her hand, held it out. The two began to dance. On their front porch.

18

Peter Stoltz was placing chunks of seed potato in the ground—working his way along a little furrow that he had dug, always being careful that the potato eye was facing up. He had never gardened before and didn't know much about it, but he was learning. Frau Schaller taught him what she knew, and much he figured out for himself. He didn't dare to say much to neighbors. If he talked to them, it might be hard to keep his deception alive, that he was a refugee from Poland.

Peter had never known such a spring. The willow trees along the stream at the back of Frau Schaller's property had blossomed, brilliant in yellow-green. He wasn't sure he had ever noticed that before, or all the birds. He didn't like some things—the mud, the lack of confidence in his own knowledge—but the world itself pleased him more than ever before. He would notice the warmth of the afternoon sun on his back and accept that little pleasure as though it were a new discovery. He had died during the winter, and now he was alive, feeling stronger and healthier all the time. It was all a gift, and he had not owned it long enough to be ungrateful. In the night he would awaken from horrifying, wild dreams, all chaos and noise, and he would breathe frantically for a time, just trying to convince himself that he wasn't in a foxhole but in a bed.

And then for a time he would look about—on some nights watch the flow of angling moonlight through the dormer window in the attic—and remind himself that he was safe and well. He would nestle under those warm blankets and tell himself that he had escaped hell, that he would never be ungrateful for that. And he would pray.

Prayer had come as a wonderful discovery. He had prayed as a boy, and then for so long, during his time in the German army, he had lived with hopelessness. When he had finally prayed again, it had been nothing but pleading and desperation, but now it was a chance to feel a closeness to a presence he had once given up on. What he felt was that he was loved, even though, for a time, he had come to believe that could never happen again.

Peter also knew that he was loved in this house. Frau Schaller wasn't really old enough to be his mother, but she treated him as though she were. And Katrina, who was fifteen, had fallen in love with him. He knew that and thought it was a little funny. She was such a skinny, awkward kid, and her attachment to him was so obvious it embarrassed both of them. But she was funny, and always happy—and great entertainment. She had not seen war in the way that he had, but she had suffered plenty. Frau Schaller had lost her husband, Katrina her father—which was sacrifice enough—but the Schallers had also struggled to scrounge enough food to stay alive. Katrina's little brothers dressed like paupers, and they had almost nothing. No toys. They played soccer with a ball of rolled-up rags. In a way, Peter felt sorry for them, but they seemed not to know they were missing anything. The Schallers laughed so often, so fervently, that it was hard not to feel that everything was all right in their home.

As a boy, Peter had gone into the country to find vegetables, to bring them back to his mother and sister. But he had been wary of it all. He hadn't liked the smell of manure, the mud, the uneducated men his father haggled with. And the families had seemed doltish. But the things he had cared about as a boy seemed frivolous now. He and his dad had sat and played chess by the hour, and Peter loved to remember those times, but he had no desire for mind games at present. He liked the feeling that his body was coming back to life, that he could experience emotion, that he could concentrate on a needed task and carry it out. In the depths of the winter and the war he had become a mindless sort of organism with a pumping heart and little else. Now, he was a person again. He longed to find his family someday, but for the present, it was enough to laugh, to work, even to smell manure, which now seemed rich and pungent to him, not at all foul.

"Do you want me to cover them over now?"

Peter looked up. It was Katrina. She was standing the way she always did: a little too straight, her arms at her sides, looking like a fence post. Her shadow stretched out behind her, a thin line. "That's all right. I'll do it."

"Why? Do you think I can't push dirt into a little trench?"

"If you get potatoes too deep, they won't grow. You have to do it just right."

Katrina laughed, and Peter looked up again. "I've been planting potatoes all my life. Two weeks ago you were asking my mother where you could get 'potato seeds' to plant."

Peter knew that was true, and he was embarrassed. "Cover them if you want to," he said. "And cover your mouth at the same time."

"I changed my mind. You can do it yourself."

He thought she really was offended for a moment, but he took one more look at her, and she was smiling. Her front teeth weren't straight, and her lips were thin—like the rest of her—but she did have an artless sort of smile. Her mother cut her hair for her and kept it short. Peter always thought she looked like a boy, but still, someone he might have liked being friends with—had he been a little younger.

"I have things I'd rather *think* about anyway—things better than potatoes."

"Like what?"

"I can't tell you. It's far too philosophical for you to understand. You farmers only understand dirt." She had turned around and was talking toward the empty field. She had stretched her arms wide, like wings, and she seemed interested in the shape she could make with her shadow. She began to sway a little, back and forth.

"Dirt and girls. That's what I understand," Peter said.

"Oh, thank you very much. And what do you know about girls?" She let her arms rise and fall, like slowly flapping wings, and still, she watched her shadow.

"That they *think* about as much as dirt does."

"That shows what you know. I can fly."

"That's girl thinking—all imagination."

"What's wrong with imagination?"

"It's not real."

"It is too. It's as real as anything. Maybe more. I can fly anywhere—see anything I want to see."

Peter straightened. He had a sling over his shoulder, full of the potato pieces. He walked back toward her, and then he picked up the hoe he had left behind, and he began to push the dirt into the furrow. He was actually being a little more careful than usual to show her that he was watching to get the depth just right.

"Here's your problem," he said. "You've never been anywhere. How can you imagine places you've never seen?"

"Now I've trapped you. You've made a blunder—a logical blunder. And it shows you're not a philosopher, like me."

"What blunder?"

"If I had seen places, I would only have to remember them," she explained. "But if I've never seen them, I can imagine them any way I wish. That's much better."

"But if you've seen nothing at all, you have no concept to start with. Have you ever seen a big city?"

"Yes." She sounded wistful, as though she were drifting to some distant place.

The kid was strong as wire, but there was something so delicate about her that he hardly had the heart to tease her. Still, he asked, "Which ones?"

"Berlin and Paris and Amsterdam and—"

"You have not."

"Oh, Peter, you are such an innocent boy. You don't know half the things I've done and seen. You *imagine* that you do, but you don't."

Peter chuckled to himself, but he didn't look at her this time. She was just a little too delighted with herself. She had a little girl's voice, sparrow-like, but her laugh was forceful, more like a crow than a sparrow.

"You've seen pictures on calendars," Peter said. "You haven't traveled and seen places the way I have. I'm a man of experience."

"You're only eighteen. That's still a boy."

"I feel older," he said, and he meant it.

"So where have you been? What cities have you seen?" She had forgotten about her shadow now. She was looking past him, toward the setting sun.

"Frankfurt, Berlin, Stuttgart—lots of places."

"All in Germany?"

"No. I've been to Switzerland, Poland, Russia, East Prussia, Lithuania, and Latvia."

"What were they like, all those places?"

But Peter wished that he hadn't bragged. He had never talked much about himself. Part of that was a fear of being traced somehow, but most of it was the fear of his memories. He didn't want to tell the Schallers anything about the war. "They're just like the pictures on calendars, I guess," he said.

"You're the philosopher. You can tell me. Are the pictures just as good?"

But the question sounded more serious than he meant it, and she accepted it that way. "No, Peter. I want to go to all those places. I want to go everywhere. What's Berlin like?"

"It isn't very far away, Katrina. You'll go there sometime."

"I know. But what is it like?"

"Katrina, it's destroyed. You know that. It's all standing walls and rubble. It's nothing you would want to see."

"Did you see it before the bombs?"

"Yes."

"Tell me about it back then."

"It was a basement. It was a hiding place. It was one day in a park. It was a jail to me."

"What are you talking about?"

"Nothing. It was a pretty city, Katrina, with a big park—the Tiergarten—and beautiful buildings. I don't know what else to tell you."

"Did you have to hide there?"

Peter had reached the end of the row again. He walked back now to make a new furrow. He watched Katrina as he approached her. She seemed concerned, and he didn't want that. He liked her better when she was joking. "I don't want to talk about those things," he said.

"You never talk about the war."

"I never will."

"Because it's so horrible?"

He stood before her and considered all the answers he could give. But nothing exactly sufficed. He could see how frayed her dress was, how worn her shoes, how frail her arms and neck. She was a symbol for this war—and she didn't know it. So finally he said, "Yes," and let it go at that.

"Did you know that *Katrina* is a Russian name?"

"I don't know. I guess I never thought about it."

"It is. I was named after a Princess. Someday I'm going to go to Russia and see all the—"

"Don't even think of that, Katrina. You have no idea what you're talking about."

"Why?"

"The Russians will be here soon enough, and then you'll know."

"Will they hurt us?"

But now Peter knew he had said far too much. Yes, they would hurt her. And it was a great worry. But not one that Katrina needed to think about yet. "I won't let them hurt you," he said.

He saw her blush, her face suddenly more red than the sunset could account for. She had taken a different meaning than he had intended. He felt sorry for her, that she would think such a thing, but she said, with touching earnestness, "I won't let them hurt you, either, Peter."

"Oh, is that right? And what are you going to do to save *my* skin?"

"I don't mean that. I won't let them hurt you in the past."

The breath left Peter's body in a steady stream. He felt the weakness in his joints. But he couldn't let her love him. He laughed. "Now that's a good trick, if you can manage that one," he said.

"I know," she said, not smiling, her narrow little face so full of adoration that Peter could only pity her. She seemed to see that. She suddenly left without a word, swiveling toward her shadow, walking straight into it, her long steps making undulations in the stretching line.

Peter wanted to tell her he was sorry, but that seemed condescending, and so he simply let her go. He finished one more furrow after that, and then he followed her inside, and he ate. Until the garden began to produce, the Schallers didn't have a lot of food, mostly just bread, but Peter could live on bread—

especially freshly baked, not the muscle-hard stuff he had known in the military.

After dinner Peter finally asked something he had been wondering about. "Do you ever go to church, Frau Schaller?" Sometimes she told him to call her Theresa, but he could never bring himself to do that.

"Not for a long time, we haven't," she said.

"Why not? Is it too far to go into town?"

"Well, yes. That's part of it. We don't have bicycles for everyone to go at the same time. But I could go by myself if I wanted. I simply feel no desire."

"I don't want to go," Rolf said. He was eleven years old, and in some ways like his sister. He was huskier, and darker, like the father that Peter had seen in pictures, and he was more animated. But, like Katrina, he loved to laugh, and he had his own way of seeing things. "The men at the church dress like birds—parrots or something—and they talk funny. Everyone gets up and down like jack-in-the-boxes, singing and saying things. If you ever go, you'll know what I'm telling you. It's all a lot of nonsense."

All this time Frau Schaller was shaking her head. "Now you know the truth. We're heathens around here. Rolf hasn't been to church since he was seven or eight. That's what he remembers of it." She looked at Rolf. "Certainly, Peter has been to church much more than you have. He knows all about it, and he probably speaks more respectfully, too."

"It doesn't matter," Peter said. "It always struck me the same way."

"What religion are you, Peter?" Katrina asked. "Catholic or Protestant?"

Peter let some seconds pass, and he considered. He didn't want to lie, not about that. "Neither one," he said, hoping that would be the end of it.

"That's what I am, too," Thomas said. "I'm nothing." He was thirteen, and he obviously took pride in his unorthodoxy. On almost any subject he would announce that he believed the opposite of his mother, or Katrina, and yet he hardly seemed to keep track of his claims. He was actually just as playful as Rolf, but he liked to take on a serious demeanor, probably to make himself seem older than he was. But he was a fragile boy, thin like his mother and sister, with eyes full of need. Peter had a notion that the loss of his father had hurt him more than the others.

"That's not what Peter said," Frau Schaller told him. "Some people believe in their own way. There are other things to believe." She looked at Peter. "You've said enough to me that I know you do believe in God."

Peter couldn't think of anything he had ever said on the subject, and so he was taken by surprise. He looked back at Thomas. "I do believe in God," he said.

Thomas glanced at his brother, and they both laughed. "So do you go to church and bounce up and down and babble prayers?" Rolf asked.

Katrina smiled, but she was clearly embarrassed. "Peter," she said, "don't listen to these two. They aren't used to being around decent people. They've grown up like rabbits, running where they want."

Peter knew that was more or less true. The boys did go to school, but the schedule had been unpredictable during the past year. Lately there had been a power failure, after a station in the area had been knocked out, and always there were difficulties keeping enough teachers. Men were pulled away, time and again, to the war, and women were often pressed into service at a local factory that produced synthetic rubber tires. But the greatest problem was that there was no bus service, with the shortage of gasoline. The boys had to walk a long way, and in the winter, Frau Schaller often let them stay home. When they did, they went outside anyway, roamed the farm, played all day, and in truth, hardly noticed that a war was going on.

Katrina, on the other hand, was now out of school. She had finished the eighth form, and now she worked in an office in the nearby town of Premnitz. She was an assistant to a bureaucrat who monitored the flow of local farm products to the military. The truth was, he wasn't that busy, especially in the winter, and he didn't spend all that many hours in his office—or expect Katrina there that often. But he also paid her accordingly, and her meager income provided little help for the family.

"My church wasn't like that," Peter found himself saying. He didn't mind them laughing at him, but he was a little defensive about their making fun of religion. He knew that these boys, sooner or later, might want to understand their world. They weren't going to have an easy time getting by, not for years to come, whether the war ended soon or not.

"What church is that?" Frau Schaller asked.

Peter was about to give a vague answer when he decided he wanted them at least to know that much about him. "The Church of Jesus Christ of Latter-day Saints."

"He thinks he's a saint," Rolf said. "But I don't see a halo around his head."

Peter smiled. "I keep my halo in my pocket—and only get it out for special occasions."

"What church is this?" Katrina asked. "I never heard of it."

"Some people call it the Mormon Church."

"*Ach, die Mormonen,*" Frau Schaller said. "I know of this." But she looked shocked, and she asked, rather hesitantly, "Isn't this the one that lets you marry as many wives as you like?"

This brought an enormous laugh from the boys. "Look out, Katrina," Rolf said. "He may want you for one of them."

"Hush, boys," Frau Schaller said, but then she looked at Peter and waited.

He could feel the heat in his face. He didn't really know what to say. "No. Of course not. We only marry once."

"But why have I heard this?"

"A long time ago—in the last century—it was this way. Some of the leaders had more than one wife. I'm not sure of all the reasons."

"When I was a girl, my father used to tell me stories," Frau Schaller said. "He told me the missionaries from this church would snatch young girls and take them on a ship back to America. And they kept them in a big building, like a prison. The old men married them and kept them in a harem."

"It wasn't so. People spread these things. But nothing like that ever happened."

Peter glanced at Katrina. She was trying to seem only casually interested, but he could see that she was alarmed. "What do the Mormons believe?" she asked. "It sounds like Mohammedans."

"No, no. I told you, it's the Church of Jesus Christ. It's Christian."

"But not like the Catholics or Protestants?"

"In many ways, yes."

"Then what's the difference?" Katrina asked, and her interest was clearly more than passing.

Peter tried to remember the things he had learned in church, back so long ago. "We believe that the other Christian churches started teaching things that weren't true. But a man named Joseph Smith was called by God to restore things the way they're supposed to be—and teach the truth." He hoped they wouldn't ask him more than that.

But of course, the next question was the obvious one. "What is this truth?" Frau Schaller asked. She looked toward the boys, who were still smiling. She waved a finger at them to hush.

Peter remembered the first thing he had known for sure about the church. "The men who have the priesthood—the missionaries and the leaders—they can place their hands on someone's head and heal them. My sister was dying, and they brought her back." But somehow this seemed too exotic to Peter. Rolf began to grin, but Thomas shook his head at him, as if to tell him not to be disrespectful. Peter also saw the concern in Katrina and Frau Schaller's eyes. "But it's all very normal. The people meet and sing, and someone preaches. There's just no bowing down and no fancy robes. It's simple and good. The people like each other, and they're all good friends."

"I like that idea," Frau Schaller said. "I think it's better for the preachers not to have such fancy outfits. I never understood that. Some of the smaller sects in Germany are like this. But we have no Mormon churches in this country, do we?"

"Yes. There are congregations in most of the cities—at least the bigger ones. Now, with the war, I don't know if they meet the way they did. But we had a group in Frankfurt, and I know there was one in Berlin."

"But it's Christian," Katrina said. "About the same as the others?"

Peter hesitated. He couldn't think what to say, but he knew the missionaries would never say it was the same. "We do have differences—important differences," he said. "God is real, for one thing. He's not just a power or a spirit. He hears you the way a father would. He's not just a spirit in the universe. When I was in trouble in the war, and dying, I prayed to him, and he heard me. I don't know many things, but I do know that."

Frau Schaller nodded. "Peter, I go to church, and I feel those cold stones, and I hear all the talk of God's mercy, and it doesn't touch me, doesn't convince me. I look around myself and ask where God is, and I don't see any evidence that he cares about us. But your words, just then—those words did touch me."

"How did you know that God heard you?" Thomas asked, and now, clearly, he was trying to be one of the adults.

"I was trying to help my friend, and I was almost dead myself. I didn't want to ask for help for myself—because I didn't deserve it—but I asked for power to pick him up. Strength came into me, and I carried him."

"And your friend lived?"

"No." The story seemed silly, and Peter could see the skepticism in Thomas's face. "But on the ship, when I was being evacuated, I knew God had been with me, helping me. And then my whole body filled up with . . . something. I felt all warm and comfortable, and I knew I was going to live. I don't know how to say it, other than that. I knew. It was more than hope or faith; it was something that came into all of me—not just my head—and filled me up."

"I don't doubt that at all," Frau Schaller said. "I think God would do that. But I don't know why so many die, and others receive this blessing."

"I don't know either," Peter said. "I watched my friend die, and I couldn't help him."

"Where was this?"

"We were in Memel, in Lithuania. And then we were carried on a ship to Pillau, in East Prussia. Almost everyone in my company died there in Memel, or before. I might be the only one left. I'm not sure. My sergeant was alive on the ship, but if he stayed in the fight, he could be dead by now."

"So you left the battle?" Thomas asked.

Peter understood the question. Every boy in Germany knew that this was the ultimate crime. This was an act of cowardice, and it was no wonder that so far, these two boys had never warmed to Peter. He knew they considered him a traitor. They didn't attend *Jungvolk* regularly, and they were hardly aware of the realities of the war, but they surely knew this much, that a German boy didn't run from the battle.

Peter had tried since the beginning to say little about his flight from the army, but having said this much, he had to defend himself or always feel ashamed. "Thomas, I was fighting for the wrong side. Hitler is as evil as Satan himself. He's led this country into destruction. He's killing innocent people by the millions. I wasn't wrong to *stop* fighting for him, but I was very wrong to start."

These were stunning words, unspeakable in Germany. The room was silent, and Peter wondered whether he would be told to leave. But Frau Schaller spoke carefully and softly. "This is what I also believe, Peter. We don't say it, and my opinion must never leave this house. But Hitler killed my husband, as far as I'm concerned. And I have seen the work of the Gestapo. If you stopped fighting for these swine, you are a hero. I've never said this to my boys for fear they would say the wrong thing sometime, but I'll tell them now. They are not going to fight in this war. If it lasts much longer, Hitler will want them, but he's not going to get them. I'll see to that."

"We have to go when we're old enough. We have no choice," Thomas said.

"Peter made a choice. We'll make one too."

"What if you're caught, Peter?" Katrina asked.

"The war can't last much longer," Peter said. "My danger now is not that I'll be caught by Germans. If the Russians come, my only papers are German military papers. And the Russians are butchers. They'll shoot me, or they'll carry me off. And you and your mother are . . . not safe with them."

"What can we do?"

"We have to hope the Americans and British will occupy this area, not the Russians."

The boys were no longer finding humor in any of this. The room was silent.

"How do you pray?" Frau Schaller finally asked. "Do you have a prayer that—"

"We don't have written-out prayers. We speak to the Lord in our own words."

"Would you be able to do that for us now?"

Peter was nervous about that. He hadn't prayed aloud since he was very young. "I can try," he said. "But I wish my father were here, or my mother. They knew much better how to do this."

"Just use your own words. You'll do fine."

And so Peter prayed. He asked the Lord that he and the Schallers might find safety, that they might have strength to deal with the danger that lay ahead. When he was finished,

Rolf and Thomas were staring at him, entirely serious, and Katrina was looking at him with awe in her eyes, as though she had felt something spiritual for the first time in her life.

* * *

Brother Stoltz was sitting in an underground bomb shelter just down the street from the boarding house where he lived. Up above, the whole city seemed to be blowing apart. Bombs had been falling for an hour, but now a grand crescendo, like the climax of a symphony, was being reached. Scores of airplanes had to be unleashing their chaos all at the same time. Inside the shelter, the sound reverberated and the dust flew, but the people who filled the place sat silent, numb.

An old man, sitting next to Heinrich on the floor, would grunt a little when a bomb seemed to hit close, hold his breath for a moment, and then let it blow out when the sounds diminished a little. "This is not all bad," he mumbled. "This is probably the last."

Brother Stoltz knew exactly what the man meant. The Allies had crossed the Rhine well north of Karlsruhe, in the Ruhr, but now Americans and French had made it across nearby, between Karlsruhe and Saarbrücken. It would be only a matter of days until ground troops would arrive. That might bring a last attack, with artillery fire, but the fact was, the end of resistance for this city was very close. What would come next, how the *Amis*, or worse, the French, would treat civilians, was the subject of constant speculation now, but no one doubted that the fall of the city was inevitable—and coming soon.

Brother Stoltz watched two little children across the room, a brother and sister. The girl, who was probably seven or eight, was holding her little brother, and he was sound asleep, with all this noise thundering around him. The girl seemed only half awake herself. She was wearing a threadbare little dress and worn-out shoes, but the dress was clean, and her hair was nicely brushed. She wasn't exactly pretty—too thin and hollow for that—but the picture was beautiful, here in this hole, and it touched Brother Stoltz.

And then the noise stopped, rather suddenly. Brother Stoltz watched as heads gradually came up, as people listened for the roar of airplanes, but those sounds were moving away, the buzz diminishing, second by second. "There could be another wave yet," the old man said, and some of the people nodded.

And they waited. But nothing more came. Finally an all-clear horn began to wail outside.

"It's been nice seeing you all," the old man said in a loud voice. "It was a lovely night—only a little noisy." He chuckled.

A woman smiled at him. "You always keep your spirits up," she said. "I don't know how you do it."

"I have nothing to lose," he said. "If I die, I die. That's easier than worrying about everything, the way you younger people do."

"I suppose," she said. "I suppose." And she followed the others, out the door and up the steps.

Brother Stoltz waited, took the man's arm, and helped him up the stairs. At the top, they both stopped and looked around. The night was quite dark, and the air was full of smoke and dust, but a block or so away, a building was burning. The light from the fire sent a glow through the clouded air. Outlined in silhouette were the broken, burned buildings, most of them damaged in previous attacks. Little of the city was left.

"Can I help you to your home?" Brother Stoltz asked.

"Oh, no. It's right here." He pointed to a building across the street that looked like the ruin of some past civilization, only fractured walls standing, the insides gutted. "My apartment is on the first floor. It's held together so far."

"All right then," Brother Stoltz said. "Sleep well—for the rest of the night."

The man nodded and laughed. "Yes, yes. I can do that. Why not?" He set off across the street, walking rather briskly for an aged man.

Brother Stoltz was moved. The German people knew how to endure. He might have helped the Allies cross the Rhine, but that had not changed his loyalty to his own people. He loved their dogged determination to survive. As he walked down the street, however, he could see another fire, and as he came closer, he saw that it was his boarding house, and the houses around it, that had been struck this time. Everything was burning. He didn't have much, only a few clothes and his borrowed Book of Mormon, but all of it was certainly gone. He stood on the street, feeling like an orphan, with nowhere to go.

Outside, his *hausfrau* was watching the place burn. Brother Stoltz walked to her. "Was anyone inside?" Brother Stoltz asked her.

"I don't know," she said. "I hope not." But she wasn't crying. "I expected this long ago, but here at the end, I began to hope that the old place might make it through."

"Have you a place to live?"

"Yes. I'll go to my sister—unless her place is gone too. What will you do, Herr Stutz?"

"I don't know. It will soon be time for me to go to work at the bakery. I suppose I can sleep in a storage room there, for now."

"Yes. That will be warm enough. Best of everything to you, Herr Stutz."

"Yes. And the same to you."

Brother Stoltz walked to the bakery. He had felt like a man without a country for quite some time, but this loss seemed to teach him the truth. Every German was an orphan now—with the country so devastated—but the fact was, the homeland wasn't in the buildings. It was in that little girl's spirit—the one who had clung to her little brother. And in the people's will. He felt more hope tonight than he had in a long time. But he wanted his son back. Once this last act of the war was finished, then he had to find Peter. He had some will of his own

19

When Anna Thomas came home from work, her mother met her at the door. "Anna, a telegram came for you this afternoon," she said. "I would have brought it to you, but I knew you would be home soon."

Anna took the telegram from her mother's hand and hurried to her room. She had received a letter from Alex a few days before. He would be coming to London, he had said. This was surely about that. But it was hard not to fear a telegram. Maybe this was to say that he couldn't come after all—or that something had happened.

She shut the door behind her, then quickly opened the envelope. Her breath had stopped. But it was what she wanted to hear: "WILL FLY TO LONDON TODAY. ARRIVE, HEATHROW, 1800. TRAIN TO VICTORIA STATION. MEET ME IF YOU CAN." Suddenly, Anna was breathing too hard.

"Anna, are you all right?"

Anna opened the door. "He'll be at Victoria Station in . . " She looked at her watch. "An hour, probably less."

"Oh, Anna. This is such good news." Sister Stoltz took Anna in her arms, but Anna pulled away quickly. "What can I wear?" she asked. "I look so terrible."

"No, no. You look pregnant, and he'll think you're lovelier than ever."

Anna put her hand over her mouth. She didn't have time to cry. She had to get moving. She only had two dresses she could wear now. She put on the lavender one that felt like a sack to her, and she ran a brush through her hair. In ten minutes she was on her way to the Baker Street Underground Station, but she reached the platform just as her train pulled away. She caught one ten minutes later, but by the time she reached Victoria Station, an hour had passed, and she was worried she had missed him. Perhaps he had taken a taxi or had caught the Underground and was already heading toward her apartment.

She hurried through the great hall. As she walked, she looked at the big boards on the walls and tried to locate the track for trains coming in from Heathrow. When she found the correct gate, she studied the schedule of arrivals. She was looking up, still reading, when she heard a voice close to her, more a whisper than a call. "Anna."

And there he was. "Alex," she said, and she reached for him, but he was already taking her in his arms. He pushed his face against hers. He kissed her and clung to her, and he kept saying, "Anna, Anna."

She felt the front of her, so big and awkward, and it was all so different to be held apart this way, not fitting together the way they always had. But then she felt him sliding down to his knees, still with his arms around her. Her first thought was that he was fainting, but he pressed his face to her belly. "Hello, hello," he said, and he laughed. "It's your daddy. You do have one, you know."

There were people everywhere, moving past them in a stream, and Anna was vaguely aware that they were looking at her, some smiling. She didn't care. She was moved by this tender touch, this love toward the baby she already loved so much herself.

Alex got up, and he kissed Anna again, and then he looked into her face. "You're so beautiful, Anna."

"No, I didn't have time to—"

"Sometimes, when I'm out there, I start to think I've made you up—that no one could be so pretty—and then I see you, and you're more beautiful than I remembered."

"It's all in your head," she said. "But I'm happy you see me that way. I love you so much." She had slipped into German; she felt closer when she used her own words. "But Alex, I don't like the way *you* look. You've lost too much weight. You look so tired."

"I am tired," he said, and the words seemed to double his weariness.

"Alex, the war will be over soon. All the papers say it. Any day now it could end. And then you can rest."

Alex didn't want to tell her yet that he had to go back, that he wouldn't be in London when the baby was born, that he could still be sent to the Pacific to fight again. "Anna," he said instead, "I have enough money to rent a hotel room. I want to see your mother, but I want some time alone."

"Of course. My mother already told me this is what we should do. But Alex, I don't want you to see me. I'm so round and fat. I laugh when I look at myself in the mirror."

Alex hardly knew how to say what he was thinking. She had no way of imagining what he felt. To hold her in his arms, to sleep next to her, to look at her over a breakfast table, to touch her skin—it was all more than he thought his senses could endure. And the truth was, he was frightened. A terrible nervousness was shaking him, and he didn't know why. He had the feeling something inside him was letting loose and that he might sink to the floor at any moment.

"Are you all right?" she was asking.

"Yes. I just . . . don't know how to do this. I'm nervous, or something. I'm not exactly sure."

"You'll be all right. I'll take care of you. We've made it

through, Alex. The worst is over, and now we just have to get better."

Alex didn't know that. What he felt was that some "worst" was still ahead, and he didn't know why all this dread and panic was in him just when he ought to be so happy.

"Let's go, Alex. Let's take a taxi. I must go back to our flat and get my things, but I won't do that now. Let's find a hotel first."

"Okay." And something in the act of moving, of doing something, seemed to pump a little confidence back into him. All these emotions—all at once—had gotten to him, he told himself, but he would be fine in a few minutes. He hoisted his duffel bag onto his shoulder.

And then, suddenly, Alex was on his face. He was curled up, his arms grasped against his chest, his knees pulled in. He knew already that it was a mistake. Someone had dropped something, a book perhaps, or a box. It had slapped on the floor and sent a popping noise through the hall. He had responded automatically.

Anna was on her knees, next to him, and people had begun to crowd around. Alex was humiliated. He got up quickly, looked about. "I'm sorry," he said, and he ducked his head.

Anna took hold of him. "It's all right," she said. "Everything is going to be all right now."

For the next twenty-four hours Alex and Anna hid from the world. Anna called her office and arranged not to work. They ate nice meals and went for a walk, but they spent most of their time in the hotel room on Regent Street, not far from Piccadilly Circus.

Alex was struggling. He didn't want Anna to think he was about to fall apart, so he went through the motions, tried to be himself, but the truth was, he felt as though he were looking at the world, even Anna, through clouded glass. He told himself that he loved the warm bath he took, the smooth sheets, and

Anna in his arms. But none of it seemed real, and all of it seemed muted, as though he were anesthetized.

But he couldn't say that to Anna, and he didn't want her to feel it. He kept telling her he was only tired, and it was true that he took brief naps all day, falling off for a few minutes almost every time he sat down. But what Anna didn't know—at least not fully—was how little he had slept since he had come out of Germany. Sleep frightened him. It was an act of letting go, giving up control of himself. Sleep also meant dreams. On his honeymoon he had awakened in a sweat, yelling, and then breathing desperately as he tried to calm himself. He didn't want to do that now. He didn't want to worry Anna, and he didn't want her to fear their future together. He needed to get himself together and show he was a man, that he was someone she could rely on, not some sniveling casualty of war.

But on the second night in bed, he was startled in the night by someone grabbing his shoulder. He twisted from the danger, and he flung his arm out to protect himself. What he struck was Anna's chest. She wasn't hurt, not seriously, but she struggled to catch her breath for a few seconds. Once she could talk, she told him that he had been talking in his sleep, moaning and gasping, and she had only meant to shake him a little to awaken him.

He got up and turned on a light. And then he sat down on the bed. "Are you sure you're all right?" he asked her again.

"It didn't hurt very much. It only took my breath away."

"I'm really sorry. It's just a reaction from sleeping out in fox-holes. I'll get over it before long. I'll be fine."

"Alex, I know this is a bad time for you. I see it in your eyes. I know how hard it is for you to hold still, even for a few minutes."

Alex nodded, and then he lay on the bed next to her and stretched out on top of the covers. He was wearing only his military underwear—the only kind he had with him. "Anna," he said, "don't worry. I'll be okay. I've been on the alert, ready for danger, for a long time. I can't let go as quickly as I'd like. But I'll do it."

"I've read articles in magazines, Alex. Doctors say this is exactly what wives should expect for a time."

"I did all right when I was in the field, Anna. I didn't like any of it, but I did what I had to do. I wasn't one of those guys who just hunkered down in his foxhole and cried."

"I know that, Alex."

"I'll be better fast, too. I just feel jittery right now."

"Alex, I'm lucky that I know what you've been doing this last month. Most wives would never know this. I understand better than some would."

"Anna, you know, but you don't know. Things happened—things I'll never tell you." He sat up again, then stood up, but he didn't know where he was going.

"I know your partner died."

"Yes. But—"

"Alex, don't think I'm so delicate. Tell me anything you want. You know *my* worst nightmare—what I did to Kellerman. It helped me when I told you. I feel like I want you to lean on me a little. It'll bring us closer together."

Alex walked across the room. He thought of sitting in the big upholstered chair, but he felt too distant by the time he got there, and so he walked back to the bed. "Anna, there are things that happened that I don't want to tell anyone, ever. I just need to let some time pass, so I can put them out of my mind." He knelt down by the bed, then bent and placed his head against her shoulder. "I don't want any of this stuff in your head, Anna. You shouldn't have to know."

"Alex, I know about war. I know what happens."

Alex didn't know what to say. Flying from France, he had sat by a civilian who worked for the army. The man had talked about the nation being weary of war, of how hard it was to go without sugar and coffee and new tires. "There's more black marketing now," the man had said, "more cheating the system than there used to be. Everyone is just fed up with doing without for such a long time."

Alex had said nothing. He knew that if he had started, he might not have been able to control his voice. He wanted to ask the guy if he had any idea how those words sounded. Were the people back in the states tired of freezing in foxholes, living in mud? Were they tired of seeing their best friends blown into bloody shreds of flesh? Tired of feeling that any second, any time—day or night—a bullet or a mortar or an artillery shell could strike? Tired of looking into the eyes of frozen corpses, knowing that their own bullets and shells had taken the lives of teenaged kids? Into Alex's mind had come the image of that military policeman Otto had killed. He hadn't been able to stop seeing that—the flesh of the man's throat dividing—and he asked himself how that compared to going without new tires or a new refrigerator.

Anna had had to cut a man's face once, had defended herself, and she had survived dozens of bombing raids, so she understood more than most. But if he told her all that was going on inside him, he wondered whether she could possibly feel confidence in him. Sometimes, in his dreams, he would wash his hands, and then he would realize that the stream coming from the faucet wasn't water at all, but blood, and that he had been throwing it over his face, spreading it up to his elbows. He could tell his mind over and over that he was not guilty for the things he had done, but his soul didn't believe it.

"Alex, you're a hero. You should—"

"Anna, don't say that. That's one thing I don't want you to think or say—not ever."

"Why?"

Alex didn't know. He sat down on the floor, next to the bed, turned his back to it. He tried to think. When she reached and touched the side of his neck, he wished she wouldn't for the moment. He really wanted to sort this out. "All your life you're taught what's right and wrong. And then someone says,

'Now it's different. Bad is good. Don't let it bother you. If you hurt people, you're a hero.'"

"Alex, you may have *done* things you didn't want to do, but you *are* good. It's the thing I've known about you since the first time I met you."

Alex tried to think about that. He didn't want to believe he was a bad person—didn't believe that. But evil was in him, on him, like that blood in his dreams, and he didn't know how to cleanse himself.

Another day passed, and Alex did sleep a little better the next night. He realized that the things he had said to Anna had helped a little. And yet he was careful not to go back to the subject. The radios and newspapers were bursting with reports that the war was about to end, that the Germans were going to surrender soon. He kept reminding himself how much he had longed for that day to come, and he tried to concentrate on a better future. Maybe his service in Germany, once the battle ended, would keep him out of the Pacific, and that might save his life. He had been through some ordeals, and it was only natural for his body and mind to require some healing time. He told himself a hundred times a day, "I'll be all right. I'll be all right."

On April 13, early in the morning, Alex and Anna were both awake early, Anna uncomfortable now as she was about to begin her eighth month of pregnancy. It was a cool morning, but clear, so they decided to walk to St. James Park before breakfast. As they passed through Piccadilly, with all its busyness, Alex saw a crowd of people gathered at a newsstand. He glanced over a man's shoulder to see the huge headline across the top of one of the newspapers: ROOSEVELT DEAD.

Alex was stunned. It seemed impossible. He grabbed Anna and said, "It says that President Roosevelt is dead. How could that be?"

"Was he sick?"

"I don't know. I didn't think so. It must have been a heart

attack or . . ." For a moment Alex wondered whether the president could have been assassinated. He stepped forward, tried to get closer to the newsstand, but people weren't moving. They all seemed as shocked as Alex was.

What would this mean to the country, to the war? How could the president bring the country this far, this close, and now, just as victory in Europe was in sight, miss the chance to share it with his people? He would have given such a fine speech, Alex was sure; he would have helped Americans understand the meaning of what they had accomplished. FDR had become a symbol of the people's will—like the flag or the Statue of Liberty.

Alex finally got a chance to move in closer. He picked up one of the papers, paid for it, and then stepped back to Anna.

"What will America do now?" she asked him.

Alex was glancing through the article. Roosevelt had apparently been more ill than anyone had been allowed to know. "I don't know," Alex said. "What's-his-name—that little guy from Missouri—will be the president. Truman. I don't see how he can step into such big shoes."

"Are you all right?"

"I don't know. I feel like someone in my family just died."

"But your father won't feel that way. He didn't like Roosevelt, did he?"

"This will hurt Dad too. He disagreed with Roosevelt's politics. But this is going to touch him. Everyone in the States is going to feel it."

"Here, too. Look." Anna pointed at the people, standing, still not walking away from the newsstand, gazing at the front page and talking in hushed tones. The crowd was growing all the time, and as people approached, they would ask, "What is it?"

"It's Roosevelt. He's died."

A hefty woman in a gray dress with a scarf over her head, probably on her way to work, said, "Oh, dear, no. What will happen now? Maybe the war isn't over after all."

For the next couple of weeks nothing official came out of Germany. Alex had to wonder whether the woman at the newsstand might have been right. Maybe Hitler had taken new courage. Maybe he felt the U.S. was leaderless now and would settle for something less than an unconditional surrender.

Alex's thirty days were slipping away, but he had mixed emotions about that. He hated the idea of parting with Anna again, but he was having trouble dealing with so many empty days. Anna had had to return to work, and while she tried to put in as few hours as possible, Alex was left alone much of the time. He spent some days with Anna's mother, and he walked a great deal, but he couldn't seem to sit still to read, and he was in no mood for sightseeing. He told himself that he loved this time with Anna, but he didn't feel it the way he wanted to. They had no future they could talk about yet, none they could begin. All was on hold until Alex got out of the army, and he didn't know exactly what he would be going back to, how long he still might have to stay. He kept telling her he was fine, feeling better all the time, but one evening, as they sat on a bench in Hyde Park, she told him, in German, "Alex, you're not *you* yet. I feel that all the time, but I understand. You don't have to try so hard to reassure me. It's going to take time for us to get back to normal."

"We don't know what normal is, Anna. We've never spent a single day together when the war wasn't hanging over us."

"We will."

"Anna, I'm sorry I've ruined this time together."

"You haven't. Listen to me." She turned to him, took his face in her hands, and gave him a little kiss. "When we can plan—when we can start our life together—you'll have things to think about. Right now, you're only waiting—and remembering. That's not healthy."

"I've been on edge for a long time, Anna. I want to stop feeling that way, but . . . . I don't know . . . my brain doesn't want to believe that I'm out of danger."

"I know. I understand. Remember—I was there. For a long time, after we came out of Germany, every little sound woke me up at night. I'm still that way a little. But we'll be okay. We'll go to Salt Lake, be with your family, and we'll have our little baby."

"Anna, I could end up going to fight in Japan."

"Maybe not. Maybe they'll need you in Germany long enough that you won't have to go over there. Maybe the fighting is over for you."

Alex had thought a lot about all that the past few weeks. He wondered what he wanted to do when he got home, what it would be like to be a civilian, perhaps to go to college again, or to work. It was all so hard to imagine. He even feared his family a little—especially his father, who wrote letters that hinted strongly that he expected Alex to be part of the family businesses again. Nothing about selling cars, or running the plant—even if it was no longer a weapons plant—appealed to him. He wanted to do something *good*—wanted to give some kind of service, do something he could be proud of. He wanted to like himself. He knew that no one would blame him for anything he had done, but he still felt the need to repent.

On May 1, word spread across world that Hitler had committed suicide the day before. Not everyone believed that, but what was clear was that the Russians had taken Berlin, and the rest of the Allies had taken control of almost all of Germany. The end was certainly very near. Rumors kept circulating through London that Germany had surrendered, and impromptu celebrations would break out, but finally, on May 7, early, Alex heard on the radio that the news was official. Surrender papers would be signed that night, and May 8 would be proclaimed Victory in Europe Day. On the tenth, Alex would be leaving. He was glad he had still been with Anna when this good news had come.

Alex and Anna had stayed on at the hotel even though they were using up all of Alex's money to do so. But they wanted this time together, and they clung to it. He had been sitting in the big chair in the hotel room when the news about the surrender had come on the radio. He took some long breaths when the announcement was over. He wanted to let the peace enter him, relax his body a little.

He and Anna ate a nice dinner in the hotel dining room that night, and they joined a little in the merrymaking. But most of people were drinking and getting more jolly than Anna and Alex liked. "Alex, let's walk to Piccadilly," Anna said. "People will be out there tonight enjoying this together. Churchill is supposed to make a statement in front of one of the buildings in Whitehall. We could stroll up that way and maybe hear him."

"I'm afraid there'll be a tremendous crowd," Alex said. "Do you want to be in the middle of all that?"

"Why not? Let's be happy. You and I, we need to be a little less tragic—and enjoy this moment. Let's start being all right."

"I just thought, with the baby, you might not want to be bumped and jostled about."

"The baby will be fine. It will like the fun."

And so Alex agreed. He knew he owed Anna this. But outside, the crowds filled up not only the sidewalks but also the streets, and Alex felt some of his anxiousness return. Piccadilly was crazy, with taxis and busses caught in the throng, unable to move, and people screaming and singing and doing snake dances. He knew what Londoners had been through—the blitz, the V-2 attacks, and the long years of fighting—but there was something too strident about all this, a little forced, as though people had pictured this celebration for seven years, and now they had their minds made up to carry it out—even if they felt more like putting their feet up and taking a rest. Only the drunks seemed unabashed in their joy, and some of those were getting obnoxious.

"It really is over, Alex," Anna yelled in Alex's ear. "I can't get used to the idea." She held his arm tight and pressed herself against him. "We made it. You're alive, and this little one in here has a daddy." She patted her belly. "This time, when you leave, I won't have to worry so much."

They had talked about the days ahead. Alex would be going into Germany before long. But he didn't know how long he would be needed there. What he didn't tell Anna was his one constant worry: if an Airborne landing were planned for Japan, the 101st might be grasping for all the experienced officers it could find. The division might want Alex back, and everyone knew that the greatest danger of all, in combat, was for lieutenants, who were often the platoon leaders. Alex wasn't like some of the green ones who came out of West Point and got themselves killed the first week, but he would be out front, and the battle to take Japan was going to be monumental. Some experts thought there would be as many Allied lives lost there as had been lost throughout the entire war.

So Alex had a hard time thinking that the war was "over" for them. But he didn't say that; he laughed and pulled Anna close, and he told her how happy he was. All the while, the noise was almost more than he could stand.

Eventually, however, it was Anna who wanted to go back to the hotel. People were yelling foul comments about Hitler, which was fair enough, but when they shouted about the "filthy Germans" and the "stinking huns," Alex saw her wince. "I thought it would be fun, but it isn't," she finally told Alex. "There's nothing left of Germany now, is there?"

"You know there isn't."

"What will happen to the people?"

"I don't know, Anna. It's going to bad there—for a long time."

"I just wanted to be happy that it's over."

"I know. But it isn't that easy. This war won't be over for a long time."

Anna nodded. "Let's go," she said, and the two worked their way out of the crowd.

Bobbi was in the officers' ward room when one of the doctors stepped in and announced, "It's official. The Germans have surrendered. We just heard it on the radio."

There was not much reaction—partly because the news had been expected. Besides, the war was over "over there," but it was far from over for those on the *Charity*. Maybe Bobbi resented that a little. But she was really too tired to be sure what she felt. Her ship had just departed from Guam for the third time since the battle for Okinawa had begun. Three times the ship had been filled to capacity, with more than six hundred patients stacked into tiered bunks, and then it had steamed to Guam and transferred the wounded to the hospital there. Now the ship was on its way back to Okinawa one more time. Bobbi had spent the day supervising the necessary cleaning and reorganizing as her staff prepared for their return to action.

Dr. Clyde Jones, a young surgeon and navy lieutenant, was sitting across from Bobbi. "We ought to celebrate," he said, almost as though he thought it was their duty to do so.

Kate Calder was sitting next to Bobbi. She laughed. "When we get back to Okinawa, I don't think we're going to feel like any war is over."

"I know," Dr. Jones said, "but just think how long we've waited for this day. A couple of years ago, we would have given almost anything to see Hitler finished off."

Another doctor, John Samuelsen, had continued to eat. But now he said, "Maybe we can throw all our strength against the Japs now and get this thing over with."

Someone at another table had managed to drum up a little more excitement. "I just talked to the cook," a young ensign shouted. "He's got a stash of beer somewhere. We're going to have a party."

Bobbi decided it was time to clear out. She didn't mind the others drinking, but she didn't have the energy to deal with the extra attractions. Doctor Jones came on strong enough to her at times when he hadn't been drinking, but give him a little alcohol and he suddenly became all hands. So Bobbi slipped away and went back to her cabin. It was awfully early to go to bed, but she thought she would anyway. First, however, she got out Richard's last letter, and she read it one more time. He had been in Utah for a while now, in Brigham City most of the time, where he was receiving skin grafts. This last letter, however, had really bothered her:

Dear Bobbi,

I'm back in Brigham after spending almost two weeks at home. I had another graft this week, and my left hand is wrapped again. But the doc said he's finished with my right hand. It doesn't look great, but it works fairly well. I can do most things fairly well with it now, and it should get even better as I keep exercising. The doc says he might send me back to San Francisco for another operation on my left hand. Right now I can't make a fist or grasp anything with it. I do have pretty good use of my thumb, though, so it's still better than if they had amputated.

I'm finally getting it through my head that I am lucky. Here at the hospital I'm one of the few guys who hasn't lost an arm or a leg—or both legs, both arms. Most of these guys are still trying to accept what it means to go on with life, with everything changed so much, and they look at me like I got off easy. Bushnell also has a big ward for patients who've broken down psy-

chologically. I've seen some guys who look like blank walls. I feel pretty lucky when I look at them.

Bobbi, I've made up my mind to start at the University this next fall. My doctor says he can probably get me out of the navy by then, and I'll get some financial help for school. I've decided I want to be a teacher of some kind. I think I could possibly do engineering work, even with my hands the way they are, but it's just not what I feel interested in anymore. I read all the time, here at the hospital, and every book I pick up looks interesting to me. I don't know how I'll ever settle on just one subject.

Bobbi, there's something I'm concerned about. I called your family the last time I passed through Salt Lake on the way home. I talked to your mom for a while, and I can see where you get your sense of humor. I really liked her. She had your dad take the phone for a minute, and he was nice too, but he talked a lot about how busy the plant is. The impression I got is that your family is really doing well financially. Since then I've thought a lot about the situation I might be putting you in. If I end up a teacher—or maybe a college professor—are you going to feel okay about that? Maybe the rest of your family will have a lot more money than we would have. You need to consider what that might mean. You don't need to feel duty-bound to marry me at this point. You might want to take my plans into account. If you would rather drop this engagement and then just wait and see when you get home, that would be something I would understand.

By the way, your mother invited me to dinner. I told her the next time I came home, I would take her up on that, so I should have a chance to meet your parents and little sisters before long.

Well, look, I just read this letter over, and I don't want it to sound wrong to you. I'm not asking to break off our engagement. I just want you to have that option. There's not a chance I would write you a "Dear Jane" letter. There are plenty of nice girls back here in Utah, but I've never met anyone like you. Now that I'm the one away from the action, and you're the one still out there, I understand what you went through waiting for me. I pray every day that you'll be safe, and that the war won't go on forever. What I want more than anything is to have you with me. At the same time, I don't want you to feel trapped. If I'm not going to have a lot of money in my life, you need to consider that. Maybe that doesn't seem very important now, but in

*the long run, it might be hard to watch your family do so well while we have
to get by on a lot less. So I guess you understand what I'm saying to you. I
want what's best for you, Bobbi, and I don't want you to marry me out of
obligation. I'm not backing out at all, but I want you to know the whole picture before you make up your mind.*

It was this passage that stopped Bobbi each time she read
the letter. Where was his passion for her? Couldn't he, somewhere in the letter, have said, "I want you more than anything"?
He had never once even used the word *love.* Maybe it was kind
and fair of him to offer her a way out, but it also seemed so
bloodless. She liked a lot better the longing for her she had
seen in David's eyes. The irony, of course, was that Bobbi was
as likely as Richard to use her head more than her instincts. But
maybe that was just the point. Maybe she needed someone
who would fire her emotions, someone more like her Hawaiian
friends.

Bobbi tried to think about the issue Richard had raised.
What she knew was that someday she might in fact feel more
concern about money, and she tried to force herself to take the
question seriously. But she had never been motivated by
"things," and she didn't know how to test her future aspirations
against the feelings she had always known. Would it matter to
her if her brothers and sisters were better off? Maybe it would.
Maybe she would change, start to wish her children had as
much as their cousins. But right now she could only think that
Richard needed to do something he cared about and not sacrifice his own needs for the sake of money.

What lingered in her head, however, was a strange kind of
jealousy. The passion in Richard's letter was all for this new-
found love of learning. Reading, right now, seemed to entice
him much more than she did. No one loved to read more than
David, but at least he knew how to look up from a book and
turn his intensity toward life—and Bobbi. Maybe Richard
would end up a distracted old professor with his head full of
nothing but ideas.

Bobbi put on her nightgown and lay on her bunk. The humidity in the room was not really oppressive, but it was annoying, uncomfortable. She longed for those spring nights that she remembered back in Utah, when the air was mild but a little bracing as it blew across the front porch all full of the smell of lilacs. She tried to think about life with Richard, life at home. What she knew was that she *didn't* care about money. What she wanted was someone who knew how to love her, someone who would *feel* more than think. Maybe David and Richard were both wrong for her. They had been perfectly willing to give her up when their reason and fair-mindedness had gotten the better of them. What she wanted was a man who would fight for her, cross burning sands to get to her—and she wanted him now. She was sick of these hot nights in her quarters, alone.

* * *

Wally's strength was returning, and part of the reason for that was that Sonbu Son was back in the mine, and he had again chosen Wally as his assistant. They worked together each day, just the two of them, and each afternoon they took a rest—just as they had done before. But some things had changed. Sonbu had no extra food to offer. He apologized for that, saying, "Not good in Japan. Many bombs."

Otherwise, Sonbu said nothing about conditions outside the mine and the prison camp. He couldn't speak enough English to say much, but he also seemed to hesitate. He had probably been warned by mine officials not to reveal anything to the prisoners. One day, however, as the two sat down to rest, he said in a solemn voice, "No war in Germany."

Wally hadn't understood the words—Sonbu's pronunciation—the first time. And so he asked him to repeat.

Sonbu said the same words, and then he added, "Hitler dead. Germany stop."

Wally had heard other rumors. Some men claimed to have heard from guards, or from men who had heard radio broadcasts, that the war in Europe was about to end, but Sonbu was reliable, and Wally was sure this was true.

"Japan no stop," Sonbu volunteered.

It was the question Wally had wanted to ask. "Too many bombs. Must stop," Wally told him.

Sonbu sat for a time. In the dim light, Wally could barely see his face. He looked worn, depleted. "No stop," he finally said.

Wally didn't know how to say what he was thinking. "Many bombs," he repeated. Then he held his hands over his head to indicate a surrender.

But Sonbu shook his head. "No stop," he said again, and this time he made a motion, as though he were fighting with his hands, swinging a stick. Wally knew what he meant, that people would fight with poles, that they would resist an attempted landing. Sonbu finished by swinging his arm in a wide arc and saying, "All people."

"No. Only soldiers," Wally told him.

Again Sonbu shook his head. "All people."

"You?" Wally pointed to him.

But Sonbu stared into the dark and said, softly, "No."

"Your son? The soldier? Will he stop?"

Sonbu looked at Wally, obviously mystified. Wally thought he hadn't understood. But when Wally repeated the words, Sonbu said, "Soldier no stop. Die."

Wally knew what he was saying, that the boy was destined to die, just as his two older brothers had done. Sonbu had no hope for anything else.

"All soldiers die," Sonbu said, softly. "All people."

Wally had no idea whether that was true, whether most Japanese would be wiped out in this war. It only made sense that at some point they would surrender. And yet, he knew what Japanese soldiers thought of those who gave themselves up. For three years the guards had told the men that they were cowards, that honorable soldiers fought to the death. Many times, when the guards were being most brutal, they—or their interpreters—would tell the prisoners that such cruelty was owed to men who had no more courage than to surrender.

But that was the attitude of soldiers. Would all the Japanese people feel that way? Would the entire Japanese nation fight to the death? That was beyond anything Wally could understand.

That evening Wally told the other men in his room what Sonbu Son had said. It was after dinner, and some of the men were sitting in their room while others took their turn digging. They were excavating a cellar beneath the barracks—a bomb shelter. The Japanese had already built concrete bomb shelters for the guards and camp officials, but now they were forcing the prisoners to dig their own refuge. These were damp, dark holes in the ground, and they required extra work that the men didn't want to do. Most of the prisoners believed the Americans knew where they were now and were avoiding the camp on purpose. They liked to point out that after that first strike, the camp had never been hit again.

"I believe it's true," Art Halvorson told the others. "Sonbu isn't the sort of man who would say something like that unless he knew."

"He's always been honest with me," Wally said. Wally was sitting on the floor, leaning against the wall, as were Chuck Adair and Don Cluff. Art and Eddy Nash were facing them, sitting cross-legged.

"So what do you think it means?" Don asked. "How much longer can Japan last?"

"Sonbu told me the Japanese won't ever quit, that they'll die fighting."

"That could be true, too," Chuck said. "Some of the guards say things like that."

"Sonbu said he would quit," Wally said. "He can't be the only one who feels that way. He's lost two sons and expects to lose another one. He's had enough."

"I'll tell you something Okuda told me," Eddy said. "I didn't take it too seriously at the time, because he's such a big talker, but it fits in with what Sonbu told you. He said Japanese pilots were being trained to fly death missions. He said they'd fly their airplanes into the decks of American ships."

"That doesn't make a lot of sense," Chuck said. "How long are you going to have airplanes—and pilots—if you do that?"

"He said that lots of young guys were being trained to make these flights, and that there was no stopping them. They would eventually destroy the American fleet and turn the tide of the war."

"Most of them would get shot down on the way in, wouldn't they?" Art asked. "You'd have to give up a whole lot of planes to destroy a fleet of ships."

"Probably so. But something like that might work, at least to knock out our biggest ships."

Wally didn't know. Years ago, before he had been taken prisoner, he had heard that almost all the American fleet had been sunk at Pearl Harbor. Obviously, a lot of production must have taken place since then. But he had to wonder—maybe suicide missions of that kind would work. Maybe Japan was far from being defeated. The men had all convinced themselves since the first bombing in Omuta that the war was in its last days, but maybe that was only wishful thinking. What if the war kept going for another year—or more? Wally wondered how many of the prisoners would last that long. The men didn't suffer as much from disease as they had back in the Philippines, but they were wearing out. Wally had always told himself that he was one of the stronger ones, but he had been weakened by the illness he had gone through, and by the brutal beating he had taken from Commander Hisitake. How much longer could *he* hold up?

* * *

The tabernacle was packed. LaRue kept turning to watch as the pews filled, and then as the standing-room areas around the edges of the building became jammed with people

President Thomas had been invited to join the funeral procession, and arrangements had been made for his family to sit toward the front of the building. Sister Thomas, with LaRue and Beverly, hadn't had to stand in line, but they'd had to arrive early, and that meant a long wait on hard benches. Before that, they had filed slowly through the Church Office Building, where President Heber J. Grant's body had been lying in state.

It was now just after noon, and the funeral procession was finally entering the tabernacle. George Albert Smith, president of the Council of the Twelve, led the way. He was followed by all the other General Authorities, who walked behind him, in pairs. LaRue recognized the apostles, but she might not have realized who the others were had Sister Thomas not leaned over and whispered, "That's Joseph F. Smith, the patriarch of the Church, and then the Assistants to the Twelve after him."

"I thought Joseph F. Smith died a long time ago."

"This is a different one. This is Joseph Fielding Smith's nephew." She smiled. "I know. It does get a little confusing." She waited for more of the men to move by, and then she said, "That's the First Council of Seventy and then the Presiding Bishopric." LaRue didn't have to be told that the last two men in front of the casket were President Clark and President McKay, of the First Presidency.

LaRue knew virtually all the General Authorities' faces even when she couldn't remember their names. Many of them—most of them, in fact—had been in her home. Mom had served them Sunday dinner between sessions of stake conference. LaRue had also seen the Brethren about town, at East High football and basketball games, at restaurants—lots of places. Always, they made a point of greeting President Thomas and his family, and it wasn't uncommon for one of them to pull Dad aside and discuss some Church matter with him.

The truth was, LaRue didn't understand why some people made such a fuss about them. They were just people. Some of them were funny and outgoing, others less so, and all were pleasant enough at the dinner table, but at conference sessions they usually gave long talks, which more often than not bored LaRue. In fact, if it were up to her, she wouldn't be at the funeral today. She rather liked the idea of missing school, but she wondered how long the service would drag on.

"All of the pallbearers are President Grant's grandsons," Sister Thomas whispered.

The men looked dignified and rather old to LaRue—to be grandsons. They walked to the center of the building in front of the elevated seats the General Authorities always occupied, and they placed the metal casket on a special stand. Flowers were on display all across the front of the building, especially at the base of the grand pipes of the organ and along the sides of the seats where the Tabernacle Choir sat.

Following the casket were the stake presidents of the Church—all who could get there. They entered the building and then filed into seats at the front. LaRue saw her father sit down, and she almost laughed at how solemn he looked. President Grant had been eighty-eight, and he had been sick off and on for the past few years. His death could hardly be a surprise; LaRue couldn't imagine why her father had to look so down in the mouth about it.

"Do you realize that President Grant was born in 1856?" Mom whispered to LaRue. "Think about that. He knew Brigham Young. He lived in this valley when it was mostly just a desert."

LaRue nodded. It *was* sort of amazing to think that his life spanned almost back to the beginning of the first settlement here in the valley. And even more, it was strange to think that anyone else could be president of the Church. That was the one uneasy feeling LaRue had had since Monday evening when word had come over the radio that the prophet had died. It was Friday now, May 18, and Salt Lake had pretty much come to a halt during this funeral. Those who couldn't get into the Tabernacle were in the Assembly Hall or outside on Temple

Square, where loudspeakers would broadcast the meeting. Others had stayed home to listen on KSL radio.

The week before, on Tuesday, Salt Lake had celebrated V-E day, but very little had happened. Government workers had had the day off, but the schools hadn't let out, and there were no parades, no special occasions. In a few places, like Times Square in New York, people had gathered and celebrated, but even President Truman, when he had officially announced the end of the war in Europe—on his sixty-first birthday—had talked about the battle being only half won. The nation couldn't let down in its commitment but had to work all the harder to defeat Japan.

First President Roosevelt had died, then Hitler had committed suicide, and Mussolini had been killed by his own people. Those deaths, all in the last month or so, had received great attention, but the death of the president of the Church had even greater impact on the Saints. Heber J. Grant had served as president for twenty-seven years, longer than anyone except Brigham Young.

J. Reuben Clark, whom LaRue knew well and considered a sort of friend, welcomed the people, and then the Tabernacle Choir sang the opening hymn, "Though Deepening Trials." LaRue was looking about, hardly paying attention, when the words of the hymn began to reach her: "Though tribulations rage abroad, Christ says, 'In me ye shall have peace,' Christ says, 'In me ye shall have peace.'"

The plaintive tone of the music made LaRue feel a little more serious than she had been all morning. She was struck with the sadness that President Grant had not lived quite long enough to see peace come—the peace that he and everyone else had been waiting for so long. She remembered something her father had said when he first heard of the death. "He almost died five years ago," he had told LaRue. "I think the Lord preserved him to get us through this war. He was the right man to do that. He's one of the few men I've ever known who actually loved his enemies."

LaRue had paid little attention to her father at the time, but now she was surprisingly moved by the thought. She remembered a time a few years back when she and her family had met President Grant. He had been in the stake to dedicate a new church building, and he had taken time to shake hands with the members there. When he had grasped LaRue's hand, he had held it and waited until she looked up into his eyes. Then he had looked at her through his little circular glasses, and she had finally focused on his eyes, not his white beard that had always fascinated her as a little girl. "You have such a pretty face," he had said. "I think your heart is just as pretty."

The words meant more now than they had then, but LaRue saw them more as a reflection of him, and the way he saw things, than as the truth about her. What she wished was that he might have lived just a little longer, to see the soldiers all come home. He would have loved that peace, that end of tribulations.

George Albert Smith was the first speaker. He would soon become the new president of the Church; everyone knew that. He was a slender man with a little white chin beard and mustache. LaRue had never felt much attachment to him, but there was a gentleness in his voice that drew her attention now. "I have never before been so subdued in my soul as I am today," he said. And the words touched LaRue. She could see in his face, hear in his voice, that he was feeling the sense of his new responsibility.

President Smith told the story of President Grant's life. His father, Jedediah M. Grant, had died a few days after Heber's birth, and his mother had survived by sewing, taking in boarders, doing whatever she could to put food on the table. Heber had inherited his mother's determination, President Smith said. He had been a devoted baseball player, a hard-working young businessman. At twenty-three he had served as stake president in Tooele County. Then he had been called as an apostle at age twenty-five, and he had served the Church ever since—most of his life.

LaRue had heard a lot of these things before—especially this week. She had also read that President Grant was one of the last Church leaders who had lived in plural marriage. He had had three wives at one time, although two had died by the time he had become president.

All the facts didn't matter much to LaRue, but she found herself responding to President Smith's kindly manner, his obvious love for President Grant. And then, after the choir sang again, President David O. McKay spoke. LaRue remembered President McKay's touching little speech at Gene's funeral. She liked this good man. She felt his gentle power.

President McKay said that he admired President Grant as a man of great character, a man who "spoke what he thought, lived up to what he professed, kept his promises, and truly believed what he taught." But that description stung LaRue just a little. She knew that she couldn't say those things about herself.

Finally, President Clark spoke. He described President Grant's great leadership as the Church had grown from a small group to almost a million members. "He was a rare spirit," President Clark said, and then, with tears in his eyes, he told how much he loved the man.

The service was not long, and the time actually passed quickly for LaRue. At the end the Choir sang "Thou Dost Not Weep Alone," and Elder LeGrand Richards, the Presiding Bishop, said the closing prayer. Then the procession left the building as it had come, with the Brethren following the coffin. LaRue was surprised to discover that she was struggling not to cry. She kept thinking what good men these were, and strangely—almost as though her dad were speaking—how fortunate she was to know them personally.

In the car, on the way home, Dad talked about all the great

historical events that had happened in the past few weeks, and he told LaRue and Beverly that they should go home and write all the things down that they had experienced, so they would remember them when they were older.

That wasn't a bad idea, but LaRue might have been more likely to do it had her dad not told her to. There was always something irritating about the way Dad would tell her what she should think about an experience—as though he thought he had to interpret it for her. What she wanted was to remember how she had felt there for a few minutes as the funeral service was concluding, when that delicate, almost tender feeling had come over her. Already the feeling was gone, and she felt her usual impatience with her father, her annoyance with Beverly, who was so quick to say how "wonderful" the meeting had been. She wondered why she could never hang on to her better self for very long at all.

"I think your heart is just as pretty," President Grant had told her. She missed him already.

The war in Europe was over, but Peter Stoltz's life hadn't changed. He didn't know how to start searching for his family. He could go to Berlin, perhaps, and try to locate members of the Church, but these days a steady stream of refugees was passing through northern Germany—mostly ethnic Germans who had lived in Poland or other eastern European countries—and they had nothing but horror stories to tell about Berlin. The Russians were terrorizing the people who were trying to survive among the ruins of the city. They were rounding up German soldiers, shipping them out on trains, probably to Russia. Peter knew he had to stay away from Russian troops. He thought, too, of making his way south to Frankfurt, but civilians weren't supposed to cross occupation zone boundaries. He wasn't actually afraid to try it, but for now he had a place to live, and food, and more than anything, he knew that the Schallers needed him. That was not something he could simply walk away from.

British soldiers were occupying the zone where the Schallers lived. The Tommys were taking prisoners, but from what Peter had heard, they were taking only those who surrendered. They weren't actively looking for deserters. It was possible that being arrested by the Brits wouldn't be so bad.

Maybe his family had made it to England and English soldiers could help him make contact with them. For now, however, he saw no advantage in embracing the chaos, of having to live in one of the barbed-wire POW camps he had heard about.

Peter's immediate concern was to harvest the early garden crop. Katrina's job in town had disappeared with the fall of the government. The family had no source of income, and German currency was almost worthless anyway. Only the garden—and the meager crops Peter might harvest later—stood between the family and starvation.

After dinner one night Peter walked outside. It was a nice evening, mild and fragrant. At first he had felt only escape here on the farm, but now, as the weather warmed, he felt something restorative working its way into his spirit. It was true that his memories tended to make him wary of confidence, of hope, but tonight, as the sun set, he felt a kind of benevolence in the soft light.

Peter needed his family, but for now he was pleased to have what he had, and to be here with these good people. He hadn't ventured out to see what had happened to Bremen or Hamburg—or any of the other cities—but he knew that Germany was a wasteland. He had seen Berlin, and that was enough. Everywhere, here in the country, urban families had migrated to the homes of relatives, or they had taken refuge in barns and chicken coops, and food was scarce. The weather had been wet for spring planting, and the chaos of the war had kept most farmers out of the fields. No fertilizer was available either, and usually no seed. Peter knew the summer would be bad and the next winter infinitely worse.

Peter was sitting on a rock fence, facing south, but he was looking to his right, at the sunset, when he heard someone approaching from his left. He was sure it was Katrina, but he pretended not to notice. She was close to him when she finally said, "It's a pretty evening, isn't it?"

Peter couldn't help laughing. Katrina was trying to sound

grown up—not as playful as usual—but it was hard for him to respond to her seriously. He smiled and said, "It *is* a nice evening."

Katrina was not the sort of girl a young man would stop to look at if she were walking by, but she had pretty eyes—huge and dark brown, with flecks of bronze, rich against her creamy skin. Someday she probably would be pretty. Peter actually liked her, but he wished that she weren't quite so crazy about him. When he left this farm he would probably never see her again, and it would only be cruel to let her think otherwise.

"Peter, tell me who you are."

"What do you mean?"

"Tell me about you. You never say anything."

"I've told you some things."

"Peter Stutz is not your name."

"How do you know that?"

"Once you slipped and said something else. It wasn't Stutz. It was Stoltz, I think."

"That is my name. Peter Stoltz."

"Why didn't you tell us that?"

Peter looked back toward the sunset. It was reaching its full brilliance. Streaks of cirrus clouds were orange now, glowing pale yellow at the edges. "I couldn't tell you part of the truth without telling you all of it. It was dangerous for you to know too much about me."

"Why?"

"People could have been looking for me. Gestapo or SD or military police."

"We already knew that. We knew you had run from the army."

"It's not just that. There's a lot more."

"Tell me now. The danger is over."

Peter had been trying to believe that for the past couple of weeks. His mind told him that his greatest danger would come from the occupying forces, no longer from the Nazis, but he had feared much too long to start thinking a new way so quickly. What he did realize, however, was how much he wanted to stop making up his past.

"Can't you tell me now?"

"Maybe it's better not to say too much."

"Why?"

"I've done things I wish I hadn't."

"Just tell me. You aren't bad. I already know that."

That seemed a remarkable thing for her to say, but he wondered whether she would say the same after she had heard. "I grew up in Frankfurt," he said, but he still wasn't certain how much he was going to tell her.

"That's what you told me before."

"I know. Whenever I *could* tell you the truth, I did, Katrina. I want you to know that."

"Thank you."

"For what?"

"For calling me Katrina. You never call me by my name."

Peter knew that. It seemed too personal. He didn't want her to think they were friends that way. "In any case, I grew up in Frankfurt. My father was opposed to the Nazis. He kept me out of the Hitler Youth as long as he could, but otherwise he kept quiet. We didn't go looking for trouble, but it managed to come to us. I won't go into the whole story, but I'll tell you this: A Gestapo agent came to our house when my sister was home alone. He made threats, tried to . . . do things to her."

"Rape her?"

"Yes."

"I know what rape is, Peter. You don't have to be embarrassed to say it."

He nodded, but he still didn't say the word. "She protected herself. She cut his face with a butcher knife. Our whole family had to go into hiding. It was our only chance to stay alive."

"Is that why you went to Berlin?"

"Yes."

"And you hid in a cellar there, didn't you?"

"Yes."

"Tell me the rest. Tell me everything."

"Let me tell it my own way."

"That's fine. Go ahead."

He glanced, and he saw that she was smiling. He knew what she was thinking—that she would get what she could of the story tonight, and then go after more later. He told himself he wouldn't do that, but then he told her much more than he intended. He told about his family's escape from Germany into Switzerland, about the Gestapo agent he and his father had injured, and he told her about being separated from his family at the French border.

"Did the others make it across all right?" she asked him.

"I don't know. There were shots fired. I always tell myself that they made it, but I don't know for certain."

"What did you do after that? How did you end up in the army?"

This was what Peter didn't want to talk about. The color was fading from the clouds. He watched the gleaming line along the dark horizon and tried to think what to say. "Katrina, I had no choice. I had to hide somewhere. Boys couldn't walk the streets without being picked up. So I used this name you know me by, and I joined the army."

"What's wrong with that?"

"I fought for the Nazis. I killed."

"That's what soldiers do. That isn't your fault, Peter."

"Think about it, Katrina. I can claim that I attacked a Gestapo agent because I was fighting *against* the Nazis, or I can say that because I loved my country I fought *for* the Nazis. But I can't claim both. It's the worst kind of hypocrisy to fight for both sides."

Peter had known all this for such a long time, but he had never put the thoughts into such simple words. Now he had defined his own treachery, what he would have to live with the rest of his life.

"No, Peter. When you fought for what you believed, that was not wrong. And then you were forced to do what every man in Germany did—what soldiers in every country do. If you're guilty for killing, so is everyone else."

"I knew better. Most of the boys in the army had come directly from the Hitler Youth. They believed what they had heard. They thought they were fighting for something good. I was killing for *me*, not for my country. That's murder."

Katrina stepped a little closer to Peter. She touched his arm. "Peter, you can't convince me that you're bad. You're the kindest boy I've ever known."

The glow of the twilight was almost gone. The sky was shading purple to black. Katrina was mostly just a voice, but Peter was glad he couldn't see her. He didn't want to look into her face right now. "You don't know what it was like, Katrina," he whispered. "You don't know what happens to soldiers in a war."

"I know some things. We had wounded soldiers here at our farm once. I saw what the men looked like. I saw the wounds. They held one man down, out in our barn, and sawed his leg off. I heard him scream and swear and rave about the *Amis*."

Peter nodded. "Everyone hates the enemy," he said. "I hated the Russians because they wanted to kill me. I didn't think about politics."

"Were you frightened?"

"Katrina, I don't know how to tell you what I felt. It was far beyond fear. It was . . . like falling into a hole—just falling and falling and finally wishing I could hit bottom so I could die and end the terror."

"But you said you had faith, that God spoke to you."

"Not for a long time. It was almost over when I finally felt that. But God *was* with me at the very worst time. That's one thing I do believe."

"God still loves you, Peter."

"Yes. It seems so."

"I love you, too."

Peter knew he couldn't let this happen. If she really comprehended what he had done—if she knew who he had been—she wouldn't be so quick to say such a thing. Maybe he seemed innocent now, but he would never be able to cleanse himself of all the filth he had wallowed in during the war. Sometimes he lay in the attic at night and felt his skin, sure that the grime was still on him. "You love me the way you would a big brother," he said, "but—"

"No. That's not what I'm saying."

"Katrina, you're only sixteen."

"You're not much older."

Peter hardly knew what to say to that. In one sense, she was right. But when he thought of himself at sixteen he remembered the boy he had been before he had filled his head with abominations. The gulf between them was actually boundless. And yet, he also knew that he liked her touch on his arm. And now she was bending toward him, her face coming close to his. He could hear her breath, cautious and slow. He knew that he should move away, but he didn't. And then her lips, stiff and tentative, touched his. He didn't kiss her back, but he didn't pull away, either.

She didn't reach around him, only held the delicate touch for a few seconds. When he did nothing, she stepped away, and then she said, "I'm sorry."

"It's all right," he said. Peter was confused. He wished he had kissed her, not hurt her this way. But he didn't love her; he only longed to have someone love him. And he knew it would be wrong to lead her on. He had come to the Schaller home for help, not to take advantage of an impressionable young girl. "Katrina," he finally said, "I'm the one who should be sorry. I've given you the wrong idea. Just be my little sister. That's all there is to this."

"Maybe for you. Not for me," she said. And then she turned and walked away. He could only see the hint of her shadow, hear her footfalls in the soft earth.

A few days later, troops marched down the road—Brits. Peter watched from the field, where he was working. He was still wearing the heavy wool trousers and worn boots that he had come to the farm with. His shirt was tattered. If the soldiers approached him, he would pretend to be a refugee. Frau Schaller would lie for him.

When a jeep turned into the lane and drove toward the house, however, Peter's impulse was to run. He had to force himself to hold his ground and then to walk toward the back door. When he entered the kitchen, he heard an English soldier speaking loudly. It took Peter a moment to realize that the man was attempting to use German.

"'Rous," he kept saying. "You must go."

Peter stepped into the living room, where Frau Schaller was facing the man at the front door. "Why must we leave?" she kept asking, and she had begun to cry.

"You go. We're going to stay here."

"Please, come in. You can sleep in our house. But let us stay."

"'Rous. Schnell."

Peter knew soldiers like this. The man was a sergeant, an NCO, and hard as a bullet. Peter could see in his face, his dirty uniform, the grit on his skin, that he didn't care about anything but having a warm place to sleep—and a bathtub. "They're taking your house," Peter told Frau Schaller. "It's what soldiers do. They'll use it for a headquarters."

"But where can we go?"

Peter walked to the man. He asked in German, "Could we sleep in the barn?" He pointed to the lean-to that was attached to the house. There were no animals in it. The Schallers had no animals.

"Nein. Nein. 'Rous. You must go."

But another man, an officer, was at the door. He said something in English that Peter couldn't understand, but the meaning seemed clear enough. The sergeant turned around and pointed to the barn. "Okay," he said. "Out there."

This was in English, which Peter and Frau Schaller certainly understood. But now the man had hold of Peter's arm. "You? Soldier?" he asked.

Frau Schaller spoke in English. Peter understood very little of what she said, but he knew the lie she was telling.

The sergeant cursed. He clearly didn't believe her. But Peter also saw that he didn't care. He spoke to Frau Schaller, and then she turned to Peter. "He says we can't take anything out there, no blankets. What will we do?"

"We'll manage. I have flour sacks in the shed. We're better off not to leave the farm to them—so they won't tear it up so much."

"Tear it up? Why would they do that?"

Peter didn't know how to answer that. They were soldiers, and victors. How could anyone understand who hadn't been there? But now the man was shouting again, demanding they move fast. Katrina had come into the room. Peter saw the sergeant glance at her, and for the first time, he felt some anger of his own. "Go with your mother, Katrina—into the barn," Peter told her. "I'll find the boys. Don't speak to these men. Stay out of their way."

Katrina nodded, and Peter saw her fright. "What are we—"

But now the sergeant was setting up a howl again, and Frau Schaller grabbed Katrina and took her out the side door into the barn. Peter faced the sergeant. *"Fräulein. Nein!"* he said. He pointed his finger at the man's face.

The Tommy was clearly amused by Peter. But now it was the officer who was barking commands to the sergeant, and the sergeant walked back outside. Peter went to find the boys. They had been playing outside when he had last seen them.

The next few days were not as bad as Peter had feared. A

whole crowd of men, mostly officers, moved into the place—twelve of them at times. They weren't gentle about what they bumped or knocked over, but they didn't purposely damage the place. Nor did they bother Katrina. In fact, they said almost nothing to Peter and the Schallers. Then one night one of the officers walked into the barn, looked around, and said something in English. Frau Schaller nodded and then told Peter, "He said I can go inside and get some blankets."

The officer was speaking again, and Peter waited for a translation. "He says we can have food, too. He has cans of meat in the kitchen. If I will cook for them, we can eat the food as well."

"All right. But be careful."

"He's a nice man. He doesn't scare me."

Peter was thinking the same thing. He knew that most German soldiers on the eastern front would not have been so considerate. And certainly the Russians would have been much worse, had they been the ones to occupy this area west of Berlin.

So that night Rolf and Thomas ate much better than they were used to. And when they played soccer with their homemade ball, some of the British soldiers joined them. Even in their combat boots, they showed some skill, too. Peter had played the game as a boy but had never had a chance since he had gone on the run with his family. He was tempted to play with the men now, but he decided he would only make a fool of himself.

Two weeks passed, and things only got better for Peter and the Schallers. Some of the officers were much friendlier than others, but the nights were getting warmer all the time, and sleeping in the barn was not a problem. It was cramped, and there was no place to wash except at the pump out back, but Peter had been through much worse times. Rolf and Thomas seemed to like the company, and they picked up all the English words they could. They also accepted all the chocolate the soldiers would give them. In some ways, they had never had life so good. Katrina gradually became less wary, too. The officers teased her a little, and she tried out her school English. In fact, she seemed to find the attention she got from the men rather appealing.

Frau Schaller was nervous, of course, and she hoped this occupation wouldn't last very long, but she made the best of it. She spoke more English than the others, and she liked talking to the officers. "It's nice to have some people more my age around," she told Peter one day. And then she admitted, "I wish I looked a little more presentable."

Peter felt sorry for her. He thought she had been a pretty woman at one time, and she was young, still in her thirties, but she had a worn look about her, sometimes even a sad look. She was too thin, her skin too papery. It was Katrina these officers liked to look at. And she was blossoming. She had no makeup, nor any way to curl her hair, or even to get a decent haircut, but she had begun to move and act more like a woman, and Peter found himself annoyed by that. He kept warning her to be careful, but one day she finally said, "Why should you care?" and Peter didn't know how to answer.

The soldiers were happy to have peas and new potatoes from the garden, and soon other vegetables would be coming on. Since the men were feeding the Schallers from their own food, Peter couldn't complain about the vegetables they used. But the refugees who passed through the area were more of a problem. Some mornings Peter would find footprints in the garden and could see where people had grubbed with their hands for potatoes. He couldn't blame them. He had stolen food when he was a soldier. But if the refugees tromped through his garden, took everything, the day might come when the Schallers would have nothing to eat. There was no predicting how long the officers would stay around.

Peter began to sleep outside, close to the garden. Some nights intruders came, but all he had to do was sit up and tell them to move on. The people were like sheep, easily driven, not aggressive—probably too weak to think of taking Peter on. But as they slumped away in the dark, he felt sick at the thought of sending them back to their little makeshift camps with nothing for their children. He began to keep a little of his harvest close to where he slept, and when the refugees came, he parceled out a few potatoes or carrots. The people thanked him quietly and then moved on.

Then one night a man accepted the vegetables but in a strange German dialect said, "My son is sick. Can you help us?"

Peter hesitated. Camps were being set up for these refugees. The British officers always made a point of reminding Peter of this. Locals didn't need to feed them. If the refugees could make it down the road a little farther there were places where they could camp and be fed. And there was medical treatment. But Frau Schaller had talked to a friend in town who said that typhus and other diseases were spreading through those camps, and thousands of people were dying. "Don't get near the refugees," her friend had told her. "They have lice. They're full of disease."

All this was in Peter's head, but here was a man in front of him, standing in the dark, his voice like a prayer. "He's only two. He can't walk anymore. He coughs until I think his chest will tear apart." The man had begun to cry.

Peter was still trying to think what he should do. He thought of little Benjamin Rosenbaum, long ago. The boy's memory would always hurt him. "Where are you camped?"

"By the road, just north of your farm."

"Stay there in the morning. I'll try to get some medicine. But I can't promise anything."

"Please try."

The man trudged away. Peter tried to sleep, but he was restless. Early in the morning he walked to the barn. "Frau Schaller," he whispered, and she sat up.

"There's a little boy dying—one of the refugees camped by

the road. Can you talk to the soldiers? Maybe they have sulfa tablets, or penicillin."

"We can't take care of all these people."

"I know. But we could help one."

"What about tomorrow, when someone else comes to us?"

"I don't know. He's only two. His father cried."

The barn was still dark. Peter could barely see Frau Schaller. He couldn't tell what she was thinking. But from across the room, on the floor of the barn, Katrina spoke. "Ask Captain Stubbs. He's the kindest of the men."

"I can't speak to him," Peter said. "I don't know enough English. Your mother needs to do it."

Frau Schaller didn't speak for some time, but finally she said, "I'll ask him. But not yet. I won't go in there until the men are out of bed."

"The boy is dying."

"I know. But if he's that close to death, medicine won't help him now. Wait a little."

So Peter waited, and when the officers began to stir inside, Frau Schaller went in. She came back after a time, and she put a few tablets, eight or so, into Peter's hand. "He made another officer give me these. Some men carry them to protect against venereal disease. He said this would be a better use."

"Thank you."

"A whole tablet is probably too much for a baby. I don't know how much you should give him."

"He's dying. It's worth a try."

"I know."

Peter walked down the road. He found the man sitting by the road holding the little boy. The child was too spent to cry. He wasn't even coughing much. But Peter hadn't thought to bring fresh water, and he realized these people didn't even have that. The man told him they drank from rivers, from puddles, wherever they could find a little water. No wonder they were dying.

So Peter went back to the farm, and he brought back a bottle full of water from the well. He helped the man break the tablet and give it to the boy. When he drank the water, he seemed to revive a little. He was a little thing, bony and pale, with huge eyes, more gray than blue.

"I don't know whether this will help him," Peter said.

The woman finally sat up, and Peter saw why she hadn't done so sooner. Death was in her face. "Thank you," she said, and she reached for Peter's hand. He didn't worry about the diseases. He let her touch him. He knelt in front of her. "Have you eaten anything?"

"We try to feed our son," she said.

"Wait here. I'll get some more food. You must eat, too."

Peter walked back to the house. He couldn't help them all, he told himself again. But he would help this family.

2 2

Bobbi Thomas had come out on deck for some air and for a moment of peace away from all the craziness in her ward. The *Charity* was waiting well off the Okinawa shore, but in the distance, closer to the island, she could see American battleships at anchor. Above the ships she could see airplanes—just little dots in the sky—with black puffs of flak bursting beneath them. She watched as one of the dots dropped out of the sky—with flak popping all around it. It disappeared, and for maybe a second, she thought it had been destroyed, but then a sharp, hard flash lit the sky in a half-circle over the ocean.

Bobbi was startled. She had seen damaged ships many times, but she had never seen one take a hit—had never seen a suicide attack. In a second or two, the sound of the explosion rolled across the sea, and then another flash followed, another roll of thunder. She knew that meant the airplane had penetrated deep and was setting off secondary explosions. She wondered how many sailors had died before her eyes, wondered whether any survivors would be brought to her ship. But it was all so unreal, like a scene in a newsreel. She looked up to the bridge of the ship and saw that the executive officer, Lieutenant Despain, was watching with his binoculars. She quickly climbed a ladder to the 02 deck, and then another to the bridge. "Did you see that?" she asked Despain. "Wasn't that a kamikaze?"

Lieutenant Despain lowered his glasses and nodded. "It sure was," he said. "It did some serious damage, too."

"How can they do that?"

"You mean the Jap pilots?"

"Yes."

"It's some kind of religious thing. They think they'll be honored forever if they die for the Empire." But then he cursed them in language that Bobbi had grown accustomed to, here on the ship, but language that still bothered her.

"I can't imagine our pilots ever doing something like that."

Despain laughed. "Japs aren't like us," he said. "I've seen our boys risk their lives plenty—to save a friend, or something like that—but we care too much about living to go out and commit suicide. Japs don't care about life the same way we do."

But Bobbi didn't believe that. She knew Ishi. And she was pretty sure she knew human beings. They weren't that different from one country to another. She almost said that to Lieutenant Despain, but she had learned to keep her mouth shut about such things. She did borrow the field glasses for a minute and take a look across the sea. She could see smoke rolling from the ship, even flames. The sight of it made her sick. She could only imagine how awful it must be for the sailors who were trying to fight the fires—or were perhaps going overboard. She also knew she had to get back to her ward and get ready.

About an hour later the first casualties began to arrive from the *Calhoun*—the ship that had taken the kamikaze strike. Some of the sailors needed surgery, but most came straight to the burn ward on litters. One man had died on the LCM, and another didn't last long after he reached the ward. The others were horribly burned over most of their bodies.

Bobbi had experienced all this so many times before—the disgusting smell of the burnt flesh, the anguish in the men's eyes, and always the disappointing knowledge that there was so little she could do—but there was something different about it this time. She had seen the explosion, the attacking plane, and she felt a closer connection.

Bobbi worked late that evening, finally grabbed a little something to eat, and then headed to her stateroom. The ship had all its deck lights on, as it always did at night. Warships tried to hide themselves after dark and shut down their lights, but a hospital ship stayed lit up to identify itself and avoid attack. A wide green line ran around the white ship, and huge red crosses were painted on both sides of the ship and on all four sides of the main smokestack.

The night was hot and humid, so Bobbi didn't bother to get into her bunk. She slipped on a cotton nightgown and then lay on top of the blanket; she slept instantly. She was still deep in sleep when a sudden jolt shook the ship, brought her awake. The sound and concussion of an explosion slammed through her passageway, shook her hatch. The ship was blowing up, she thought. Suddenly she was out of bed, looking about herself, trying to think what to do. Sirens had begun to howl, and she heard movement in the passageway outside her state room. Would the crew have to abandon the ship? Would other ships come to their aid?

She grabbed for her white dress, which she had dropped on a chair the night before. She had no idea how much time she had. The ship seemed to be listing a bit, but she had no sense that it was going down. Ideas flashed through her head: what could she, should she, take with her? Was there some way to get the wounded off the ship?

She had her dress on by then. Without putting on her shoes, she ran into the passageway, which was full of smoke. A young corpsman was hurrying toward her. "We've been hit," he yelled. "We're on fire."

"What should we do?"

"I don't know. Get off, somehow."

But Bobbi was thinking better by now. "No! Go to your ward. Check on your patients." And then she tried to follow her own advice. But the burn ward was aft of where her stateroom was, and she couldn't go that way. Smoke was billowing toward her, getting thicker.

She climbed to the main deck and saw that sailors were already working hard, pulling hoses, carrying injured men away from the fire. A large section of the top two decks, right at midship, was blown away and billowing smoke. What sickened Bobbi, however, was the realization that the operating rooms had certainly been hit. Doctors and nurses had to have been in there. Surgery had been going on around the clock. She had no idea who might have been on duty, but her first thought was that Kate could have been, that she might be dead.

But Bobbi had no time to consider the possibilities. Men were carrying a screaming sailor toward her, and her instincts came alive. "Bring him this way," she shouted. The ship wasn't sinking—not yet, anyway—and no one was going overboard. The crew was getting after the fire, and her role was the one she knew. She had to save this life if she could.

She led the men toward the stern of the ship, had them put the sailor down on the deck, under a light. "Who can get morphine? And bandages?"

A young sailor, probably a corpsman, dressed only in his underwear, said, "I'll try to get some." He took off running.

Bobbi tore away the shreds of the injured man's shirt. His chest and face were burned and black, and blood was pumping from a wound at the base of his neck. "Hold him," she told the men around her. And then, in a gentler voice, she told the sailor, "You're all right. We'll give you something for the pain in just a minute or two. Hang on until then and you'll be all right."

"Mama! Help me!" the man screamed.

Bobbi had heard this many times before—men calling for

their mothers—and it always broke her heart. "We need to stop this bleeding," she said. "What can we use to—"

One of the men was already pulling his undershirt off. Bobbi took it and pressed it to the wound. She kept talking to the sailor, reassuring him, but he didn't seem to hear. "Help me," he kept yelling. "Do something. It *burns!*" He was fighting the men who were holding him down.

The corpsman returned rather quickly. He had a first-aid box. He set it down and tore through it quickly until he found morphine in a syrette. He broke the top off the little vial and jabbed the exposed needle into the man's arm. In only seconds Bobbi saw the sailor begin to relax. She pulled the undershirt away from his wound and replaced it with a compress from the first-aid box. The bleeding had already slowed, and she wasn't too worried about that now. She got out gauze and bandages and began to wrap him as best she could. That was all she could do for now.

Not far away another man was screaming, and no nurse, no doctor, was there to help, so she hurried to that sailor, and she repeated the process. This was different from what she was used to, seeing these men before they were out of pain, before the bleeding and burns had been treated once, and she felt the chaos and terror around her, so different from the control she usually had over circumstances in her ward.

"How's the ship?" she kept asking, but no one seemed to know.

Finally one of the crew, an ensign, came by. "The fire is under control," he said. "We're all right. But for now we'll have to keep the injured out here on the deck."

"What happened?" Bobbi asked. "Was it a bomb?"

"No. A kamikaze."

Suddenly Bobbi was enraged. It hadn't registered with her until that moment that a pilot had purposefully flown his airplane into a *hospital* ship—an easy, defenseless target. All of the men around her were cursing, using vile language. She heard a sailor near her ask, "What's wrong with these filthy Japs? Aren't they human?" Bobbi felt the same rage, even some satisfaction that these men could say the things she could only feel. What if some fanatic Japanese pilot had killed Kate? He deserved to burn in some sort of hell forever if he had. "Who was in the OR?" Bobbi asked the corpsman by her side.

"I don't know. I was off shift."

"What about Dr. Calder? Have you seen her?"

"No. But she was cutting all afternoon. I doubt she was still in the OR."

That didn't prove anything. Bobbi had seen Kate work thirty-six hours with only an occasional nap. She could still have been there when the airplane struck.

But Bobbi had other things to think about. The deck was thick with sailors and patients, nurses and corpsmen. Many of the patients had been forced from their wards by the smoke. But Bobbi was able to work her way through the chaos and make it to her ward. She found it mostly empty, but not very smoky, and so she hurried back up to the deck and began finding burn victims who needed to return. Many who had left had been able to walk, and some of them didn't want to return. Others had been carried out on litters by corpsmen. Bobbi talked most of those into going back. She also began to find new burn victims who needed to be brought to her ward. There was no organization to any of this, no one doing triage, so Bobbi did her best to bring a little order.

The new patients needed care. Bobbi worked hard with them the rest of the night. Most of her staff eventually showed up to help. By then rumors were spreading. All the doctors and nurses who had been in the operating rooms had apparently been killed. Other corpsmen and crew members had also died. No one really knew how many, but Bobbi heard numbers from twenty to fifty. And she kept asking, "Has anyone seen Dr. Calder?"

One of the corpsmen told her, "I think I saw her out on the

main deck, not long after the plane hit." But he didn't sound very sure of himself, and Bobbi was left to wonder. At least no one had reported that she was one of the ones missing.

When Bobbi finally found her way out of the ward long enough for a break, she went to the officers' ward room. There, in the back, she spotted a little cluster of officers—but no Kate. She walked to them and asked, hesitantly, "Has anyone seen Dr. Calder? Is she all right?"

A nurse, a young woman named Ilene Cowens, looked up from her coffee. "She wasn't in the surgery," she said. "She's all right. She's probably operating now—but I don't know where they've set up to do that."

"Who did die?" Bobbi asked.

One of the doctors, Glade Dunham, was also hunched over a cup of coffee. Without looking up, he said, "There are four doctors and six nurses unaccounted for—and certainly dead—and a bunch of corpsmen. Altogether, about thirty people dead, and maybe twice that many injured." He named the four doctors. One of them was Dr. Jones, who had been so eager to celebrate the end of the war in Europe.

Ilene listed off the six nurses, reciting the names in her tired voice, the sound like the thudding of a mallet. Each name hurt Bobbi. She knew all of them well. She had eaten breakfast with some of them the previous morning. One of the women, Lois Sutterfield, had talked to Bobbi about her brother's wedding. Lois had been feeling bad that she couldn't be home for it. At breakfast she had joked about West Texas, where she was from. "It's so flat out there," she told Bobbi, "you can stand on a chair, look hard, and see the back of your own head." But then she had said, with her Texan intonation, "But I'll tell ya, I'd *shore* love to be back there rat now."

"I'm sorry," Bobbi told the group before her now. "I know you were close to all of them."

"I keep thinking about Alice," one of the nurses said, a woman named Eva Curley. "I've seen that picture of her family in her quarters, and I keep wondering how her parents are going to feel when they get the word."

Bobbi had been thinking the same thing about Lois's relatives, out in west Texas. What would this do to their wedding celebration?

When Bobbi finally located Kate, she was at a bedside in a temporary post-op area. "I'm glad to find you," Bobbi told her. "I was afraid you were operating when that plane hit us."

Kate was kneeling by a man who was lying on the deck, a pillow under his head. She glanced up. "Thanks," she said. "I was pretty sure you weren't in there, Bobbi, but it's still good to see you with my own eyes."

"Can you take a break?"

"If I do, I might fall asleep."

"Walk out in the air with me for a minute."

"All right." Kate got up slowly, with obvious effort. The two climbed the stairs to the main deck and then walked toward the stern, where the air wasn't full of smoke. The morning was already hot, but the breeze off the water was rather pleasant.

Kate had taken off the apron she had been wearing in surgery, but Bobbi saw little spots of dried blood on her face and neck. "I'm so sick of this," Kate said. "I don't want to see any more."

"Why would someone attack a hospital ship?" Bobbi asked.

And that seemed to release Kate's anger. "Why not, Bobbi? If you shoot a man once and he doesn't die, why not *blow* him up? It's just as logical as anything else in this war."

"Kate, we had all our lights on. The pilot knew we were a hospital ship. There has to be some line people don't cross—even in a war."

"*Why?*" Kate turned toward Bobbi, her eyes full of fury. "Is it civilized to burn people out of caves with flamethrowers but wrong to kill doctors and nurses? What's the difference? Who makes up these rules? Emily Post? What's the proper *etiquette* for killing your fellow man?"

"But we have to—"

"What we ought to do is kill off *everyone* and then let some civilized animal take over: rats or rattlesnakes or cockroaches. We're really not worth the trouble to worry about, if you ask me."

Bobbi nodded. The words seemed about right. But she was mostly feeling disgust with herself at the moment. She had always been able to watch this war as a spectator—and feel morally superior to someone like Lieutenant Despain, who despised his enemy. But tonight she had been *in* the war, and her very first response had been hatred—burning, fierce hatred. And the worst part was, she was in no mood to give it up, just yet. Kate could find her disgust with all humanity if she wanted, but Bobbi was still outraged with the Japanese.

* * *

Beverly was nervous. She had been wanting to meet Richard Hammond for such a long time, and now he was coming to the Thomas's house for dinner. She had seen his picture, in his white uniform, looking handsome but serious, and she was a little worried that she wouldn't like him. She was in the kitchen with her mother now, helping to prepare dinner. She had peeled and boiled potatoes and was getting ready to mash them. "Where's your sister?" Mom asked her. "She promised to set the table."

"She's home," Beverly said, "but she just came through the door about five minutes ago. It'll take her half an hour to get ready."

"Oh, dear. If you'll start the table, I'll finish the potatoes. And then I'll get the rolls out of the oven. Maybe LaRue will be down in a minute. She knows I got home from work late tonight."

Beverly knew better than to hope for any help, but she was better at setting a table than LaRue anyway. She stepped toward the door to the dining room, but as she did the doorbell rang. Sister Thomas moaned. "Oh, wouldn't you know it? He's early. That's what I didn't need tonight."

"It doesn't matter. Dad can talk to him."

Mom was pulling off her apron. She whispered, "*That* is exactly what worries me. You stay out there with the two of them, and if Dad starts to do a stake president interview on the poor man, you change the subject."

"Mom, I—"

"Oh, honey, I'm just kidding." She walked to the sink and quickly washed her hands. "But stay out there. He'll want to talk to you a little, too. And if your dad does start asking too many questions, you step in, okay?"

Beverly liked the idea of being in the room where she could listen, but she wasn't sure she could think of anything to say. She followed her mother out through the dining room. As they reached the entryway, Dad had already opened the front door and Richard was stepping in. But Beverly couldn't believe what she saw. It was the man in the picture all right, but he was smiling—and he was *beautiful*. His picture had been black and white, but Richard was *Technicolor*—his eyes a misty pastel blue and his skin rich and tan. Beverly had never seen anyone so handsome—not even Victor Mature.

She stood and waited while Richard shook hands with Dad and then hugged Mom. His right hand was bandaged, lightly, and his left hand was wrapped entirely, even his fingers covered. "I'm so happy to meet all of you finally," he said, and then he turned and added, "This has to be Beverly. You look so much like Bobbi, I can't believe it."

Beverly nodded, didn't move, and she saw him make a decision not to step toward her. An instant too late, she finally began to raise her hand, but by then Mom was already taking his attention away. "Come in, Richard. Sit down with Al for a minute. Bev and I have to finish getting dinner ready."

So Richard and Dad walked into the living room. Dad sat in his big gray chair, and Richard sat across from him on the couch. Beverly followed her mother to the kitchen. "Oh, Bev, he's *so* handsome," Mom whispered.

But Bev couldn't give words to what she was feeling. That smile of his had started her knees quivering.

"Did you hear what he told you—that you're as pretty as Bobbi?"

"No, he didn't. He didn't say I was pretty." But Beverly was searching her memory. Had he said "as pretty as Bobbi" or just "look like Bobbi"?

"Well, *he's* prettier than either one of you. I might steal him for myself."

"Mom!"

"Who knows? I might want to get me a new model—something without so many miles on it."

Beverly laughed, but then she said, "No wonder LaRue says things she shouldn't say. You teach her."

"Speaking of your sister, go tell her to hurry. And then get that tablecloth on. I'll help you with the dishes in just a minute."

Beverly walked through the living room and took another quick glance at Richard. As she hurried up the stairs, she heard him say something to Dad about needing another operation on his left hand. She trotted along the hallway on her tiptoes to LaRue's room, knocked, and then pushed the door open. "He's here," she said. She was about to say how handsome he was but realized she didn't want to. LaRue would take all of Richard's attention, once she got downstairs. She always did. "Mom wants you to help me set the table."

LaRue was looking into her mirror, standing with a brush in her hand. "I look so awful," she said. "Is he nice?"

"Yes."

"What's wrong? You look like you got hit by a truck."

"Nothing. But Mom says to come down."

"Just a minute. I've got to do *something* with my hair."

Beverly turned and walked away, and then she took quiet

steps down the stairs, listening as she walked. "Well, that's true," her dad was saying, "with so many boys coming home, jobs might not be all that easy to come by for a while. But a lot of these girls who are working will be excited to get married and stay home, and the minute we get permission to start normal production, I think there's going to be a real boom in this country."

"That's good to hear," Richard said quietly. He glanced at Beverly again as she reached the bottom of the stairs. He smiled just a little, and she felt her face turn hot—which mortified her. She wished she didn't blush so easily. She hurried to the buffet at the back of the dining room and opened the drawer where Mom kept her tablecloths.

"Do you have any idea what Alex plans to do when he gets home?" Richard asked.

"Not exactly," Dad said. "But he was working with me when he left. By law I have to give him a chance to come back." President Thomas laughed in that big, deep voice of his. "I hope that's what he wants to do. I'm certainly going to need him. The way things are looking, I'm going to be hiring a lot of help to keep both my businesses operating—and not just on the line. I need managers, too. I want to take things a little easier, and I think Bea will want to get away from the rat race herself. I see a lot of expansion ahead for us in the parts business. We've just entered an agreement with Bendix that could double or triple the size of our operation."

Beverly chose a white tablecloth with pretty lace around the border. She unfolded it and spread it over the big table. Then she peeked at Richard again. He was wearing a brown suit with a white shirt and tie, and his wingtip shoes were as shiny as Mom's hardwood floors. Beverly thought he looked sort of stiff, the way he was sitting up so straight. But he was looking at her again. "So Beverly," he said, "how's everything with you?"

"Fine."

"Let's see, you're in what grade now?"

"Eighth."

"So you start high school next year?"

"Yes."

"You're growing up."

"I guess." She hesitated. "Well . . . I've got to get the dishes."

"Say, I'll help you." He stood up.

"You don't need to. You can just—"

"I don't mind." He walked toward her, so Beverly turned and pushed through the door and then stepped into the kitchen. Over her shoulder, Richard said to Mom, "I'm here to help set the table."

"You'd better not," Mom said. "This house might not stand the shock. No man has ever offered to do such a thing since this place was built."

"Well . . . let's chance it. I've got at least one hand that works pretty well."

"And it's better than being interrogated by my husband. Right?"

"Oh, no. It's not that." But he laughed a little more than he really needed to.

Mom got out dinner plates from the kitchen cabinet, and Richard carried them out to the table. As he passed Beverly, he whispered, "I'd better not drop these and break them." He smiled and winked. She felt a tingle rise up her back, and she knew she was blushing again. She wanted to think of something funny to say, but she swallowed the stupid words that did come to mind, and as usual she said nothing at all.

By the time the table was set, and Mom had helped carry the food out, Beverly had had to pass by Richard half a dozen times, but she hadn't looked again—she didn't want to blush anymore. She had seen enough to last her for now anyway.

But then LaRue arrived. "Hi," she said, "I'm LaRue." She had stopped, was standing stiff, and it wasn't like her to sound so out of breath.

"I'm Richard." LaRue didn't move toward him. She just looked. "Wow, LaRue," Richard said, "you're as pretty as Bobbi said you were."

Beverly felt the blow, knew the truth.

And by then LaRue had found her tongue. "Bobbi? I never heard of anyone named Bobbi. But I'm free tonight."

Beverly couldn't believe it. How could LaRue *say* such a thing? It was so embarrassing. But Richard was doing the prettiest thing Beverly had ever seen. *He* was blushing. "Actually, I do have a date," he said. "And she's a good cook." He looked at Sister Thomas and smiled.

"You'd better try my pot roast before you make a decision," Bea said. But Beverly could see that her mother was turning into butter right before her eyes. That was even *more* embarrassing.

"If it's as good as it smells, I'm sure I'll love it," Richard said. He was now avoiding *all* the eyes that were on him.

Even LaRue seemed to know she had gone too far. "It's fun to meet you after hearing about you for such a long time," she said politely.

"Well, thanks. That's how I feel too. Bobbi sure loves her family."

Dad came into the room then, and after Mom dashed back to the kitchen one more time for a serving spoon, everyone sat down. Dad said the blessing, praying a little too long, as usual. He even blessed Richard's "injured hands." Beverly worried that might make Richard feel awkward. She noticed how quietly Richard spoke, afterward, when he said, "Sister Thomas, I'm wondering if you could do something for me. I can eat all right, one-handed, once I have food on my plate. But if you could maybe fix up a plate for me—and cut up my meat—that sure helps."

"Oh, sure. I should have thought of that."

"How did you get a roast, anyway? My mom said that meat is the hardest thing to get these days."

"Connections," Dad said, and he laughed. "I got that directly from the source—a friend of mine who raises cattle."

"So you're into the black market, are you, Dad?" LaRue asked.

"Well, not exactly." But he actually did seem a little embarrassed, and all Beverly could think was that LaRue had done it again. The girl could be such a sap sometimes.

As everyone else passed the food around, Richard asked about Wally, and Brother and Sister Thomas told him what they knew—which was almost nothing. Beverly loved the soft way Richard spoke, the richness of his voice, even the attentive way he listened.

"There's someone else I wanted to ask you about," Richard said. "Bobbi told me about a Japanese fellow who was a friend of your family—and about his brother who was interned in California. What's happened to them?"

"Well," Dad said, "Mat has done all right. He's grown his fruit and stayed pretty much to himself. He can tell you stories about being treated pretty badly sometimes, but he lets it go and just goes about his business. But Ike is still in the internment camp. Some are starting to be released, but Ike, with a wife and a baby, is still sitting in that camp, waiting to start his life. From what Mat says, Ike has a pretty good attitude about it. Both of them just want a chance, after the war, to prove what good citizens they are."

Richard was chewing. He waited a moment and then said, "I've been reading the *Deseret News* since I got back to Utah, and I notice every day that ten or twenty boys—sometimes more—are listed as either killed, missing in action, or wounded. What surprises me is to see how many Japanese boys from around here have been killed or wounded. During that last week of the war in Europe, I saw a Japanese boy from the 442nd listed—killed in action—and his parents' address was an internment camp in Alabama."

"I know," President Thomas said. "I saw that too."

"Can you imagine how those parents must feel?" Sister Thomas asked.

"There are lots of different kinds of victims of this war," Richard said. "When you're out there in the battle, you don't realize how many of them are back at home."

"What I hope is that people will give Ike and boys like him a chance," President Thomas said. "But when we land in Japan, we're going to lose thousands—*hundreds* of thousands of lives— and I hate to think how much anger that's going to create in this country."

"But we don't hate Germans who are Americans," LaRue said.

"I know. That's what Mat told me a long time ago. And he's right."

"You used to say that we *had* to have those camps. You know you did."

Beverly couldn't believe it. Why did LaRue *always* have to spout off like that? Richard was ducking his head, and poor Beverly could see how hard Dad was trying not to react. "In the beginning it did seem right to me, LaRue," he said. "It was partly for the protection of the Japanese people themselves, and we didn't know—some of them might have been spies."

"No one has ever caught a single Jap spying in this country. My teacher told me that in civics class."

"I know, LaRue. I think Ike—and all the rest of them— should be released now."

"Sure, you—"

"LaRue, don't," Beverly said, the words popping out unexpectedly.

"Don't what?" she said.

"We'll talk about it some other time," Dad said, and Beverly saw him glance at Richard with a "you know how teenagers can be" kind of glance. But then he said, "Richard, how much longer will you be in the navy?"

LaRue was glaring at Beverly, but Beverly didn't care. LaRue didn't have to cause trouble all the time, start fights right in front of someone like Richard, who just getting to know the family.

"I don't know," Richard answered. "I'm going back to San Francisco for one more operation, and then I'll be at Bushnell again for more skin grafts. I'm thinking it still might be two or three more months."

"What are you going to do after that?"

"I'm not exactly sure about that either, President Thomas." Richard took a sip from his water glass. "I am planning to go back to college for a while."

"But you have your college degree, don't you?"

"I do. But I'm not sure I want to be an engineer now—or whether I can be. So I want to look at some other possibilities."

"A guy like you, who's served as an officer, has a lot of management skills. You'd be a natural in business."

"Well . . . not really. I tried to do my job as an officer, but I was anything but a natural. As much as anything, it showed me what I wasn't good at."

"But the business world is a lot different from the military. A fellow like you could get in at the right time and do *very* well."

"Richard knows himself, Al," Mom said. "He knows what he's interested in." Then she turned to him. "I want so much to meet your mother. Tell me about your family."

Beverly was relieved, in a way. Mom had gotten Dad away from asking too many questions, but she had hurt Dad's feelings, too. Bev could see that in her father's eyes.

For a time Richard talked about his parents, about growing up in Springville, but when dinner was over and everyone was still sitting at the table, Richard cleared his throat and, with some hesitation in his voice that was obvious to Beverly, said, "I do want to tell you something. I wrote Bobbi a while back, and I told her that I didn't feel that I should hold her to our engagement. My life is kind of up in the air right now, and I'm not sure

I'm much of a catch." He looked at Dad. "Your family is doing very well, and I'm just not sure I'm going to be able to meet those kinds of standards—if you know what I mean. So I told Bobbi that it might be better if we wait until she gets home before we settle anything for sure."

Beverly felt sick—and scared that someone was about to say the wrong thing. But Mom said, "Richard, you and Bobbi have to work all that out. But I can tell you right now, we already love you, and we welcome you to our family."

And then Beverly's voice acted on its own again. "Yes, we really do," she said. But the words had come out sounding entirely too sincere, even a little dreamy. Beverly heard the tone in her own voice, and she was engulfed in humiliation.

But Richard reached across the table, touched her hand, and said, "Thanks, Bev." And then he smiled. "When you blush like that, I can just *see* Bobbi. I guess I'll have to come and see you often—so I won't feel so lonely."

But now, just when she needed it, Beverly's voice had quit again. She wanted to say, "You're welcome here anytime," or something else really nice, but she couldn't even look at him. What was going through her head was a little fantasy. Bobbi would choose not to marry him, and Beverly would . . . but that was stupid even to think about.

23

"We've got a mess on our hands here in Germany, Lieutenant Thomas. It's ten times—a hundred times—worse than I ever imagined. We don't even know where to start working on all the problems."

"I got some idea of it on the way here," Alex said.

"No. You didn't. You thought you did, but there's no way to grasp the whole picture. I read the reports, look at the numbers, but I can't start to comprehend what it means."

Alex nodded, but he actually thought he did understand more than Colonel Whitefield thought he did. Alex had known this country before, and as he had traveled by jeep across much of it to Frankfurt, he had understood more than others might. The cities were graveyards, with gutted buildings standing like rows of tombstones among the rubble. The devastation was more complete, more pervasive, than Alex had expected, but what had shocked him most deeply were the German people. This was now a nation of women and children, with almost no men to be seen anywhere, and the faces of those women, those children, were all the evidence Alex needed. He saw their ragged clothes, their emaciated bodies, but he comprehended even more in their resolute expressions. The people were hungry, of course, and disheartened; they survived only by the force of sheer determination. Never had it occurred to Alex that the victory could be so complete.

Alex was sitting in a beautiful room, what had once been a bedroom in a luxurious villa outside Frankfurt. Elements of his new military unit had taken it over and turned it into a headquarters. Colonel Whitefield was with the army Counter Intelligence Corps, and Alex's understanding was that he would be working on a "denazification" project, part of the Allied "big three" agreement to govern Germany and bring it back into the world of civilized nations. Germans were to be "democratized" and "demilitarized" and forced to pay reparations for the war. Leading Nazis had to be found and punished, and local Nazi leaders had to be removed from public influence. All the people, but especially young people, were to be reeducated to understand the falsehoods they had been taught, and to accept the guilt for what their nation had done.

Alex didn't disagree with any of that. But outside, he didn't see Nazis. He saw hungry women and children who were trying to survive in the ruins, living in cellars or bomb-damaged apartment houses, or even in sheds and makeshift huts. No one was offering the Nazi salute. No one was saying, "Heil Hitler."

"I don't know how to tell you what your job is right now," the colonel said. He was sitting behind an antique desk—dark cherrywood—in a huge chair that wrapped around him. On the desk was a glass ashtray filled with cigarette butts. One thing Alex had learned already was that cigarettes were now the main medium of exchange in Germany. German Reichmarks, enormously inflated, were almost useless. Seven cigarette butts could be traded for a full cigarette, and a cigarette was worth more than a person could make in two days' work—in the rare case that work could be found. The contents of the colonel's ashtray could feed one of those hungry kids outside for several days.

"Aren't we supposed to track down Nazi leaders?" Alex asked.

"Yes. Apparently. But no one knows exactly who's supposed to do what right now. The soldiers in the field are taking a lot of that sort of thing into their own hands. They occupy a town, ask around, and grab up any Nazis they can find. We've got reports of our soldiers shooting some of the 'big fish' they've been able to land. They figure that if it gets into our hands, we'll let them off, so they carry out their own justice."

Alex nodded. "That doesn't surprise me.'"

"Hey, let them shoot all the Nazis they want, if you ask me. The trouble is, it's all so haphazard. There are guys getting away—big-time party leaders. They're moving into the countryside and taking on new identities. They may be slipping out of the country, too. We have almost no control. This whole continent is on the move."

"I saw all the refugees on the roads."

"What you saw, the direction you came, was a drop in the bucket. There are *millions* of people displaced in Europe right now. I'm not talking two or three million, either. I'm talking maybe fifty or sixty million—something like that." The Colonel had been leaning back, but now he put his elbows on the desk. He was in his forties, apparently a career soldier. All the edges of him seemed hard, but his voice rumbled from his chest, moist and thick, and something told Alex that he was trying to sound a little more staunch than he really was.

"I don't understand," Alex said. "How can that many people be displaced?"

"Well, it's complicated." Colonel Whitefield had stubbed out a cigarette as Alex had first entered the room. But he reached, already, for a pack of Lucky Strikes on his desk. He tapped the pack, and a cigarette slid out. This he bit with his lips and pulled from the pack. Then he reached across his desk and offered the pack to Alex. Alex shook his head and then waited for the colonel to light up. "See, the only thing anyone is talking about right now is all the Jews—and that *is* a mess. Some people think five million Jews were killed, maybe more, and there's maybe a million or two still alive, most of them in concentration camps—a lot of them still dying. But we've also got something like ten or eleven million foreigners in Germany—Russians, Estonians, Latvians, Poles, Czechs, Frenchmen, you name it. DPs, we call them—'displaced persons.' Most of them have been slave laborers for Hitler—building his bombs and airplanes, doing his farming. And some of them have been cooped up in camps themselves—especially the ones that were POWs."

"Are they trying to get back to their own countries now?"

"A lot of 'em are. A lot more will be setting out before long. But it's crazy. Most of the Russians don't want to go back. They're scared to death of Stalin. He's demanding we send them back, and the DPs themselves are claiming he'll kill them."

"Why would he do that?"

"They think he'll see them as traitors—because they worked for Hitler while they were here."

"They didn't have any choice, did they?"

"No. But some fought for Hitler—because they feared Stalin even more. What a choice, huh? The Cossacks did that, and they probably will be killed if we send them back." Colonel Whitefield took a long draw on his cigarette, then leaned his head back and blew the smoke into the air.

"If a lot of refugees leave Germany, won't that ease some of the food problems?" Alex asked.

Colonel Whitefield shook his head, and for the first time Alex thought he heard a hint of compassion. "Thomas, we've got all those people boarding boxcars or heading east on foot. But there are even more coming the other way, *into* Germany."

"Why?"

"Ethnic Germans live all over Europe. The boundaries of these nations have changed a lot over the centuries—especially after the first World War. You've got something like eleven million Germans living in an area that's considered Poland, and

Stalin has Poland now. It's the same in Czechoslovakia, and there are big pockets of Germans in a lot of the countries that Russia has taken over in these last few months of the war. As the Russians came through, a lot of the Germans moved out ahead, and now the people in those countries are demanding that the rest of the Germans leave. Most are on foot, with nothing but the clothes on their backs, and they're dying of malnutrition and disease. Some of them make it to camps that we've started to set up, and then typhus goes through the camps and kills half of them."

He took another draw on his cigarette. As he spoke, the smoke seeped from his nostrils. "We could have more people die in Europe *after* the war than died during it. Something like half a million civilians died from our bombing raids. That could be a drop in the bucket compared to all the Germans who are going to starve to death."

Alex was stunned. "Aren't we going to feed them?"

"We're going to try. But how can you get that much food over here? And how can you treat all the disease? There's no way to keep up with it."

Alex was thinking of all the ragged kids he had seen outside. The one thing he had told himself, as he had traveled across the country, was that soon the Allies would be getting food to them. "Isn't there some way we can—"

"Listen, Thomas, the Germans brought this on themselves. I know the kids didn't choose Hitler for their leader, but their parents did. And now what they're receiving are the wages of war. But it's not our fault. The Germans are just lucky that we're going to do as much as we can. A lot of nations wouldn't."

"Yes, sir. I know that's true."

"You're here because you speak German—and because you lived here before the war. You know Frankfurt, maybe have some contacts. We want you to find out who the Nazi leaders were in this area. These men are criminals, and they can't be allowed to run this country again. That's all you need to worry about. Other men have to decide about feeding the kids. It's not easy to see what's going on in the streets out there, but there's nothing you can do about it. For one thing, you're not allowed to carry food out of here. Do you understand that?"

"Yes."

"All right. Then grow some thick skin. You're going to see some terrible things in the next few months. You can't shed tears about all of it. You've got a job to do."

"Yes, sir." Alex got up. "Could I ask you one question?"

"Certainly."

"How long do you think I'll be here?"

The colonel stood now, too. "I can't say. You have a special assignment, so the point system doesn't apply to you. If it did, you'd be one of the first to go. As it is, you could be here . . . I don't know . . . maybe a year, maybe longer. I just can't say."

Alex took a deep breath, drew in more of the stale tobacco smoke than he wanted. "My wife is going to have a baby—any day now. She's in England."

"Maybe you can get a leave at some point. But you just had your thirty days. I don't see any chance of your getting out of here for quite some time."

"Yes, sir."

"Look, Thomas, I don't want to be here either. My wife keeps writing me, asking when I'm coming home. I have to tell her the same thing I just told you. I have no idea. But a war doesn't end when the shooting stops. You and I got stuck with some of the mop-up work."

Alex nodded. Then he saluted, and he left the room.

Over the next few days Alex saw a lot of Frankfurt, or what was left of it. It was miles of wasteland where the walls of buildings stood like ancient ruins, the windows gone, the interiors burned out. Many of the old church spires were at least partially intact, and the grand old fourteenth-century cathedral had survived fairly well. But that was only a reminder to Alex of what the city had once been.

Alex was traveling about in a jeep. Some of the streets were impassible, but he could usually find a way to get through. The people had no way to start rebuilding homes, but their instinct was to clean things up, bring some order back into their lives. So every day people worked among the ruins, often carrying off the debris in handcarts and wheelbarrows. Everywhere Alex went, children gathered around him. He gave them what he had: crackers from K-ration boxes, hunks of chocolate, little cans of Vienna sausages or Spam. Colonel Whitefield had told him not to leave the headquarters with food, but he sneaked all he could anyway, and no one really tried to stop him.

But he also ran out of food quickly every day, and then he had to say he was sorry. One afternoon he had a meeting scheduled with local police officials, in the city. They were working out of the first floor of a building that was destroyed from that level up. After the meeting, as he walked back to his jeep, a little girl approached him. She was wearing a ragged dress and broken-down shoes, with the soles flapping. Her hair was dirty, but her face was wonderful. She had eyes like robin eggs, and knobby little cheeks. "Cigarettes?" she said in English. "Chocolate?"

"I have nothing," he told her in German. "I'm very sorry."

He saw her surprise that he had spoken German, but he also saw the despair. She hadn't expected anything. This was merely a ritual for the children. They asked every soldier, and once in a while they actually got something.

"Where do you live?" he asked her.

She was only eight or nine, but she was wary. Alex saw the doubt in her eyes. She stepped away from him.

"Do you have a family?"

"My mother and a little brother."

"Where's your father?"

She shrugged, and then she said, "Russia." But Alex knew what that meant—he was probably already dead, or at least he wasn't coming home anytime soon.

"Come with me to the bakery. I'll buy you a loaf of bread you can take to your mother."

The little girl backed farther away, but she didn't say no. "There's a bakery around the corner. I'll walk there. You wait here and I'll bring you the bread. Is that all right?"

She nodded this time. But then, as Alex walked to the corner, she followed, staying at a distance. There were not many shops left operating, but he had stopped at the bakery once before, knew where it was. It was making only bread, but it was staying busy. Some people were finding ways to earn some of the inflated German money, mostly by selling off their possessions, or they were using cigarettes—mostly American soldiers' gifts—as barter.

Alex went inside and bought a large round loaf of black bread. The woman who waited on him also seemed surprised that Alex spoke German. "I'm buying this for the little girl outside," he said. "But I'm afraid she'll never get it home to her mother. I'm worried that someone will take it from her."

"It could happen," the woman said, nodding. "People are desperate."

"I would walk with her to her house, but she's afraid of me."

"Yes. I understand." The woman had once been heavier than she was now, Alex thought. The skin on her cheeks, her arms, seemed loose. Her dress hung slack around her. But she had a kindliness about her, a tranquil voice. "I have a son," she said. "I will send him with her."

"That would be a great help," Alex said. "Give this to him." Alex set an American dime on the glass counter.

"No, no. There are others who need it much more than we do. My son won't mind doing this." She pushed the dime back toward him.

"Thank you," Alex said, and he picked up the coin.

"I would feed everyone if I could," the woman said. "I would give them the bread. But then we would starve. I don't know what to do."

"There will be more food. We're going to help. But it takes time."

"I know this. Some of your soldiers are hateful to us, of course. That's only natural. But most of the young men are good. They remind me of our sons—the way the boys were before all this."

"All they want now is to go home," Alex said.

"Yes, yes. That's clear." The woman stepped to a door at the end of the counter. "Johann," she called. "Please come here." As she waited, she looked at Alex and said, "Tell me, is your family German? How did you learn our language so well?"

Alex glanced to see that the little girl was still waiting. "I was a missionary here in Frankfurt, before the war."

"Missionary?"

"Yes. For the Mormons. Do you know this church?"

"Only by name. And I know a member. Herr Meis."

"You *know* him? Do you know where he is? I've been looking for him."

"He comes here. He buys bread for his family—and for others."

"Do you know how I can find him?"

The woman's son had appeared at the door. "I want you to do something for me," she told him, and then she explained the errand. He seemed less thrilled with the idea than his mother had claimed he would be. All the same, he agreed, and he returned into the apartment behind the store. His mother had told him to be sure to take his coat—and to hide the bread inside it.

When she looked back at Alex, she said, "Herr Meis told me that his building was destroyed. He is now renting a downstairs room from a family, somewhere around here. I know only one thing. He said his church meets in this neighborhood, too—in a *Gasthaus* that was damaged by bombs and is closed to customers. It's called the Black Swan. You will see it if you go around the corner and down the street. It's not far at all."

Alex was overjoyed. Suddenly the aroma of the baking bread was wondrous, what he remembered from his days here before the war. He had tried all week to locate the Church or the Meis family, and he had made no headway. Now, by accident—or maybe not by accident at all—he had found them. When Johann returned, he tucked the loaf of bread under his coat. Alex walked out with him and explained to the little girl what the boy was going to do.

And then he gave Johann the dime after all. The boy suddenly looked much more pleased about his errand. And if that much joy could be created by a dime, Alex dug into his pocket for another one, and he gave it to the little girl. She grasped it tight in her hand and said *"Danke,"* nothing more. But Alex saw the life that had come into her pretty eyes. She had a loaf of bread—and money to buy more. For a few days, life was going to be better.

On Sunday, at seven-thirty in the morning, Alex was waiting at the Black Swan. But no one came, the old schedule apparently changed. It was a few minutes before nine when Alex finally saw a stout little man striding down the street, limping a bit. Alex turned toward him, and then he waited. He was curious to see when President Meis would recognize him.

But President Meis kept coming, even nodded to Alex and said *"Guten Morgen"* before he suddenly stopped. As he did, his arms jerked up and out, automatically, and he whispered, "Oh, is it true?"

"Good morning, President Meis," Alex said, and he laughed.

"Brother Thomas, I can't believe this." He stepped forward and grabbed Alex, tossed his arms around him. He pounded on Alex's back as he said, "This is too wonderful. Too wonderful."

"I'm so happy to see you," Alex told him. "I wondered whether you would be all right."

President Meis stepped back. "I got pulled into the war at the end," he said. "Everyone did. I was on the western front. But

I was more fortunate than most. I was shot through the leg, and they sent me home."

"We have something in common. I was shot in the leg too. But in my case, they fixed me up and sent me back."

"Yes. This would have happened to me also. But the war ended in time."

They stood looking at each other. There were so many memories jumping back into Alex's mind, but also a strange realization. "Where were you when you were shot?"

"In the Ardennes offensive. I was hit by a machine gun."

Alex nodded. He stood silent for a time. "I was there, too. In Bastogne."

The irony didn't need to be stated. They looked into each other's eyes and accepted it. "Now it's over," President Meis said. "In time, things will be better."

"I told you once that I would never be your enemy."

"And you weren't. You're not."

Alex wanted to believe that. It was so good to hear his old friend say it. Tears spilled onto his cheeks. President Meis took hold of him again, this time by his shoulders. "It's we here in Germany who have much to be ashamed of. Not you. By the time I was forced to enter the army, it was the last thing in the world I wanted to do. But I had no choice."

"If those who wanted to fight had done the fighting, maybe the war could have been held in a boxing ring," Alex said. He tried to laugh.

"Or at least a football field," President Meis said. He reached into his pocket then, and he found a large key, which he used to open the door of the *Gasthaus*. Then he motioned for Alex to step inside. "I have no presidency, only myself," he said. "But I still come here before services, and I try to think what I need to do. And I pray. It makes me feel better prepared. I give the sermon almost every week in sacrament meeting, but for now, I don't mind that."

"Why don't you have a presidency?"

"We haven't been able to reorganize. For a long time, we didn't even try to meet. The Miller family was bombed out. They moved away from Frankfurt. The Stoltz family left the area early in the war, and—"

"President Meis, I just realized—you don't know. I'm married to Anna."

"Anna Stoltz?" President Meis had pulled a chair away from a table and had been ready to sit down, but he stopped halfway. He was clearly astounded. "How can this be?"

"The Stoltz's got out of Germany. They made it to London. It was during the time I was in a hospital in England."

"I knew they were trying to leave, and I was afraid for them. Are they all right?"

"Peter didn't make it out, and we don't know where he is. You haven't heard from him, have you?"

"No."

Alex told the story, as briefly as he could, and admitted to President Meis that Brother Stoltz was also probably in Germany somewhere. But again, President Meis hadn't heard from him.

"You have to understand," he said. "It would be very difficult to find me. Toward the end of the war, all the registering of moves ended. Everything was in chaos. Our district president was pulled into the war too. He was on the eastern front, and his wife has heard nothing from him for a long time. He could be dead. There's no mail right now, either."

"Then you don't know about President Grant?"

"No. What?"

"He died two weeks ago. I just found out myself."

"Who is president of the Church, then?"

"George Albert Smith. He's a good man. I've known him all my life."

President Meis finally sat down, and he motioned for Alex to do the same. "You're *married* to Anna—beautiful Anna. I knew she had feelings for you, but I never imagined anything like this could happen."

"We're going to have a baby, President. In less than a month. But I won't be there."

"Oh, my goodness. That is difficult. All the same, it's good for us to have you here. We need your help. How long will you stay?"

"I don't know. Maybe a year or more—unless I'm transferred to another part of Germany."

"Could you speak to our members today? It would mean so much to them."

Alex was taken by surprise. He looked away. "President Meis, I don't feel worthy to do that. I need to *hear* good sermons, but I don't feel ready to give any right now."

"What's happened? What do you mean?"

"I don't know exactly." He stuck his hands into his pants pockets and looked down. "I can't really say that I feel the Spirit, President Meis. I feel as though I have to be rebuilt on the inside—like all these buildings."

"We all feel that now. But we have to heal each other. No one can do it alone."

Alex knew that was right, but he also knew what he felt about himself. "I feel all alone right now. I pray, but I get no answers."

President Meis took a long look at Alex. He seemed so very much older now. He had been a strong man, always intense, but now he was thinner, more subdued, and the lines around his eyes had folded into deep creases. He had lost a tooth in the front. "Brother Thomas, listen to me," he said. "We need you. Some of what you say sounds like self-pity, and there's no time for that. We have to put things behind us and get the Church going again."

Alex nodded. He thought for a time, and then he added, "Maybe I *could* speak to the branch for a few minutes. Maybe it's what I need to do."

"That's good. I can't tell you how much it will mean to our members."

There was still some time before the people would start to arrive. Alex and President Meis had time to discuss the members of the branch, and Alex ached as he heard all the sad stories. Every family had suffered, and so many had lost sons or fathers—or both. Alex also had time to ask whether President Meis knew anything about Agent Kellerman now. "He disappeared," President Meis said. "I used to see him about, and I hoped the day would come when some justice could be served. But I've been back here since January, and I have never seen him once. He's certainly a marked man—with that wicked scar across his face. Wherever he goes, he can be identified."

"He's one man who ought to be punished," Alex said.

When the members of the branch began to arrive, Alex found that he didn't know them all. Some were refugees from eastern Germany—people who had fled the Russian invasion. A few were new converts, taught and baptized by the members, without help of the missionaries. But Alex did know many of the people he saw, and not one of them spoke to him without breaking down in tears. He hugged them all, talked with them, heard more of their stories.

The branch was not holding Sunday School yet, and they held their sacrament meeting in the morning. When President Meis stood, after he and another brother had blessed and passed the sacrament, he said, "You have all seen our beloved Brother Thomas—one of the great missionaries who served here with us before the war. He is a good man. He wears an American soldier's uniform, and that may seem a little strange to the young people here. But the uniform matters nothing to us. He is our brother. He was our brother before the war, and is again after, but he was also our brother during the war. I know he never stopped loving us, and we never stopped loving him."

When Alex stood, he felt the rightness of his being there, and something awakened inside. It was not a powerful manifestation but a simple reassurance that he was doing what he ought to be doing. He told the members that food and clothes and blankets would come in time. The army was working on that, but he also knew that the Church would provide help as soon as it could get permission from the government. "During a war, there is always much hatred expressed," he said, "but I have heard our members pray for our brothers and sisters in Germany many times during this war. I heard it in America and England and even in France. I'm not saying that the war has created no bitterness between our countries, but it has never split us apart as people who seek to follow Christ."

Alex looked around the room. The light was natural, coming only from the windows. There was no electrical power to the building. But the people sat in the dim light, gathered around the big wooden tables, as though ready to share a meal. No one was dressed well, and some may have even been embarrassed by their tattered clothes. But everyone was sparkling clean, and even the children seemed intent to hear every word that Alex had to say. He knew he symbolized an end to them, and a beginning, and they were desperate to believe that better days lay ahead.

"I'm certain that no one here got through this war without wondering at times whether God had given up on us. But we created the war, not God, and now I know that he is waiting to welcome us back to him. I have seen horrifying things in these last two years. You have seen far more, and I know you are suffering now. But God is waiting for us to return to him. We must give him back our hearts."

When Alex sat down, he tried to let his words sink in to his own mind, his own spirit. He needed to go home, needed to be with Anna, needed to see something other than suffering all day. It was so hard to find God in these ruins. Still, he had felt a wonderful comfort with these good friends, a sense that he did belong here right now. And that was something. There had been times in Belgium and France, and later in Germany with

Otto, when he had felt utter despair that he would ever be himself again, but today he felt, not for the first time, but stronger than before, that it might eventually happen.

* * *

Anna was lying back in her hospital bed, resting now—tired, but very pleased. She had a son. Alex had a son. She had seen the baby only briefly when he was still all wet and angry, and then the nurse had taken him away to clean him up. She was waiting now, wanting to see him again, have a chance to hold him.

"He was pretty, wasn't he, Mother?" she asked, in German.

Sister Stoltz took hold of Anna's hand. "They only gave me a little glimpse at him," she said, "but to me he was beautiful. His eyes were wide open, and big like yours were when you were born. And I have to tell you, that doesn't seem so long ago to me."

"Mama, I wish so much that Alex were here."

"I know. And I keep wishing Heinrich were here. But *Liebling*, we know they're both alive and well. And we know they will be coming back to us. We have to be thankful for that."

"I am, Mama. I am." But all Anna could think was that she needed Alex right now. This was such a strange time, so frightening. Her mother could help her with the baby, but she wanted Alex with her to share this time. She wanted him to know what she had experienced, to understand what it all meant. That was something he had missed, forever—just one more thing that they should have shared and couldn't.

In a few minutes the nurse came in. She was carrying the baby in a little white blanket, wrapped up tight. She came to Anna and placed the bundle in her arms. For the first time, Anna saw the baby's little face, at peace, quiet. His eyes were shut, and his face was still puffy and red, but she could see how lovely he was. She could see Alex in his chin, his jaw, even in his almost formless little nose.

"He looks so much like you," Sister Stoltz said. "I thought there never was a prettier baby than you were. But this one might be."

"He looks like Alex, I think," Anna said, but suddenly Alex's absence struck her full force. His war *should* be over. This wasn't fair. She pulled the baby to her chest, gripped him tight.

"You might want to check him over," the nurse said. "You know, just make sure he's got all his fingers and toes, all the proper plumbing. We wouldn't want to short change you in any way."

Anna did want to see her little son, and so she set him on her lap, folded back the blanket, and inspected him closely. His little body was so wondrously perfect, every little fingernail a charm to her. But all the movement awakened him, and his eyes came open wide again. "Oh, yes, those are your eyes," Sister Stoltz said.

And Anna did see some of herself in the roundness of his eyes. And it was that as much as anything that brought her to tears. There they were, both of them, she and Alex, brought together in this little person. She wanted him to be a wonderful child, a noble boy, a good man. She wanted to give him all the love he needed, all the guidance. But she wanted Alex. The three of them needed to be together.

LaRue Thomas slept in late on the Fourth of July. She had been dancing at the Avalon with Reed the night before, and she had gotten home rather late. She was thinking of getting up, had been for half an hour, when her mother came to the door. "LaRue," she said, "you need to start getting ready."

"For what?"

"Our picnic. Remember?"

LaRue *hadn't* remembered—until now. She had promised Reed that she would go swimming with him and his friends—the same group that had been together the night before. The whole gang was going to drive down to Saratoga Springs by Utah Lake.

"Your dad would like to leave before it gets too hot, so why don't you get up and get ready."

LaRue didn't answer. She waited until she heard her mother's footsteps on the stairs before she sat up and dropped her legs over the side of the bed, but she wasn't sure what she was going to do. She didn't want to argue with Dad this morning, but on the other hand she knew she would rather go swimming with her friends than go on this picnic he had thought up. She also knew that she'd better take her stand right away. She grabbed her seersucker robe, tossed it on, and then walked downstairs. She peeked into the kitchen, where Mom was frying chicken for the picnic and creating a wonderful smell. Dad was not there. He had probably eaten his breakfast hours before, and since he wasn't reading his paper by the radio, he had to be in his office—where he spent most of his time when he was home.

LaRue decided to take the breezy, friendly approach and hope she could pull off a quick escape. She gave the door a little knock, waited for her dad to say, "Yes?," and then opened the door a crack. "Dad," she said, "I promised Reed I'd go with him and the gang today. But you have fun. Just leave me a little fried chicken."

She quickly pulled the door shut, but she heard the pronouncement. "No, LaRue."

She stood by the door a few seconds, but her decision was instant. She wasn't going to let him win this one. If he hadn't spoken quite so harshly—and authoritatively—she might have decided it was one of those times when she needed to back down, but his tone of voice fired something resolute, stubborn, inside her. She reached back and opened the door again, and by then he was coming around his desk. "Dad, I'm sorry. I made other plans."

"Unmake them. I talked about this all week, and you never once said anything about having other plans. I want this to be a family day." But the words were hardly out before he seemed to think better of the approach he was taking. He softened his voice and added, "LaRue, we need to get together—just the four of us. We don't do that often enough."

But it was that conciliatory voice that maddened LaRue the most. It was his attempt to cover his real reaction, which had come first. "Dad, I don't see why it makes any difference whether I'm there or not."

President Thomas stepped forward, through his office door, close to LaRue, and he whispered, "Beverly won't have any fun with just us. You need to go, LaRue. It's one of those times when you need to put the family first."

But he couldn't have chosen words that would anger LaRue more. "Oh sure, Dad. You mean, the way *you* always do?"

She saw him take that blow like a boxer. He flinched a little, but he didn't back off. "Listen, LaRue," he said, "I've told you many times that I'm sorry how busy my life is. You know I regret being gone so much. If I could—"

"Look, let's not do this. It doesn't matter. I really don't care."

"If you don't care, why do you always bring it up?" *His* anger was building, too.

LaRue was struck by the question. It took her a moment to realize her answer, but when she did, her rage began to seep away. "I used to care, Dad. I don't anymore. I won't bring it up again."

"Well, I care. I worry about it all the time." But he seemed thrown off-guard by LaRue's change of tone. His eyes disengaged from hers.

"Do you *want* to spend the day with us, Dad?" LaRue asked. "Or do you just think you ought to?" But there was no challenge in her voice now. It really was a question.

"How can you ask me that?" He still wasn't looking at her.

"Why don't we just be honest with each other," LaRue said. "You don't want to spend the day with me, and I don't want to spend it with you."

"That's simply not true. Not in my case."

"Oh, come on, Dad. You don't like me and you know it. You haven't liked me for a long time."

Something like panic was in her father's eyes now, and LaRue actually felt sorry for him. But she didn't want to talk anymore. She turned to leave. "Wait a minute," he said.

She looked back at him.

"Listen, honey, I know we've had our troubles over the years, but we've done better lately. Haven't we? I've been very proud of you, the way your grades have been coming up—and the maturity you've been showing. I don't tell you that enough, I know, but it is how I feel."

LaRue was suddenly furious again. "That's good to know, Dad. You do love me after all—as long as I get good grades."

"I didn't say that."

"Didn't you?"

"No. Of course not."

"Well, that's what I heard. So I might as well explain *why* I've been working harder in school lately. My only goal is to win a scholarship and go away to college."

"What?" He was obviously taken by surprise.

"I want to go somewhere else to college, and I know you won't pay for it. So I'm going to do it on my own. What I want is to get away from Salt Lake. But mostly I want to get away from you. That's the whole truth of it. So what do you say? Do you still want to take me on a picnic?"

"LaRue, just calm down. You lose your temper, and then you say things you don't really mean. What we need to do is sit down and talk about all this. Maybe you *could* go away to college. Maybe that would be a good thing. But that's two years away."

Suddenly LaRue had lost the high ground in the argument, and she couldn't think what to say. But she didn't trust any of this. Her dad still hadn't heard her. "Dad, how could we change anything by *talking*? I *know* when someone doesn't like me. It's not that hard to tell." She was starting to cry, and she didn't want to do that.

"Honey, I have no idea why you'd think such a thing. I know I—"

"Don't! Just don't!" She spun away and ran from the room. What she had heard in his voice was his own lack of conviction.

LaRue dressed quickly and then hurried back downstairs. As she reached the front door, she heard her mother say, "LaRue, come back here. Where are you going?"

But LaRue stepped out and shut the door behind her. She wanted to talk to Cecil. She jumped off the porch and ran all the way to the corner. After that, she walked the two blocks to Cecil's home quickly, stood on his porch, still out of breath, and knocked on the door. Sister Broadbent soon appeared. She was always a little more formal than LaRue thought she needed to be. "Hello, LaRue," she said. "May I help you?"

"Is Cecil here?"

"Yes. Just a moment. Please come in and sit down." But something in her voice also seemed to say, "I'm surprised that you—a girl—would come calling on my son."

"No. That's all right. I'll just wait out here."

That idea obviously didn't please Sister Broadbent either. "Well, then, have a seat out there, and I'll ask him to come down."

LaRue sat in one of the wicker chairs on the front porch. The Broadbents lived in a two-story frame house, much like the Thomases', with a similar front porch. Sister Broadbent kept the yard in beautiful order, with pansies and marigolds planted in neat little beds, and irises and four-o'clocks along the side of the house. Out back, Brother Broadbent had an extensive orchard of cherries and apricots, pears and apples. He was known for the quality of his fruit, and even for his own bottling, but he was also a professor at the University of Utah, some sort of scientist. He was a quiet man who came to church every Sunday but rarely said a word and never held a calling that LaRue was aware of.

When Cecil pushed the screen door open a few minutes later, he was already smiling. "Good morning," he said. He didn't voice his question, but it was in his face: *What are you doing here?*

What LaRue liked about Cecil was that he didn't confuse their relationship. He knew he was her friend, not her boyfriend. When they had first started taking walks together, he may have wanted something more than that to develop, but he had obviously accepted things the way they were, and maybe he had even come to prefer the arrangement. Neither one of them felt a need to impress the other.

"I just had a fight with my dad," LaRue said. "I had to get out of my house. I'm going to take a walk for a while; I just thought you might want to go with me."

"Sure."

"Is your family doing anything for the Fourth?"

Cecil laughed. "Not that I know of."

"What's so funny?"

"I don't know. My family is sort of strange now. I'm the tail-end kid, and I pretty much keep to myself. I think my parents like the idea that they don't have to do family things anymore."

LaRue laughed. "That sounds wonderful to me. So what are you going to do all day?"

"I don't know. Dad's probably reading, or he's out in the orchard. And Mother is puttering around. She was out weeding her flowers at some unthinkable hour this morning. I had my window open, and I could hear her humming hymns— 'Today, While the Sun Shines'—before the sun had hardly come up. I had to put a pillow over my head."

"My dad wanted to take us on a picnic, but I'm not going."

"Just a second." Cecil walked back into the house. LaRue didn't hear the conversation he had with his mother, but she did hear the end of it, when Cecil said, "Not long. I don't know." And then he stepped out through the screen door again. "Come on. Let's go," he said. "You walk and I'll follow."

But their walks had become a kind of ritual. They almost always walked up the hill past the prison, and then either into the foothills or down into Parley's Ravine. She thought she would take him into the ravine today, where it would be cooler.

"What was the fight about?" Cecil wanted to know as soon as they set out.

But LaRue didn't tell too much of the story. She described the conflict over the picnic, but she couldn't bring herself to tell the rest. It had all been a little too emotional, and she didn't want Cecil to make fun of that.

Down in the ravine, the two sat on rocks along the creek, and they watched the water run. There was not much volume now. It was a quiet little stream, and LaRue liked the peace. The morning was beginning to heat up, but in the shade of some big cottonwoods, the temperature wasn't bad.

Cecil sat and tossed little pebbles into the water and didn't say much for a time. LaRue was going back over the conversation with her father. Usually, after one of their outbursts, she thought about all the things she wished she had said, how she might have made a better argument, but what she felt now was that there was no going back, nothing more for them to argue about—she had split them apart forever.

"LaRue," Cecil finally said, "I don't understand you sometimes. You don't care that much about being with Reed. Why didn't you just go with your family? What did you have to gain by making a big fuss?"

"I don't like to be forced. Dad always thinks he can boss me around."

Cecil laughed. "The more you buck him, the more he feels he has to keep you in line. Me, I don't fight my parents, and they mostly just forget about me. Then I pretty much do what I want."

"Do your parents like you?"

"Like me?"

"Yes."

"I don't know. I can't imagine that they would." He laughed again. "No one else has ever found me particularly charming."

"Cecil, that's the way you talk. But if you really thought your parents didn't like you, you wouldn't laugh about it."

"So what are you saying? Do you think your dad doesn't like you?"

"I know he doesn't."

"No. You don't know that."

Cecil was sitting on a rock that was higher up the bank. LaRue had to twist around to look at him. "Don't you think I can feel something like that?"

"I don't know. I doubt it's that simple."

"What's that supposed to mean?"

Cecil shrugged. He picked up another little rock and flipped it with his thumb, as though he were shooting a marble. LaRue heard the pebble plop into the water. "He's your dad. He thinks he has to teach you things, guide you in the right direction—all that kind of stuff. It's not a matter of him liking you or not. Probably no dad exactly *likes* his own fifteen-year-old kid."

"Oh, and *I'm* being too simple?" She turned around and looked at the creek.

"Hey, all I mean is, parents think they have to control their kids. And kids get to an age where they don't want to be controlled. So then the fight is on. It's like that in most families."

"Thanks, Uncle Cecil. You're so old and wise. You're *seventeen*."

"Well, no—I'm not old and wise. But you're acting like you're about ten." He changed his voice to a mocking falsetto. "'I'm so sad. My daddy doesn't like me.'"

"Shut up."

Cecil was laughing again, and LaRue didn't like that at all. But she knew she would only prove his point if she lost her temper, so she said, coolly, "You may call me a kid, but at least I'm standing up to my dad. Bobbi waited until she was a lot older before she finally did that. Now he knows that I'm planning to leave when I get out of high school. He even told me that he might be okay with that." She bent and picked up a little handful of gravel, and she tossed one of the little stones into the pool, near her feet. It hit the water and set off a series of little circular ripples.

"Well, then, it sounds like you did just fine. You got what you wanted."

"Shut up."

"Now what did I say?"

"You don't really think that. You're being sarcastic."

She waited for his laughter, but it didn't come. In fact, he didn't say anything for a long time. And when he did, he sounded serious. "LaRue, tell yourself the truth. You want your dad to love you. You don't have to act tough around me."

"Maybe I am tough," she said. But suddenly she threw the rest of the rocks, a dozen or so, and they splattered across the surface of the water, like rain. "What my dad wants is for me to fit some picture he has in his head. If I can do that, then I *qualify* for his love." She looked around at Cecil again. "But I don't need that kind of love. I don't want it."

Cecil was merciful at that point. He didn't say anything. And when she started to cry, he didn't comment, didn't even let on that he knew that's what she was doing. She stared at the water and fought the tears, mad at herself that she was giving in that way.

"Look, LaRue," Cecil finally said, "maybe your dad bosses you, but at least he takes some interest. If I'm gone all day, my dad won't even notice."

"That's how you want it, isn't it?"

"Yup. That's how I want it."

She twisted to look at him. "Are you happy, Cecil?"

"I don't know. I never ask myself that question. I don't think I'm unhappy."

"You don't sound happy."

"Yeah, I think I do. Most of the time. At least I don't spend all my time trying to be someone I'm not."

"You mean, the way I do?"

"Yeah."

LaRue looked away from him, looked up toward the mountains. She tried to think about that. The strange thing was, she actually was happier when she was playing the role she had created for herself. It was like walking onto a stage, escaping reality. Cecil made her think too much. And her dad made her question herself, her behavior—made her think about herself in ways that she hated.

"You say your dad doesn't like you, LaRue. But I know what you've told me at least a dozen times: You don't like yourself."

That wasn't the first time that thought had crossed LaRue's mind today. Maybe she just wanted to blame her father for her own problems. She was trying to think about that when a rock hit the water—a boulder. Water splashed everywhere, spraying LaRue. She cringed, automatically, but sort of liked the surprise, the change of mood. She looked around to see Cecil grinning at her. "What did you do that for?" she asked.

"I don't know. It seemed like a pretty good idea at the time. I don't go in much for slobbering and moaning."

"Let me just say, one more time—*shut up!*"

"No thanks. I've got one more piece of advice for you."

"Good. I promise not to listen."

"Understood. But I'm still right. What you should do right now is go home. Then you should say, 'Let's go on that picnic. I'm sorry I got the day off to a bad start.' Don't make this into a fight when it doesn't even have to happen."

"You sound like those 'young, red-blooded Americans' they talk about on the Ovaltine ads."

"I'm right, and you know it." He sat down on his rock again.

"No, you're not. You don't solve problems. You avoid them. And you're not happy. I know you're not. So don't try to tell me how to deal with my problems."

Cecil was still trying to smile, but he wasn't doing very well. He leaned over and put his elbows on his knees. "LaRue, if I say I want to go away to college, my dad will say, 'That's fine. Drop us a line sometime.' And he won't miss me for one second. I think maybe I'd rather have your situation than mine."

"Cecil, you're exaggerating. Your dad's just quiet. He doesn't tell you how he feels. But he'll miss you."

"No. You don't know him, LaRue. I've never been close to him. We never talk about anything of any importance."

"Maybe that's just as much your fault as it his."

"Oh, it is. I know that. I'm not close to anyone. These little walks we take—they're the best thing I've got going in my life. The very best." He nodded, forced a grin. "That's pretty pathetic, don't you think?"

LaRue knew what Cecil was saying. She felt the breath leave her chest. She didn't want to hurt Cecil, too. He had always been so in control, so rational about everything. She hadn't expected him to be as susceptible to her as other boys.

"Well, anyway, you should go home," Cecil said.

"I can't."

"Why not?"

"Because Reed has started calling by now. If I go back, I either have to face my dad and tell him I'm going with Reed, or I have to face Reed and tell him I'm going on a picnic with my family."

"You're probably right. The best thing to do, in a situation like that, is to hide out in Parley's Ravine. With me." He laughed, but the sadness was still in his eyes.

"Let's walk some more," she said.

He nodded and then stood up.

"Cecil, maybe *you* ought to be my boyfriend. Is there any chance at all that you're going to stop wearing such awful clothes?"

"What's wrong with these?" He looked down at himself and really did seem to take the question seriously. He had on a worn-out pair of corduroys and a cotton shirt that looked like it had been in the family since pioneer days.

"I guess that answers my question," LaRue said, and the worst thing was, she knew that clothes really did matter that much to her.

LaRue was gone for two more hours, and by the time she finally returned home, there was no question that the picnic had been canceled. The car was still out back, and the midday heat was on. She thought about going to her dad, opening up to him. Maybe a talk would make a difference—especially now that she had thought things through a little more. But she had said too much that morning. She didn't know what she was ready to take back. Or whether, if she started talking, she wouldn't get angry all over again.

LaRue stepped quietly through the screen door, and then she walked quickly upstairs to her own room. Not two minutes had passed before she heard her mother's quiet little rap. "Come in," LaRue said, but she walked to the window and looked into the thick growth of the apple tree outside her window.

"LaRue, Reed has called three times."

"I'm sure he has."

"Well, you'd better call him. He stayed home from the swimming party in hopes he would catch up with you. Our picnic is off, so you might as well do something with him."

LaRue could almost always guess her mother's motivations. It was like her to entice LaRue back out of the house so there would be no more Fourth of July fireworks at home.

"I don't want to go with him, Mom."

"Now? Or ever?"

"I don't know. But at least not now."

"That isn't fair of you, LaRue. He—"

"I know, Mom. You don't need to tell me."

There was a long silence. LaRue waited and hoped that her mother would disappear, but she could hear Mom's breath, coming in measured pulls, as though she were trying to control her anger. "LaRue," she finally said, "some of what you said this morning was true. If you had talked to your dad the right way, you might have accomplished something. But what you've done all day is treat people badly. You let your tongue get away from you, and I know that you hurt your father. And then you left all of us hanging, not knowing what to plan. You ruined

Beverly's day entirely. I don't know whether you care about any of that, but you should."

Actually, LaRue did care, but she didn't know how to make that claim, so she said nothing. But she made a decision. She would break up with Reed. She needed to let loose and allow him to go with someone who would treat him right.

"LaRue, your dad has changed a great deal in the last couple of years. And he's worked at it. You give him no credit at all for that."

LaRue thought that was probably true, too; she wasn't sure. But she didn't want to argue, so she said, "Mom, I don't know what to tell you. I'm sorry—again. I wish I didn't cause so many problems."

It was her father who spoke. "I'm sorry, too."

LaRue turned around. Her dad was standing in the doorway. She couldn't think what to say, but finally she looked down at the floor and told him, "I don't know why we have to go through this over and over."

"I don't either."

"I just wish you didn't feel that you have to change me all the time."

"Is that what makes you think I don't love you?"

"I guess so."

"Well . . . that's interesting. I've been thinking the same thing all morning. 'Am I such a terrible father that she feels she has to correct me all the time?'"

"Maybe that's what we both need to stop doing."

"I suppose, LaRue. There are some things that just can't be changed, and we don't need to harp on each other about those. But I am your dad. I don't know how to forget about that. I don't think I should."

"Dad, I'm going to make some decisions for myself. I don't mind living by your rules. I've stopped fighting you on that. But when I graduate from high school, I'm going to decide what I want to do with my life."

"Wouldn't you appreciate some advice from me and your mother?"

"I don't know. Maybe. But you usually give a lot more than advice."

"I know. But that's something you'll understand better when you have your own kids."

That was fair enough. LaRue could admit that was probably true. She nodded and said, "I guess."

"I do love you, LaRue."

But she didn't feel that. She wondered whether she ever would. And she couldn't say the same to him, even though she knew how much he wanted to hear it.

25

Alex Thomas was on his way to Karlsruhe. Since returning to
Germany, he had spent most of his time in Frankfurt. His work
was tedious and, to Alex, almost pointless. He interviewed
local citizens, tried to learn the names of prominent Nazis in
the area, and then tried to locate them. But everything was
made complicated by the state of the destruction. Communi-
cation was still disrupted. Most information had to be passed
along through military channels because civilian telephone and
mail systems were still almost nonexistent. What he did have
was more freedom than most military people. He could move
rather freely around the American zone, and he had a jeep at
his disposal. Fortunately, Karlsruhe was in the American sector.
The only problem was, he hadn't found a good excuse, until
now, to justify a trip there.

It was a warm afternoon in July when Alex had finally gotten out of a meeting he had scheduled with the Karlsruhe
police captain, and now he had a little time to seek out his
father-in-law. He had letters from Anna, and he had important
news that he wanted to carry in person.

Alex had struggled a little to find the bakery where Brother
Stoltz worked. The streets were difficult to identify, and some
were still blocked by rubble and craters. Eventually, however,

he found the place. The bakery had taken some damage in the last weeks of the war, and the front window was boarded up, but the business was now back in operation. Alex was excited, even a little nervous, when he stepped inside. Anna had told him, in her letters, the name Brother Stoltz was using, so when he saw a tall, strongly built woman at the counter, he asked, "Does Herr Stutz work here?"

"*Ja*," the woman said. "But he's resting now. He gets up every morning at four." It was just after three in the afternoon.

"But is he here?"

The woman seemed wary, almost frightened. Alex knew that was partly because of the uniform he was wearing, and probably the fear Germans had learned, over time, of anyone in authority. He smiled at her. "I'm his friend," he told her. He wasn't sure how much more he should say. "If you'll wake him, I promise you, he'll be pleased."

She seemed to respond to Alex's smile, but she hesitated before she said, "All right then. May I tell him your name?"

"Alex Thomas."

She nodded, and then she walked to the end of the counter, opened a door, and stepped into another room. She soon returned, smiling. "He wants to see you," she said, but by then Brother Stoltz was already behind her. He was wearing his white baker's clothing, and he looked rumpled and tired, but he also looked amazed. "Alex," he said. "I can't believe this." He hurried around the counter and grabbed Alex in his arms. "Oh, my goodness. This is too much!"

But he was also quick to say, "Come outside with me. I must talk to you." And outside, he told Alex, "I don't want to explain everything to my friends in the bakery—not yet. They don't know who I really am."

"I understand."

"Alex, it's wonderful to see you. You made it. You survived the war. There were so many times when I feared that you never would." He held Alex by the shoulders. "What about

Anna? And the baby? I've gotten word out to them, through
the OSS, but I've had no letters. Nothing is coming through
yet."

"I have a letter from Anna."

"Has the baby come?"

Alex smiled. "Read the letter," he said.

"All right. But come with me." Brother Stoltz walked down
the street. At the corner was a little square, with a fountain that
had survived the bombs, and some benches. The two sat down,
and Brother Stoltz opened the letter. Then he put his glasses
on. Alex sat next to him, and he too read the letter, though he
had read it many times before:

Dear Alex,

*You have a son. He was born last night, June 26th, at 9:06 P.M. He
weighed eight pounds, two ounces, and he is twenty-one inches long. He is
beautiful, Alex, with not too much hair but big eyes. Mother says he looks
like me when I was a baby, but I see only you. He has your chin and the
shape of your face, and he is very strong. He takes hold of my finger and
squeezes hard. When I held him in my arms the first time, I cried and cried. I
was happy to see him, but I felt so bad that you cannot be here then.*

*But I will not complain. I asked the Lord so many times to keep you
alive, and he did. I can live without you for a little longer. Many women
have had their babies alone, and I was not that unlucky. My mother was
here, and your heart was here. That will be enough for now, and once I have
you back with me, I will keep you forever.*

*Is there any way you could tell my father about our baby? You told me
when you were here that you would try to visit him. I can't get letters to him
right now, and it would be so wonderful if you could see him. You could tell
me if he is all right, and carry this news to him. If you do see him, tell him
how much we love him and miss him.*

*Alex, there is something I think we should do. We should name our little
son Gene. This would mean so much to your family, and I think, to you. Is
there any chance that you could come back to us, even for a short time, to
bless your son and give him this name? I think I know the answer, but please
try.*

I nursed the baby a few minutes ago, Alex, and he's a good eater. When he was full, he was like a lump—like a little fat man after a big dinner. He fell asleep, still against my chest, and I cried so hard I was afraid I would wake him. I couldn't believe I would ever know this much joy. He is you, Alex. He is you and I. And before long we can start a life together. I know that hard things happen in life, but we have faced the worst, and we have made it through. Now we must only be strong through the last of this, and then all will be well. I know it. Think of me every minute, Alex, and think of our wonderful little boy. I never stop thinking of you.

Love, Anna

Brother Stoltz was crying, and so was Alex. They sat next to each other for a long time. Brother Stoltz read the letter a second time before he finally said, "This is right, I think, to name the baby after your brother."

"It's what I wanted. But I hadn't told Anna. I didn't know whether she would feel the same."

"Anna is wise for her age. She'll be a good mother."

"Since I got the letter, all I think of is my little son. I want so much to see him."

"Yes, of course."

"I wonder all the time now, what kind of world we're going to give him. I don't want him to go to war. I don't want him to see anything like this." Alex gestured at the destruction around them.

Brother Stoltz looked across the little square toward the fountain—from which no water was flowing now. "This is all so terrible, Alex," he said. "I should have spoken up. I should have denounced Hitler. All of us who saw what kind of man he was—we should have done it. We were cowards, and now look what it's all come to."

"You couldn't speak out against him. You would have been shot."

"I *should* have been shot. If more of us had been shot back then, maybe the people would have seen what was happening, and more would have joined us—and all these *millions* wouldn't have died."

"But there was no knowing that then."

"We *should* have known. We can see the future now. We have barely begun to pay the price for what Hitler did."

That reality had certainly set in with the German people. Some still hated the Allies, the pilots who had bombed their country, and especially the Russians for their brutality, and most of the people still said, "There was nothing *I* could do." But privately a number of Germans had told Alex, "I don't know how we allowed this to happen." There were those who still refused to believe what they were hearing about the death camps, about the murder of millions of Jews, but Alex was well aware that many had known what was happening in the camps and hadn't dared to speak out. That would be Germany's shame forever.

"I can't tell you how relieved Anna and your wife were to find out that you were all right," Alex said. "Let's concentrate on that now—think about the future."

"Yes. It's what I'm trying to do."

"You did so much more than most."

"I did more harm than good, Alex. That's what I will always have to remember."

"You tried. You put your life in danger. You didn't have to come back here, once you had escaped and were safe."

"It *is* true that I have been in serious danger—many times. I'm lucky I survived. I'll tell you that, but I won't ever tell Anna and Frieda what I've seen, what I've done." What he gave Alex was an account of the mistakes he had made in Berlin, how he had lost his cover, how he had found his way to Karlsruhe, and about his work with the resistance.

"What are you going to do now?" Alex asked him.

Heinrich shook his head. He looked considerably older to Alex, aged perhaps by what he had gone through in the past few months, and thinner—even weak compared to what he had once been. He had lost much of the bulk in his shoulders and chest. The lines around his eyes had deepened, too. "I don't know what to do. I refuse to go back to England without Peter, but it's almost impossible to look for him right now. I went to one of the prison camps—manned by the French. There were thousands of German boys there, and I asked whether I could see a list of their names. The guards told me no. I tried to explain who I was, what I've been doing, but they wouldn't listen. To them, I was merely one more German. They threatened to throw me in the prison with the others."

"I can do some looking," Alex said. "I'll get better cooperation. But if he was in the east, the Russians may have him. They're much harder to work with."

"Most of the soldiers in the camp I went to had come from the eastern front. They had fled to the west so they wouldn't be taken by the Russians. Peter might have done that too."

"There's no telling. He could also be somewhere in Russia or Poland or eastern Germany."

"I know that. And I know the Russians are shipping their prisoners back to their own country." He didn't have to explain the danger in that possibility. Stories had spread across Germany about the inhuman treatment POWs were receiving at the hands of the Russians.

Alex tried to think what he could do. He knew even better than Brother Stoltz that a search like this was almost hopeless, at least for the present. The Red Cross was trying to compile names of displaced persons, Jews, and prisoners of war, but the lists were months away from being of any real help. And Peter had no idea where his family was, so he wouldn't know how to make the contact himself.

"I keep thinking," Brother Stoltz said, "if he was fleeing ahead of the Russians—like so many others—that he might have tried to contact the Church at some point. That would be his best hope of finding us."

"Where would he go? Would he try to get to Frankfurt?"

"Yes. If he could. I think he would try to find President Meis or some of the other members there."

"I've seen President Meis, Heinrich. I've been to church in Frankfurt. No one has had contact with him there."

"Tell me about those families. How well did they survive?"

"They all have losses. President Meis was drafted into the Wehrmacht. He was wounded in the leg, but he's doing quite well now." Alex listed off some of the families, tried to account for everyone he could. Tears filled Brother Stoltz's eyes as he listened to the stories.

"But no one there has heard from Peter?"

"No."

"His only other contact would be in Berlin. And there, he only knows President Hoch. We didn't get acquainted with the other members."

"I have no idea whether the Hochs survived the war—or whether they are still in Berlin. Most people had to leave the city."

"He might have looked for the Church, wherever he could find it. But are the branches in touch with each other?"

"No. Not yet. Some of the leaders are trying to reestablish the district organizations, but there are no membership lists— and people are scattered. You know how it is. It's going to be a while before we can learn anything through Church headquarters. My father has talked with some of the Brethren in Salt Lake, and he's given them the information I send him—about the state of things here. President Smith wants to help. Do you know that George Albert Smith is president of the Church now?"

"Yes. We have started holding meetings again in an old building that's half destroyed. We've had Mormon soldiers— Americans—visit our branch. They told us that President Grant died in the spring."

"President Smith wants to send help, but from the look of things, that won't be happening right away. The military is in

control, and they want to establish order before they let civilians come in. They think other organizations will just create
more confusion."

"Alex, do you have any idea what Germany is going to be
like this winter? The people are going to starve if we don't get
food."

"Yes, I know. I know far too much."

"How soon can the Church do something?"

"I don't know, Heinrich. The bridges are all gone. The rail-
ways are destroyed. It would be hard to distribute food, even
if the army let us bring it in. We could help our own people if
we could find them, but there are so many others in need. The
poor Jews must wonder whether they've been liberated. Most
of them are still behind barbed-wire fences, with guards at the
gates."

"You mean they're still in concentration camps?"

"No. They're called 'displaced person' camps. But General
Patton is afraid to let them free. He says they'll stir up
trouble—try to take revenge on Germans. They're eating better, but their camps are crowded and filthy. I've been inside
them. The stench of those places is disgusting."

"I keep thinking about the Rosenbaums. Is there any way
to find out whether they're alive?"

"I contacted the Red Cross about that. They had no record.
But that doesn't mean very much."

"They're probably dead, aren't they? All three of them."

"I don't know, Papa. I just don't know." It was the first time
Alex had called Brother Stoltz "Papa"—the name Anna always
used. Alex saw the man's eyes fill with tears again. He took
hold of his hand. "Some made it. And the Rosenbaums were
strong. I'll try to find out what happened to them, too."

"This is all worse than after the first world war. We had
little food then, but our nation wasn't devastated. What we've
done this time is cut ourselves off from our own past. We had
such a grand tradition—in philosophy and music and poetry—

and now we'll be known forever as thugs and murderers. How do we get our spirit back after this?"

Alex continued to hold his father-in-law's hand. He felt close to him, but he also felt his own link to Germany deepen. He remembered the Germany he had loved, before the war, and Brother Stoltz's words brought the tragedy into focus, the loss. "People can repent," Alex said. "Nations can too. And no one in this war is without sin. We all have to put this in the past."

"Yes, of course. But I wonder whether Germany can *ever* recover."

"When I was a missionary," Alex said, "you spoke of all this—what could happen."

"More than anything, I didn't want Peter to have to fight for Hitler. But I couldn't protect him from it, could I?"

"Are you *sure* he joined the army?"

"Yes. That much is a certainty. Whether he had to fight, I don't know, but if he did, it must have been unthinkable for him. What I do believe, though, is that he's alive, and I won't ever stop looking for him."

"Heinrich, I can do that better than you can. You need to go home to your family. Let me find Peter."

"Not yet. I don't want to face Frieda until I have some sort of answer for her. I've failed at everything else; I can't fail at that."

"Heinrich, you have to stop thinking that way. You've done your best. You got information back to the OSS, didn't you?"

"Some. But not as much as I wanted to. I did help to blow up tracks one night—when the Allies were crossing the Rhine. But I killed Germans doing it, and that was the one thing I didn't want to do."

"That's what we all have to face. That's what happens in war." There was so much Alex could have told his father-in-law about his own failures. He wasn't allowed to talk about any of that, but he knew he wouldn't have anyway. Alex had already vowed that many of the things he had done he would never tell anyone, not even Anna, and try never to think of again, if he could do it.

"I did find out, later, that the damage to the track—and to the repair crew—delayed a train that was bringing equipment and ammunition to the front."

"Heinrich, I can't tell you what I know about the Rhine crossings. But I'll tell you that I was involved in a certain way. What you did—along with the other resistance people—did make a difference. I can't say that you saved *my* life, but you certainly did save lives."

"What I hope is that I saved German lives as well as American ones—at least a few."

"Yes. That's exactly the right way to look at it. And there's no question that you did. You helped to shorten the war. Every day that was cut from the length of the war saved lives."

Across the square Alex could see a brigade of workers—all women. They were using hammers to knock the mortar off brick, to salvage it. "Rubble women," they had come to be called, and Alex had seen them in every German city. They earned a little money that way—very little—but it was something to keep their families alive. The sound of their tapping, so pervasive across the country, had become for Alex a symbol of German will. So many of the men were dead or in prison camps, so the women were making the best of things, doing what they could.

"How long will you be in Germany, Alex?"

"I have no idea. It could be quite some time. The army needs people who can speak the language."

"But you're longing to see Anna and your new son, aren't you?"

"Yes, of course. I miss the men I fought with, too. If I have to be here, I'd rather be with them."

Alex could hardly express how lonely he had been. He'd had no contact with anyone from his old squad; he had no idea how many of his men had survived. His battalion was occupying Hitler's "Eagle's Nest" in Berchtesgaden, on the Austrian border. That he knew, but nothing else.

These recent weeks, after his time with Anna in London, had been the emptiest he had ever known. It was not good for him to be on his own, with time to think. Everything kept coming back to him now—all that had happened in the past year of battle—and there were so many things he didn't know how to think about, how to live with. Without warning, images would appear in his brain: pictures of battles, of dead friends, of dead enemies. He wanted the Spirit back, wanted to put all those things behind him, and he tried, but the pictures came no matter what he did.

"Are you all right, Alex?"

"Heinrich, I've . . . gone through some bad times. It's a little hard to imagine right now how I can ever be the same person I once was."

"You won't be, Alex, but you can be better than before. That's what life is for. Isn't that what you taught me?"

Alex nodded. But he wondered. He didn't seem to be making a lot of progress.

"You have a son to raise. That will help you. It will change your heart back to what it was."

"I hope so, Heinrich. I'm trying very hard. But what about you? Are you going to be all right?"

"Yes. I must do this, too—the same as you. At the last, it was very bad here. I was hiding in a bomb shelter on the night my boarding house was blown apart. I lost everything—even the Book of Mormon I borrowed from the branch president."

"I can get you one."

"Oh, yes. That would be good."

"Do you sleep at the bakery—in that little room?"

"That's my home—the only place I could find. I'm lucky to have it. Some of the people in our branch don't have as much. I'll at least be warm this winter. And I'll have bread to eat."

"Heinrich, go back to London. Be with our family. I promise you, I'll do everything that can be done to find Peter."

"It's my responsibility. I feel that I have to keep trying."

"I have my own responsibility. I should be with Anna. I should be a father to my little son. You go and take my place for now. I'll look for Peter."

"I don't know, Alex. I've made promises to Frieda, to myself. I don't want to give up."

"I'll find him, Papa. If he's alive, I'll find him. If he's not, I'll at least find that out."

Heinrich didn't speak, but Alex saw in his eyes that he was adjusting to the idea, accepting that it might be right.

"They need us both in London, and I *can't* go. Please, go for us. Give my son a blessing. Name him after my little brother. That would do my heart more good right now than anything else I can think of."

· CHAPTER ·

2 6

Early one July morning Peter was hoeing weeds in the garden. He had gotten out of bed just after sunrise. It was better for him to get away from Frau Schaller and Katrina when they were getting dressed, but even more than that, Peter found it difficult to stay in bed very long. He usually fell asleep, dead tired in the evening, but at night his fears came, sometimes as dreams, sometimes as sounds and voices in his head. He would struggle to stay down, to control the panic, but eventually it was always easier to get outside into the mild morning air. He didn't know how long he would have to live with this kind of agitation, but once he was up and working, he always felt much better.

This morning, however, he looked up from his work and saw Frau Schaller walking toward him. It was still very early, before the British soldiers usually ate breakfast. When she reached Peter, she stood before him and folded her arms across her middle, over her old black apron. She seemed worried, upset. "Peter," she said, "Captain Stubbs just warned me. There's a problem."

"What?"

"The zones have been changed—the borders. The British are withdrawing today. The Russians will be moving in."

"Why?"

"I don't know. He said that the first borders were only temporary. Now, there's been an adjustment. The Russians are taking more of this region west of Berlin. He told me that I should warn you. He thinks you should leave."

"Leave?"

"He's sure you were a German soldier, not a refugee. It didn't matter to him, but he says the Russians will arrest you and ship you to their prisons back in their own country."

Peter knew all about that. He had no doubt that Stubbs was right. "When are the Russians coming?"

"He doesn't know. They start taking over today. He says you should go immediately and get across the new border."

"That's not legal. I'll be stopped." But Peter's mind was busy. That wasn't the real problem.

"You can get off the road, cross in the woods. Many are doing it. You'll be crossing into the English zone again, and they don't enforce the zones carefully, especially right now, before new guard stations can be set up."

"You have to go too. Didn't he tell you that?"

Frau Schaller looked past Peter. She had pretty dark eyes, like her daughter's, and at times her face was as lively as Katrina's, but she was more than solemn this morning; she looked discouraged. "Yes, he said that. But how can I leave? How can I walk away from my farm? It's all I have."

"You know what the Russians will do."

She looked out across her land. She was still gripping her arms against her body. "I don't know what Russians do. It's all just talk, so far as I know. Why would they be any different from the others? My people, way back, were Russians. I can tell them that. I speak a little Russian."

"It's not just you. It's Katrina—what they'll do to her."

Frau Schaller turned back and looked at him. "Do you know that? Are you sure? These Englishmen made eyes at her at first, but they've never bothered her."

"The Russians aren't the same. They're bitter. They *hate* all Germans. They think it's their right to have the women. I saw it in the east, and I heard it from the refugees—over and over. In Berlin the stories were horrible. There was hardly a woman there, of any age, who wasn't raped."

"Where would we go? Where could I take my children?"

"I'll help you. We'll find a place. Perhaps I can get work."

"I won't live in those displaced person camps. You know what will happen to us if we do. Those people are dying."

"Yes, but they're exhausted. They came here sick and worn out. We're not like that. But we'll find some other place. I can work at something—on a farm or in a mine."

"For how long? You want to find your family."

"I won't leave you until you're all right."

Frau Schaller seemed locked in place, her breath caught inside her, but Peter could also see that she was trying to adjust to this new reality. "I'd have to leave *everything* behind—not just my land and my house, but every plate, every picture. How can I do that?"

"Maybe you'll be able to return in time. Maybe the armies will withdraw."

"No. If I leave, I'll never have this place again. You know it's true."

Peter didn't know, but he thought she might be right. He couldn't imagine the Russians giving up what they took. They weren't like the Americans, eager to get home. They were spreading their power across Europe. "Frau Schaller, I camped one night with some refugees—in East Prussia. There was a man in the camp, just a young man, but he was talking to himself, acting crazy. I asked what was wrong with him, and his friend told me that some Russian soldiers had grabbed his wife and raped her—a whole group of them. They had held him, made him hold his little baby, and made him watch. When the baby cried, one of the soldiers grabbed it from the man and killed it—crushed its head."

Frau Schaller raised her hands to her face, cupped them against her cheeks. She began to nod her head. "All right. Don't say anymore. Fill some flour sacks with potatoes. We'll go as soon as I can get the boys ready."

"Ask the officers for food. Cans of meat and fruit—anything they can spare."

"Captain Stubbs already told me. We can have all we want."

"All right, then. I'll dig potatoes. But we can't try to carry too much. We have to move fast. Does he know how far away the border will be from here?"

"About twenty-five kilometers. Maybe thirty."

"We can walk that in one day if we keep up a good pace."

"Can the boys do it?"

"They won't want to, but they can. Better than you or me, probably." He tried to smile at her.

She took a long breath. He could see that she was trying to summon strength, but he could also see how devastated she was.

"It'll be all right, Frau Schaller."

"No, Peter. It will never be all right. I'll do this for my children, but it will never be all right for me. I got through the war, always holding onto one hope—that I would have this place, the food here, that my children wouldn't starve. Now we're no better off than these poor refugees we see walking past here every day."

Peter didn't argue. He knew that in many ways she was right. But he would do what he could for them. They had saved his life, and now he had to save theirs.

Peter and the Schallers set out in less than an hour. Peter worried that they were trying to carry too much, but he knew it would be easy enough to lighten their load if they had to. They could feed a few of their fellow travelers on the road. He kept his own little group moving much faster than the others, however. The refugees had traveled hundreds of kilometers, and they weren't able to walk more than a few each day now. A certain part of the day was given to foraging for any kind of food they could find. Peter hardly knew what to do as he and the Schallers passed the people on the road. But Frau Schaller made the decision for him. When she saw people by the side of the road, looking starved, she gave them two or three potatoes. "Don't give away our food," Rolf told her. "We need it."

"They're dying," she would say, but Peter worried too. They had to get outside the Russian zone, and they needed to survive until he could find some way to feed themselves. He had worried they had brought too much, but now he could see their provisions shrinking fast.

Katrina was strangely silent. Peter knew she was going through a process, trying to accept this change in her life. He remembered his own flight from Frankfurt, with his family, many years before, and he knew the ache she was feeling. In the middle of the afternoon, after a short break to eat a little, she finally came alongside Peter and said, "What's going to happen to us?"

"We'll be all right," Peter said. "We'll figure something out. I'll get a job."

"You don't know how to do anything."

"Be quiet. You're not funny."

"I'm not trying to be funny. There are no jobs. You know that."

"There's work to be done. We have to rebuild our whole country."

"Who's going to pay you to do that?"

It was true, of course. There was no pay for such work, not yet, and factories weren't operating. Those places that hadn't been destroyed in the war had no capital, no clientele, no way to get started again. The occupying forces had frozen the currency, to avoid inflation, but the only thing that had done was render the *Reichsmark* worthless. The Allies had brought Germany to its knees, but no one had given much thought to saving the German people once the regime was crushed. America and England were beginning to disperse food, but supplies were far short of adequate, with little promise of improvement for a long time to come. Peter knew he would have to find some way to get more than the handouts they might receive. The truth was, he was as worried as Katrina was—probably more—but he knew he couldn't tell her so.

But if Peter had his worries, he also liked what was happening to him. He felt like a man. He had a family to look out for, and in spite of some self-doubt, he was also determined. He had a purpose that was better than anything he had achieved in his life, and he was not going to let the Schallers down. There was something redemptive in the idea that after taking life, struggling so long against his better self, he could finally make an attempt at preserving life, at doing what he knew was right.

"I'll take care of you, Katrina," he said.

"You will? Really?"

"Yes. Of course."

"Do you want to marry me?"

Peter shook his head and laughed. "I want to take care of *all* of you. That's what I meant to say."

"But if you want to marry me, my answer is yes. Just in case you're wondering."

He glanced at her. She was smiling, and something in that touched him. She was strong, this little girl, no matter what else he might say about her. "You should look for a boy your own age," he said. "Some little boy who hasn't started to shave yet."

"Your cheeks look pretty smooth to me."

Peter ignored that. He glanced at Rolf and Thomas, who had started the day cranky and upset about leaving home but had settled into a steady tempo and moved along quite well all day. They were too tired to act up now, but they were also frightened. Peter could see that in their serious faces. That morning they had both kept saying, "But for how long? When can we come back? Where are we going?" Frau Schaller had only said, "We don't know exactly. In time. Certainly, in time, we'll plan to come back." But they had obviously sensed that their lives would never be the same.

The afternoon heat and humidity gradually got worse. Peter had told Frau Schaller not to carry water because it was too heavy. And so far, finding drinking water had not been a problem. But now, in the oppressive heat, the boys were complaining more often. Finally Peter let them stop and rest by a little stream. The boys stripped to their underwear and jumped into the cold water. That revived them, but afterward, they were reluctant to put their clothes back on. Frau Schaller had obviously been thinking ahead when she had told them to wear their long pants that morning. It was hot now, but winter would come, and then there might not be other clothes available.

Still, the boys seemed a little refreshed when they began to walk again. The group had not been walking long, however, when Peter looked back and saw a vehicle coming. It was traveling fast and raising a plume of dust, like smoke, behind it.

Peter wanted to believe that these were British Tommys, moving out, but he kept watching and saw that it was a Russian truck, a type he had seen many times on the eastern front. He scanned the countryside. If there had been a wooded area near enough, he would have had the family hurry off the road. But there were open fields on either side. "A Russian truck is coming," Peter told the others. "Walk with your heads down. Don't look up at the truck. Trudge a little. Try to look tired." He saw the boys exaggerate their motion, and he barked at them, "Not like that. Try to look like the refugees we've passed today."

The boys glanced back at him, clearly alarmed by his severity, but they made more effort to drop their gaze, to slow their pace. Peter could hear the truck coming now, rattling and kicking up rocks, and he hoped that it would merely speed on by. He could also hear his own heart beat in his ears. He had not been close to this enemy for a long time, and all his old feelings returned.

The truck kept coming, the roar of the engine louder all the time. "Step aside," Peter said. "Keep your eyes down."

As the big truck wheeled on by, spreading dust, Peter thought the threat was over. He wondered where the Russians were going, however, and whether he should lead the Schallers off the road.

Then the truck slowed abruptly and stopped. Peter tried to think what to do, but he had no choice but wait to see what the men wanted. He heard the door slam on the driver's side of the truck, and in a moment a soldier walked back to Peter and the Schallers. He stepped up to Frau Schaller, looked her straight in the eyes. *"Du Deutsch,"* he said.

She didn't answer for a moment. She glanced at Peter. "Polish," she finally told the soldier.

"Nein."

The back of the truck was full of Russian soldiers. Most of them had crowded to the rear. They were peering over the tailgate, leering at Katrina. One of them said something in Russian. And then, in German, *"Frau. Komm."* The other men laughed.

The soldier on the ground, a sergeant, turned toward Peter. "Go back," he said, and he held up his hands, the palms toward Peter. "Go back."

Peter nodded. He thought it might be best to turn around and start back to the east. Once the truck had moved on, he and the Schallers could cut across a field, find another road, or maybe stay in a wooded area until nightfall. He figured that they weren't more than seven or eight kilometers from the new zone, and the Russians would certainly not be able to cover the whole boundary—at least not right away.

But Frau Schaller said "Polish" again, and she pointed west. That was a mistake. The Polish refugees were bedraggled, emaciated. It was not hard to see that Peter and the Schaller family had not been on the road long.

"*Deutsch!*" the sergeant screamed into her face. She had let her sack full of food rest on the ground. He grabbed that and looked inside. The sack was full of potatoes and carrots. He walked the few paces to the truck and handed the sack up to one of the soldiers, and then he walked back to Frau Schaller. "You German," he said. "You go back." He pointed again to the east.

Frau Schaller seemed to accept that. She nodded. The little scene seemed to be over. Peter turned back and said to the boys, "Come on. Let's go." Like the Russian, he pointed to the east.

But Katrina said, "They can't make us go back. We can go wherever we want to."

She had said this to Peter, not to the Russian, but the soldier had apparently understood. He bolted toward her and gave her a shove. She stumbled backward, and Peter grabbed her to keep her from falling. "Go! Now!" the sergeant said. But two of the soldiers were climbing over the tailgate of the truck. They dropped down to the ground, and then another followed them. The three swung their rifles off their shoulders and moved in close. One of them spoke in Russian and gestured, pointing up the road.

"We'll go. We'll go," Frau Schaller was saying.

But a young Russian, a dark-haired boy with a hawkish nose, stepped to Katrina and took hold of her arm. "*Komm,*" he said. He looked at the sergeant and nodded, then spoke in Russian. The sergeant laughed; he nodded too.

"*Komm, Frau.*" The man pulled on Katrina's arm and took a step toward the side of the road, but Katrina twisted quickly, broke the man's grip, and ran a few steps away.

The soldier spoke in Russian, loud and harsh. Clearly, he was demanding that she come back to him. Katrina seemed to know that she had no hope to outrun the man. She stood several steps away from him, facing him, and she said, "No. You can't do that to me."

Peter didn't move quickly, but he took a step to his left, so that he was between the soldier and Katrina. Peter glanced to see Frau Schaller step to Katrina, wrap her arms around her shoulders. "We'll go now," she said. "Come on, boys. Let's leave."

But the sergeant shouted, "*Nein.*" This was the same man who had told them to go before, but now he was apparently interested in having his fun, along with the other soldiers. Two more were climbing over the back of the truck now.

Peter stepped back to his right, so he was facing the sergeant, who was about three steps away. "No," he said. "Leave them alone."

The sergeant was a bulky man with a great, round head. He hadn't shaved for a few days, and the bristles were thick across his chin. Peter could see that he liked this little game. He smiled and motioned with an easy wave of his hand for Peter to step aside.

Peter shook his head. "No."

The other soldiers had collected around the sergeant, five of them, and now their rifles came up, all pointed at Peter. Peter knew all about Russian soldiers. He believed they really would shoot him. But it didn't matter. He had no chance against all these armed men. They would do what they chose to do. But he wouldn't watch it happen. He wouldn't step aside and *let* it happen. He would die instead.

The sergeant waved him aside again, and Peter wondered why the man didn't just step forward and knock him down. There was nothing he could do to fight off more than one of them, even if they didn't use their weapons.

"Leave them alone," he said again, in German. It didn't matter to him whether any of them understood the words. They certainly saw that he wasn't moving.

Rolf and Thomas had retreated to their mother and sister.

Peter glanced over his shoulder. "Start walking," he said. "I'll do what I can."

"No," he heard Katrina say.

But now the sergeant was reaching for the holster on his belt. He unsnapped the leather strap and pulled out a pistol. Then he raised the gun, held his arm all the way out, and aimed at Peter's head. Peter stared into the round opening of the barrel. He felt himself shaking, felt the panic, and he wanted to duck, to run, but he held his position and waited.

Again the sergeant spoke in Russian, and with his free hand he waved Peter aside. Then he pulled back the pistol's hammer with his thumb.

All the rifles were pointed at Peter, too, at his chest.

"Please don't shoot him," Peter heard Katrina whisper. She was crying.

Seconds passed. Peter squinted and waited, expecting the worst, but his thoughts were simple and clear: *I can't stop this, but I won't give Katrina to them.*

The sergeant barked at Peter, and whatever the words were, clearly this was the final order. Step aside or die.

Peter had been so close to death before, and lately he had begun to hope for a full life. But he knew death well enough to accept that it had to come, sooner or later. He could do this. "*Nein*," he said quietly.

Another second passed. Two. Three. *Lord, help me,* Peter was thinking. And he meant "help me to do this."

And then the sergeant lowered his pistol. And he laughed. "You, a man," he said. He gave Peter a nod, what seemed a sign of respect. Then he spoke to the other soldiers. They laughed. "Go back," he said to Peter. "You. Frau. You go back." He pointed to the east.

Peter nodded.

The soldiers returned to the truck. They climbed up and over the tailgate. When they were all on the truck, the sergeant stepped to Peter. He laughed, and he held out his hand. "You, a man," he said again. Peter shook the Russian's hand.

The sergeant walked to the truck and motioned for a soldier to toss him the flour sack. He handed it to Peter, and then he went back and got into the truck. Peter turned around to Katrina and the others. The starter on the truck whined, and the engine chugged a couple of times before it caught and roared. Gears clanked, and the truck rolled away.

The Schallers, all four of them, were staring at Peter, seemingly overwhelmed.

"Let's start back to the east," Peter said. "There's a road north a little way back. We can head up that way and find a different road to the west." But he saw the exhaustion, the fear in all their faces. "We can hide out until dark and then make our way west more slowly."

But still they were staring. "I thought they were going to shoot you," Rolf finally whispered.

"They were just trying to scare us," Peter said. "Let's go."

Katrina was clinging to her mother. She had begun to shake and cry, but her eyes were on Peter. He could see what she was feeling, the relief, the gratefulness. It touched him, but it embarrassed him too. "Let's go," he said. "Other trucks could be coming."

He walked past the Schallers and then walked ahead. He couldn't stand to have them all looking at him the way they were. "That's the bravest thing I've ever seen in my life," Frau Schaller said to his back, but Peter knew better. There had been at least as much cowardice as bravery. Death had seemed easier than regret at that moment. He had piled up enough regrets in his short life, and he had known very clearly that he couldn't take on another one—not one like this. The Russians might have made him watch; death had to be easier than that.

So he walked on ahead, turned at the road to the north, and kept going. He was setting a rather fast pace, but he could hear the others behind him. The boys weren't complaining, not even talking. They were certainly still shaken by what they had seen.

Before long Katrina increased her pace and came alongside him. He didn't look over at her. He was still too self-conscious. "Thank you," she said.

"They wouldn't have shot me," he said, trying to sound unconcerned.

"You didn't know that."

He didn't answer.

"I think you love me."

He certainly wasn't going to answer that.

"I know I love you." And then she took hold of his hand. He didn't resist. He walked next to her, holding her thin little hand. But now the emotion had finally come. Fear was filling him, jolting through him like an aftershock, and at the same time, he felt weak from the relief. Those men hadn't harmed her after all, and here she was holding his hand—after what he had thought was going to happen to her. But he didn't say anything to her. He really couldn't at the moment.

Bobbi Thomas heard the commotion, people yelling up and down her passageway. She was sleeping in the middle of the day because she had been up all night. On the previous evening the ship had arrived in Manila Bay, in the Philippines, and the medical staff had worked much of the night moving patients to the Manila hospital. But now some sort of news was spreading, and Bobbi had never heard quite so much excitement on the ship.

She got up, slipped on her robe, and stepped to the door. "What is it?" she asked. "What's happened?"

A corpsman was in the passage in only his trousers, without shirt or shoes. "I just heard it myself. I guess it came over the radio. We dropped some new kind of bomb on a city in Japan. People are saying it destroyed the whole place. One bomb!"

Bobbi had actually heard something about this possibility, that the United States, along with Germany at one time, had been working on a powerful new bomb.

"Everyone is saying that the war could be over right away, that the Japs can never hold up against a weapon like this," the corpsman said.

Bobbi felt a kind of chill go through her. This was what she had looked forward to for so long. If the war ended soon, her whole life would change. She was committed to stay six months after the end, but maybe the navy wouldn't really want her that long. Maybe she could be home by Christmas. And Wally—maybe Wally would be released. That was the best thought of all.

But it was all a little too good to be true. What if one of these bombs hit the city where Wally was—wherever that might be? Or what if, after all this waiting, the family finally learned that he had died long ago right here in the Philippines?

Bobbi went back inside her state room. She knew she needed to sleep longer, but she was too excited now, so she got her toiletries and walked down the passageway. She showered and quickly did what she could with her hair, and she got dressed and walked to the officers' ward room. People were gathered there listening to the radio. But the same news was merely being repeated over and over. The new bomb was called "atomic," and announcers said it had harnessed the basic power of the universe, but no one seemed to understand exactly what that meant.

One doctor, a man named Nolan Healy, told the others, "It doesn't matter. We destroyed Tokyo with fire bombs in March, and that didn't stop the Japs. This won't either. We'll still have to invade those islands." But others disagreed. This new bomb put a power in America's hands that no one could hold out against. The story was that it had created an enormous fireball over the city and wiped out absolutely everything for miles around. The idea was startling, and frightening. Bobbi could hear the awe in people's voices as they spoke of it.

Two days passed, but nothing changed. Radio broadcasts and newspapers were full of speculation, but no one knew much more than the rumors passed around that first day when the city—now known to be Hiroshima—had been bombed. But on August 8 Russia declared war on Japan. This was Stalin's response to Japan's unwillingness to accept the declaration announced at Potsdam, Germany, a couple of weeks before. Stalin had met with Truman and Churchill, and the three countries had issued a demand that Japan surrender unconditionally or face total destruction. Everyone seemed to feel that Russia's declaration would also hasten the end. Russia could attack the Japanese in Manchuria and drive them out of China.

On the following morning word came over the radio that the Russians were doing just that. A massive attack had been unleashed all along the Manchurian border. And then, that afternoon, news bulletins filled all the radio stations: another atomic bomb had been dropped. This one had leveled a city called Nagasaki.

Bobbi found a crowd gathered around the radio in the ward room once again. Dr. Healy was still not convinced that the end would come soon, but he said, "I gotta hand it to Harry Truman. He's a tough little cuss."

Bobbi didn't know, but the radio announcers kept talking about the devastation and probable death. No one knew the number, but certainly tens of thousands of lives had been taken.

Bobbi thought of Ishi—how she must feel about this. Maybe it had always been inevitable that Japan would have to suffer this way, but Ishi had family in Japan. She must be horribly worried.

Bobbi felt a hand on her shoulder. She turned to see Kate. "What's happening?"

"We've dropped another atomic bomb," Bobbi told her.

"I know. But what are they saying?"

"Just that. Another city was destroyed."

Kate had a cup of coffee in her hand. She motioned for Bobbi to come with her. They walked away from the group and sat down at a table. "Do you think this is going to end the war?" Kate asked. She looked tired. Her short hair was messy, like that of a kid who had just gotten up from a nap.

"It's got to speed it up—don't you think?"

"I hope so."

But Bobbi felt strange about all this. She kept remembering that kamikaze pilot who had attacked their ship, how she had *hated* him. He had attacked a hospital ship, killed her friends. So how could she celebrate now when whole cities full of people were being blown up? The people dying were not soldiers but ordinary citizens. "Kate, do you think it's right to use a weapon like that?" she asked.

"Bobbi, if this ends the war, it just might be the thing that will save your brother's life. Now multiply that by all the families that will see their sons come home. And it won't just save our boys. In the long run, this will save Japanese lives. It'll end the war so much faster."

"I guess that's right. But doesn't it scare you a little—the idea of a bomb that powerful?"

"No. It doesn't scare me a little. It scares me half to death." She set her cup down and rubbed her hands over her face. "It's one more monstrosity to come out of this war."

* * *

After the atomic bomb had dropped on Hiroshima, the whole world had waited to see what would happen next. In America, the speculation on the radio and in newspapers—and across back fences—was that the war would soon be over. LaRue Thomas felt the excitement. She could hardly believe that the day she had imagined since she was twelve years old might finally come.

President Thomas had never said much of anything positive about Harry Truman, but he was praising the man now. "Roosevelt never would have had the backbone to use a weapon like that," he told LaRue. "But this new bomb is going to shorten the war by months, maybe years." Then the second bomb dropped, and the talk had changed. Maybe Japan would not capitulate. Maybe the leaders would allow the destruction to continue. Hiroshima had been struck on a Monday, Nagasaki on Thursday. All through the weekend, everyone waited and wondered. On Sunday evening a report came that the Japanese might have accepted surrender terms, but by Monday those reports had been denied. It was Tuesday, August 14, when the official announcement finally came.

LaRue was in her room alone that afternoon, listening on the radio. She had certainly hoped the declaration would come that day, but when the announcer broke into a music program and said, "Ladies and gentleman, we have an important announcement," she assumed it would be another "development," not the final word. And then a deep, serious voice said, "Word has just come from the White House. Japan has announced its unconditional surrender. The war is over."

LaRue was too shocked to do anything for a moment, but downstairs she heard Beverly whoop with joy and then come charging up the stairs. When she appeared at LaRue's door, her face was flushed and her eyes wide with excitement. "Did you hear?"

LaRue was already running to her. "Yes!" she shouted, and they threw their arms around each other. Then they hopped up and down, turning in circles. "It's over. It's really over," both of them kept squealing.

When they finally stopped and looked at one another, LaRue said, "Let's go downtown. Everyone's going to be heading down there."

"Maybe Dad will want us to—"

"Never mind about him. Let's just go."

"Okay. But we'll need to get back before too long."

"That's fine," LaRue said, but she had no intention of cutting the fun short. She had been waiting far too long for this moment. "I need to change my clothes first. What are you going to wear?"

"I don't know. Just this, I guess." Beverly looked down at herself, as though she couldn't remember what she had on. It was an old cotton dress—something she wore around the house in the summer.

"No, no," LaRue told her. "Let's wear one of our new school outfits."

Beverly suddenly smiled. "Okay," she said, and LaRue was pleased. The two had shopped together this year, and LaRue was starting to make Beverly at least vaguely aware of clothing styles. "Which one?"

"Wear your pleated skirt, and one of your new blouses."

"But if there's a big crowd, I could get something on it. Mom would—"

"Hey, it's okay. This war is only going to end once."

"All right." Beverly still looked wary but rather pleased with herself as she hurried off to her room.

LaRue changed quickly. It was a hot afternoon, and yet she put on the new cashmere sweater she had not planned to wear until school started. She didn't put on the whole outfit, not the wool skirt she would wear with it in the fall, but she found a cotton skirt that went with it just as well.

In a few minutes Beverly was back, beaming with pleasure. Her skirt was cream colored, and her blouse a soft shade of rose. "You look *pretty*, Bev," LaRue told her. "Come here. She took her sister to her bureau and had her stand still while she touched her lips with the same red lipstick she had just applied to her own lips. "Okay. Now press your lips together like this."

Beverly was laughing too hard to do it for a moment, but she finally mimicked the motion that all girls knew from watching their mothers.

"Now blot it a little on this," LaRue said.

"There won't be any left."

"Yes, there will. You don't want it to show up too much."

Beverly had worn lipstick before, but never in the daytime, never when she wasn't all dressed up. She obviously liked the idea of putting it on now.

"Do you think your friends will be in town?"

"You mean my *boy* friends?"

"*All* of your friends," Beverly said, but she smiled.

"They'll be there, sooner or later. But those boys are way too old for you."

"Reed's friend from the football team, Rulon Wilkerson, came to our MIA dances a couple of times this summer."

"He didn't ask you to dance, did he?"

"No."

"See. He knows you're too young for him. He'll be a senior this year."

"He talked to me once. He said, 'So, are you going to start high school this fall?' Then he started telling me I was going to be popular with the boys, like you. All my friends just about died when they heard him."

"Don't be popular *like* me, Bev."

"What do you mean?"

"I don't know." LaRue didn't want to talk about it, not now—not when she was getting ready to celebrate.

"What's wrong with the way you're popular?"

LaRue walked to her bureau and got her little purse. She made sure she had enough money for the trolley, but when she looked up, Beverly was still waiting for an answer. "Bev, I act the way I think the boys want me to act," she said. "I flirt with every boy who comes near me."

"But I thought that's what you liked to do."

"I'm sick of it, if you want to know the truth."

"I'll never be popular. But I don't care."

"Don't care, Bev. Really. Find some good friends—some nice kids. But don't try to prove anything. Just stay the way you are."

But Beverly looked a little disappointed with the advice. And when she said, "I know I'm not as pretty as you are," LaRue decided she didn't want to get into all that with her. LaRue suddenly thrust both her thumbs into the air. "Hey, never mind about that stuff today. It's time to let loose. We need to have some fun." She headed for the stairs, and Beverly followed her. They were almost to the front door when the phone rang. It was the Thomas ring on the party line, so LaRue walked into the dining room and picked up the receiver. "Hello," she said.

"LaRue, it's Mom. Did you hear the news?"

"Sure we did."

"What are you planning to do?"

"Bev and I were just going out the door. Everyone's going to be downtown. We're heading down there."

"Your dad wants you to wait for a few minutes."

"Wait?"

"Yes. We're going out to the car right now. We'll be home in ten or fifteen minutes. Dad wants to, you know, just have a little family meeting for a few minutes before you leave."

"Family meeting? You're kidding, aren't you?"

"No. Please just wait that long. There's plenty of time to celebrate."

"All right. But get him out of there right now, okay? I don't want to be sitting here for an hour." She slammed the receiver back on the hook. "Good old Dad!" she said. "Him and his family meetings."

"It's okay," Beverly said, and LaRue knew what she was thinking: "Don't get mad, LaRue. Don't get into one of your fights with Dad."

The truth was, though, LaRue wasn't nearly as bothered as she had pretended. She knew what this was about.

The girls sat in the living room and listened to the news on the old Philco radio. Live reports were coming now from New York about the celebration in Times Square. "That's where I'd like to be," LaRue told Beverly. "Right in the middle of that big crowd." But LaRue knew, even as she spoke, that she was playing her LaRue role. What she really felt was a kind of uneasiness, and actually some disappointment that after all the anticipation she wasn't really as excited as she was pretending to be.

It was Beverly who finally put LaRue's worry into words. "Do you think we'll hear from Wally pretty soon?"

"I don't know."

She knew what Beverly was thinking, what they were both worried about, but neither of them said it.

When President and Sister Thomas got home, they sat down in the living room with LaRue and Beverly, and Dad turned the radio off. "Girls, I'm sorry," he said. "I know you want to leave, but I thought we needed to get together for a few minutes first."

"Good excuse for one of your speeches. Right, Dad?" LaRue actually meant to sound playful, but the irony in her voice seemed stronger than that—even to herself.

"No, LaRue," Dad said. "I just want to say a couple of things." He was sitting next to Mom on the big gray sofa. The fabric on the arms was worn thin and dark, and the cushions were flattened, even frayed in spots. For all Dad's improved income, he still hadn't bought new furniture, and LaRue knew why. He wanted to leave the house unchanged until Wally came home.

"I don't know whether you girls remember," Dad said, "but last fall the First Presidency asked the members of the Church not to celebrate when the war finally ended."

No matter what LaRue had been feeling, this rubbed her the wrong way. She couldn't imagine Church leaders saying something like that.

"Don't roll your eyes, LaRue," Mom said, and then she winked.

"It's mostly a time to feel thankful," Dad said. "War is never anything we ought to celebrate."

"The end of one is," LaRue said. "We're just happy it's over."

"I know. And you can go on downtown in about five minutes. But I just wanted to have a prayer with you before you go."

"A prayer for Wally?" Beverly asked.

"Yes. We also have a lot to be thankful for right now."

"I'm scared about Wally."

"I know. We all are. But we'll have to accept whatever comes. We don't know what's happened during these bombings over there. And we've had no word of him for a very long time."

Beverly looked at her mother. "You always said he would come back," she said.

"I know. And I still feel that way."

"Well, anyway, I wanted to have a family prayer," Dad said. "Let's kneel down."

So they got down on their knees, the four of them next to each other in front of the long couch. LaRue bowed her head and closed her eyes. She waited for Dad's big voice. But he said, softly, "LaRue, would you be willing to say the prayer for us?"

LaRue opened her eyes, looked up. She could hardly believe this. She didn't want to do it. She wasn't the one to ask something like this. That was for Dad to do. But she was also touched—even honored. "Okay," she said. And she bowed her head again.

"Father in Heaven," she began. For a moment, however, she couldn't think what to say. And then, she was too moved to say the words that came to her. She held on, let the tears run down her cheeks for a time, and then she began again. "Father in Heaven, we are so thankful that the war has finally ended and that Alex and Bobbi are all right. We pray that they both might be able to come back to us soon."

She waited, trying to keep control. "We also pray that Wally is safe, and that he will come home." She didn't want to add to that, but she knew what her dad would want her to say. "But Father, if Wally isn't well, and can't come back, we pray that we can understand and accept that, the way we did when Gene died." But the words cost her, and now she was crying hard. She wanted to tell God that it would be unfair if Wally didn't make it back after all he had been through, and after all the prayers the family had offered. She thought of adding something stronger, of making something of a demand on God, but she couldn't do it. "Father, we just want our family to be together again. We pray that our new little Gene will come to us soon, too . . . and that he will never have to fight in a war. That no one will. Ever again." She tried to close the prayer but couldn't. She put her face into her hands and sobbed.

Her dad was next to her, and she felt the weight of his big arm as he reached around her and gripped her shoulder. "In the name of Jesus Christ, amen," he pronounced, and then for a long time he held LaRue close, and LaRue felt his body shake, as he too cried.

When LaRue finally got to her feet, she hugged her mother, but emotions were still storming inside her. LaRue wanted the war to be over now, really over, and that could only mean that Wally would come home—no matter what she had said in her prayer. And the truth was, what she really wanted was to find out that some horrible mistake had been made, and that Gene was actually still alive. He had gone to the place called "the war," and it had swallowed him whole. No matter how hard she tried to accept that, she had never stopped feeling that the war, that God, should give him back.

"Thank you, honey," Mom was saying. "I'm so glad you thought of little Gene. It's what we need now. We need him with us."

But LaRue didn't want to talk anymore. She didn't want to hurt.

"Maybe Beverly and I can cook dinner," LaRue said. "We could have something special tonight."

"Aren't you kids going downtown?" Dad asked.

"We can go later."

She looked at Beverly, who nodded back to her. "Yeah. That'll be better," Beverly said. She was still crying.

After dinner Dad surprised everyone by saying, "Why don't we *all* drive downtown and just see what's happening. This is a day to remember."

So Mom agreed to leave the dishes on the table for now, and they all piled into the old Hudson. But as they drove toward town, north on State Street, they got bogged down in a terrific traffic jam. Cars were filling the streets, and so were people. At Fifth South, Dad gave up and turned east, but traffic was thick there, too. He finally parked the car, and the family walked into town. People had especially jammed State Street between First and Third South. LaRue could hardly believe how wild everyone was acting. Music was blasting out from stores, from speakers, and people were dancing, forming snake-dance lines, or just milling about, shouting and laughing.

"Look at that," Beverly said.

LaRue looked to see where Beverly was pointing. A man in a white sailor's uniform had hold of a girl who was maybe twenty or so, and he was kissing her—just like in the movies. He had thrown her back, and he was leaning over her. She was clinging to him and kissing him back, and LaRue thought maybe she was his girl. But when the sailor finally stood her up and looked at her, he grinned and said, in a loud voice, "Say, it's nice to meet you."

"Same to you," the girl said. She grabbed hold of him again, and they went for another one. She was a slim girl, and she had on a pretty polka-dot dress with heels, white gloves, and a cute little hat, which she had to hold onto with one hand as he bent her back again.

"Isn't that Clarence and Vivian Wadham's girl, from our stake?" Mom asked Dad.

"I hope not," Dad said, and he looked away. LaRue and Beverly both laughed. But a conga line was coming their way, the people singing as loud as they could to make their own music. The end of the line snapped as it turned, and a man bumped against President Thomas. "Excuse me, sir," he said, in a slurred voice. He tipped his hat and then chased after the line. "Whew! Did you smell that guy?" Mom said.

"Maybe we should go," Dad told her.

"Oh, come on, Al. Don't be such a stick-in-the-mud. People need to let loose a little."

"They don't have to use alcohol."

"I know. But most people aren't drinking. Let's walk on up the street. It sounds like there's a band playing up there."

There was a band all right, and it was playing a jazzy version of "You'd Be So Nice to Come Home To." It was not at all the sort of music Dad liked. But as they got close, LaRue grabbed his hand. "Come on," she yelled in his ear. "I'll teach you how to *swing*."

She spun around backward and pulled him off the sidewalk and into the street. She was mostly just teasing him. She was sure he wouldn't really dance with her. But he took hold of her, and off he went. He wasn't doing a jitterbug, but he certainly knew how to keep up with the beat. He spun with LaRue, moved her through the crowd, knew exactly how to lead—like no boy her age ever did.

"You're good, Dad," she yelled at his ear. "You're really good."

He looked down at her and smiled, and then he spun her again, but maybe a little too wildly. They crashed into another couple, and LaRue was thrown off balance. He hung on to her, kept her from falling, and then gave her a hug. "Sorry, honey," he said.

"That's okay." She was laughing, feeling happier than she could ever remember.

"I love you, LaRue," he said.

And the words were out before she even thought. "I love you too, Dad," she said. "I'm sorry I worry you so much."

"I'm sorry you worry me, too."

LaRue laughed again. "I hate to tell you, but I'm just getting started."

"Do you think I don't know that?"

But they were dancing again, twirling, and LaRue wondered where in the world her dad had learned to dance so well.

Wally was glad when his crew got an early train ride into the mine. They reached a big pile of timbers early and were able to get enough to keep them going all day. That meant they wouldn't have to dig any out from caved-in sections of the mine—something all of the men hated to do. All the same, the crew put in a hard morning. They cut the big logs to size and prepared the wedges they would need to timber the ceiling and walls of the mineshafts they were now preparing.

Wally was with Chuck, and the two of them were working with their foreman, about to raise a timber into place, when a young Japanese guard came running down the mineshaft. He was shouting commands in Japanese. The men knew enough of the language to understand what he was telling them to do: to stop working and take their tools back to the toolshed.

"*Nan no?*" Wally asked the man. What was going on?

The guard shrugged, but the thought struck Wally immediately: maybe this was it. Maybe the war was finally over. He had always tried to imagine what would happen when the war ended, and this seemed a possibility, that the prisoners would be called from the mine. Then again, once before the men had been called out, and it had been nothing, only the guards demanding to count the prisoners—because one had disappeared. So Wally told himself not to get his hopes up. "What do you think it is?" he asked Chuck.

"Probably someone missing," Chuck said. "You know how the Japs are—scared one of us might actually get away. Where do they think we would go?"

But Chuck's words didn't fit the tone of his voice. He sounded more intense, more alive, than he had in a long time. Of course, anything that changed the routine was exciting to the men.

At the toolshed other crews were gathering, and everyone was speculating. One man had the audacity to say, "This isn't like the Japs. This could be the day we've been waiting for." But the others were quick to put the idea down.

Wally saw the mine supervisor for this section talking to the Japanese foremen, so he moved closer. He was an older man with a raspy voice, and he was talking very fast. Wally couldn't pick up much of what he was saying, but the man did seem excited, maybe even happy. And then Wally heard the words. *"Senso yamu."* Or at least he thought that's what he heard. He took another step closer, and he heard it again.

"Come here!" Wally grabbed Chuck and pulled him closer. "I think they're saying the war is over."

They listened closely, and then they both heard it again. Chuck grabbed Wally, looked into his face. Chuck's eyes were wide with elation, but he said, "Would they know? Maybe they're just talking. Maybe they just *think* that's what's going on—the same as us."

But the word was spreading through the prisoners, and the talk was getting louder, more excited. The foremen weren't stopping them, either, weren't yelling for their silence. That had to mean something.

Once the tools were all put up, the supervisor commanded the POWs to take the train out of the mine. It was a long walk through the mineshafts to reach the loading dock, but all along the way the idea was building among the men that this was it.

"*Something* is up," the men would say. "You could tell that from the way that supervisor was talking to the foremen."

"You can't assume anything," others would answer, but they were walking faster than usual, not hobbling along.

When the crews reached the loading dock, they met men getting off the train. Recently the mine supervisors had begun bringing in a second shift of prisoners at noon. These men worked a shift late into the night. When Wally saw them, he felt the disappointment. Why were they coming down, as usual? He grabbed one of the men by the arm. "What's going on out there?" he asked.

"What do you mean?"

"They're sending us out of the mine. Don't you know why?"

"No. No one said anything."

"We heard a supervisor say that the war was over."

The man shrugged. "I can't say. But we haven't seen anything. I didn't even hear any airplanes this morning."

He was an Aussie, a little man with crooked, stained teeth. The arm that Wally had grabbed was all bone, and the man's face, like so many, was full of defeat. All Wally's hopes disappeared. He turned to Chuck. "It's nothing," he said. "These guys haven't heard a thing."

Chuck was nodding. "That's what I was afraid of," he said.

But now the supervisor was shouting to the noon-shift men to turn around and take the train back out of the mine. Both crews, together, crowded onto the train and packed themselves tight. Some were making the case that it didn't mean anything that the noon shift hadn't known anything. "Word is just getting around. That's what I think," Wally heard someone say.

"Let's not get carried away," Chuck told Wally once again. "We'll know soon enough."

Wally knew that was good advice, but as the train jiggled and rattled, as it had done for so many days—so many months—Wally had to fight himself. He wanted to say, "This is it—the last trip out of this stinking mine." At the same time, he and the other men had always wondered what might happen at the end. Maybe the guards were waiting up above to take their revenge on the prisoners.

The train finally angled upward and reached the topside loading dock. Wally ducked his head and squinted for a time until his eyes adjusted to the light, and he could look outside. He was watching for some sign of change. He didn't see any until he reached the equipment shack. The men turned in their lamps, as usual, but there were no guards to shake them down for stolen tools or contraband.

Then one of the prisoners shouted, "The boy in the shed, he's saying the same thing. He says the war is over."

"He's crazy," Chuck told Wally. "He doesn't know."

But the guards at the gate were telling the prisoners not to bathe, to put on their clothes and get ready to march to the camp. A couple of the guards, with no explanation, began to hand out cigarettes. Surprisingly, the guards seemed as happy as the men, and a kind of looseness was spreading. Wally couldn't help it any longer; his excitement was at the bursting point. Nothing was happening the way it always had before. There was no way the guards would suddenly let down their vigilance—unless something big was going on.

Chuck was not the only man cautioning everyone. "Something's up. That's for sure," men would say. "But that doesn't mean the war is over."

And then one of the prisoners said, "Hey, look. There's no spotter up in the lookout tower. They wouldn't stop watching for bombers unless they knew that none were coming."

That idea seemed right, and now everyone was almost frantic for something definite, some sort of announcement that would make the suspicion official. The parade of men kept streaming from the train, but there was no fall-in order from the guards. The prisoners stood in groups, talking, speculating, many of them smoking, and the change in everyone was obvious in their faces, the tone of their voices.

An hour passed, but the prisoners didn't let go, didn't start to celebrate. They had been watched and controlled far too long to let that happen. When the fall-in order finally came, they began their long hike back to the camp, but this time it was not an orderly march. Everyone merely strolled along at a casual pace.

Along the way, a Scotsman shouted to the other men, "If we get back to the camp, and the camp commander finally breaks loose with that Red Cross chow we're supposed to have been getting, then you'll know the war is over."

Some of the men laughed and shouted their agreement, but others argued rather gruffly to lay off the stupid talk. "Those Japs are probably setting us up," one man told Wally. "They'll let us think something has changed and then fall on us like vultures."

"Why would they do that?"

"Maybe they're upset about something. Maybe they're looking for an excuse to shoot some of us. Who knows what they think around here?"

"They can't afford to kill us. If the war isn't over, they need the labor."

"They've killed plenty of us before."

Wally had to admit, all that could be right. He did have just a bit of apprehension that some sort of trap could be laid and the men were walking into it. But that's not what his instincts were telling him. It just wasn't the way the guards— or the commander—operated.

At the camp the men lined up in front of the guard house, as always. But a guard waved them on. There was no count, no search. The men walked into the compound, still talking loudly, laughing. They were heading for their barracks when the camp commander began to shout. He was standing on the porch of the headquarters building, and Mr. Okuda, his interpreter, was next to him. "Each prisoner please come forward to receive Red Cross boxes."

A wild cheer went up. The Scotsman's prediction had come true. The commander hadn't announced anything official, but this was close enough. The men were now shouting and slapping each other on the back, and no guard stepped in to stop them. In fact, Wally saw relief on the guards' faces. These men so full of hatred and anger, it always seemed, were actually smiling. It was over for them, too.

"Now what do you say, Chuck?" Wally yelled.

Chuck was grinning. "I think it must be over," he said. "It almost has to be."

The two grabbed each other, embraced, swatted one another on the back. When they stepped back, Wally saw tears on Chuck's cheeks, and he felt his own chest begin to heave with sobs. It was too good to be true—simply too good to be true. But the Red Cross boxes were being distributed. If nothing else was true, this was. He had extra food in his hands—real food, not just rice.

The men tore the boxes open, but most of them chose carefully, didn't eat the food all at once. Wally sat on the ground and opened a tin of meat. It was so powerful and tasty that the flavor almost overwhelmed him. He wanted to eat some other things, but he promised himself he would keep the rest of the box for later. He and Chuck took a bath and then went back to the barracks. By then he could no longer resist. He decided to eat just a little of a Hershey's chocolate bar. But he ate half of it before he could stop himself, and a charge went through him like electricity, making his head spin. He knew he had to save the rest of the chocolate for later. Before the evening was over, however, he had traded his cigarettes for more chocolate, for powdered milk and jam. He tried not to eat too much, but he kept nibbling away at the food all night.

No one went to bed. It was a hot night, August 15, and the barracks were sticky and miserable as usual, but it didn't matter. Wally got together with Chuck and Art, Don and Ray and

Eddy. They sat in a circle in one corner of their room and talked—and ate from their boxes. Ray and Eddy smoked.

At some point, late in the night, Eddy asked, "How long before the government can get us out of here?"

"It's going to take a while," Chuck told the others. "I just hope we get supplied with food. The commander and all these guards might just high-tail it out of here, and we could be left high and dry."

This didn't seem like Chuck. For so long, he had kept Wally going, always helping him believe they would make it. "What's with you?" Wally asked him. "You worry too much. America isn't going to let us starve to death—not after all this. They'll drop food in here long before they haul us out."

Chuck smiled. "That's probably right," he said. "But let's just keep ourselves under control a little bit. We still need some discipline if we're going to get through the end of all this. I'm not ready—absolutely—to admit the war is over. Maybe the Japs have just given up on this mine and they're closing it down. Something like that."

"Oh, sure," Don said. "And they're letting us do anything we want for a few days—just for a little vacation. The *only* way they pull back on us, the way they did today, is if the war is over."

"All right. I pretty much agree," Chuck said. "But we still need to keep control. For one thing, I'm afraid some of the men might go after these guards. I don't blame 'em too much if they do, but they could get themselves shot or beaten to death, and I don't want anyone else to die."

"Not even the guards?"

"No. Not even the guards."

Wally agreed with that, but he hoped someone, sometime, would take care of the commander. The guy was guilty of war crimes, and he ought to end up in jail, at the very least. Still, Wally didn't want to think about that tonight. "Hey," he said, "here's something to think about. Won't the army give us all our back pay when we get home?"

"They have to," Eddy said, and he obviously liked the idea. Poor Eddy's face was thin and withered, almost like an old man's, and he had lost a lot of his hair, but his eyes were bouncing around like pinballs tonight.

Ray said, "Sure, we'll get some money, but I wonder what people back home will be saying about us. Maybe we're just the yellowbellies who gave up in the Philippines."

"You've listened to the Japs too much," Eddy told him. "We didn't have any choice about that."

The question had not seemed very important during these years in prison, but going home might change all that. Wally hated to think that he might have to apologize for surrendering all the rest of his life.

"If I get a bunch of back pay I'm going to buy me a nice car," Eddy said. He was grinning, gazing over the others' heads, as though he were seeing it all. "A nice little Chevy coupe, maybe. I'm going to date a different girl every night. Eat steaks. Go dancing. Man, I'm going to live it up."

"Slow down," Wally said. "You've only got twenty-one bucks a month coming. You've got it spent ten times already."

"No. I'm already thinking ahead. I'll use some of it for a down payment on a car and use the rest for good times."

"You'll spend it all in two weeks, and then what?"

"Hey, I'll get me a good job. I'll be all right."

"Yeah, I can see where the girls will be chasing after you," Chuck said. "They like a man who's nice and trim."

All the men laughed, but they also agreed that putting weight back on was going to be easy enough, and they were ready to get started.

"I want a job with no heavy lifting," Ray said. "And outside—where there's plenty of light."

But Wally wished the men wouldn't talk too much about realities. He wasn't sure what to expect at home, and he felt a little worried about the transition that might lie ahead. For tonight, he just wanted to feel the relief of having so many bad things behind him. He had concentrated on the end for so many years, told himself that he had to keep hanging on. Now, he wanted to think of seeing his family, of being human again, but he didn't want to think about jobs, about making his way in the real world. He knew his body was weakened, that his health wasn't good, he hoped he could rebuild himself, learn to be a normal person.

"All I keep saying to myself," Don said, "is that maybe, before long, I'll see my wife and kids. I hope they're all right." His voice broke a little, and he looked down.

"Do you think your wife even knows you're alive?" Chuck asked him.

"I don't know. I don't know what she's gone through. I've thought about it every single day for all these years. I don't even know whether the Japs sent any of my letters to her."

Wally knew the feeling. He wondered what was happening in Salt Lake. Had the end of war been announced? Were people celebrating? He had no idea what life had been like back there all during this war. Maybe the Japanese had bombed San Francisco or San Diego, maybe even Salt Lake. Maybe there was as much devastation there as here in Omuta. What he wanted to think was that his house was exactly as it had always been, that no one in the neighborhood had moved. He wanted his life back, wanted to be Wally again, wanted to sleep in a nice bed with clean white sheets, get up to a breakfast of bacon and eggs. He wanted to sit with his old friends in his ward chapel and hear a sermon—even a boring one. He wanted to take the sacrament.

"Let me say something to you guys," Wally said. All the men looked at him, sensing that he wanted to be serious for a moment. "I just want to thank you guys. Anyone who made it through this thing had to be lucky, to some degree—and had to be pretty tough, too. But I know I couldn't have made it without you—you and some of my friends back at O'Donnell and Cabanatuan, and out in the Tayabas jungle. Some of those guys didn't make it, but they got me through, the same as you did."

"Wally, you did more for us than we ever did for you," Don said. "You and Chuck and Art have taught me more about life than I ever knew before."

But Eddy said, "Hey, it's going to take a lot of work to keep you Mormon guys from messing up my conscience. How am I going to have any fun when I get home?" Everyone laughed, and that was just as well. For now, Wally didn't want to think too much about all his friends who hadn't made it but had once longed, as he had, for this day.

"Wally," Don said, "what about that girl you used to tell me about? Do you think she's waiting for you?"

"She never was waiting for me. We broke up before I left."

"I know. But you used to talk about her all the time."

"Don, I left home in 1940—five years ago. Lorraine is twenty-four now, and she's *beautiful*. What do you think the chances are that she's still single?"

"Well . . . you've got a point."

"I can't imagine being around a girl now anyway. I can't even think what I would say."

"It'll all come back," Eddy said. "All of it will. And I do have to admit, I had what it took when it came to the girls."

Wally tried to think of himself going out on a date—but the picture simply wouldn't come into focus.

When Wally and the others finally tried to sleep, there were a thousand such things to think about. Wally did finally drift off, however, and it turned out there was no early call to work, and that was like heaven. Once he did get up, the day was strange, with nothing to do. By now, the guards were assuring the men that the war really was over, and even though nothing official had occurred, no one doubted any longer that it was true. The guards issued Japanese NCO uniforms to the prisoners, complete with underwear. It was strange to put on the very uniforms they had long hated, but the clothes were clean and fresh and felt wonderful. Wally especially loved the leather shoes with rubber soles. He made up his mind that he was going to have comfortable shoes the rest of his life, and he was going to wear gloves—work gloves and dress gloves—to pamper his beat-up hands.

The men spent the day trading and eating, sleeping and talking. No one knew what to expect. The great question was how much longer they would be there. But for now, this was enough, this leisure, this chance to eat from Red Cross boxes, this relaxation of all the rules they had lived under for such a long time.

On the following day, the seventeenth of August, the men were called to the parade ground. Commander Hisitake—the man who had beaten and tortured Wally and Chuck—stood before them. He was dressed in his full Imperial Army dress uniform, with braid and decorations, and with a long sword at his side. He looked like a comic fool. Wally had sometimes imagined himself putting the man through some kind of pain— just enough to show him what torture was like. He wouldn't really do that, of course, but he did harbor enough hatred to wish he could somehow humiliate Hisitake, let him feel what the men under his control had felt.

As Wally moved closer, however, he was surprised to see how broken Hisitake appeared. He was attempting to look stern and straight, but his eyes were distant, and his pride was clearly gone. He spoke through his interpreter and read the official declaration of Japan's surrender. Then he told the prisoners, "I know that we have not treated you as well as you might have liked. We had limited supplies, however, and we fed you the best that we could. We believe in discipline, and so it was necessary to keep order here."

Wally heard some of the men react, swear under their breaths. One man nearby called the commander a filthy name, shouted it out. But Wally was stunned by his own reaction. The commander was a proud man, trained in the Japanese military tradition, and now he was, in effect, surrendering to these POWs he had long considered cowards. It was surely the most humiliating moment of the little man's life, and Wally felt something he *never* could have predicted. He actually felt sorry for the man.

Wally fought the impulse. He didn't want to let Hisitake off the hook that easily. What he had done to the men—to Wally personally—was inexcusable.

But then Wally saw that Hisitake was crying, tears sliding over his wrinkled cheeks. A kind of tingling passed through Wally's body, and he hardly knew what to make of it. It was a spiritual feeling, a change coming over him. Some weight seemed to lift from inside his chest. Wally actually fought it, told himself he didn't want this. He wanted to hate this man, always. But what had started as a hint, an idea, began to build into a powerful emotion, as though his spirit were being altered. He felt calm and right, and the thought that began to fill his head was that he never wanted to hate *anyone* again.

Wally wasn't deciding, wasn't reaching this state on his own; a force beyond himself seemed to be working on him, refining him. He realized he was receiving a gift—one he hadn't earned—and now even his reluctance was slipping away. What he felt was free—stripped of all the hatred he had felt for so long—and he was overwhelmed with gratitude. He didn't exactly forgive Hisitake; he simply felt the burden of his hatred lifted from his soul. He couldn't help it when he began to cry. He realized that the war was not only over but that it was over *for him.*

* * *

Anna was sitting at the kitchen table. She and her mother were eating breakfast. Anna had been up twice in the night with the baby, and she was tired. She sipped at the peppermint tea her mother had made for her, and she ate the last of a breakfast roll, spread with a bit of marmalade. "When you finish that, I want you to go back to bed for a while," Sister Stoltz told her. "If the baby wakes up, I'll take care of him."

"It's all right. I'm up now."

"Anna, you sound discouraged this morning. Are you?"

"The doctor said I have the blues a little. He said new mothers get that way."

"I know that. Every mother knows it. But darling, I thought it would give you such a lift to know the fighting is over for Alex."

"It did, Mama." Anna took another sip of her drink, then pushed it away, unfinished. Summer had come slowly this year, and now, already, fall seemed in the air. The sky was overcast, and occasional sprinkles of rain had fallen during the night and again this morning. Sister Stoltz always kept the flat cold, except for the kitchen, but this morning even the kitchen was cool. "I've always told myself that when the war is over, Alex will come home, and everything will be all right. But now I have no idea when he'll be released. I didn't mind so much when I thought he was being saved from fighting in Japan by being in Germany, but now the war really is over, and I keep thinking about the baby, how much he's changed already, and his father has never even seen him."

"That's not such a terrible thing, Anna. There are children four years old, and older, who have never known their fathers. And Anna, remember—there are so many children in this world who will *never* know their fathers."

Anna was suddenly annoyed. She said, rather curtly, "I know, Mama. I know." Then she got up and began to clear the table.

Anna, of course, was well aware that her mother was right, that she shouldn't feel sorry for herself, but it seemed that she had been waiting all her life for life to begin. It had been four years since she had taken on Agent Kellerman, cut his face, and her family had been forced to hide. The first three years after that had been hellish, and then miracles had happened and

Anna had gotten what she had wanted: Alex for her own. She had known that he would have to return to the war and she would have to wait once again, and she had dealt with that. But now the war was over, and the baby was here; it was time to be a family, to be together. She found comfort in her son, loved to hold him and rock him, but she had never realized how much work a baby was, how exhausted she could be from nighttime feedings and long evenings when he would cry incessantly for no reason that she could understand. Sister Stoltz was a huge help to Anna, but she seemed to think she knew everything about babies, seemed to feel that Anna's instincts were always wrong.

But Anna was being petty, and she knew it. Her mother had so much to deal with herself. "Mama," she said, "I'm sorry. I don't mean to be grouchy. I'm just tired."

Her mother had set the dishes in the kitchen sink, and now she was running hot water over them. She turned off the faucet and looked around at Anna. "It's all right," she said. But Anna knew she was offended. Mama was always fighting her own discouragement. But there was no use talking about all that. It wouldn't do either one of them any good.

The morning was quiet, with the baby asleep, not at all according to the schedule Anna was trying to establish for him. Anna didn't go back to bed, but she walked into the living room, wrapped a quilt around herself, and lay on the couch. She was drifting but still half awake when a knock came on the door. She started, then sat up. Then she realized that it was probably Mildred at the door. The girl had a habit of leaving for work and then returning, all out of breath, having forgotten her card for the Underground, or some such thing.

Anna was pulling the blanket back over herself when she heard her mother open the door, and then she heard a gasp and a little shriek. It sounded joyous, not fearful, but still Anna couldn't think what it was. She got up quickly and walked down the hall. By then she was hearing a man's voice. "Papa," she whispered, and hurried to the door. Her mother had thrown her arms around him and was saying, "Oh, Heinrich, oh, Heinrich." Brother Stoltz had hold of her, but he was looking over her shoulder, smiling at Anna as tears ran down his face.

In a moment, Sister Stoltz stepped back and let Heinrich go to Anna. He took Anna in his arms, gripped her tight. He was shaking with sobs by then. When he could speak, finally, he said, "Where's my grandson?"

"Come with me," Anna said, and she led him to her bedroom. She opened the door quietly and then walked to the little wooden cradle in the corner. She turned back the blanket and carefully lifted the baby, who let out a cry before he settled into her arms. She turned then and let her father look. He leaned close and whispered, "Oh, my. What a beautiful boy. So much like you were."

"Like Alex, I think."

"I see that, too." He held his hands out, palms up. "May I hold him."

"Yes, of course." Anna put the bundle into his arms. For a moment the baby's eyes came open as he nestled against his grandfather's chest. Suddenly Brother Stoltz was crying hard again, his body shaking. Sister Stoltz put her arms around his shoulders and held him, tried to steady him. Anna, of course, understood what was happening, that her father was thinking about Peter.

"Why did you come now?" Sister Stoltz asked.

"We need to talk," Brother Stoltz said. He was getting himself under control, but he continued to stare into his grandson's face as though that were the only thing he wanted to do for now. After a minute or so, however, he handed the baby back to Anna, and she put him down again. Then all three walked to the kitchen. There, Sister Stoltz took her husband in her arms once again, clung to him. "Why didn't you tell us you were coming?" she asked him.

"I did. Didn't you get my letter?"

"No."

"I've gotten here faster than the letter, then. I thought you knew."

"No. Sit down. Tell us what you wrote."

Brother Stoltz walked to the table and pulled out a chair. Anna sat across from him, his wife next to him. She took hold of his hand. "Heinrich, it's so good to have you here. But you said you wouldn't come yet. I don't understand."

"Yes. This is what I want to tell you." He didn't look at his wife, however; he looked at Anna. "Alex came to see me. He brought your letter. He told me about our grandson. And then he told me to come home, to look after you—and to bless the baby for him."

"Papa, does that mean he can't come?" Anna asked. "He told me he would try to get another leave."

"He can't, Anna. Not even for a short visit. His commanding officer told him that he's had his leave, that he can't have another for quite some time."

Anna had expected this. It was what Alex had told her would probably happen. But she had held out hope. "It's all right," she said. "At least you can give the blessing—that's almost as good. What did Alex say about the name? I call the baby Gene, in my mind, but I never say it. I wanted Alex to decide."

"Yes. That's the name he wants. Eugene, after his little brother—and call him Gene. It's what Alex wanted all along. And Alexander for a middle name, if you want."

"I have thought, maybe Peter," Sister Stoltz said.

There was a long, difficult pause. Anna knew what her mother was saying, and Brother Stoltz, of course, understood too. "Frieda," he said, "I haven't given up. Don't think that. It was almost impossible to look for him, the way Germany is now. Alex can look more easily than I can. He has a better chance to find him. He promised me he will do everything he can. But if he can't find him, I'll go back again. I'll keep searching."

Sister Stoltz got up from the table. She walked across the room.

"What is it, Frieda? Do you think I should have stayed?"

"No."

"Then what?"

She tucked her hands into the pockets of her apron, and she looked toward the window. "Heinrich, we have to accept things as they are. We have to go on. Sooner or later, we have to do that. We can't give this pain to ourselves forever."

"Frieda, there's no reason to give up yet. There are millions of German soldiers in prison camps. There's no reason to assume he's dead."

"What will the Russians do with their prisoners?"

"In time, they'll let them go, I would think."

"You know what's in the newspapers—how the Russians starve these boys, or work them to death. They're shipping them to Siberia to work camps. What makes you think Peter could live through something like that?"

"But Frieda, the Russians will surely soften before long. They are bitter now, but those feelings will pass away."

"Peter doesn't have forever." Anna had thought all these things before. Maybe it *was* time to accept, not to spend her whole life wondering.

"Frieda, there are so many possibilities. We don't know that he was taken by the Russians. He could be—"

"He could have been killed, Heinrich. He could have frozen to death. You know that *millions* died in the east."

"Yes, but—"

"He could have been caught, long ago—discovered for who he was. And if that happened, the Gestapo wouldn't bother to hold a trial. They would shoot him, and how would we ever find that out?"

Anna was shocked by her mother's voice, the seeming bitterness in it. She couldn't remember her mother ever sounding this way.

Brother Stoltz got up. He walked to his wife, took hold of her shoulders. "Why are you doing this? You have always believed that he was alive, that he would come back to us."

"I trusted you, Heinrich. Your feelings." The harshness in her voice was suddenly gone. Tears spilled onto her cheeks. "But the war is over, and why wouldn't we hear something now—if he's all right?"

"He doesn't know where we are. How could he find us? The Red Cross couldn't tell him. No one could."

"So what are you saying, Heinrich—that we'll wait for years and years, and no matter how long we do, we still won't know?"

Brother Stoltz pulled her into his arms. "No. I'm saying this: Trust me for a while yet. I believe the Lord spoke to me. I still think he's alive."

"I thought that too, but now I don't know. Maybe it's only what I wanted to believe."

"I know. I could be wrong. But I don't think I am. And Alex will keep his promise. He can move about Germany more than most people can. He can check at camps. When records are available, he can get them. Maybe, in time, the Russians will provide names."

"I just want to know," Sister Stoltz said. She began to sob much harder. "I'm so tired."

Anna felt much the same, in truth, but she said, "Mama, we'll name the baby Eugene Alexander. That's a hopeful name. Let's be happy that Papa is here with us. It's what we've wanted."

But now little Gene had begun to cry, and Anna knew that she needed to change his diaper, perhaps nurse him again, although it seemed too soon. The thought that he might be fussy again today was difficult for her.

"Let me get him," Sister Stoltz said. "I'll change him." Then she looked at her husband. "I'm sorry. I'll be all right." Sister Stoltz pulled a handkerchief from the pocket of her apron and dabbed at her eyes. "I can get through this. We all can."

"Frieda, I still think we'll find him. If Alex doesn't locate him, I'll go back. I'm not going to give up."

"Heinrich, you think you can always make things right. But some things can't be fixed. The war came, and it changed everything. Now we have to live with what it's done to us."

Brother Stoltz nodded, accepting that, but he looked heartbroken. Anna went to him, put her arms around him again. "We'll be all right. We'll be fine," she told him.

Wally could walk around the compound—anywhere he felt like strolling. He still couldn't leave the camp, but just having this much freedom—no work to do, no more trips to the mine—was wonderful enough. Commander Hisitake was now letting the cooks use the bulk food sent by the Red Cross, and this meant meat with the rice, and other food in much greater quantities. For most of the men, it also meant all the cigarettes they wanted. The only problem with that was, with so many cigarettes available, Wally had lost his trading power. But he could get plenty of chocolate, and his body was getting used to it. He craved the stuff. He ate lots of it—and anything else he could get his hands on. Some things upset his stomach, his system not used to richer foods, but it was a great feeling to have a full stomach, actually to eat enough not to be hungry.

The Japanese guards finally got around to marking the camp with big letters, "POW," on the parade ground and on top of the mess hall. That would have been a good idea back when the bombers were attacking, but at least now it meant that supply planes might spot them.

The better conditions were great, but everyone wanted to get home, and there had been no contact from Allied forces. After a couple of weeks, Hisitake turned over all the weapons in the camp, and the Japanese disappeared from the place. The prisoners had often spoken of retribution, if they ever got the chance, but that didn't seem top priority for most of them. The men in greatest danger were Langston, the mess hall officer, who had treated his fellow prisoners so badly, and Honeywell, his crony. Both seemed to disappear with the Japanese. Some said they were hiding out in Langston's quarters, but Wally didn't care. He never wanted to think about those two again.

When the prisoners took control, the highest-ranking American officer, a dentist, took command. He ordered the prisoners to wait in the camp, not to leave, and to await the arrival of Allied troops—or for some instruction from the military. But a few days after the guards had left, the food ran out—and the cigarettes. This brought on some rage. The men had lived too well lately to go back to starvation rations. Wally was in on some of the discussions about what the men could do to feed themselves. Everyone agreed that the mine owner owed them food after all the work they had been forced to do for him. So they sent a representative to the mine owner with a demand for food and a warning that they would take over the mine and shut it down, should he not comply.

On the following day five large trucks pulled into the compound. Two trucks were loaded with rice, and two more with canned goods. The fifth was full of nothing but cigarettes. With the food had also come cooks, and the prisoners began to eat well again. But the anxiousness to get out of the camp, to go home, was only increasing. The American commander did give the men permission to go to the nearby beaches, where Wally began, every morning, to dig clams. That was a great treat—fresh clams, shucked and boiled—and he liked the activity. It was something to occupy his time. Some of the men organized a program with lots of funny performances one night, but most days were long, as everyone talked about only one thing: getting home.

Finally one day a B-29 flew over and released magazines

and a note that told the prisoners to clear the compound for a drop. The big flying fortress came in again and dropped fifty-five-gallon cans of food and clothes, but it came in far too low, not giving the parachutes time to deploy. The cans slammed into the dirt and blew apart, or crashed and rolled. Most of the food was ruined.

The next time supplies were dropped, however, crates were let go from a reasonable height, and they drifted into the compound. By now, the men had all the food they could eat—and more. More drops only kept them well supplied.

Men who had been released from other camps also began to show up. They were simply wandering about, looking Japan over, and they, like everyone else, were trying to figure out how to get home. No one had the answer for how to do that, but the men of the Omuta camp decided their own commander was being entirely too strict. They started wandering out themselves.

One morning Wally and Chuck took cigarettes, soap, and some big GI overcoats, and they headed out. The overcoats had been dropped with other supplies by American pilots. Wally wondered what that meant—was the military expecting the men to stay through the winter? But most assumed it was a typical army supply foul-up, and they used the coats for barter on the local market. Wally and Chuck wanted to trade for fresh vegetables or fruit, or maybe some chickens. They weren't hungry, but they wanted to do something interesting, see some of the area, and eat some things they hadn't tasted for a long time. They walked through the demolished city to the train station, and they caught a train—although they had no idea where it was going. At a little town they got off, and then they walked into the country. Both were impressed with how beautiful and green the farmlands were, with rolling hills, a few little groves of trees, and farmhouses scattered about. The houses were certainly more than shacks, but they seemed insubstantial compared to homes in the States.

When they passed a house where chickens were running about, Chuck said, "Let's go in and see if these people will trade for a couple of those little hens."

So the two approached the house, and they knocked at the door. In a few moments a young girl, maybe fifteen or so, and pretty, opened the door. She was clearly alarmed. She waved her hand before her face as though she were pleading with them not to hurt her.

Wally spoke to her calmly, tried to reassure her. He knew a simple Japanese greeting, and he kept repeating it, and he bowed. She bowed, too, without ever looking them straight on, and then she hurried away, but she left the door open. In a short time a man came to the door. He bowed, and then, in English, he said, "Please. Come in."

When Wally and Chuck stepped inside, Wally could see how beautiful the house had been at one time but how sparsely furnished it was now. The three men sat on the floor together. Wally and Chuck set the coats and the package of soap and cigarettes on the floor next to them. The Japanese man said, "We bring you something to eat." Wally thought the man seemed too old to be the girl's father. Maybe he was her grandfather. Or maybe he was merely worn down. His skin was creased, like the folds in dry leather.

"You don't have to feed us," Chuck told him. "We're not hungry."

The man bowed from the waist. He was dressed in a baggy pair of cotton trousers that buttoned at the calf, and in a loose blouse that tied across at the waist. "We are honored," he said. "No more war."

"Yes. We're glad it's over too."

"Many people in Japan, no food. In winter, no warm, no clothing. Very, very bad."

"What about you? Did you have to go hungry?"

"No."

Wally wondered. Had he been selling off his possessions?

Is that why the house looked so bare? On the wall he saw a picture of a young man—handsome, in a navy uniform. "Is that your son?" Wally asked.

"Yes."

"Did he come through all right?"

But the man didn't seem to understand.

"Is he alive?"

Now the man looked down. "We do not know. His ship . . ." He hesitated, and then he pointed down.

"Oh, my," Wally said, "that must be difficult. How long has he been missing?"

"Long time."

Wally suddenly felt strange. "Your son could be a prisoner. Like us," Wally said.

"Yes. We hope."

"We were prisoners almost three and a half years."

The man looked confused.

"Three *years*. Four months."

The man nodded solemnly. "Very long time."

"Bad food," Chuck said. "Hard work."

"Yes. I am sorry. War very bad."

"But we're going home now," Wally said. "We hope your son comes back."

The man bowed again, but then he said, "Not come home." Now he was saying what he really believed, and Wally suspected he was right.

The young woman appeared again. She was carrying a tray with bowls on it. There were cooked vegetables and rice in the bowls.

She bowed before Chuck, then got down on her knees and offered the food. "Oh, no," he said. "We're not hungry. We have plenty of food now."

"Please," the man said. "Please, eat."

Wally got up. He wasn't sure whether he was supposed to do that, and not sure that it was right to turn the man down.

But this family didn't have much to eat, and he couldn't take what they had. "We brought something for you," he said.

The man was getting up. Wally knew there were rules of etiquette about that. He feared that he wasn't being respectful. He bowed to the man. But this caused the man to bow low himself.

"We have cigarettes and soap. And we thought you might like these coats—when things get colder."

"This is wonderful gift," the man said. "Thank you. Please eat."

But Wally couldn't do it. He was afraid that he was hurting the man's feelings, but he couldn't take any of his food.

Chuck was already moving toward the door, and Wally followed. They both stopped and bowed again, and the man and the young woman bowed too. "Thank you very much," Wally kept saying.

"I do hope your son makes it back," Chuck said, and he stepped outside the door. Wally followed him, and then, outside, Chuck said, "Oh, man, I wish we had brought them some food. Maybe we can come back here some time."

Wally glanced at the chickens. He was glad now that he hadn't offered to trade before he had learned a little more. The man surely would have had the chickens killed for them.

Wally and Chuck didn't return to the train immediately. They walked farther down the road and looked at more of the countryside. What they could see was that most families were worse off than the one they had met. By the time they got back to the camp, they were subdued and not saying much. This time, the walk through Omuta had caused Wally to think more about all the homes that were lost, about all the other families in Japan affected by the war.

Just as Wally and Chuck were coming into camp, they spotted a little band of American GIs—in their Japanese uniforms—approaching from the opposite direction. They were leading a cow—a big white animal with brown splotches on its back and sides. The Americans seemed to have found some alcohol, too. They were in a merry mood.

"Look what we got," one of them yelled. Wally didn't know most of the men, but he had worked with one of them, a man named McMurrin. He was a loudmouthed old army sergeant.

"Hey, Wally," McMurrin said, "if you two want in on this, come and help us slaughter the old girl. We're going to eat steak tonight."

"Where did you get it?" Wally asked.

"Off a farm out here, not far from town." He laughed. "She may be an old milk cow, but I figure she'll taste like corn-fed beef to us."

"McMurrin, these people here are starving. That cow might be the only source of income for that family."

"Well, I got a solution for that. Let the little Nips starve to death."

"Hey, don't talk like that," Chuck said. "The *people* didn't start the war. Don't take it out on them."

McMurrin still had hold of a rope that was tied around the cow's neck in a crude, tight knot. He stepped closer to Chuck and said, "Don't give me any of that. These Japs starved me for three years. Now, I say, let them starve."

The other men with McMurrin had plenty to add to that, most of it disgustingly foul and profane. And then they walked with their cow toward the mess hall.

"Is that what's going to start happening now?" Chuck asked. "Are our boys going to make life miserable for all these poor civilians?"

"I don't think so," Wally said. "Some of them will. But most won't."

At least he hoped that was true. What he found after that, however, was that he was more aware of all the Japanese families, especially the kids, who were hungry. He and Chuck went on lots of walks, each time taking with them cans of meat, chocolate, soap, and other things, and giving them out where they saw need. The only problem was, the need was everywhere, and they could do only a very little.

Even more supplies were coming now. Every two or three days an American bomber would fly over and drop crates, usually about twenty at a time. The men would watch for them in the compound and then hope the drop was on target. It was fun to gather the big boxes and see what had come this time. The men were getting braver about staying on the parade ground and watching the cases descend.

And then one day one of the crates broke loose from its parachute. It dropped like a stone, and everyone ran. But one man slipped and fell, and as he was scrambling up, the box struck him. It hit him across the hip and smashed his leg.

Wally wasn't there, didn't see it, but he knew the man. He was an American, a kid from Virginia named Weatherby who had been taken prisoner with all the others in the Philippines. He had survived the death march on the Bataan Peninsula, some terrible illnesses at Cabanatuan, and this long, hard year in Japan. Wally prayed that he could survive this.

But Weatherby lost too much blood, was too weak from all he had been through. He died the next morning. For Wally, of all the deaths he had seen, this one seemed the saddest. Everyone in the camp felt the same way.

* * *

Alex Thomas was sitting at his desk in Frankfurt when his assistant, Sergeant Morrey, stepped to his door. "Lieutenant Thomas," he said, "there's a Sergeant Duncan here. He says he's a friend of yours. I told him how busy you were this morning, but—"

"No. It's all right." Alex stood up and in a loud voice said, "*Sergeant* Duncan? I never heard of a *Sergeant* Duncan."

And then Duncan appeared at the door, behind Sergeant Morrey. He was grinning, but what Alex saw was the scar next to his Adam's apple, a jagged and lumpy red line. "Hey, the real question is, how did *you* ever get to be an officer?" He slipped around Morrey and held out his hand.

But Alex didn't shake Duncan's hand. He stepped closer and grabbed him in his arms. The two laughed and slapped each other on the back. When they stepped back from each other, Alex said, "I got a letter from Curtis a while back. He told me you were alive—which I hadn't even known for sure until then—but I thought you'd be long gone by now. Curtis was shipping out."

"Yeah, well, I should be gone too. You know how the army fouls everything up. They've got me down for about half as many points as I'm supposed to have. By the time they get it straightened out, I could be here another month or two."

"Yeah, well, I'm worse off than that. Sit down. Tell me what happened that night you got hit. I tried to find out, and no one knew."

"It's pretty, ain't it?" Duncan said. He stretched his neck a little to give Alex a good look at his scar. Then he stepped to Alex's desk and grabbed a wooden chair. He turned it around and sat on it backward, leaning his arms on the backrest. "There's one good thing about it. I got official permission not to wear a tie—a signed letter from General Taylor. Down in Austria, officers are always after me about that, but I just pull out my letter and those guys have to back off."

"But is it a problem for you? I wondered whether it might have ripped up your vocal cords."

"Naw. It nicked my throat, but they fixed it up. It grazed a bone in my neck, too, but it didn't really hurt anything. It was another one of them things where if the bullet had been over just a little, maybe a quarter of an inch, I'd be dead now. It could have cut my spinal cord right through—or tore up my throat and choked me to death."

"What happened that night after you got hit?" Alex sat down at his desk, across from Duncan. The room had once been an elegant bedroom, with tapestry on the walls, but the desk was a piece of army junk—gray metal. It smelled of stale coffee, apparently spilled at some point into its crevices.

"They took me to that aid station where you saw me, and they got the bleeding under control. Then, the next morning, they trucked me over to France to one of those big temporary hospitals. I had an operation that same day, and then I had to lay around there for about six weeks. When I got released, they put me in one of those Repo-Depots, but I just kept arguing with 'em, telling everyone I wasn't going nowhere but back to Easy Company. I think they finally got sick of me and just let me go."

"I thought you'd be on your way home."

"Yeah, well, I probably coulda been. But I told 'em I wanted to go back. Of course, now that I'd rather go home, they can't fix it up for me."

Alex smiled at the irony of it all. But he didn't like what he was seeing. Duncan looked pale, and he had lost weight. In most ways, he was still his old self, but he seemed a little more subdued, maybe tired. "Why in the world did you want to go back to the five-oh-six? You had your million-dollar wound."

"I don't know." Duncan ran his hand over his chin and then along the scar. "At the time, I think I was worried about our squad—especially the young guys. I thought we were going into some hard fighting, and I . . . well, I don't know." He shook his head, looked at his hands, which he gripped together. "It seemed like I was cutting out on all you guys. And I didn't want to do that."

"When did you get back to the company?"

"Not until they were over in Mourmelon. I don't know if you know what happened."

"Curtis told me a little about it."

"Those guys got pulled back for R and R in February, I think it was—not too long after you got transferred. Then in April, after the 17th dropped into Germany, they sent us over to occupy an area by Düsseldorf, along the southern part of the

Ruhr. But that was nothing. We lived in houses. Most of the guys spent their time drinking and chasing Fräuleins. It was kind of a mess, actually. It's all been that way ever since then."

"What do you mean?"

"I don't know. Just the way a lot of the men have been carrying on. I guess you know, we went down south into the Alps and occupied Hitler's Eagle's Nest for a while, and then they stationed us in a place called Zell, in Austria. It's kind of a resort town, on a big lake. You can't help but feel like you're on vacation down there. The brass told us we had to make it to the Alps before a bunch of renegade Germans hid out and tried to keep the war going, but there was none of that. When we were at the Eagle's Nest, we were sleeping in quarters the SS had used—better than any place you and me stayed in the whole war—and Summers found a cache of wine that could have kept the whole 101st drunk for years. He told the guys to go easy on it, but everyone kept grabbing it up and drinking like they wanted to finish off the whole thing overnight."

"I never thought you'd complain about having a good supply of alcohol."

Duncan laughed. "Well . . . I don't drink much anymore. I don't like what I see it do to people. But it wasn't just the wine. Everyone was all messed up—nervous and jumpy. I saw things down there that were worse than anything we saw in the whole war."

"What are you talking about?"

"Some really sick stuff. A guy in D Company needed some gas for his jeep, and he was drunk. He told a couple of Germans to siphon gas out of their car and give it to him. They tried to tell him the tank was empty, and he wouldn't believe it. So he killed them."

"Just shot them?"

"Yeah. Now he's up on charges. I think some of these dogfaces got certain things in their heads during the war, and now they don't know how to stop, just all at once. Some other guys

I know tracked down a big-time Nazi who lived down by Berchtesgaden. They figured if they turned him over to military police, or something like that, nothing would happen. So they told the guy they'd give him a chance, that he could make a run for it. They let him run a little ways, and then they just stood there and chopped him down with Thompson machine guns."

"I know about some of that kind of stuff. My CO says we're going to get more justice that way than we will from any war trials that we hold."

"Maybe he's right, for all I know. But a few months ago, we all knew what we were fighting for, or at least thought we did. Now, I don't know. I just want to go home. Too many guys are acting like they've lost their marbles."

"What are you going to do when you get home?"

"I don't know."

"Have you thought about—"

"I just don't know, Deacon. All those years have gone by, and I don't know what home is anymore. My mother is going to take a look at me and wonder who I am. It's the same thing I think, every day, when I look in the mirror."

"You'll be okay, Dunc. It's just going to take a little time for all of us."

"I'll tell you something interesting—something I sort of hate to admit. But it's one reason I wanted to see you before I ship out. By the way, I *borrowed* a jeep to drive up here. It wasn't exactly a legal arrangement. So if I get caught, you'd better pull some strings for me."

"Hey, I'm no big shot, you lamebrain. I'm a lowly second lieutenant. Any string I tried to pull would break off in my fingers."

"Well . . . anyway . . . I wanted to see you. You know, to say good-bye, see how you were and all that. But there's one thing—and I know it's stupid to even bring up after all this time—but it's something I wanted to clear up with you."

"What?"

"I found out I like Germans. I remember that whole thing we got into back at Taccoa." He grinned. "You know, when you smashed my nose."

"I got you with a sucker punch."

Duncan laughed. "Yeah, that's right. You did. But that whole thing was about you saying you liked the German people, and I couldn't handle that back then. Now, I've been around here for a while, and I like the Germans better than anyone in Europe—except maybe the Dutch, and they're a lot the same."

"Why? What do you like?"

"There's something sort of bull-doggish about the way they're fighting to survive. They're battered down, and they ought to throw in the towel, but they just don't. They're out there in the streets, cleaning up and doing whatever they have to do to stay alive."

"You don't sound like the old Duncan. I hope you're okay."

"Oh, yeah. I am. I just feel about twenty years older than I was back when we started this whole thing. And I don't know—I always told you I had to hate Germans to kill them. Now I talk to these people, find out what sort of folks they are, and I don't know who it was I thought I was shooting. I know we had to do this, but in a way, I wish I'd gone home that night I got shot. I don't think I'd be feeling so . . . confused . . . or whatever it is I'm feeling. It sounds stupid to say, but I keep wishing all this had never happened—that I'd never killed anyone. I don't like the idea of thinking about it the rest of my life."

"I'm afraid of that too. Maybe some guys can let it go. But all kinds of pictures keep coming back to my mind."

Duncan nodded. "I still have bad dreams," he said. "But everyone does. Some guys say they don't, and then I hear them yelling in their sleep." He leaned back, was quiet again for a time. And then he said, "Deacon, I need something more like what you've got. Something I really believe in. Religion, or something like that."

"A wife and little son might help."

"It was a boy?"

"Yeah."

"What's his name?"

"We've named him Eugene, after my brother."

"Yeah, of course. That's really good, Deacon."

"I think it means a lot to my family back home."

"Sure. I can see how it would. Curtis told me, when he gets home, he's going out there to see your family. He said he wants to be a Mormon."

"Maybe you ought to think about that yourself." Alex smiled.

"My ma would kill me if I did something like that. I'd better just go to the Baptist Church." He glanced away and then said, seriously, "But I do plan to go to church."

"Let's get in touch when we get home, Dunc. Let's keep track of each other. Okay?"

"Yeah. I'd like that. I think I might drive out to Utah some time myself. I'd like to see that part of the country. You're taking Anna there, aren't you?"

"Yeah. If I ever get out of here."

"That's a bad deal. You're supposed to get extra points for being a father."

"I know. But they say I'm needed."

Duncan shook his head. "The army," he said with disgust. "Say, listen. Have you got time to go get something to eat?"

"Not really. But let's do it."

"Okay. But Thomas, I might not say it later, so I want to say it now." Duncan stood up, but then he looked down at the floor. "You're the best man I've ever known. You and Curtis. I figure I'll never again have a friend as good as you guys. That's half of what's bothering me. This war is the worst thing I've ever been through, but it's the best, too. I'm scared I'm never going to know anything as good again as what us guys had when we were all together."

"I just wish our whole squad had made it through."

"We lost a lot of guys from that first group," Duncan said. "General Taylor told us, before D-day, that a lot of us were going to die. I figured that was probably right, but it didn't really sink in. I had no idea what we were up against."

"No one did."

Alex looked at Duncan, and the two simply nodded. But Alex was sure there were things between them, things they understood about each other, that no one else ever would.

The days continued to drag for Wally and the other prisoners. Wally wanted more than anything to feel like himself again, to get back to some sort of normal existence. And he wanted to see his family. For the present, however, he would have been satisfied if he could at least let his parents know that he was alive, but there was no way to do that.

Most of the former prisoners, however impatient, were orderly and controlled, but some were trading food and winter coats for *sake*, and that was creating some problems. The other group that bothered Wally, and worried him, were those who were obsessed with the idea of taking retribution against their former supervisors in the mine. Some of those men walked to the mine one day and lined up all the mine officials they could find. Then they rated each according to his treatment of the prisoners. Those who received good ratings were let go, but those who were found guilty of brutality were beaten unmercifully.

On September 14 a reporter from the *New York Times* arrived at the camp. The next day he stood in the compound and gave the prisoners a long lecture. He told about the campaigns of the war, about D-day and the victory over Germany, and about the many Pacific battles, including Douglas MacArthur's return to the Philippines, where remaining prisoners had been released. When he told of the atomic bomb and the destruction in Hiroshima and Nagasaki, the men became quiet. Nagasaki, they were told, was on the same island, Kyushu, across the bay, only about fifty miles away. But the men had never known.

All of this, in fact, was new to the men, and astounding. The world had been locked in the greatest conflict in history, and they had known almost nothing about it—only rumors and sometimes arrogant claims by their captors.

The reporter also said that the occupying army was not likely to arrive in Omuta for another month, but that the Army Air Force, as it was now called, had established bases at the southern tip of Kyushu island. "They're flying C-47s and C-46s in there every day," he said. "They're coming in with supplies and going back empty. If you can get yourselves down there, I see no reason you couldn't catch a ride to Okinawa. General MacArthur has authorized you guys to use any means of transportation you can find to get to those bases."

Wally nudged Chuck, who was sitting next to him on the ground. "Let's go," he said. The meeting wasn't over, and men were still asking questions, but Wally and Chuck stood up and slipped away. Others were doing the same. Art, Don, and Eddy followed Wally and Chuck back to the barracks. "Let's get to the train station before everyone else does," Eddy told the others as he came through the door.

"That's what we're thinking too." Wally said. "But we've got to know where we're going. How can we get a map?"

"What about Horikawa? He must know the island. He could draw something up for us."

Horikawa was one of the guards who had marched back and forth to the mine with the men. He was no longer a guard, but he was still working at the camp, supervising maintenance work. He was friendly, and he spoke a fair amount of English.

"I'll find him," Eddy said, and he headed out. As the men

packed together the things they wanted to take with them, it was pretty clear that most of what they had collected in the past few days—the coats and even some of the souvenirs—were too bulky to pack into bags and take along. Eddy came back with Horikawa and got him to sit down and draw out a map, and then the men started unloading anything and everything they didn't need. They gave it all to Horikawa. He was overwhelmed with joy and appreciation. He cried as he shook the men's hands. He could sell the coats and food and other gear and be better off than almost anyone else in Omuta.

"Old Horikawa is set for life," Chuck said as the men left the barracks.

Wally knew that was true, and he wondered whether they couldn't have divided the loot among more of the people. But at least it was a reward for the man's goodness. "He deserves what he got," Eddy said. "He was as decent as any guard we ever had."

The group hiked through the battered city and arrived at the train station, only to find that about a hundred former prisoners from the camp were already there. Most of them were wearing Japanese army uniforms, but they were easily identifiable as Allied troops and not Japanese. They were milling about in the station and out on the loading platform, talking to one another, and most of them were discussing the same questions: How could they get to the bases in the south? What train should they take?

Wally was asking some men he knew what they thought when an old Navy chief, a man named Bruce Potts, walked out to the platform. "I got us a train," he announced. "I talked to the station master, and he told us we can pretty much take over this next southbound train." Potts laughed. "I think he wants us out of here as much as we want to get out."

There was a general cheer, and the Japanese who were waiting must have wondered what was going on. "What about all these people who are standing here with tickets?" Wally asked his friends.

"Hey, we've been waiting for over a year for this train," Eddy said. "Them folks can wait an extra hour or two."

Maybe that was true, but Wally kept watching the people. He could see how beaten down they looked, and he wondered how long they would have to live with their own hardships—certainly much longer than a year.

Wally was still waiting for the southbound train when he saw a Japanese army officer walk down the platform. He was an older man, with graying hair, and he was wearing his full dress uniform. At his side was a long, ornate, two-handed sword. Wally liked the man's bearing. He seemed resolute and dignified in spite of the embarrassment he must have been feeling with so many former enemies staring at him.

A young American stepped up to him. He was still mostly skin and bones, and he was ragged looking, his Japanese uniform already quite dirty. In a loud voice that attracted the attention of everyone on the platform, he said, "Hey, you. I want that sword for a souvenir. Hand it over to me."

The officer stood straight, looked up into the American's face. He didn't move, didn't react.

"You heard me. Give me that sword." He pointed to the sword and then to himself. "You Nips aren't supposed to keep any of your weapons. That was part of the surrender."

The officer placed his hand on the handle of the sword almost as though he planned to protect it. It crossed Wally's mind that he might pull it out and try to fight off the American.

"That's mine, you yellow little creep." And then he called the officer a string of obscene names. "Hand it over. I'm taking it home with me to hang on my wall."

The officer took a long, deep breath, and then he released the belt that held the sword on his hip. He handed the sword, belt and all, to the young man. And he bowed his head in deference.

Wally felt sick. He knew what humiliation this Japanese officer, this old man, was obviously feeling. All around, people were watching, Japanese as well as POWs, and the Japanese officer could do nothing but accept the stares.

The American snatched the sword, pulled it loose from its scabbard, and admired it. He said something to his friend, and both of them laughed. The Japanese officer was still standing in the same position, as straight as ever.

Wally understood the American's motivation, of course. He knew that when a war was over the victors took the weapons from the defeated. And after all the humiliation the prisoners had put up with, the American surely felt he deserved what he was taking. But Wally couldn't imagine how the boy could humiliate an elderly man that way. He thought of saying something to the officer, but he didn't want to bring any further attention to him.

The old man finally turned away, faced the railroad tracks, and stood waiting, still dignified. But another American stepped up to him. "Hey, I want your boots," he said, and he laughed.

The officer turned toward the man, looked at him, and again showed no reaction. Wally was not sure whether he had understood.

"Your boots," the American said, and he pointed to them. "Turn them over to me."

Wally had noticed the high boots, black and beautifully polished. The officer looked down, studied them for a moment, and seemed to consider.

"Come on. Pull 'em off."

The officer bowed his head again, accepted his fate, and then stood on one leg and began to pull at his right boot.

Wally stepped close to the soldier. "Don't do this," he said.

"Why not?"

"You're humiliating this man. Don't leave him standing here in his stocking feet."

The officer handed over the first boot, and now he shifted his weight and began to tug on the left one.

"Humiliated? What do you think we've been for three and a half years? These cocky little Japs need some humiliation."

"He's an old man."

"Hey, we ought to kill these little rats. He's getting off easy."

Chuck had come alongside Wally. "Those boots won't fit you," he said. "What are you doing this for?"

"I got a sister, likes to ride horses. She can use 'em for riding boots. Or I'll hang 'em on my wall."

The officer was offering the second boot now, and the American took it and walked away. Wally looked at the officer. "I'm sorry," he said. "I . . . I'm sorry."

The officer took one long look at Wally, then acknowledged his concern by bowing his head. In that instant, Wally felt the same tingling sensation, the same sense of relief he had known when Hisitake had stood before the men, back at the camp. And again the thought filled Wally's head: I never want to hate again. And what was even better, he felt no need to hate. This man was not his enemy, and twice now God had sent him that sweet clarity—the love of a brother. The American boy had a pair of boots that would eventually mean nothing to him, the other a sword, but Wally had a greater gift. He had escaped the bitterness that he had feared he might harbor all his life.

The Japanese officer turned back toward the tracks. He stood in his stocking feet, staring off toward the distant hills. Wally knew this had to be the worst moment of the old man's life, but he bore it with composure.

Wally stepped away. Some of the soldiers on the platform were laughing, even making fun of the man, but Wally heard one man say, "That kind of stuff isn't necessary. That's as bad as what they did to us."

Wally thought about that, thought about the officer's dignity, thought about himself. What he felt at the moment was that his imprisonment had refined him, that it had actually been worth the pain. He would never be thankful for the things that had been done to him, but he was thankful for the result. He just hoped he could cling to what he had gained. He thought of his father. He wanted to look his dad in the eye, and he wanted him to see the change. He wanted to see all his family, hold them all in his arms, but more than anything he wanted his father, finally, to be proud of him.

When the train finally arrived, the POWs filled it to overflowing. Without tickets, they simply loaded on and took every empty seat, the aisles, even the engine and the coal cars. They sat if they could, or stood, and they looked triumphant and relieved. Then they were heading out. The men in Wally's car began to sing—any song they could remember. "Wait for the sunshine, Nelly," they belted out. And "You are my sunshine." Along the way, someone began to sing "Nearer My God to Thee," and most men were able to join in. Wally heard all this, even enjoyed it, but he was spending the time inside himself, picturing the man he wanted to be when he got home.

Home. It really was going to happen. He thought of his parents, his brothers and sisters, tried to think what they were like now, how old, what they had been doing. He hoped that all of them were all right. He hoped they were home now, and before too much longer he could see all of them.

At about midnight the train stopped, and a conductor told the men, in English, that they would have to change trains in this station in order to continue south. "We have held a train for you," he said.

And it was true. The other train was not nearly so crowded, and so now there was even more freedom to join together and laugh and sing. All night the craziness continued—and on until nearly noon the next day. Outside the train, all the cities were leveled. Wally wondered where the people could be. How many had died? Where were the survivors? Were they living in the rubble out there, or had they found some other shelter? He tried to think what it would have been like if Salt Lake had been demolished this way.

At the end of the train line, the men were told they would have to cross a large bay if they were going to reach the southern tip of the island where the American base had been established.

Everyone grabbed up their bags and packs and headed toward the bay. Now it was time to find a boat—a ship, really. There were more than a hundred men, and that large of a group was going to require a big vessel. When the men spotted some freight ships docked below, someone yelled out, "Wally, why don't you go down there and see what you can work out?"

"All right," Wally said. He had grown accustomed to people choosing him to step forward and represent the other prisoners, so he didn't think much about that. Chuck and Don went with him, and they walked on down a little incline to the ship. But what they found was that the civilian crew was entirely unwilling to help. "We'll pay," Wally told them. "We have yen." But the men only shook their heads, and they hardly looked Wally in the eye.

Wally knew what he and his group would have to do, but he didn't want to make the decision himself. He and Chuck and Don walked back to the others. "They say no, and those other two ships are too small. I guess it's up to you, but we have authority to demand help. Can any of you navy boys sail that ship, if they won't do it?"

"No problem," Potts said. "Let's go."

This time it was Potts who walked on ahead. He was carrying a souvenir sword of his own. When he stepped onto the deck, he shouted, "We need to talk," and he slammed his sword into the deck, sticking it up by its point. The four men who had turned Wally down came to something like attention. "Listen to me, you guys," Potts went on. "General Douglas MacArthur has authorized us to use any means we find necessary to reach American troops. We're going to cross this bay with you or without you. If you want to take us across and get paid for your troubles, fine. If you don't, get off the ship, and we'll take her across ourselves."

Wally had no idea how much of his English these men had understood, but apparently it was enough to force them into a little conference of their own. After only a minute or so, one of the sailors turned back toward Potts, bowed his head, and said, "Yes. We take you. Three yen. Each man."

"It's a deal," Potts said.

It was a wide bay, and the crossing took all afternoon. At one point the engine suddenly stopped, and it was Potts and his men who got it going again. But when the ship finally docked, the crew was obviously shocked by what happened. The POWs had no need for yen now; they were getting off this island. So most of them unloaded all their money on the sailors. One of the sailors was standing by the ladder that the Americans used to disembark. He was there to collect three yen from each, but the passengers were throwing hundreds at him instead, the bills piling up on the deck. Wally gave the man a thousand yen, almost everything he had. Once again it occurred to him that he should have spread the money around a little more, with so many in need, but he hadn't known until now whether he would need to pay for his travel. So he kept a couple hundred yen and let these sailors have the rest. They stood watching, their eyes full of wonder and joy.

A large city had once existed just beyond this port, but it was gone now, flattened. The men walked through the debris and ashes and then on down the road. They kept up their march well into the evening, and they kept guessing that they couldn't be far from the base, but their map lacked the detail to give them an exact idea how many miles they had to go.

Eventually, along the road, they found some Japanese army trucks. Close by, in a hillside, were some large tunnels that seemed to be used as some sort of military establishment. Wally walked to the tunnel and yelled, "Anyone here?"

In a moment a Japanese officer appeared, looking wary. Wally told him they would like to use the trucks to drive the rest of the way to the tip of the island. He didn't warn or threaten; he simply asked. He watched the officer consider and hesitate, but then he finally said, "I will give you men to drive the trucks. They will return them to us."

"Hey, that's fine," Wally said. "Do you happen to have anything we could eat?"

Before long the men had transportation again, and the officer tossed large boxes of hardtack into the back of the trucks. These were crackers, more or less like saltines, but with little flavor. The men didn't seem to mind that, however; they were hungry after having not eaten since the day before. That was something they knew how to live with, but not something they'd had to deal with for a while, and no one liked the idea.

The four trucks were not really big enough for the large number of men, but they crowded in, and all of them were still having fun. They stood and sang and yelled and laughed, and all the motion had a tendency to toss the trucks around. At times Wally thought his truck was likely to tip over, and he tried to warn the men. The driver obviously thought the same, and he drove very slowly.

But that wouldn't do. Finally the caravan had to be stopped, and the Americans took over the driving. Now they were *moving*, but the men in the back didn't change their behavior. The laughing and singing continued. Wally knew these men had to be exhausted, but they were full of the raw pleasure of freedom. They were going home, and nothing could quiet them down.

Eventually the trucks came to a roadblock manned by Americans, and now Wally finally saw what he was looking for: big men, dressed in American army uniforms. This was a home of sorts, like the first familiar landmark after a long trip away.

"What's this all about?" Wally heard one of the soldiers say when he saw who was in the back of the trucks: Americans in Japanese uniforms.

"Hey, we're POWs," one of the men shouted. "If you think we look bad in these clothes, you should see what we've been wearing the last few years."

"How long have you guys been prisoners?" the guard asked.

"Most of us, for the whole war."

Wally saw the young man stare. He was a clean-cut fellow with a sharp new uniform—well-pressed khaki, with a necktie. Wally looked at Art, who was standing next to him, both of them still in the back of the truck. "How are we ever going to explain all this—what we've been through—to anyone back home?" he asked.

"That's exactly what I was thinking," Art said.

But the Americans were very welcoming, even respectful. "We heard you guys coming, and we thought some crazy Jap soldiers had decided to come at us on a kamikaze mission," one of the guards said. "We set up this roadblock and got ready."

Everyone was laughing now. The Americans, in their jeeps and halftracks, became a military escort for the prisoners, and the whole convoy rolled on into the air force base. By then it was midnight, but not long after the men piled down from their trucks, they saw an officer walking toward them. "I was in bed," he told them, "but I got up to see this. I wanted to welcome you men personally."

Wally could hardly believe it. Kindness from someone in authority was something he had almost forgotten. As it turned out, the officer was a major and the base commander. He didn't organize the men into any sort of military formation, but he stood before them and said, "On behalf of the government of the United States of America, I welcome you and salute you. I know what you men went through in the Philippines—the death march and all the rest. You may not know it, but you are heroes at home, and always will be. You've put up with terrible conditions, I know, but we're going to try to make up for that a little now. From this point on, you're getting first-class treatment, all the way. You're going to get whatever you want, if we've got it. I'm going to get the cooks out of bed right now and get them working on an early breakfast. What do you want to eat?"

The response was amazingly unified. "Hotcakes!" almost all the men yelled.

"All right. That's what you'll get. And while we're getting that going, anyone for a hot shower?"

It was just too wonderful to imagine. Things had been a lot better for a month or so, but Wally could hardly contain his joy at the thought of a shower, a truly hot shower with plenty of soap, and afterward, a good old-fashioned American breakfast. The nightmare really was over.

"Men, we're flying out of here every day, and we can get all of you to Okinawa in the next day or two. I wish I had uniforms for you here, but you'll have to wear those awful things you've got until then. I need a list of your names and service numbers so the military will know you're on your way. From what I understand, they're setting up a repatriation camp in the Philippines, so you might be flown there for a few days, but no one is going to hold you up any longer than they have to. You're going home."

Wally put his arm around Chuck's shoulder, held onto him. Wally was crying, so he didn't want to say anything. He could feel Chuck shaking, and he knew that he was crying, too. Art was nearby. He stepped over to them, and the three all wrapped their arms around each other. "We made it," Chuck said.

"We're not just alive, we're in pretty good shape," Art said. "I didn't know whether that would ever happen."

"It's like resurrection morning," Wally said. He had meant the words almost as a joke, but they struck him as true, almost exactly right.

The men took their hot showers, and the pleasure of it was

just as grand as Wally had hoped. Then everyone was assigned to a tent. Soldiers had been rousted out of bed to set these tents up. No one was about to ask the POWs to do it themselves. Inside the tents were cots and blankets, mattresses. And pillows! Wally didn't have a real bed yet—and there were no sheets—but he had thought a thousand times in the past three years how much he would love to have a pillow to put his head on. And clean, white, crisp sheets. That would come soon, too.

Breakfast was more than hotcakes. It was also ham and eggs and juice, jam and syrup, coffee for the men who wanted it. And all the food the men could eat. Wally ate until he couldn't stuff in anything more. The hotcakes tasted better than anything he ever remembered eating.

And then he went to his bunk, and he lay on the soft mattress. He didn't want to sleep immediately. He wanted to lie on this bed, with his head on a pillow, and just feel the pleasure of it. But he was exhausted, and in only a few minutes, sound asleep.

When Bobbi's ship docked at Pearl Harbor, she felt as though she had come home, but the war was not over for her. For the present, she would continue to sail back and forth across the Pacific, her ship transporting wounded soldiers and sailors from the many islands to Hawaii, or on to the mainland. For many of the men she was treating, the war would never end; they would deal with their wounds and emotional scars for the rest of their lives. But Bobbi's great relief was to know that the battles were over, that at least no new wounds were being inflicted.

On this trip the *Charity* had been transferring serious medical cases from Guam to the navy hospital at Pearl Harbor—her old hospital—where more difficult burn and trauma cases could be handled. When she entered the hospital, she walked with a blinded young man, holding his arm. She was acquainted with most of the nurses, of course, and everyone greeted her. Afton, they said, was in post-op, so as soon as everything was settled, Bobbi hurried to that part of the hospital. When she arrived, she stood at the door and watched Afton, who was talking to a patient. Bobbi heard her familiar cheerfulness, but she was also struck by how much Afton had changed in the past three years. She had been such a young girl back when she had come here, naive about almost every-thing, and she would never be particularly sophisticated, but Bobbi watched how confidently she patted her patient's shoul-der and then strode to the nurse's station.

She was writing on a chart as Bobbi stepped up to her. When Afton glanced up, her eyes didn't accept, didn't believe for a moment, and then she squealed, "Bobbi!" and threw her arms around Bobbi's neck. "I've missed you *so* much," she said, and already she had begun to cry.

Bobbi had little sisters at home, but they were growing up without her really knowing them. It was Afton that Bobbi felt closest to. The girl had been a pain in the neck sometimes—like any sister—but the two had survived some of the hardest days of their lives together.

"How long will you be here, Bobbi?"

"I don't know. No one knows what's going to happen now."

"Do you think they'll ever let us out?"

"Well, sure. But there's a lot left to do."

"I know. We keep getting more men in—just like the war never ended." Afton pushed some loose hair behind her ear. She looked tired, but she was prettier than ever. She seemed a little less animated than she had once been—softened a little. "Are you going to get married as soon as you get home?" she asked.

"I don't know," Bobbi said. "I'll have to talk to you about that."

"Is something wrong?"

"I just don't know, Afton. I can't figure out what he's think-ing."

"What about Wally? Have you heard anything from him?"

"No. Not yet. But I haven't heard from my parents for a while either. My mail hasn't caught up with me for a couple of weeks."

"I heard we're finding POWs all over Japan, in camps and everything, and that it's going to take a long time to get them all out."

"I know. That's what everyone is saying. But you'd think they'd know more by now." Bobbi didn't want to say any more, but she was worried. She knew that mail could be on the way, and should catch up with her here in Hawaii, but she never went a day now without wondering how she would handle the news about Wally, if it was bad.

Bobbi glanced at the patient in the closest bed. He smiled and nodded. Bobbi could see that both his legs had been amputated, just below his knees. It crossed her mind that she had always expected to get used to such things, to become hardened to such realities. But something in the boy's face—the hint of embarrassment she had seen—touched her. She hoped his life was going to be okay.

"What about Alex?" Afton asked.

"He got through all right, but he's involved in the occupation. He felt bad that he couldn't be with Anna when she had her baby—but everything went fine. She had a little boy."

"Good."

"The best thing is, they named him Gene."

"Oh, Bobbi." Afton took Bobbi in her arms again. "That's so wonderful. It's exactly right."

Bobbi felt the same, of course. But she never mentioned the baby, his name, without tears coming to her eyes. She wanted so much to see him, hold him, and she had no idea when she would finally have the chance to do that.

Afton stepped back, patted Bobbi's arm. "Listen," she said, "I have a million things to do. You know how it is around here. But I'm working six to six today, and I should get off on time. Can you spend the evening with me?"

"I think so. Once we get the ship cleared we've got some cleaning and resupplying to take care of, but I'm pretty sure I can get shore leave tonight. I'd like to see Ishi. Is Daniel still all right?"

"Yes. Ishi found out after the fighting stopped in Europe that he had been wounded again—for the third time. He didn't tell her until he was recovering. But now he's admitted that he might walk with a limp the rest of his life."

"But he's alive," Bobbi said. "I guess the three of us got what we wanted. Our men have all been wounded, but they made it. When are you going to get married? I thought you might have done that by now."

"We *are* getting married, but it's all such a mess. I'll talk to you about it later."

Bobbi went back to her ship, but shortly after six that afternoon she was able to get permission to go ashore. She put on a civilian dress—a little beige shift she had bought in the Philippines—and walked through the navy base, past the white buildings. Returning here, she was reminded of all the things she had loved: the trade winds, the delicate smell of plumeria, the almost constant rustle of palm fronds, and the memories associated with everything she looked at. She decided, before she went on to meet Afton, to walk to the back of the hospital and sit down on the bench where Richard had proposed to her—the same bench where she had talked with Gene the last time. But when she sat down, she was unprepared for all the emotions that came over her. Many times, after Gene had been killed, she had come here to remember him, and his loss had always brought to mind the vulnerability of all the others she hoped would make it through the war: Alex and Wally, Richard, Daniel. She wished so much now that those worries could end. The killing was over, but Wally was like a fictional character, so long invisible that he hardly seemed real. Maybe he was dead. She had to admit that. And maybe that was the next great pain she would have to deal with, after all these years of waiting.

Maybe it had been a mistake to come to this little spot. Bobbi was certain that she needed to get up and walk away from the bench before long, but she didn't do it yet. Two or three times, sitting here, she had felt the touch of God, and that was absolute in her own mind. It was something to build her life upon. Most of the faith she possessed, she had learned here at this navy base, or in her ward in Honolulu. She would always be thankful for that. So she said a prayer. She thanked the Lord for the things she had learned, and she prayed that she might not ever lose what she had gained during the war. She prayed for Wally. She prayed for Richard. She prayed for her family. And then she offered a kind of benediction on the war. "Let *all* of us learn from this," she said.

She got up, but she took her time, walked around the base a little more before she finally was ready to break with the revery she was feeling. But when she finally sat down with Afton, in the room where the two had lived together so long, another set of concentrated, potent memories came back.

Afton seemed to feel that too. "This is how it ought to be, Bobbi," she said. "I wish you had never left."

"What about Marla? Hasn't she been all right?"

"Not really. These have been some rough months for me, and she's not understanding about it the way you were. I know she doesn't approve of me marrying Sam. She makes fun of Hawaiians all the time, like they're all stupid."

"What are your parents saying now?"

"Well . . . that's the problem. I think they've said what they have to say, and now they're hoping I'll back down."

Afton was lying on her side, on her bed. She had showered, and she had on a faded blue terrycloth robe. She had always loved to lounge around that way, with her hair wrapped in a towel, rather than to get dressed quickly, the way Bobbi always did. Bobbi sat down on the wooden chair, by the little desk where she had sat to write so many letters.

"Haven't your parents softened at all?" she asked.

"Not really. Mom tries to be understanding, but she keeps saying, 'Come home for a while before you decide,' and I know what she's thinking: If I get back to Arizona, I'll remember how people feel about Mexicans and Indians and Negroes, and I'll see that marrying a Hawaiian is a big mistake."

"They need to meet Sam."

"That's what I've said to them over and over. But I think it scares them to think of having grandchildren who aren't *white*."

"Afton, for people who grew up when they did, and—"

"You don't have to tell me. You know how I felt the first time I had dinner with Ishi. I'm not blaming my parents for how they feel. I just wish they understood my feelings."

"So when are you going to get married?"

"I still don't know. But I think I do want to go home once before we do."

"Maybe you *will* change your mind."

"No. I'm not going to do that. And that's part of what I want my parents to see. But also, I've been here all these years, and you know how homesick I was at first. Now, I just want to have what I dreamed about for so long—that moment of walking back into my house, feeling completely *at home* again."

"And then give it up forever?"

"Yes." Afton sat up. She looked at Bobbi resolutely. "I can do it. I like Hawaii. I can live here all my life. But I don't know whether my parents will ever come to visit us. And if I go home with Sam, I know how people will look at me, and how awkward my parents will feel. So I want one trip home, as soon as the navy will let me go, and then, if my parents won't support us, we'll get married anyway."

"And Sam is okay with that?"

"Sort of. But if the navy won't let me out pretty soon, then I don't know. I keep hearing that if women have definite plans to be married that's supposed to be taken into consideration, but I guess half the girls in the nurse's corps are claiming they're engaged. They probably are, too."

Bobbi laughed. "How would *you* like to make the decision about who gets out? All these loved-starved women can't be easy to deal with."

"Oh, Bobbi, I swear, Sam and I are both going to bust something if we don't get married pretty soon."

Afton could still embarrass Bobbi, who laughed, but she knew she was blushing. "Get dressed," she said. "Let's go see Ishi."

Bobbi and Afton took the bus into Honolulu—which brought back more memories. Afton had called ahead, so Ishi was waiting when they arrived. She was dressed in a pretty brown dress and high heels, as though she felt the occasion was too important for everyday clothes. She hugged Bobbi, and then Lily approached—smiling but hesitant. She had grown taller and skinnier in the past six months. "You're so *beautiful*," Bobbi told her, and she took Lily in her arms.

"Our daddy's coming home," she told Bobbi.

"Yes, I know. Do you know when?"

Lily looked at her mother. "We're not sure," Ishi said. "He's in the States, but he's still in a hospital. He has enough points to get out immediately, but they want to do another surgery on his knee."

Bobbi had spotted David. He was standing across the room by the kitchen doorway. His hair looked recently combed, still wet. When Bobbi looked at him, he looked away. "Hey, none of that. I'm your Aunt Bobbi, and you have to hug me."

He walked forward and stood before Bobbi, let her take him in her arms, but he said nothing. "Since when did you get shy?" Bobbi asked.

"He's not," Ishi said. "Just give him a minute to remember you a little. He'll talk your leg off."

But now he retreated, back to the kitchen door, and everyone else sat down, Bobbi and Ishi together on the couch, with Lily between them, and Afton on the big chair facing them. "Ishi, how bad is Daniel's leg?" Bobbi asked.

"I wish I knew. He makes it sound like it's hardly anything. But a shell fragment must have torn up his knee really bad. They've operated on it three times."

"The important thing is, he's coming home. Think how many times we prayed for that."

"I know. And I'm not worried about a limp. But I can tell that he is. He only mentioned it once, but I know it hurts his pride to think that he won't be quite the same."

"Ishi, that's what Richard is going through, and I guess I'm not as understanding as I ought to be, but I saw so many men who were hurt worse."

Ishi looked down, and Bobbi remembered the quiet, diffident way she would speak when she disagreed. "Bobbi, we've never had our bodies damaged. We don't know how we would feel to have something like that done to us."

"I know. I try to tell myself that. And Richard is worrying about making a living. But I think what he's most ashamed of right now is that he's lost his bearings a little and doesn't know what he wants to do with his life. To him, I don't think that's a manly thing to admit to."

"Bobbi," Afton said, "what about you two getting married? Is he having second thoughts about that?"

"I guess so. I don't know for sure. He's got it in his head that my family is rich, and I might not want to marry a guy who doesn't have his future all planned out. He told me I could back out if I want."

"But you would never think of that, would you?" Afton asked.

"No. Not for that reason. But I might back out if he won't even fight for me. I'm just not sure he's that committed to me."

"Oh, Bobbi," Ishi said, "I just think these guys are coming home confused and nervous about everything. It's a big adjustment. I keep hearing about so many men who come home without a scratch but all changed inside. They'll be all right, I think, but we just can't push them too fast."

"All these years, all we talked about was the war ending. We didn't take into account all the ways the war would come home with the warriors."

Bobbi looked at Afton, who nodded, and then at Ishi, who whispered, "Yes. But we still have plenty to be thankful for."

"I know. I won't complain anymore," Bobbi said, and she thought of all the times the three of them had tried to imagine this day. What they had now was more complicated than they had wanted but so much better than what they had feared.

Bobbi asked Afton and Ishi about the ward and about all the families she knew. What Bobbi was beginning to notice was that Afton was not as animated as usual, and in fact, she seemed to become more subdued as the conversation continued. Finally, Bobbi asked her why.

But Afton wouldn't look at her. "Bobbi, there's something I need to tell you. I thought it might be better if I waited until we were here with Ishi."

"What are you talking about?" Bobbi heard the reluctance in Afton's voice, and she was suddenly frightened. Had her parents contacted Afton somehow? Was this news about Wally?

"I don't know how to tell you this."

She paused again, and Bobbi was suddenly irritated. "Just tell me. What is it?"

"Bobbi, David Stinson was here, in our hospital. He was shot in the abdomen, in Okinawa. He had surgery in Guam, and then they flew him here and operated again."

"Is he still here? Is he all right?"

"He's alive. But they've flown him to San Francisco for more surgery. His insides are really in a mess, Bobbi. He might not make it. If he does, he's going to be in for a rough time, probably all his life."

Bobbi took a deep breath, tried to find her equilibrium. She bent forward, put her face in her hands, but she was too stunned to cry.

Afton came to the couch and sat next to Bobbi, put her arms around her. "I want to tell you what he told me. I know this isn't easy, but I promised him I would tell you, and I think you'll want to know."

But Bobbi didn't. She knew what Afton was going to say.

Afton took her time before she said, "He told me he wished

he could have believed in the Church, so he could have married you. He wasn't all tragic and sad about it. He kept laughing and making jokes about this being his deathbed repentance. He knows he's in trouble. We kept pumping blood into him the whole time he was here. But he did mean what he told me. He said, 'The one thing I feel bad about is that I made another little pitch for her. And I shouldn't have done that. I know she'll be a lot happier with Richard.' Then he told me, 'If I don't make it through this next operation, tell her that the best single thing that happened to me in my life was knowing her.' I might not have said some of it the way he said it, but that last part was exactly what he told me. I've said it over and over so I wouldn't forget."

Bobbi felt a wave of frustration go through her. For a moment she was angry at Afton for telling her this. But mostly she was angry at David, who couldn't resist this indulgence. Life was always a kind of performance for him, and he had probably liked doing a death scene—even laughing, sounding brave and noble—and all the while expecting to live.

But that was unfair—true and yet not true—and Bobbi knew it. David *had* loved her, and he had given her up, long ago, for unselfish reasons. She tried to think what he must be going through. She wondered how he felt about God now, whether he was afraid of going on to nothingness. Maybe he would live, and maybe this was the experience that would finally humble him, bring him to believe.

Bobbi let her anger shift, let it focus on the war. David loved ideas and music and literature. With so many brutes in this world, why couldn't such a harmless man have been allowed to come home whole?

"Bobbi, how do you feel about David now?" Afton asked. "I liked him so much."

"Don't do that to me," Bobbi said, but she was already doing it to herself. She wanted to go to him now, to help him live. And she didn't know what it meant that she felt that way.

Ishi finally moved Lily, gently, and then slid closer to Bobbi. "Remember when we sat here together on Christmas day and talked about inviting the whole world over for a good cry?"

Bobbi nodded. It was a funny memory—one of those things they had done to deal with their worries.

"Well, it's time. The killing is over, so maybe the crying is worth it now."

"I've lost too much," Bobbi said. "I still might lose Wally—and maybe David, too. I feel like I can't take a good, healthy breath until I know for sure they're both all right."

There was nothing to say to that, and neither Afton nor Ishi was naive enough to try. But they did cry for the world again, for David and Gene, for Daniel and Richard, and for all the rest. No one said anything, but each had known young men who had died, and each had memories to deal with.

What Bobbi knew, however, was that the crying wouldn't help. This loss of David, if it came to that, was just one more scar she would have to carry around with her. But she also knew what she had learned many times in the past few years: she was not alone, and there were many who had dealt with more. She would not wallow in self-pity. She had read about the starvation in Europe, the death of so many Jews, the devastation in Japan and the islands of the Pacific. Her suffering was nothing compared to all that.

"Let's laugh," she finally said. "I don't want to cry anymore. Did I ever tell you about the time David kissed me the first time—in his office at the U?"

"Bobbi! No, you never told me that. I can't believe you didn't."

Bobbi laughed. "It's worse than you think. I was engaged at the time, to Phil. I even went to David's apartment once and then showed up late to a family party. I kissed him that night, too. And then I *lied* to my family about where I'd been."

"Bobbi! That's the worst thing I ever heard about you. And

you didn't even *tell* me? You aren't as holy as I always thought you were."

Bobbi laughed. But the emotion was finally too much for her. She leaned forward, put her face into her hands, and sobbed.

Wally didn't wake up in time for breakfast, but then, he had eaten all those hotcakes in the middle of the night. When he did get up, he went back to the showers, and this time he stood for a long time, soaping himself and scrubbing, then just standing in the hot water, letting it run down his back. There were all sorts of things to think about: the trip home, seeing everyone again. But mostly for now, he just wanted to bask in all the pleasantness of life. Certain things, like the warm water and the good food, he hoped he would never take for granted again, never experience without feeling thankful.

When he returned to the mess hall, he was offered either breakfast or lunch, but both looked so good he took everything. He ate eggs and bacon and more hotcakes, and he also made himself a sandwich of baked ham and cheese on white bread. He tasted mustard for the first time in all these years, and the intensity of the flavor was almost shocking. He knew he had to be careful about stuffing himself too full. He didn't want to make himself sick, but he just couldn't resist eating while he had the chance. It was hard to believe that more food would be available later.

Chuck and Art had gone with Wally to the mess hall, and they had met Don and Eddy there. As soon as they had eaten, all of them walked over to the camp administrative office and asked about getting out that day. A sergeant asked them, "How soon can you be ready to go?"

"We *are* ready to go," Wally told him. They had brought their packs with them, and that was everything they owned. All five were still wearing their Japanese army uniforms, and they couldn't wait to get rid of those.

"Get in the back of that truck out front," the sergeant told them. "We're taking a group out to the airfield in just a few minutes."

Wally looked at his friends, and they all laughed. This was it. They were getting out of this place at last. Wally wondered whether it wasn't too good to be true, but the only hitch was a short delay at the airfield. The men boarded a beat-up C-46, and the big bird lumbered down the airstrip and lifted into the air. There was lots of rattling and whining, but the thing held together. Wally was glad to be traveling this way—as fast as possible. "Remember the last time we crossed this water?" Wally yelled to his friends over the noise of the engines.

"Oh, man, what a difference!" Art said.

Wally was thinking, of course, of the hell ship—all those weeks down in the hold, with the heat and the stench and the starvation rations. His seat now was a fold-out chair that hung from the wall of the airplane. It was anything but comfortable, but Wally shut his eyes and said a prayer of thanks. He was leaving Japan. There was no way he could imagine anything worse ever happening to him than what he had been through here.

Once the plane was well underway, and the noise quieted some, one of the crew, a lieutenant in a khaki jumpsuit, came back and asked the men how they were doing. All the men were happy, and they were laughing and talking and enjoying themselves. Wally asked the officer, "What happened to the POWs who were left in the Philippines—the ones who didn't get shipped to Japan—do you know?"

The lieutenant walked closer and spoke loudly to be heard over the rumble. "As far as I know, they were all freed. I don't think the Japanese dared to do anything to them. I know that big camp—whatever it's called—"

"Cabanatuan?"

"Yeah. It was liberated before the island was entirely secured. I was never up there, but I saw pictures of a lot of guys coming out of there looking like scarecrows."

"Like us?"

"No. You guys look pretty good by comparison."

"That's because we've been eating for over a month." Wally knew he had gained at least twenty pounds. But he doubted he weighed one hundred thirty yet. "Did our troops have a hard time taking the Philippines back?"

"Yeah, they did. The Japs held on as long as they could. They didn't declare Manila an open city the way we did, back at the beginning of the war. They stayed in the city and fought, and so the whole place got blown apart. It's pretty much flattened now."

Wally couldn't imagine that. Manila had been so beautiful. He had hoped to see it again on the way home and remember the good times he had experienced there.

"What's life been like back in the States?" Art asked. "Has the war changed things much?"

"Well, the folks back home thought they had it pretty hard, and I guess they did in some ways. You couldn't get much gas to drive a car, and buying a tire was like trying to hold up a bank. Lots of other things were rationed, too: sugar, coffee, butter, meat."

"Oh, those poor babies," Eddy said.

All the men around the lieutenant laughed, and he seemed confused for a moment. "Hey, you gotta understand," Wally said. "We've hardly eaten a pound of meat—all of us together—during this whole war."

"Look, I know. But when you get back, you need to be

careful about what you say. People—even the kids—had to give up a lot. Everybody worked together to get this victory. People held drives to collect metal, paper, rubber, string. They even saved their cooking fat, poured it off into cans, and carried it to the butcher. They got a few ration points per pound, but mostly they just did it because the government asked it of them. And it was always, 'We're doing this for the boys overseas.' Most people couldn't take a vacation or even drive a car on a pleasure ride. I know that doesn't sound as bad as you fellows had it, but there was a lot of effort put in, and you guys need to respect that."

Wally thought that was right, but he also thought of the people of Japan and the suffering there. He was relieved to know that the folks back home hadn't had to experience anything like that.

"What I want to know," Chuck said, "is whether there are still some girls back there waiting for Johnny to come marching home."

"No problem. But I'll tell you, girls ain't the same as they used to be. Most of 'em have been out working, building airplanes, pumping gas—everything. You guys don't even know about Rosie the Riveter, do you?"

"Who?"

"It's just a name they used on posters and—but you don't know about all the posters, either."

"What do you mean? What posters?"

"There were signs up everywhere. 'Buy bonds' or—"

"Bonds?"

"Yeah. The government sold bonds to pay for the war. You could pay eighteen bucks for a bond that would come due in so many years and would be worth twenty-five by then. That kind of thing."

"But who was this riveter girl?"

"Rosie. She was a symbol. A lot of women had to go to work, so they used this picture of a woman in her overalls, working for the victory. It was something to be proud of, women getting out and doing their share for the war effort."

All of it was more than Wally could imagine. Somehow, even though he had known a war was going on, he had pictured life back home pretty much the same as it had always been.

The men had hundreds of other questions, and the time passed quickly. Wally had flown a couple of times before—just quick flights for the fun of it, back when he was in the Philippines—but he had never actually traveled this way. He couldn't believe how quickly the plane was landing in Okinawa—a place he had never heard of, but which he now knew had been the site of a major battle.

When the men piled out of the C-46, they were told to walk across the field to a Red Cross wagon. "They've got doughnuts and coffee, maybe some sandwiches for you," the pilot told the men.

Wally hadn't thought to be hungry again already, but a doughnut was something he had almost forgotten about. He found himself hurrying, as though the food would disappear before he got there. But halfway across the field, he realized what he was seeing. There were four women, Red Cross workers, standing near the refreshment wagon. His first thought was that they were amazingly tall, and then he realized they were Americans. These were the first American women he had seen for almost three and a half years.

Chuck was walking next to him, and the two slowed automatically. "Look at those girls," Chuck whispered. "They're *beautiful*."

Wally was suddenly all too aware of how he looked. He could only imagine how horrified these women would be to see men in Japanese uniforms, their hair so crudely cut, and so emaciated. He was embarrassed, but as he neared, he saw they were smiling. "Welcome home, boys," one of them said, a gorgeous young woman with red hair and freckles. "Life is going to get better now. Eat all you want."

Wally turned his head. She was looking right at him, it seemed, and he was afraid he had been staring—gaping—back at her. He couldn't think of anything to say, any normal way to respond. What did people say at times like this? How had he ever talked to girls before? He honestly couldn't imagine ever doing it again. But he kept taking quick glances at the four women, especially the red-haired one, who had perfect teeth, white and straight—a smile so beguiling it hurt to look at it. He thought of Lorraine Gardner, who didn't really look like this girl, but whose smile had always had the same effect on him.

Wally took a proffered doughnut and a Coca-Cola. He could hardly believe the taste, like explosions in his mouth. And then he saw Hershey bars. He tried to wait, not seem too eager, but others were already starting on their second doughnut, and so he got himself a candy bar. He stuffed the rest of the doughnut into his mouth and tore the wrapper on the Hershey bar. His impulse was to eat fast so he could get another one before they were all gone. But he knew that was stupid, and he had to stop thinking that way. There were lots of candy bars, and there would be from now on. He couldn't start eating too much candy and soda pop; he knew it wasn't good for him. All the same, he was eating the chocolate quickly, and then he edged in close and got two more. He was embarrassed, but he knew just one was not going to satisfy the desire he had for sweets.

Chuck was still eating doughnuts, and he had taken a second Coke. He and Wally stood together and kept eating, neither one saying a word. Wally could see that Chuck was doing the same thing he was: watching every move the women made. They were so friendly and lovely; they joked with the men, touched them on the arm, encouraged them to take more. And they never stopped smiling or laughing in voices that were

wonderfully musical. Wally wanted to say something to one of
them, make a joke or ask about the weather—just anything to
speak directly to them. But he couldn't do it, and when one of
the girls circulated among the men with a tray of doughnuts,
he took another one, but he could only manage to say "Thank
you" and nothing more.

When the men finally broke themselves away from the
refreshments, they were led to a supply depot. There, a supply
sergeant was much less melodic than the women had been.
"Strip them ugly Jap uniforms off right now," he told them.
"What you guys got for brains, running around in them things?"

Wally and Chuck laughed. No one could upset them now.
This guy had no idea how nice the uniforms had seemed after
the way they had dressed for the past few years. They walked
through a line, all of the men stark naked and skinny, and were
happy to get a complete army uniform and a barracks bag.
Once they were dressed—and looking magnificently better
than they had for a long time—they were led to a row of tents
and assigned bunks. Wally and Chuck were together and got
placed in the same tent, but their other friends were assigned
to the next tent in the line. It was strange to be separated. The
five men had come to depend on each other constantly. Wally
wondered whether he would be able to separate himself from
them when the time finally came.

But now the men were being told to go to the mess hall—
to eat once again. Wally thought he couldn't eat much so soon,
but the food smelled wonderful, and he piled his tray high.
Behind him, at another table, he heard some men who were
stationed at the base complaining about the quality of the food.
"Can you believe that?" he asked Chuck.

Art, who was sitting across the table from Chuck and
Wally, said, "How long are we going to feel this way—like
everything we get is just too great to believe? I don't want to
complain about *anything*, ever again."

That, of course, was what Wally kept wondering. He

hadn't slept on a bed yet, with sheets, and he hadn't seen his family, but he was almost sure he would *always* appreciate such simple pleasures for the rest of his life.

After the men ate, they walked outside, stuffed and happy and wondering what to do. "Let's walk over to the Red Cross hut," Eddy said. "I heard you can get toothbrushes and stuff like that."

"Is it a toothbrush you want, or do you want to look at those girls again?" Chuck asked him.

"I want a toothbrush for now." He grinned. "But someday, I want to be brushing my teeth in the morning and have a girl like that redhead to share the mirror with me. Do you think, if I proposed to her, she'd go home with me?"

"It's worth a try," Chuck said, and he laughed. "But you'd better hurry before everyone else beats you to her."

"No," Wally said. "We're all too afraid to talk to her."

"I'd like to ask her where she's from, or something like that," Chuck said. "But I gotta keep my lips tight—so she won't see how bad my teeth are."

Wally laughed. He would have sworn they were all fifteen years old again.

At the hut, the men did get toilet articles: toothbrushes and toothpaste; bars of soap; shaving soap, with mugs; safety razors; and even after-shave lotion. They got writing paper, too, and pencils. The red-haired woman wasn't there, but another one, almost as pretty, told Wally, "There are plenty of candy bars. Take some back to your tent with you."

Wally was almost sure she had watched him eat three of the Hershey bars earlier, and he was embarrassed, but still, he took a whole pocketful again. He would eat them slowly this time, but he would have them all evening.

All the men turned when another young woman walked into the little supply shack. She was wearing an army uniform, and that was something none of them had ever seen before. Wally had had no idea that women, other than nurses, had begun to serve in the military. He thought of his sister Bobbi and wondered how the war might have changed her life. And that brought to mind something he had begun to worry about. He turned back to the desk, where the young woman in the Red Cross uniform was standing. "Excuse me," he said without really looking at her directly.

"Yes."

"Is there some way I can send a telegram to my family? I don't think they even know I'm alive."

"Sure you can." She reached down and pulled out a pad of forms, and then she said, "Why don't all you guys fill these out? Keep your messages short, but let your family know you're okay and coming home. I'll get them all sent just as soon as I can."

Wally wished he could actually telephone his family and talk to them, but that was one treat he would have to wait for. At least a telegram would relieve their minds. So he jotted down the address and then wrote a quick note.

* * *

LaRue and Beverly were the only ones home when the telegram came. "Should we open it?" LaRue asked.

"I don't think we'd better. It's addressed to Dad and Mom."

LaRue knew that was right, but she had a feeling that whatever was in the envelope would change her life forever—for better or worse—and she hated the idea of waiting. "Let's take it down to the plant," she said. But she didn't want to wait for a bus, which would take forever. "I'll drive the Hudson."

"LaRue! You can't do that. You don't know how to drive."

"Yes, I do. Reed taught me."

"But you don't have a *license*."

"That's okay. We won't get caught."

"Dad will just about die."

"Just come on, Beverly. Think what might be in here." She held the envelope up to the light, tried to see through it, but she couldn't make out any of the words.

"Let's have a prayer that it's good news, LaRue."

"That's stupid, Beverly. Whatever is in here isn't going to change now, just because we pray. Come on. Let's hurry."

"I need to get my coat."

"It's not cold. What do you need a coat for?"

"It's cloudy. It might rain."

LaRue couldn't believe it, but Beverly ran upstairs to get her coat, and LaRue found the extra keys that Mom kept in the kitchen. Mom had a driver's license now, and Dad had actually given the Hudson to her. With gas rationing coming to an end, he had decided to buy a second car. There were no new models coming out yet, but he had taken in a nice trade, and he decided it would be more convenient to have two cars in the family. It was something almost unheard of, but Dad was doing things like that these days. All the same, Mom almost always rode to work with her husband. The plant was being converted now—for the production of washing-machine parts—and President and Sister Thomas were spending almost as many hours at the place as they had at the height of the war.

The truth was, LaRue had driven only once before, and the clutch on the Hudson had quite a different feel from the one on the Plymouth that Reed's dad sometimes let him drive. She jerked and bounced and killed the engine twice before she managed to get the car backed out the driveway, and then, in first gear, going forward, she was even worse. As the car lurched down the road and LaRue ground the gears shifting into second, Beverly muttered, "You're going to *break* it, LaRue. Dad's going to kill us."

But LaRue didn't worry. She would get the hang of it.

And gradually her driving did smooth out a little. Once she got into third gear and was rolling along, she had time to think about the telegram again. There was no way of knowing, from the envelope, where it had come from, so it might not be about Wally. But things were okay for Alex now, and Bobbi probably wouldn't be sending a telegram. It was always possible that some emergency or accident had happened, something with baby Gene, but it seemed most likely that this was about Wally. Dad kept saying that the family should hear something "any day now," and once he had even admitted, "If we don't hear soon, it could be bad news."

But now, here was a telegram, which Beverly was holding in her lap. Beverly had not only put on her coat, but she had also quickly changed her dress. LaRue was the vain one, not Beverly, but LaRue knew what Beverly must have been thinking. Beverly had a powerful sense of propriety. She would want to have proper clothes on for such a crucial moment in all their lives.

"Do you think it's good news?" Beverly asked. She had begun to relax a little, not brace herself with her hands on the dashboard.

LaRue didn't answer for the moment. She had to stop at State Street and then make a right-hand turn. She popped the clutch too fast again, sending the car into a series of little jumps, but once she got to third gear, more easily this time, she said, "I don't know, Bev. I hope it is. What do you think?"

Beverly didn't answer for quite some time. When she did, she said, "If it isn't, I can't stand it, LaRue."

LaRue had been thinking the same thing, but she felt an impulse to say what Mom would have said, for Beverly's sake. "We won't have a choice, Bev. We'll do what we have to do."

"I don't want to," Bev said, her voice tight with anger, or maybe just tension.

LaRue didn't try to respond. She knew what Beverly meant, and her own response was much the same. After all these years, finally to know was terrifying. This was the time to explode with joy and relief, and if that wasn't going to be allowed to her, there was something wrong with the world.

When LaRue parked the car outside the plant, she found that she was no longer hurrying. Neither was Beverly. They walked to the front door of the plant, neither one saying a word now. LaRue felt lightheaded, almost faint, by the time she walked into her mother's office. But Mom wasn't there, and the secretary said Dad was out on the floor of the plant somewhere.

That was almost more than LaRue could stand. It was five minutes before the girls found Dad, and then he went looking for Mom. The girls went to his office and waited, still not speaking. LaRue didn't want to look at Beverly, who was gripping her hands together and shaking. When Mom and Dad came in, Dad closed the door. He stepped to his desk, and Mom stayed by the door. Bev and LaRue, rather automatically, stood up. LaRue saw her mother's eyes go shut, saw her lips moving.

Dad picked up a letter opener and carefully sliced the envelope open. He pulled out the telegram and unfolded it. There were a couple of horrible seconds, when his face showed nothing, and then in a whisper, he said, "It's from Wally. He's all right."

LaRue had always thought she would shout for joy, but she didn't have the strength. She dropped into a chair and began to cry. Beverly ran to her mother, and the two clung to each other, both sobbing. Dad stepped behind his desk and sat down. He was still looking at the telegram, but now tears were running down his cheeks.

"Read it," Mom finally said.

"DEAR FAMILY," he read. "I'M ALIVE AND WELL. FLYING TO PHILIPPINES TOMORROW. WILL WRITE SOON. HOPE EVERYONE IS WELL."

"Oh, dear," Mom said.

LaRue knew—everyone knew—what Mom meant. The news from Wally was wonderful, but their news for him was going to be devastating.

"We need to pray," Dad said. Everyone slipped to their knees immediately, as though they all knew that's what Dad would say—and what they wanted to do. "Bea, would you like to say it?"

"No. I can't. You do it."

LaRue knew what Mom meant. She was still crying hard, for one thing, but there were also difficult things to say.

Dad took a long time himself before he finally said, "Oh, Father, we thank thee." But he couldn't get any more out. He rested his head on his desk and cried. LaRue was crying just as hard. She was so relieved, and she felt *blessed*—not something she acknowledged very often. But she also felt so bad for Wally that his first step back into life would be to deal with Gene's death.

* * *

Wally's flight landed at a base near Manila, and from there he and the other men were trucked to a POW expatriation camp. The treatment he and the others received was beyond anything he could have imagined. Men carried his bags for him, even made his bed. The mess hall was open twenty-four hours a day, and the cooks even took orders. True, Wally had to go through a lot of tests and get half a dozen shots, but every time he had nothing else to do, he ate. He just couldn't stop. He felt as if life was a constant celebration, an ongoing feast.

He was interviewed by an officer and asked to give his witness against Commander Hisitake, and he did tell about the ordeal he and Chuck had been put through—kneeling on the bamboo poles—but he played the experience down, didn't really admit how terrible or life-threatening it had been. Perhaps the man had committed "war crimes"—Wally wasn't sure—but he felt no need to press the issue.

A little later, a radiogram came from his parents, carried by a young private to his tent. Wally was thrilled. He sat down on his bunk, and he was already smiling as he tore it open. "So happy you are well," the brief letter began. "We eagerly wait for you to arrive home." And then, "Sorry to tell you that Gene was killed in action, in Saipan."

Wally moaned and dropped onto his side. He had seen so

much death, for so long, but this one was different. A picture flashed through his mind: Gene, just a boy, standing across the back lawn from him, grinning, his arm cocked as he was about to throw a football. Not Gene. He couldn't lose Gene. "Oh, please no," he groaned.

Chuck was lying on the next cot. He sat up. "What is it?" he asked.

Wally was trying to get his breath. "Gene," was all he said. "Oh, no."

Wally rolled onto his back and put his arm over his face. He needed to cry, but all his strength, his breath, had been knocked from him. Just when he had thought his ordeal was over, there had to be one more test. "He was just a kid," he told Chuck. "Just a little boy." And those words released his tears.

Bobbi was still in Hawaii when the telegram came. She was on her ship, in the burn ward, when a corpsman brought it to her. She opened it with trembling fingers but then let out a little cry of joy when she read the words: "WALLY ALIVE AND WELL. HEADING HOME. LETTER TO FOLLOW."

She sat down and took a long breath. "Your brother?" the corpsman asked.

"Yes. He's safe." And then, like a delayed reaction, the reality struck her. The war was over. The war *really was* over. She cried, of course, but her reaction was not what she expected. It was as though the tension of all these years had finally been released, and she was suddenly overwhelmingly tired. She needed to sleep, but more, she needed to go home and sleep. She wanted to get out of the navy right now. She wanted to share this with her family. She wanted to *see* Wally. And more immediately, she wanted answers to all her questions: Where was Wally? Would he come through Hawaii? Would she still be at Pearl Harbor if he did?

She knew what she had to do. She got permission to leave the ship, and then she hurried—ran half the way—to the office on base where she could place a long-distance call. A young sailor placed the call for her, but Bobbi listened to the phone ring for some time before she heard an operator, with that distinctive Utah intonation, say, "I'm sorry. The party you are calling is not answering at this time."

"It's all right. Thank you," Bobbi said. And then, on impulse, she asked, "Could you put the call through to Springville, Utah, instead. To the Hammond home. I don't have the number, but it's Ruel Hammond." She wasn't sure Richard was there. He might have gone back to Brigham City by now. But she had received a letter from him that week, and he had said he was going to be home for a while.

"Thank you very much," the operator said, and then, after a short delay, the phone was ringing again.

"Hello," a woman's voice said, in a kind of searching tone, as though she weren't expecting a call.

"Sister Hammond," Bobbi said. "It's Bobbi Thomas, calling from Honolulu. Is Richard there, by any chance?"

"Who did you say it was?" Sister Hammond almost shouted.

"Bobbi Thomas. You know, Richard's—"

"Oh, Bobbi. Yes. My goodness. Let's see. I think Richard is down in the orchard. Can you wait for just a minute?"

"Sure."

But it was more than a minute, and very expensive time. Bobbi was thinking that she never should have done anything so impulsive. But when she heard Richard's voice, she wasn't sorry. "Bobbi?"

"Richard. Yes. I just had to call you. Wally is all right. He's coming home."

"Actually, I knew that. Your dad called down here this morning. He said he thought I'd want to know. He told me that he sent a telegram back to Wally—to tell him about Gene."

"Oh, dear. Poor Wally. What a time to have to get the news."

"I know. But your dad didn't think it was fair to let him come home not knowing."

"I guess that's right."

"How are you, Bobbi?"

"I'm okay. I'm so happy about this. But now I want, more than ever, to get home."

"I know. That's what I want, too."

"Really? Do you still want to marry me?"

"Sure I do. I just think we need to talk a few things out— so you know what you're getting into. That's all I've been trying to say."

"You sound so tentative, Richard. I don't know how you really feel about me." She glanced at the young man who had placed the call for her. He had moved across the room to another desk. He was pretending not to listen, but she knew he was hearing every word. She wished so much she could just have Richard to herself.

"Nothing's changed, Bobbi. I'm just trying to figure some things out."

"Are you okay?"

"I think so. My hands are doing a little better all the time."

"Then what's wrong? What's all this fuss about whether you're going to make enough money? You'll do all right. I don't worry about that."

"Well, it's easy to say that. But it might become more important than you think. I went to see your folks again, and your dad offered me a job. I told him I'm going back to school, and he talked to me about working for him part-time while I do that. That might be all right, but I can see what he wants. He's trying to bring me into the business and make sure that you're fixed up for the future."

"Richard, I know my dad. Sometimes you just have to say no to him. He doesn't back off until you do."

There was a long pause, and for a moment Bobbi thought the line had gone dead, but then Richard said softly, "Bobbi, we need to take a hard look at all these things—when we really have time to talk."

"Why don't you fight for me, Richard? Why do you keep offering me a way out?" Bobbi ducked her head. She didn't want the sailor hearing all this, and even more, she hated the way she had to beg Richard to say what she wanted to hear.

"Bobbi, I'm trying to be fair. I don't want you to start down a road and find out that's not where you want to go." His voice had taken on some force.

"David Stinson *wanted* me. And now he's been shot. He might not even live."

"What?"

Bobbi suddenly felt like such a fool. She had no idea why she had said such a thing, and even more, why she had sounded so angry.

"Bobbi, if you're still thinking about him . . ." But he didn't finish his sentence.

"All I'm saying is . . ." She turned around, whispered into the phone, "If you love me, we can work things out. We don't have to talk about money and jobs or anything like that. All those things will take care of themselves."

"But what's this about David Stinson?"

"Nothing. I shouldn't have said that."

Now there was silence again, and Bobbi knew she had made a huge mistake.

"Bobbi, it sounds like maybe you're the one who's not so sure about us. Maybe you need to make some decisions."

"No. That's not true. You're the one who keeps thinking up excuses. But I'm not going to beg you anymore. Just tell me— are we getting married or not?"

"For heaven's sake, Bobbi. This is no way to talk about something like that."

"Oh, never mind. I can't stand to listen to any more of this!" She slammed the receiver down on the telephone and walked from the room and on outside. But it only took about two minutes for her to regret what she had done. Now the engagement was off, she supposed, and nothing was clear in her life. All she had wanted was for Richard to say, "I love you, I do want you," and he couldn't even come up with the words.

And in San Francisco David might be dying. This was supposed to be such a great day, when she finally found out that Wally was safe, and now everything had been turned upside down.

* * *

Peter was sitting in the kitchen at a little walnut table. Frau Heiner set a bowl of potato soup in front of him. He looked up at her and said *"Danke,"* but he wondered whether he had the energy to feed himself. It was after seven in the evening, and he had just returned from working a twelve-hour shift in a potash mine. The Schallers and the Heiners had already eaten. Katrina and Frau Schaller, however, were sitting at the table—just to keep him company.

"You look so tired," Katrina said.

"It's not so bad. I'll get used to it a little more each day."

"But we need to find more food for you, somehow, or you'll never manage."

"In the war, I made long, long marches, sometimes with very little food. I got through that. I can do this."

But it was not what Peter felt. He was thinking that one more dark passage in his life had begun—symbolized by the miserable mine. He felt confined and frightened so far under the ground, and he didn't know whether he would ever overcome those fears. The work was hard, but it was the lack of adequate food that made the labor seem impossible.

Frau Heiner—a tall woman, big-boned but thin now—spoke from across the room. "I'm just so thankful that he will do this for us."

"Yes, yes," Frau Schaller said. "We all are."

"I feel lucky to get the work," Peter said.

And that was true. Several weeks had passed since he and the Schallers had crossed the border into the British zone and escaped the Russians. They had survived on the food they carried with them for a few days, but they knew they didn't want to enter the refugee camps that the British military had set up. Too many people were dying from the diseases there.

They had kept going, worked their way toward the area south of Hannover, where someone had told them Peter might find work in the mines. Outside Hildesheim, however, they had started running out of food, so Frau Schaller had begun to enquire at farms whether anyone needed farm labor. She had gone to Frau Heiner's door and asked, but Frau Heiner had laughed, sadly, and said, "This only looks like a farm. I planted a few potatoes—and I had some chickens—but when the *Amis* came through, they took all my chickens, even dug away at my garden. I hid what I could, but I have little left now—nothing I can plant, not even any seed potatoes."

Frau Schaller had stood at the front door, nodding, saying that she understood, and she had been ready to leave.

But Frau Heiner had told her, "You can sleep here if you want—if you have nowhere else to go."

"Yes. That would help us. Could we use your barn?"

"No. Come inside. If you have anything with you to eat, we could share a little of that."

"We have almost nothing now."

"I have some potatoes. We can make do with that."

"But what will you do this winter?"

"I don't know. The English, they give out some food, but it isn't much."

"Could we each get some and combine what we have? Would we be better off that way?"

Frau Heiner had leaned against the door frame and looked out toward Peter and Katrina and the little boys, who were standing a few paces back, off the porch. "There is some work—in a potash mine not far from here. If that young man could work, he could buy a little food and add that to the rations. We could possibly survive the winter that way."

Peter had stepped forward. "Yes. I can do that," he had told her.

But now, more than a month later, he had been in the mine only a week. Getting a job hadn't been as easy as he had hoped at the time. The first time he had gone to the nearby Siegfried-Giesen mine, he had learned there were waiting lists for those seeking work. And he had no experience, no training. But Peter had gotten lucky. He had gone back to the mine every day, mostly just to keep checking, to tell himself he was making an effort. As he had stepped into the shack near the mouth of the mine one day, an elderly man had said, "Are you here for work?"

"Yes. I was here before. I filled out—"

"It doesn't matter. I need someone now. Today."

Peter hadn't known why the job had opened for him until later. He had thanked the Lord for the opportunity but then had learned that a mineshaft had collapsed and two miners had been killed. The cave-in scared him, but he didn't turn the job down, and he was struck by the strange whims of fate—as he had been in the war. Someone's terrible misfortune had opened up a way for him to feed his friends, and himself.

But now, sitting in this little kitchen, exhausted, it was hard to feel grateful. What he said, however, was, "I'll be paid in a few more days. Then I'll be able to eat more. We all will."

Peter began to eat his soup, and the two women stepped outside. The evenings were cooling off now, and the women liked to sit outside and enjoy the air. But Peter also understood something else. It was their nightly ritual, their way of giving Katrina and Peter a little time together.

Katrina waited until they had closed the door, and then she said, "Peter, I have something for you." She walked to the cupboard, opened it, and then knelt and reached far to the back. "I bought this for you today. It's not much, but you need it."

She came to the table with one of the flour sacks they had carried from the Schallers' farm. She reached inside and pulled out bread—a quarter of a loaf, it appeared—and a small cut of *wurst*.

"Bought it? What do you mean?"

"On the black market."

"How could you *buy* it? Where did you get the money?"

"I went to the train station. I kept watching, and I picked up cigarette butts. It took me all morning, but I got seven. That's the same as one full cigarette to the buyers. It was enough for this."

"I can't eat that. Rolf and Thomas are going hungry. You all are."

"You have to eat it, Peter, or you will drop, and then what will we do?"

"I can last a few more days. I'll take my share of this—but nothing more. Divide it with everyone."

"No, Peter. I didn't tell anyone. I'm so worried about you. I see how you look each night. You're so thin, there's nothing left of you."

He smiled. "No thinner than you."

"Eat it. And tomorrow I'll look again for cigarette butts. Then I'll share what I can get with everyone. But tonight, you eat. You have to."

"Katrina, I can't. Not behind everyone's back."

"Peter, you saved me. Let me do this. Just this once."

Peter understood what she meant—understood her need. He nodded. And he ate the bread and wurst, while she watched. But when almost all of it was gone, he said, "Please eat the rest of this."

"No," she said. "I'm not hungry. It fills me up to see the color come back to your face."

So he ate the rest, feeling the guilt that went with it, but he told her, "Thank you, Katrina."

"Tomorrow I'll try to get more—for everyone. Maybe I can find cigarette butts every day."

"Be careful. I don't like you staying around the train station by yourself."

"Why?" She smiled, and some of her old playfulness came

into her eyes. But Katrina was much older now than she had been a few months before. She looked worse in some ways, paler, even thinner, but she was stronger, deeper. He could see that in her face.

Peter couldn't imagine that he would ever care for anyone more than he cared for Katrina. But he didn't tell her that. She was still too young, and there were too many uncertainties in their lives. He knew if he worked hard enough now, he might be able to find a way to locate his own family, but he didn't have that leisure. For now, his days were going to be full of nothing but mining. He couldn't let the Schallers and Frau Heiner down.

* * *

Anna Thomas had quit working for the OSS before the baby was born. Her father had received back pay for his time in Germany, however, and now he was finding more translation work, both with the OSS and the British SIS. So the family had enough to eat—but only just enough.

All England had celebrated when the war had ended but ironically, war's end had brought on greater shortages of some foods—especially bread. Crops had been bad all across Europe that year, partly because of the war, and partly because of the weather. But the great burden now was for the English and other Allies to try to feed all the displaced peoples on the continent, and to feed the defeated Germans. It was an act of generosity for England to sacrifice in order to feed a recent enemy, but political leaders in the west also saw a need to stabilize Europe. They were beginning to fear that Russia might make a power move to consume even more of the continent. If that happened, Stalin could be as great a danger to world peace as Hitler had ever been.

Anna had watched little Gene become more of a person all summer, begin to show his personality. He was anything but a sleepy baby, and strong willed. He could put up a howl when he wasn't pleased and stay with it for a full hour. But he also knew his mother, and he did love to nestle next to her. When she nursed him in the night, sometimes she listened to his gentle little grunts, felt his pull, and marveled that this little life was hers. She found herself weary of the demands he placed upon her, but when she looked at him, saw the shape of his face, the little grimaces she took for smiles, she saw Alex, and this was the best thing she had in life right now.

In September Alex wrote to her, telling her some things she didn't want to hear—and some things that gave her solace:

Anna, I see no chance that I can get out of the army any time soon. I know I've told you that before, but I've continued to hope that I might get a pleasant surprise. My CO is Regular Army and figures he'll be left in Germany a long time. He doesn't care whether I'm stuck here or not. He has trouble finding people who can speak German, so he isn't about to let go of me. He can't keep me forever, but I'm almost sure he will hang me up until next year some time—maybe even longer. Dad wrote and said he was going to talk to some politicians he knows and see whether he can't do something, but he was talking about my medals and my "heroism," and all that really bothers me. I told him not to get involved, but I'm sure he won't listen.

But Anna, I'm so relieved about Wally being safe that it's hard to begrudge anything right now. I figure this time will pass, and then we'll take Gene to Salt Lake, and life can go on. And I feel like maybe I'm being kept here for a reason. Maybe God is answering your prayers, and your parents' prayers, by keeping me where I can look for Peter. I can do that better than anyone else, and I'm pursuing leads that could get me somewhere before long. If I'm right—and I'll admit, I don't know for sure that I am—and God wants me to be here, maybe that means Peter is alive, and I'm supposed to locate him. At least that's what I like to think. I certainly won't give up until I've tried everything I can to find him.

Anna, I know you remember how I was when I was in England. I'm not going to lie to you and say that I'm fine now and not having any problems. But I am doing a little better, and I promise that I'll keep working to get myself back to where I ought to be. Maybe that's another reason that it's good I'm here. Maybe I need to keep working some things out before my son knows me. It's also good for me to be involved with the Saints here. The branch brings back so many of the best moments I've known in my life. There are times when I feel a return of my old self, and it's the happiest sensation I know. So don't worry too much about me. I'm going to be all right, eventually.

So be strong, as you always are, and I'll try to be worthy of that strength. Kiss my little son for me and tell him about his daddy. Tell him I'm a fine guy, and by the time I get back, maybe I can live up to that.

I love you,
Alex

Anna loved the letter, and she read it every day, even when some others had come. It said to her, over and over, that everything was going to be all right in time—both for Alex and for Peter. She feared that Peter might be in Russia by now and might not be released for a long time. But when she read the letter, she found more hope that God was involved and would bring about a better end. Mostly, she loved the last lines about Alex's love for her and Gene. And certainly she followed his advice. When she nursed little Gene, or held him on her lap, she told him all about his daddy. She would tell him in English, and then in German, and then start over. It was all a joke to her, and when she did it in front of her parents, they laughed, but she actually believed that Gene's little spirit could comprehend at least the essence of what she told him—in both languages.

* * *

Alex was alone. He was supposed to be tracking Nazis, but he was more a researcher than a policeman. He spent much of his time processing papers. All the same, he was finding the names of Nazi leaders throughout the zone. More often than not, tips came from neighbors or local policemen, and then Alex called in military police to make arrests. He had a lead now on Agent Kellerman, and that was one piece of business he actually did want to finish if he could—although he never mentioned that to Anna. If he were given the chance to go home rather than stay and take care of that loose end, he would definitely choose to leave, but he did want to see Kellerman behind bars.

But justice was unclear to Alex right now. He often worked with military police, and he was seeing a side of life that was disillusioning. With so many Allied troops roaming about now, many of them drinking too much, acts of looting, of violence, of rape, were occurring. It wasn't easy to take the high ground, and seek out wrongdoers, when he saw American boys taking out their own brand of vengeance on the German people.

But the corruption wasn't all on the side of the victors. Prostitution was a major source of income for destitute women, and black-market trading, theft—abuse of power of almost every kind—all these were part of the world he lived in. He wanted to believe in goodness, to be honorable, to forget what the war had required of him—and he had promised Anna that he would do just that—but it was not easy to feel much of the Lord's Spirit when his life was so full of ugliness. He had promised Anna, President Meis, Brother Stoltz, his parents— and especially himself—that he would be himself again soon, and he wrote optimistic letters that put the best face on his situation. But the fact was, he was struggling. He couldn't go back to being the person he had once been; he had to find a way to move forward. But his head was still full of images more powerful than thoughts. He tried to keep his mind occupied, always, but without warning the pictures would push their way into his consciousness. And every picture reminded him of what he had done, who he had been, for the past year. People kept telling him that he was a hero, that he had helped save the world from evil, and he understood what they meant. But he kept seeing the faces of the boys he had killed, kept remembering the hatred he had felt. He had fought like an animal, had fought to stay alive, the same as every soldier, and his heart told him he was anything but a hero. But he could make it through the days, tell himself the right things, push the thoughts away; it was at night that everything came back on its own: the noises and the chaos and the panic—and the blood. He never went to bed without dreading what would come.

Church services were good for Alex, in some ways, but difficult, too. He felt glimmerings of himself when he was with the German members, but that reminded him all the more of the spiritual self that was missing most of the time. One Sunday a sister named Ursula Knapp sat near him at one of the *Gasthaus* tables. She had married during the war, and now she had a baby, a boy only a month or so younger than Alex's little son, Gene. Her husband was not a Church member and didn't come to the meetings, but she brought her baby every week, sometimes sitting away from the others to nurse him. But on this day he had been sleeping soundly, and Alex couldn't stop watching him.

When Sister Knapp leaned toward Alex and whispered, "Would you like to hold him," he was taken by surprise. The idea frightened him a little. He wasn't sure what he would feel. But he nodded all the same, and he took the baby, wrapped in a faded little blanket. The baby jerked a little during the jostling, then made a little sucking motion with his mouth before he settled down again. Alex smiled.

But it was the smell, the baby smell, that suddenly brought everything back. He thought of baby Gene—his brother Gene—the day he had come home from the hospital. Alex had been nine years old, and he had waited impatiently those five days that his mother had been in the hospital. He had wanted to see his new little brother, but children weren't allowed to visit. Mom had come into the house, walking slowly, looking tired, and holding the baby in a blanket. "Do you want to hold him?" she had asked, and Alex had sat down on the big couch in the living room. Then his mother had placed the baby, mostly blanket it seemed, into his arms. Alex had smelled that sweet baby smell, the milk or powder or whatever it was, and he had wondered at a person so little, with fingers so tiny.

Alex could remember it all so clearly. "Gene," he whispered, meaning both. But he liked the pain he felt. He hadn't felt this pure in a long time.

* * *

Wally was kept in the repatriation camp in the Philippines for three days. He was able, during that time, to see Manila—but it was a painful sight. The city had been turned into a battlefield, and not much was left of it. When Wally got a chance to ship out, he actually felt strange about doing it. He had come to the Philippines all those years ago and had been treated so well here; now he felt as though he owed something to the people. Maybe he ought to stay for a time and help rebuild. But he couldn't do that. The military wasn't about to let him, and he knew he needed to get home. But as the old freighter sailed from Manila bay and past Corregidor and the beaches at the tip of the Bataan Peninsula, where he had started his ordeal, he felt a strange sense that he had left things unfinished here and would never get the chance to do anything about it.

The passage was not an easy one. Compared to the hell ship that had taken him to Japan, it was a luxury liner, but conditions were not pleasant. The ship was extremely hot. He was lucky enough to have found a top bunk with an air vent over it, so he didn't sweat in his bunk as much as most of the men did, but it was still not comfortable. Food lines were long, with two thousand men aboard—but there was always plenty of food. Showers were supplied by salt water, which wasn't all that pleasant—but there was plenty of water and soap, too. All in all, the men were jovial, and no one complained. How could they?

When the ship reached Pearl Harbor, all the men wanted to get off and see the sights in Honolulu, but the captain knew better than to let such a mob of men loose on the city. How would anyone ever round them up again? So the ship took on supplies and fuel, and then it went on its way. Wally had still not had any letters from his family. He didn't know where anyone was or what had happened to everyone during the war—other than Gene.

The crossing took twenty-three days, considerably longer than Wally would have liked, but it was time to rest and eat, and he enjoyed himself. All he had to do was remember that he had made it, that he had survived all the illnesses, the starvation, the beatings, the torture, and then he would remember that he was one of the lucky ones. In the Philippines he had found some men from his old squadron, and together, with all of them putting their knowledge together, they could account for only about forty of the men from their squadron who were still alive. There were probably more than that, but they had started with two hundred. Certainly over half, maybe two-thirds, were now dead. Wally knew that all kinds of factors had come into that, and one of them was luck, but he also knew that his faith and his family had often given him the strength to get through when he otherwise might have given up.

He and his friends still spent a lot of time together, but sometimes Wally would sit on the deck alone and watch the rolling water. Over the years he had often thought of Warren Hicks and Jack Norland, who had died at O'Donnell, and Alan West, who had apparently died on a work detail after surviving Tayabas with him. He thought of George Robbins, who had died in the jungle and had asked Wally to go see his parents when he got home. Wally was going to do that, too. Through all these years he had been too intent on surviving to devote much of his mental energy to grieving. Now, however, all those deaths were coming back, all the friends he had watched die, all the men of his squadron he had known as young, joyful guys. He felt an overwhelming sense of thankfulness, partly that he had been blessed to stay alive, but even more for who he was, coming home, compared to who he had been, sailing the other direction five years before. He had missed a great deal and hardly knew his family anymore, but in some ways he was more a part of them now than he had been then.

More than anyone else, however, he thought of Gene. During all these years, his family had been a sort of collective whole, and he hadn't really missed one of them more than any other—except perhaps for his mother. But now he felt so cheated to have missed those years when Gene had grown into manhood. Wally's relationship with Alex had always been complicated; he had felt such a competition with him. But Gene had been pure little brother, a kid who looked up to him, who laughed at his jokes, who was always ready to tag along with him from the time they had both been little. And it was mostly those younger years Wally thought of now.

He and Gene had built a tree house once, or at least tried to. Gene had ended up falling from the tree and breaking his arm. The project had ended with the fall, Dad telling Wally to pull down the boards they had managed to nail into the big old apple tree. But Wally remembered the day they had finally gotten something of an off-balance platform established in the tree. Wally and Gene had made themselves sandwiches— peanut butter and jelly sandwiches—and they had climbed that tree, using the rungs they had nailed to the trunk. They had sat there together and eaten, and they had told each other time and again how "neat" it was to have their own place. But once the sandwiches had been finished, they couldn't think what else to do, and the project had lost some of its momentum.

Somehow, maybe a day or two later—Wally wasn't sure now—Mel had come into the picture, and he and Wally had dominated the play after that. They had hidden out and played war, and they hadn't sent Gene away, but they hadn't included him as fully as they might have. Wally had known that, even then, and had felt a little guilty, but not enough to do much about it. Gene, however, had never gone to the house crying. He had stayed with the bigger boys and not complained about the treatment he was getting. What Wally remembered now was the day—probably the next day after Gene had broken his arm and Dad had demanded that the tree house be dismantled—when Gene had told him, "Sorry, Wally," meaning sorry that he had fallen and caused such trouble.

Wally could still see Gene's innocent face, his sincerity. Wally hadn't cared that much. The treehouse hadn't turned out to be all that great, and he and Mel were on to something else, but now he pictured Gene's sorrowful face, and he longed to have that little brother back. He thought if he could just have one day with him, just enough to remember, then he could wait so much easier for his chance to see him in the next life.

And what about Mel? What about all his friends? Where were they now? How many of them had died? It was all too much to comprehend—so much had happened while he had been in prison. He was learning from newspapers and radios, from talking to people, about the tremendous scope of the war, all the countries, all the fronts, all the people who had been involved. Millions of Jews killed. Millions of civilians. Millions of soldiers. How could all this have happened?

On the twenty-third day of the trip, Wally heard someone shout, "There's the Golden Gate." The men crowded out to the deck, and all of them waited to catch sight of it. Chuck and Wally stood together and watched the bridge grow larger as they approached. "Are you scared?" Chuck asked Wally.

Wally was surprised. He thought maybe he was the only one who felt that way. "Yeah," he said. "The closer we get, the more scared I keep feeling."

"Same here."

"What are we scared of?"

"I don't know. For all these years, I've been able to say, 'Once I get released, everything will be all right.' But now we've gotta get back to reality, and I'm not sure how well I'll handle that."

"Everything is going to be coming at us, all at once, isn't it?"

Wally said. "We're going to have to figure out what we're going to do with our lives now. I keep thinking I ought to go to college, maybe, but I'm not sure what I'd study."

"I want to get married, Wally. I just keep thinking about that. I want to have a normal life. I want a family. But maybe we're too strange now. Maybe no girl will ever want me, the way I am now."

Wally knew exactly what Chuck meant. They could put on weight, get their dental work done, buy some clothes. But how did they stop thinking like POWs? How did they get used to people again? To life? How did they learn to relax around women? What did people say when they just chatted? It was like starting over on life. The world had kept going, and they hadn't been part of it.

"We'll just take it one step at a time," Wally said. "I don't know what the army is going to do with us for a while, but everyone says we'll be sent to a hospital first, not home. Maybe that'll give us a chance to get back to normal a little before we face everyone."

"Yeah. That's what I've been thinking."

As the ship neared the bridge, and San Francisco, Wally could see a blimp flying overhead. On the side of it was painted, in huge letters, "Welcome home, POWs."

All the men cheered and laughed and slapped each other on the back. How long had they been dreaming of this moment? "Still alive in '45!" men were shouting. It really was too good to be true. Wally told himself he wouldn't think too far ahead now. He would just take things as they came and try to enjoy it all.

The ship passed under the bridge, and then, in the bay, a smaller ship approached. It was loaded with young women. The men shouted and waved at them, and the girls threw kisses. They were calling out, and mixed into all the noise, Wally heard a clear, mellow voice shout, "You boys are heroes to all of us. Welcome home!"

It was more than Wally could handle. He cried unashamedly, and as he looked around, he saw that all the men were doing the same thing. He told himself that whatever else happened in life, he had this moment to remember. He was almost home.

When a missionary departs or a loved one is about to go away, it's common for Latter-day Saints to sing the hymn "God Be With You." It's a way of praying that God's presence will accompany the loved one "till we meet again." The lyric is comforting: "When life's perils thick confound you, Put his arms unfailing round you. . . ." In the chorus, however, the consolation takes on a higher meaning: "Till we meet, till we meet, Till we meet at Jesus' feet, God be with you till we meet again." We put our trust in God, in other words, even in the case of the ultimate separation—death. We don't say "*if* we meet again" but "*when* we meet again," because we take to heart the hymn's promise.

There were so many hardships during the war, but maybe the worst were all the separations. Young men and women were away from home; couples were pulled apart; friends were divided. Kids missed their big brothers and sisters; young people missed their sweethearts; parents and grandparents worried every day about the soldiers gone from their families. Everyone dreamed of the day when it would all be over and those separations would end. Most Americans prayed that God would protect the ones they loved. But faith required that those who waited at home accept that other consolation—that if the loved one didn't return in this life, families would still "meet again."

We do our wars "quick and clean" now. We watch them on CNN, and we get impatient if the bombing lasts more than a couple of weeks. We expect no American to die, we get upset if the smart bombs miss by an inch, and above all, we expect life to go on without any change or inconvenience. For all those reasons, it's difficult for most of us to comprehend fully the commitment that was required during World War II. *Everyone* was affected by that war. Every life changed. When the separations ended, friends and lovers saw each other again, but that meant new challenges as relationships had to be rebuilt. Some feelings were easily renewed, but many memories, many experiences, were better forgotten. And yet, all in all, the end of the war was glorious. Soldiers and civilians alike had done what they had to do, the victory had been won, and basic freedoms seemed a wonderful blessing, not something to take for granted.

The story of the war didn't end in 1945, and my story won't end there either. There will be one more book, volume 5, in my series. It will be about meeting again and about the difficulties and wonderful joys in doing that.

In past volumes I listed some of the resources I have used to understand the history I have covered in these books. Let me add a few more to the list. Two excellent books about the closing months of the war have been published in recent years. To comprehend the conditions in Europe when the war ended there, see Martin Gilbert's comprehensive *The Day the War Ended, May 8, 1945—Victory in Europe* (Henry Holt, 1995). A fascinating book about politics at the close of the war is J. Robert Moskin's *Mr. Truman's War: The Final Victories of World War II and the Birth of the Postwar World* (Random House, 1996).

Charles Whiting wrote a number of fine books about the latter stages of the war in Europe. Two that helped me were

Siegfried: The Nazi's Last Stand (Stein and Day, 1982) and *The End of the War, Europe: April 15–May 23, 1945* (Stein and Day, 1973).

In trying to understand Germans and the affect of Hitler on the people, I have found three books insightful: *The Burden of Hitler's Legacy* by Alfons Heck (Renaissance House, 1988), *The Tragedy of Children Under Nazi Rule* by Kiryl Sosnowski (Howard Fertig, 1983), and *Voices from the Third Reich, an Oral History* by Johannes Steinhoff, Peter Pechel, and Dennis Showalter (De Capo Press, 1989).

A book I enjoyed, even though it is a little sloppy in its research at times, was *What They Didn't Teach You About World War II*, by Mike Wright (Presidio, 1998). It explodes some clichés and provides a lot of interesting background about life at home and at war.

I am always trying to understand the mind of a warrior. We have often gotten false ideas from movies, and even from reticent soldiers, who don't like to talk about the psychology of combat. One honest and fascinating writer on that subject is Paul Fussell. I have especially enjoyed his books *Wartime: Understanding and Behavior in the Second World War* (Oxford, 1989) and *Doing Battle: The Making of a Skeptic* (Little, Brown, 1996).

There are a number of books about behind-the-lines espionage in World War II, but the book that helped most in writing this volume was *Piercing the Reich: The Penetration of Nazi Germany by American Secret Agents During World War II*, by Joseph E. Serpico (Viking, 1979).

One book I bought recently but wish I had owned all along is a wonderful general reference in encyclopedic form: *The Oxford Companion to World War II*, edited by I. C. B. Dear (Oxford, 1995).

My wife, Kathy, has been my partner again on this volume. She helps me work out plot detail, brainstorms with me, and sometimes helps with research. She also reads my drafts and criticizes gently but directly. Jack Lyon, Emily Watts, and Tim Robinson, all editors at Deseret Book, were not quite so gentle, perhaps, but supportive and wise in their advice. A number of my friends and relatives also read the manuscript and offered advice and lots of enthusiasm: Tom and Kristen Hughes, Amy and Brad Russell, Rob Hughes, Dave and Shauna Weight, Richard and Sharon Jeppesen, and Pam Russell.

This book is dedicated to my daughter Amy Hughes Russell, her husband Brad, and their two little boys, Michael and David. Amy knows the characters in my books as well as I do, and we talk about them as though they were our old friends. Brad has also become interested in the books and likes to join in the discussions of plots and outcomes. Michael and David, along with their cousin, Steven, are the best compensation for my "loss of youth." Of all the roles I've played in life, I like "Papa"—as they call me—the very best.